Praise for Garry Kilworth

Kilworth's versatile skill at navigating between genres, his outre imagination, his deft and evocative handling of the exotic, his keen insights into human behaviour, his affecting ability to inhabit and communicate an impressive breadth of perspectives across cultural and genre spectrums, and, finally but certainly not least, his deliciously elegant prose, all combine to present a selection of stories whose diversity, originality and poignancy leave me breathless with awe. (Claude Lalumiere, *Locus*)

Garry Kilworth is arguably the finest writer of short fiction today, in any genre. (*New Scientist*)

His characters are strong and the sense of place he creates is immediate. (*Sunday Times*)

Kilworth is a master of his trade. (*Punch Magazine*)

Kilworth is one of the most significant writers in the English language. (*Fear Magazine*)

There is something very special about this collection of stories, which span twenty years of a little-known author's 35-year career. Many superlatives spring to mind but quite simply Mr Kilworth's imagination is a treasure to behold. (KM Knight)

Moby Jack

AND OTHER TALL TALES

GARRY KILWORTH

infinity plus

This edition published by infinity plus
First published by PS Publishing
This edition also includes the previously uncollected 'When the Music
Stopped' © Christian Lehmann and Garry Kilworth

www.infinityplus.co.uk

Follow @ipebooks on Twitter

ISBN-13: 978-0995752238
ISBN-10: 0995752230

Billy Pink's Private Detective Agency
The Phantom Piper
The Electric Kid
The Brontë Girls
Cybercats
The Raiders
The Gargoyle
Welkin Weasels Book 1 – Thunder Oak
Welkin Weasels Book 2 – Castle Storm
Welkin Weasels Book 3 – Windjammer Run
Welkin Weasels Book 4 – Gaslight Geezers
Welkin Weasels Book 5 – Vampire Voles
Welkin Weasels Book 6 – Heastward Ho!
Drummer Boy
Hey, New Kid!
Heavenly Hosts v Hell United
The Lantern Fox
Soldier's Son
Monster School
Nightdancer
Faerieland Book 1 – Spiggot's Quest
Faerieland Book 2 – Mallmoc's Castle
Faerieland Book 3 – Boggart and Fen
The Silver Claw
Attica
Jigsaw
Hundred-Towered City

Horror Novels
The Street
Angel
Archangel

Short Story Collections
The Songbirds of Pain
In the Hollow of the Deep-sea Wave
In the Country of Tattooed Men

Hogfoot-right and Bird-hands
Moby Jack and Other Tall Tales
Tales from the Fragrant Harbour
Dark Hills, Hollow Clocks
The Fabulous Beast
The Best Short Stories of Garry Kilworth

Fantasy Novels as Kim Hunter
The Red Pavilions Book 1 – Knight's Dawn
The Red Pavilions Book 2 – Wizard's Funeral
The Red Pavilions Book 3 – Scabbard's Song

Historical Fantasy Novels as Richard Argent
Winter's Knight

Historical Sagas as FK Salwood
The Oystercatcher's Cry
The Saffron Fields
The Ragged School

Historical War Novels
Jack Crossman series
The Devil's Own
Valley of Death
Soldiers in the Mist
The Winter Soldiers
Attack on the Redan
Brothers of the Blade
Rogue Officer
Kiwi Wars

Ensign Early series
Scarlet Sash
Dragoons

Memoirs as Garry Douglas Kilworth
On my way to Samarkand: memoirs of a travelling writer

CONTENTS

THE SCULPTOR

(I took the shanty-tower from my writer pal Peter Beere, who carries a bagful of ideas into a pub and scatters them amongst friends like wild seeds. The rest of the story wrote itself, as many of them do.)

NICCOLÒ REACHED THE PALE OF the Great Desert at noon on the third day. He dismounted and led his horse and seventeen pack camels towards the last water he would see for six weeks. There at the river's edge they drank. Some would have said that so many camels was an expensive luxury, but Niccolò knew the value of too many over too few. Only eight of them were carrying the statuettes. Of the remaining camels, two were loaded with his and his mount's personal supplies, three were carrying water, and three were loaded with fodder to feed the other camels. The last camel was packing fodder for the fodder-carriers but not for itself. It was possible that this camel, or one of the others, would die of starvation before he reached the Tower.

Niccolò had had to call a halt at seventeen. When he had consulted the sage, Cicaro, the old man had recommended that to ensure survival he take an endless string of camels with him. Distance, food-chains, energy levels, temperatures, humidities, moisture loss—when all the relevant information had been given to Cicaro, and the calculations made, the result was camels stretching into infinity. Impossibilities were not the concern of the sage. He merely applied his mathematics to the problem and gave you the answer.

At least they were flesh and blood. Towards the end of the journey Niccolò could begin eating them, if it became necessary. At that moment he found the thought distasteful, though he was no sentimentalist, and had refrained from even naming his horse. Niccolò knew, however, that when it came to the choice between starvation or butchering one of the beasts, whatever he promised himself now, he would use the knife without hesitation. He had eaten worms, even filled his stomach with *dirt*, when he had been without food. Man is a wretched creature when brought to the level of death. When he has shed his scruples he will eat his own brother, let alone a horse or a camel.

Yet there was a mystery there. Man also perplexes himself, Niccolò thought, as he filled his canteens from the river. When he and Arturo had almost run out of water in this very desert, they had fought like dogs for the last few mouthfuls, would have killed each other for them. Then rescue had come, at the last moment, preventing murder.

Yet, not two months afterwards, Arturo ironically committed suicide, hung himself in the back room of a way station, for love of a whore.

Why does a man fight tooth and nail to live one day, and kill himself the next? It was as if life was both precious and useless, not at the same time, but in different contexts. Life changed its values according to emotional colours. In the desert, dying of thirst, Arturo had only one thought in mind—to *live*. It had been a desperate, savage thought, instinctive.

Yet that instinct had vanished when Arturo had climbed on that ale barrel and tied a window sash around his neck. Why hadn't it sprung out from that place in which it was lurking, waiting to perform, to kill for life? Perhaps it is hopelessness that kills the instinct in its lair? In the desert, if he fought hard and callously enough, the water might eventually belong to him. The love of the lady though, no matter how savagely he battled, could never be his. If she withheld it, could not feel such for him, then he was helpless, because he could never in a million years wrench *love* from her grasp like a water bottle.

A craft came along the river, silently, the helmsman apparently happy for the most part to let it follow the current. The cargo was sheltered from the sun by a palmleaf thatched cabin, which covered the deck with an arch-shaped tunnel. The sail was down, unnecessary, even a hindrance in the fast flow.

As the boat went by, Niccolò was able to peer inside, through a window-hole in the thatch. A giant of a man sat in the dimness within: a clumsy-looking fellow, appearing too big for his craft, but a man with peace, contentment, captured in his huge form. He was knitting. His great hands working the wooden needles while his elbow occasionally twitched the tiller, as if he could steer sightlessly.

It seemed he knew the river so well—the meanders, the currents, the sandbars and rapids—had travelled this long watery snake for half a century—he needed no eyes. Maybe he could feel the flow and know to a nautical inch, a fraction of a fathom, where he was in time and space? Perhaps he navigated as he knitted woollen garments, both by feel, on his way to the sea.

Niccolò signalled to the man, and received a reply.

Afterwards he made camp by the river that wound beneath the star patterns visible in the clear sky. The campfire sent up showers of sparks, like wandering stars themselves, and though Niccolò did not know it they gave someone hope. A lost soul was out there, in the desert, and saw the glow in the heavens.

The following morning, Niccolò woke to the sound of camels grumbling, kicking their hobbled legs, shaking their traces. The horse took no part in this minor rebellion. A nobler creature (in its own mind) it held itself aloof from dissident camels. Niccolò fed the camels, then he and the horse ate together, apart from the other beasts.

THREE DAYS OUT INTO THE desert, Niccolò came across the woman. Her lips were blistered and he had trouble forcing water past them. When she opened her eyes she said, 'I knew you would come. I saw your fire,' then she passed out again.

In the evening he revived her with some warm jasmine tea, and soon she was able to sit up, talk. She was not a particularly pretty woman. At a guess she was about the same age as he was, in her very early thirties. Her skin had been dried by the sun, was the colour of old paper, and though it was soft had a myriad of tiny wrinkles especially around the eyes and mouth. Her stature was slight: she could have been made of dry reeds. She wore only a thin cotton dress.

'What are you doing out here?' he asked her.

'Looking for water,' she said, sipping the tea, staring at him over the rim of the mug.

He gestured irritably.

'I can see that, but how did you get lost? Were you part of a caravan?'

She shook her head, slowly.

'I was searching for my mother's house.'

'Here, in the desert?'

Her brown eyes were soft in the firelight.

'It wasn't always a desert,' she said. 'I thought there might be something left—a few bricks, stones, something.'

Niccolò nodded. He guessed she was one of those who went out searching for their roots. Lost now, but lost before she even came into the desert. One of those who had been separated as a child from her family during the exodus, and had found out her father's name, where her parents had lived, and had gone looking to see if there was anything left.

He stared around him, his eyes sweeping over the low and level plain. Only a short three decades ago there had been a thriving community here, the suburbs of a city. On the very place where they were sitting buildings had stood, streets had run. The city had been so vast it took many days to travel by coach-and-six from its centre to the outskirts.

Now there was nothing but dust.

'I can't take you with me,' he said. 'I'm heading for the Tower…' he nodded towards the marvellous structure that dominated the eastern sky, taller than any mountain in the region, so tall its heights were often lost in the clouds. Since it was evening, lights had begun to encrust the Tower, like a sprinkling of early stars.

She said timidly, 'I can come with you.'

'No. I don't have the food or the water to carry a passenger. I have just enough for my own needs, and no more. I'll point you in the right direction. You can make the river in five, maybe six days, on foot. The first refugee camp is two days on from there.'

She looked at him with a shocked expression on her face.

'I'll die of thirst.'

'That's not my fault. I came across you by chance. I didn't have anything to do with your being here. You might make it. I'll give you a little water, as much as I can spare.'

'No,' she said firmly, hugging her legs and staring into the fire, 'you'll take me with you.'

He did not answer her, having nothing more to say. Niccolò of course did not want to send her out there, and he knew she was right, she probably *would* die, but he had no choice. His mission depended on him making the journey safely. To ensure success, he needed to do that alone, without any encumbrances. She would hold him back, drink his water, eat his food, spy on him, probe for his secrets. He would probably have to kill more than one camel to get to the Tower, if he took her along too. It was not in his plans.

Finally, he spoke.

'We must get some rest, we both need it.'

Niccolò gave her the sleeping bag and used a horse blanket himself. Once the sun was down, it was bitterly cold, the ground failing to retain the heat. She moved closer to him for warm, and the fire blocked his retreat. He had not been with a woman for so long, he had almost forgotten how pyrotechnical the experience could be. Just before dawn she crawled under the blanket with him and said, 'Take me—please,' and though he knew that the words had a double-meaning, that he was committing himself to something he wished to avoid, he made love with her.

In the morning, he knew he could not send her on her way. He wanted her with him, in the cold desert nights, and afterwards, in his bleak life.

'You'll have to ride on one of the pack camels,' he said. 'Have you ever been on a camel?'

'No, but I'll manage.'

'What's your name?' he asked, almost as an afterthought, as he helped her up onto her perch. He had chosen one of the less vicious camels, one that did not bite just out of pure malice, though it was inclined to snap when it got testy at the end of a long hard day's walk.

'Romola,' she smiled, 'what's yours.'

'Niccolò. Now listen, Romola, we've got a long way to go, and your... you'll get a sore rump.'

'You can rub some cream into it, when we stop at night,' she said, staring into his eyes.

'We're not carrying any cream,' he said, practically, and swung himself into the worn leather saddle.

They moved out into the desert, towards the wonderful Tower, whose shadow would stretch out and almost reach them towards the evening. He and Arturo, eight years ago, had set out on a mission of murder, and had failed even to cross the desert. This time he was well prepared, but carrying a passenger. If anything happened, he would have to abandon her, for the mission was more important than either of them.

The city was still there, of course, he reminded himself. It was vertical, instead of lying like a great pool over the surface of the continent. It was as if the houses had been sucked up to the clouds, like water in a waterspout, and now stood like a giant pillar supporting heaven. The city had become the Tower, a monument to artistic beauty and achievement: a profound and glorious testament to brilliant architecture. Perfect in its symmetry, most marvellous in its form, without parallel in all the previous accomplishments of man. It was grace and elegance, tastefulness and balance, to the finest degree possible this side of heaven. The angels could not have created a more magnificent testimonial to art, nor God Himself a splendour more pleasing to the eye.

And at its head, the great and despised architect and builder himself, its maker and resident.

The Tower had been started by the High Priest designate, da Vinci, when he was in his early twenties.

'We need to get closer to God,' he had told his contemporaries and the people, 'and away from the commerce and business of the streets. We have the cathedral's steeple of course, but think what a great monument to the city a tower would be! We could use the bricks and rubble from condemned buildings, to keep the cost of the construction low. The air is cleaner up there.'

Da Vinci was now truly a 'high priest' living at the top of the Tower, away from the people, protected by his army of clergy. It was said that oxygen had to be pumped to his chambers, night and day, in order to breathe up there. It was also very cold, and fires were maintained constantly, the fuel coming from the stored furniture of a million inhabitants of the old city.

He had begun the work, as he had promised, by using the debris from demolished houses, factories, government buildings, but gradually, as the fever for greatness took him, so he had urged his priests to find more materials elsewhere. Gravestones were used, walls were pillaged, wells were shorn of bricks. The people began to complain but da Vinci told them the wrath of God would descend upon any dissenter, and since he was God's instrument, he would see to it that the sentence was death.

By this time the Tower had become a citadel, within whose walls a private army grew. The Holy Guardians, as they were called, went forth daily to find more building materials, forcing people from their homes around the Tower, and tearing up whole streets to get at the slabs beneath.

Not all the citizens were unhappy about da Vinci's scheme, or he never would have got as far as he did. Many were caught up in his fervour, added fuel to his excitement and determination. The guild of building workers, for example, a strong group of men, were totally behind the idea of a Tower to God. It promised them work for many years to come.

Also the water-carriers, with their mule-pulled carts; the tool makers; the waggoners carrying supplies for the builders and the Holy Guardians; the weapon makers; the brick workers; the slate and marble miners. All these people put themselves behind da Vinci with undisguised enthusiasm.

Da Vinci began recruiting more youths, and maidens, as the Tower's demands for a larger workforce grew, and these came mainly from the city streets. When the guild could no longer find willing, strong people to join them, they sent out press gangs and got their labour that way. Eventually, they had to get workers from the farms, around the city, and the land was left to go to waste while the Tower grew, mighty and tall, above the face of the world.

Churches were among the last buildings to be stripped, but torn down they were, and their stained-glass windows and marble used to enhance da Vinci's now fabled monument. The High Priest strived for perfection in his quest for beauty. Inferior materials were torn out, removed, shipped down to the ocean in barges and cast into the waves. No blemish was too small to be overlooked and allowed to remain. Every part of the tower, every aspect deserved the utmost attention, deserved to meet perfection at its completion.

Flawlessness became da Vinci's obsession. Exactness, precision, excellence. Nothing less would be accepted. There were those who died, horribly, for a tiny defect, a mark out of true that was visible only in certain lights, and viewed at certain angles, by someone with perfect vision. There was no such thing as a small error, for every scratch was a chasm.

This was the form that his obsession took.

By the time the tower was half-built the population had already begun to leave the city. Long lines of refugees trekked across the wasteland, to set up camps in the hanging valleys beyond, where there was at least a shallow surface soil for growing meagre crops, though the mountains cast cold shadows over their fields, and high altitude winds brought early frosts.

Or people made their way to the sea and settled on a coastal strip that could barely support the fisherman who had lived there before the multitudes arrived. Many of them died on the march, some travelled by river and drowned when the overcrowded rafts were thrown by the rapids; others perished of starvation when they arrived at the camps; thousands went down with the plague and never raised their heads above the dust again.

And still the Tower grew.

'WHAT DO YOU THINK OF da Vinci?' asked Romola on the third night they were together.

'He's a genius,' said Niccolò without hesitation. 'He is the greatest architect and builder the world has ever known.'

'Does his genius come from God?'

She peered at him through the firelight.

'What do you mean?' he asked.

'I mean does God give him instruction?'

'That sounds close to blasphemy,' he said, staring hard. 'You're suggesting that God, not the High Priest, should take credit for the Tower. It is da Vinci's work, not the Lord's.'

He drew away from her then, away from the fire, despite his fear of the night snakes amongst the darkness of the rocks.

She continued to talk.

'I used to be one of the Holy Guardians—until I was thrown out on my ear...'

He looked at her, then behind him at the Tower, then back to her again.

'Ah,' he said, 'you didn't come from the refugee camp? You came from the Tower itself?'

'I... I didn't know what else to do, when we were told to leave, I thought about looking for my parents' former home, thinking it was a long way from the Tower and something of it might have survived.'

'Why were you asked to leave?'

'New guards were recruited, from distant places. The old Holy Guardians have been disbanded. We are no longer permitted to remain near the tower. Most of my friends have gone down to the sea, to try to get work on the ships, guarding against pirates. Fighting is all we know. I intend to ask the High Priest if some of his—his closer Companions at Arms can return to our former posts. We were his Chosen, after all.'

Niccolò smiled.

'You mean he doesn't call you to his bed any more?'

She lifted her head and shook it.

'No, that's a privilege reserved for the Holy Guardians.'

'I see. So the fact that you, and most of your companions, had reached the age of thirty or thereabouts, had nothing to do with you being asked to leave? The new men and women, they're not young, handsome or pretty of course?'

She stared at Niccolò.

'He recruited a new army for very logical reasons. They now consist of many small groups of men and women from different regions, different tribes.'

'Now why did da Vinci do that?' asked Niccolò, softly.

'It's said that he's afraid of plots being formed against him, even amongst his trusted Holy Guardians. The separate new groups do not speak each other's language, they use many different tongues. If they can't communicate, they can't conspire against the High Priest, can they?' she said. 'Since he has control over a small group of interpreters, he has complete control over the whole army.'

Despite himself, Niccolò was impressed. It certainly was a clever strategy on da Vinci's part. There was much to admire about da Vinci, no matter how much he was hated. The Tower was a product of a brilliant mind. The architecture, the engineering, was decades ahead of its time. Where an old support might have proved to have been too weak, da Vinci had designed a new one. He was responsible for inventing the transverse arch, the buttress, the blind arcade, and many other architectural wonders. The absolute beauty of the work—the colonnades, the windows, the ceilings—was indeed worthy of a god.

Such a pity a million people had been sacrificed to feed his egoism.

ON THE THIRD SUNDAY NICCOLÒ confronted her, waking her from a deep sleep.

'You've been meddling,' he said, angrily. 'You've been sticking your nose in amongst my goods.'

She shook the sleep from her head, staring up at him. Comprehension came to her gradually. He could see it appearing in her eyes.

'I was just curious,' she said. 'I didn't mean any harm.'

Niccolò pointed to one of the packs that had fallen from a camel. Its contents had spilled out, over the desert floor: marble statuettes, of angels, of cherubim, of seraphim.

She stared where he was pointing.

He said, 'When you retied the knot, you used a knot that slipped—there's the result.'

'I'm sorry. I just wanted to...'

'To spy,' said Niccolò.

He could see he was right by the expression on her face and he grabbed her and pulled her to her feet. She immediately struck him a sharp blow with the heel of her hand behind his ear, then as his head snapped to the side, she kicked him in the groin. He went down in the dust, excruciating pains shooting through his neck, a numbness in his genitals which quickly turned to an unbearable aching.

She had been, after all, a soldier.

'Don't you dare try that again,' she cried. 'My mother was an assassin. She taught me the martial arts. I could kill you now...'

In his agony he didn't need to be told.

By the time he had recovered, she had gathered his statuettes, carefully wrapped them in their protective rags, and tied them inside the pack. He hobbled over to it and inspected the knots, satisfying himself that this time they were correct and tight. Then he swung himself into his saddle, winced to himself, and then gestured for her to follow on with the camels.

'THOSE FIGURINES,' SHE SAID, OBVIOUSLY trying to make friends with him again, 'they're very beautiful. Where do they come from?'

'I carved them myself,' he said, 'from the finest block of marble the eastern quarries have ever disgorged.'

She seemed impressed, though she was obviously no judge of art, nor could she know the work that went into just one of the three hundred and thirty-three statuettes. There was admiration in her tone.

'They're very beautiful,' she repeated.

'They're flawless,' he remarked as casually as he could. 'It took many years to carve them all, and I have only just completed them. They are a gift, for da Vinci. He can no longer carve minutely, the way one needs to be able to carve if one is to produce a piece just six inches tall—objects that need a younger steadier hand—especially since he developed arthritis.'

She was silent after this.

The Tower grew in size and height, as they drew nearer to its base, until it filled the horizon. Its immensity and resplendence overawed Niccolò so much that he almost turned around, forgot his mission, and went back to the mountains. It would now take him a day to ride, not to the end, but to the edge of the Tower's shadow. The Tower was like a carved mountain, a white pinnacle of rock that soared upwards to pierce the light blues of the upper skies. Its peak was rarely visible, being wrapped about with clouds for much of the time. The high night winds blew through its holes and hollows, so that it was like a giant flute playing eerie melodies to the moon.

By this time they had begun to eat one of the camels, and two others had been set free, their fodder having been consumed and their usefulness over. The water was almost gone.

Romola showed him how to produce water, by using the stretched membrane of the dead camel's stomach. She dug a conical pit in the sand, placed a tin cup at its bottom, and shaped the membrane so that it sagged in the centre. Water condensed on its underside and dripped into the cup.

'I'm an artist,' he stated, piqued by her superior survival knowledge, 'I don't know about these things.'

'So, an artist, but not a survivor?'

'I make out.'

THEY REACHED THE TOWER, FOOTSORE, weary, but alive. The Holy Guardians immediately took them into custody. Romola protested, saying she was a former soldier, but she could not get them to understand what she was saying. All around the tower was a babble of voices, men and women talking to each other in a dozen different tongues. Romola's pleas were ignored and she was thrown into the dungeons.

Niccolò found a Holy Guardian who spoke one of the three languages he knew and explained to them that he had brought some gifts for the High Priest and that da Vinci would be greatly angered if Niccolò were not permitted an audience with the one on high.

'I am the High Priest's son,' said Niccolò, 'and I wish to pay homage to my father.'

Messages were sent, answers received, and eventually Niccolò found himself being hoisted in silver cages up the various stages of the Tower: pulled rapidly aloft by winches through which ran golden chains with counterweights. An invention of his father. With him went his bundles of statuettes.

He reached the summit of the tower and was ushered into a huge room on his knees, before the powerful presence of the High Priest, da Vinci. The room was decorated to the quintessence of perfection, its ceilings painted by great artists, its walls carved with wonderful bas-relief friezes, and on the cloud-patterned marble floor stood statues sculpted by the genius da Vinci himself.

A thin middle-aged man stared at Niccolò with hard eyes, from a safe distance. He rubbed his arthritic hands together, massaging the pain, while the guards stood poised with heavy swords, ready to decapitate Niccolò if their master so gestured.

'You claim to be my son,' he said, 'but I have many sons, many daughters—bastards all of them.'

Niccolò replied, 'It's true, I'm illegitimate, but how could it be otherwise? You've never married.'

The old man laughed softly.

'That's true. I loved only one woman—and she failed me.'

Niccolò assumed a puzzled expression.

'How did she fail you, my lord?'

'She scarred herself, making her loveliness ugly to my sight. She was a vision of beauty, that became horrible to my eyes…' the memory was obviously painful to da Vinci, for he paused for a moment in deep thought, a frown upon his face, then his mood changed, and he said, 'What? What is it? Why did you request, no *demand* to see me?'

'I bring you a gift, my lord,' said Niccolò. 'A present for my father. Three hundred and thirty-three statuettes, all carved with great skill by a talented artist—a genius—every one of them a masterpiece.'

'Who is this artist? Raphael? Michelangelo?'

Niccolò raised his head and smiled.

'I am the artist, my lord.'

This time da Vinci roared with laughter.

'Let me see the gift.'

The guards unwrapped the rags and the statuettes, began to appear, were placed carefully upon the marble floor, until they covered a huge area of the great room. Eventually, they were all on view, and the High Priest motioned for the guard to bring one to where he stood. He studied it, first while it rested in the guard's hands, then taking it in his own and turning it over and over, cautiously, but also admiringly.

'This is indeed a beautiful work of art,' said da Vinci, holding up the figurine so that the soft light caught the patterns on its buffed and polished surface. 'How many of them did you say are in the set?'

'Three hundred and thirty-three.'

Da Vinci smiled.

'You know the value of numbers. Three—the Perfect Harmony.'

'Or union of unity and diversity...'

'Both. And here we have the perfect number—three threes.'

'Angels, cherubim, seraphim,' said Niccolò. He began to arrange them in a large circle on the marble floor. 'As you see,' he continued as he worked, concentrating, not looking up at da Vinci, 'they are also an interlocking puzzle. Each angel fits into another, but only one other. You will notice that the pattern of the marble flows through the figures, like an ocean current, following the holy circle. I defy you to find where the pattern begins and where it ceases, for it is one continuous flowing band.'

'Marvellous...' Niccolò heard the High Priest breathe.

There were angels of every kind, some nude, some clothed in flowing robes, some wielding swords of justice. There were seraphim brandishing spears of truth, and cherubim with little wings, drawing on cupid bows with tiny arrows.

'But look closely my lord, at the features...'

The High Priest did as he was bid.

'…every one of them,' continued Niccolò, 'has your face, when you were a young and beautiful youth.'

There was silence in the room for a long time.

Finally, da Vince walked past his prisoner, looked down on the multitude of marble figures at his feet, all bearing his features from a time when he was at his most handsome.

'Superb,' he whispered, stroking the one in his hand lovingly. 'Wonderful—,' but then he cried out, as if in pain, as he plucked a cherub from the holy ring.

'There's one with a broken wing,' he cried.

A guard near to Niccolò moved uncertainly, as if he believed he was expected to do something about his master's anguish, but da Vinci held up a withered arthritic hand.

Niccolò spoke quickly.

'An accident, father. I shall carve another to replace it. I brought enough of the marble with me to carve three more statuettes, should it be necessary.'

'But the patterns…?'

'I can match them. As a sculptor of figurines I have no equal, save yourself in the days when your joints were supple. I am you, when you were younger, without your arthritis.'

Once more the middle-aged man studied the statuette, minutely, weighing it in his hands. Then he picked up another and did the same.

'This is truly a great work of art,' he said when he had finished, 'but I shall have them inspected closely before I allow them into my chambers. After all, you may have hidden a spring-loaded trap amongst them? One of those cherubs perhaps, lets loose its arrow as I hold it up to my eye? Or some devious device to administer poison? Perhaps if I pricked my finger on one of those spearpoints? I have lived so long, because I am without trust.'

'It is part of your genius.'

'Which has rubbed off on you, it seems.'

'Am I not my father's son?'

Da Vinci placed a hand on Niccolò's head.

'You are indeed. You took a great risk coming here, to give me these. I almost had you beheaded before I saw you. There are many plots against me. Many. But there was something very audacious in the manner in which you *expected* an audience. I was curious to see you before you died.'

'Am I to die, my lord, for being your loyal son?'

Da Vinci snorted.

'Don't put too much faith in flesh and blood. You can't prove I'm your father, and it means nothing to me anyway. There are a thousand like you, by women whose faces I hardly looked at.'

He paused and strolled across the room.

'However, you have, as you say, great talent—no doubt inherited from me. I am an artist too. A genius. I have decided to let you live, at least until you carve the last figure. What use is three hundred and thirty-two? A broken circle? It must be 333—all with *my* face. Go down from the tower, find your marble, and do the work. Once you have completed your task, we shall see if you are to live.'

'I understand, my lord.'

The High Priest then said to his guards, 'When you take him down, send me up a stone mason. I want to construct a raised circular platform, to display these pieces.'

They then led Niccolò away.

THEY RELEASED ROMOLA, AND SHE found Niccolò. He was pleased to see her. She had holes in her hands and feet, where they had tortured her, trying to extract some kind of confession. She knew the ways, knew the limits, having been one of them herself. She professed a profound hatred for her old master, wishing he would rot in hell for his treatment of her.

'I sent him a message, telling him I was in the dungeon, and he ignored it for the first few hours, knowing they would torture me.'

She went with Niccolò and watched him, as he spent the next week, carving the final figure to complete the circle. As he worked, he told her what had passed between his father and himself, high in that room above the world. They were staying at an inn, on the far side of the river. Accommodation for those not directly connected with guarding the Tower, was on the north bank, while the Tower itself stood on the south bank. It was another safety measure, to protect the High Priest. All river traffic ceased at sundown, and anyone found on the south bank, after dusk, was immediately put to death.

'When we were out in the desert,' she told him, 'I often wondered… well, why didn't you bring the statuettes by river, on a barge? Why risk that terrible journey over the wasteland?'

Niccolò had left the carving of the facial features until last, and this he had completed within the last five hours of close work. He held the statuette up to the light coming through the dusty window, inspecting it. The piece, as always, was pristine, immaculate. It would fit, patterns matching exactly, into its place in the holy ring of angels. It was the sibling of the other 332 figurines—with one exception.

Instead of da Vinci's youthful countenance, it had the face of a monkey. Worse still, a monkey whose features resembled those of the High Priest. A cruel caricature.

He wrapped the statuette in a piece of cloth, before she could inspect his final work, and answered her question.

'The river is crowded, full of his agents and spies. I know how fanatical they are. I knew I could convince *him*, once I was here, but they would never have allowed me to reach this far.

Besides, one is only permitted to carry agricultural goods by river craft, unless one bears the authority of the High Priest. I had no such authority. They would have killed me simply on suspicion, before I reached the Tower.

'The river is a deadly place, as you know. Then there are the pirates... I stood far more chance of being murdered on the water, than I did from dying of hunger or thirst out on the sands.'

'That's true, and it's also true that you could cross the desert relatively undetected, until you came within sight of the Tower, of course. Yet... you took me along with you, knowing the risk. I might have been one of his spies.'

He stared at her.

'Yes, you might. I think you were—and still are. It is fascinating, and horrifying to me, that people like you are prepared to go through torture for the sake of discovering his enemies. It's an enigma I don't think I shall ever solve... but I am glad for my father's sake that he has his devoted servants.'

'You wrong me,' she said, looking into his eyes.

'No,' replied Niccolò, 'I don't think so. You are still besotted with the mystique of the man, and you think that if you can uncover some plot against him, he will reinstate you, and you'll return to his favour. You have been blinded, Romola, but I shall restore your sight.'

Niccolò dispatched the statuette to da Vinci by courier. Then he asked Romola to walk down to the river with him, so that they might cross, and gain audience with the High Priest, once that man had had time to gaze upon the final figurine.

On their way down to the river, Niccolò said to her, 'You have been asked to guard me, haven't you?'

She stared at him, then nodded.

'Yes. That's why they let me out of prison.'

'I thought so. Da Vinci would never let me run around loose, of that I was sure. So it had to be you.'

They reached the jetties, and waited for a boat to come which would carry them across.

A short while afterwards a barge came down the river with a giant man at the tiller. He had a gentle face, a good face, and he was wearing a knitted waistcoat that looked new. When his boat reached the jetty he clambered ashore. The Holy Guardians swarmed over his craft, inspecting every spar, every beam, before allowing the dockers to unload his cargo. The only goods permitted to be carried by river barge, were food and drink, and if you were found with any other freight you were executed on the spot, no excuses accepted. The big man nodded to the two people who watched him amble past them.

When the big man returned, his barge had been unloaded, and his craft stood high in the water.

'Will you take us across?' asked Niccolò.

'Two sesterces,' growled the giant.

'Agreed.'

The three of them boarded the barge, and the giant raised the lateen sail, and the craft caught the current. They headed downriver, towards the sea.

Romola looked puzzled, stared at the far shore, then into Niccolò's face.

'Where are we going?' she snapped.

'Away from here,' answered Niccolò.

'Out to sea?'

'Yes. We shall be island-hopping for as long as necessary, staying one jump ahead of da Vinci's people, I hope.'

She nodded towards the giant at the tiller, with his knitted waistcoat and benign expression. Romola became angry, clenching her hands, making them into fists. Niccolò stepped away from her, warily.

'The two of you are together—conspirators?' she said.

'We came to help da Vinci destroy himself, and now we are making our escape. Now, I realise you're an ex-soldier, and I still have the lumps to prove it, but my friend Domo here...' he indicated the giant, 'is not an effete artist. He could snap you in two, like a twig, so no violence please.'

She stared at Domo, who smiled broadly. He did indeed appear to be a man of enormous strength, and while all three of them knew Romola would put up a spirited fight, the outcome could not be in doubt. Especially since Domo had a wicked-looking baling hook in his free hand.

Niccolò said, 'We don't want to kill you, Romola—at least, I don't, though gathering from the looks Domo has been giving me, he thinks I am a fool, and jeopardising our mission. I'm afraid you got under my skin, out there in the desert, and I've fallen in love with you. However, if you try anything, anything at all, Domo will kill you where you stand, and throw you to the fish. Is that understood? I shall be unable to prevent him, or help you.'

She stood a long while, as if weighing up the situation, and then turned her head.

The craft eventually reached the ocean, and Domo set a course for the outer islands, behind which the sun was settling for the night. Niccolò stood in the bows, watching the prow cut through the water as the wind carried them westwards, into the red glow of the evening. When it was almost dark, Romola came and stood beside him.

'How did you do it? The assassination?' she asked.

'Oh, he's not dead yet, but he will be.'

'How? Did you poison the statuettes?'

Niccolò shook his head.

'No, I gave him a gift—an imperfect gift. Perfection is an obsession with him. Now he is caught in a cycle of madness. He will not destroy the gift, for the angels have his face and it would be like destroying himself. Yet one of the figures mocks him—resembles him in a crude way, but actually has the face of a monkey. Without this figure the ring of angels is incomplete, an obscenity—three hundred and thirty-two statuettes. The pattern on the marble is broken, the circle unfinished, yet with it, the art is marred, twisted into a joke of which he is the brunt.

'He will go mad, it will destroy him.'

Her eyes were round.

'You're sure of that?'

'I'm certain of it. He loved my mother very much—my friend the sage Cicaro was there at the time—but he had her executed after my birth, because… because her beauty was marred.'

'In what way?'

'Stretch marks,' said Niccolò. 'In giving birth to me, she was left with stretch marks on her abdomen. He destroyed her because she was imperfect, blemished by a natural act of which he himself was the author. He killed someone he loved because of his madness for perfection. Now he will destroy himself—he's caught in the web of his own vanity. He *has* to have the circle of angels, for they immortalise his youth and beauty, yet he cannot have them, because one of them is a mockery. He will rage, he will consume himself with frustration and fury. He will destroy himself…'

'You are a genius,' she said.

'I am… subtle.'

They stood, watching the water sliding beneath the craft, as darkness fell. When it became cooler, once the sun had finally gone, she put her arm around him.

BLACK DRONGO

(Written during my years in Hong Kong, where I used to watch the black drongos fighting amongst themselves. Hong Kong was seething with ideas for short stories: one just had to reach up and pluck them from the air.)

'SO WHAT YOU WANT TO do is take Marcia's personality and put it in the body of a bird?' said Steve. 'What are you trying to create, some monster freak? Some creature that'll think, like… like Marcia?'

We were at dinner, just the three of us, in a small restaurant off Mody Road in Tsim Sha Tsui. My brother Steve and his girlfriend Marcia were flying out of Hong Kong the next day. They were going on a business holiday, to some remote place in the Philippines, which was incidentally Marcia's homeland.

I explained patiently, 'I'm not transferring her *psyche*, Steve, there are laws against that. All I want to do is copy Marcia's persona, and superimpose it upon that of the drongo's.'

'Okay Einstein, what's the difference?' he said.

'Her persona is simply her personality. A *psyche* is someone's conscious and unconscious, someone's *mind* or *self*, if you like. I'm not allowed to screw around with psyches, although it is

35

possible to make a transfer under controlled conditions. Only the GRL, the Government Research Labs, are permitted to dabble in that. This won't hurt her in the least, and she'll have the satisfaction of knowing she's furthering my studies of behaviour patterns in wild birds.'

'What if I don't want you to mess around with my girl's persona?'

'Stevie...' said Marcia, in that soft voice she has, but he cut her off, with, 'No, wait, *I* want to hear what Einstein here has to say about it. You just keep quiet for a minute. No, I'm sorry Marcia, this is for me to decide whether it's right for you to do this or not. You don't understand these things like we do.'

Steve can be a real pain in the ass, when he wants to be, which is most of the time, but he is my brother and I put up with him because I love him. He is unbelievably insecure, and this manifests itself in hostility and aggression. Tonight, he was being nice: any other time he would have blown his stack and started throwing things around the room. He always mellowed a little prior to travel, gradually becoming as pliant as he would ever be with Marcia, or any woman.

Men could take him better than women: they recognised the apprehensive hunter-gatherer in him as something they had within themselves, though often not to the same extreme. Steve was one of those people who believed you had to prove yourself all the time, against the competition. If you didn't, you would be taken advantage of, and eaten alive. They would fall on you like jackals while you were exposed to them. You had to keep your defences up, show them you were a man to be reckoned with, never let them see your vulnerability.

He played squash as if to lose would mean the guillotine. He was merciless against business rivals. My older brother was still living in a world where you clubbed a man senseless and took his meat and his woman and made sure you felt damn good about it.

Any weakness in you would be exploited, and you would become carrion for the vultures.

I did not consider Steve a *bad* man, and most other men liked his company, many women too if they were the kind who preferred being told what to do, but there were others who considered him an aggressive thick-skinned bull.

I hadn't told Steve that the reason I wanted Marcia's persona, as opposed to any other, was because of my observations of their relationship. Steve had always been a bully, and the person who took the brunt of his obnoxious behaviour, was Marcia. She, on the other hand, had soaked up his abuse with not a flicker of annoyance or retaliation. I used to sit and watch her being verbally attacked, Steve imposing his will on her with unbelievable insensitivity, and yet she took it all calmly, letting it all wash over her, leaving her unmoved. She wasn't submissive, not in a way that was visible, she just allowed it to happen while seemingly unimpressed.

'I think it's for Marcia to decide, not you Steve. I'm not asking you for your persona, and Marcia is a grown woman. She doesn't need your permission.'

'Yeah, but she's my girl, Pete. I've got to look after her interests.'

'You don't need to do anything of the sort. She's a capable person.'

Steve was typical of many expatriates living in a far eastern enclave consisting mostly of other expats. He was conservative, thoroughly conventional, and about a hundred years behind the times. His passport said he was an Amer-european, but in truth we had long since left our original nationalities behind, and had become something else. I'm not sure what. *Gweilos* I suppose, which is the Cantonese term for all Caucasians living in their society. Literally it means *foreign devil*, but language is dynamic and it has become a quick description of a western businessman living on the China coast, out of touch with reality, holding on to out-of-date values, talking in clichés like: 'Your average British workman is lazy, but take the Chinese, they'll flog their guts out for you for a few dollars a day, and they can live on it you see, because they know which markets to go to get cheap vegetables, they don't pay the same prices as me and you...'

There are Chinese businessmen like Steve, who exploit the local labour, but they don't make excuses for the poor pay they offer, they simply do it. Steve thought the Thatcher-Reagan years of the last century were wonderful, but of course he only went to Britain and America for business conferences, a few days, nothing more.

'Is that what you think?' said Steve, his tone belligerent. 'Well, okay, I'll leave the decision to her, but I'm going to come along. I only have her best interests at heart.'

Steve being a man's man, a hard drinker, naturally believed eastern women were toys to be played with, but Marcia was the immovable object, who took all he had to throw at her, and remained intact, without reprisal, without going under. She was a small woman, even for a Filipino, with a gentle smile. She withstood the storms and remained undaunted. I had great admiration for her in one way, though I felt she lacked the spirit to kick Steve in the balls, like many *gweilo* women I knew would have done ages ago. The Filipino maids, fifty thousand of them in Hong Kong, were an accommodating group. Most of them considered a little abuse worth pursuing the romantic dream of marrying out of the terrible poverty which was their cultural heritage. Even if the man be a boorish old fart like Steve, twice her age and with a body ravaged by too many gins.

'That's what I think, Steve...'

In the end, I had my way, and Steve even drove us to the lab in his new Mercedes, chatting quite amiably on the journey under the forest canopy of neon branches that grew from buildings either side of the street. The night watchman was a little surprised to see us, at eleven in the evening, but he let us in, and stood by the lab door in that guarded manner of the Cantonese security worker dealing with the unusual, wondering whether he is going to get into trouble for allowing someone to enter the building after hours, even if that someone was perfectly entitled to be there. The Cantonese like to live lives of complete order, within a vast sea of chaos.

Marcia went into the scanner cubicle a little nervously, though it is one of the newer devices produced by Walker and Quntan, in which the subject stands upright, rather than one of the more common horizontal coffin affairs of Stebling Inc. Steve chatted to the night watchman, while I took the reading, then when everything checked out, proceeded to take a facsimile of Marcia's persona on disk.

When I had finished with Marcia, I asked Steve to step into the cubicle.

He stuck out his jaw.

'Why? What do you want my personality for? I thought you considered it pretty shitty?'

'Don't make a fuss, Steve, I'm not going to hurt you.'

This struck at the core of his manhood, as I knew it would. He went straight into the cubicle to prove he was not afraid of anything, even if his brother was a mad scientist.

'Okay,' he growled, from within, 'but if I start growing hairs on the palms of my hands Pete, I'm coming looking for my little brother to eat.'

It was all over by twelve, and we went for a final coffee at the Peninsula Hotel on Nathan Road, where the string quartet plays on a balcony above patrons surrounded by the ornate glitz and opulence of yesteryear.

I saw them off at the airport the next morning, Steve grumbling at the taxi driver most of the way, because he wasn't driving fast enough for him, and Marcia talking to me in that soft tone quite unlike the voice she used when talking in Tagalog to her fellow Filipinos. Steve was *definitely* more mellow now. In the old days he would have taken time out to snap at her, and ask me what I found so interesting in her 'drivel', but that day he simply gave her one or two side glances, not without a trace of fondness in them. They were to be gone for the whole of July and August, the terrible months in Hong Kong, when the temperature is over 33 Celsius most days, and the humidity in the high nineties.

A week after they had left I began my experiment.

The Chinese government had employed me as a lecturer on Animal Behaviour at the University of Hong Kong, but of course I was permitted, even expected, to carry out my own research. Any findings would of course be credited to the University as well as myself, thus gaining face for my Chinese employers.

My specific interest at this time was *animal aggression*. What I wanted to do was to superimpose a placid persona on an aggressive wild creature, in order to study the reactions of the creature's own kind, and to see whether there was any change in their behaviour towards the subject, and indeed whether the subject showed any signs of reverting to type.

The creature I had chosen was a black drongo (*Dicrurus macrocercus*), a bird about the size of a jackdaw. It is a quarrelsome creature, known in India as King Crow, because of its habit of mobbing the much larger members of the *Corvidae* family. It fights amongst its own kind, for scraps of food, though there are no recorded combats ending in fatalities. The black drongo has an unusual cat-like hissing call, which is quite disturbing to other birds.

I had three black drongos, caught on the Mai Po Marshes of what used to be the New Territories, when Hong Kong was a colony. The marshes, founded as a bird sanctuary in the last century by a man called Peter Scott, are a resting place for thousands of migrating birds on their way to and from SE Asia. The black drongo and hair-crested drongo, are summer visitors however, and stay in the area for breeding. The other birds must breathe a sigh of relief when the drongos leave for other parts, at the end of the hot season.

I chose a female for the subject (for no other reason than Marcia was a female) and called her Yat Ho, or Number One. The other pair were of course Yi Ho and Sam Ho—Two and Three. Marcia's persona overlaid that of Yat Ho's, and I introduced the subject back into the aviary, while my students put themselves in charge of the video cameras, ever eager to record experiments and pore over the results. They are a good bunch, this year. Some undergraduates spend much of their student life in the gaming halls of Wan Chai district, risking failure for the sake of glitz, but then many of them are from remote villages in the north, and the bleeping and pinging of the gaming machines in the neon-lit halls act like syrens on them.

At first, the expected happened. Yat Ho's strange docile behaviour kept the other two birds at a distance. The unusual was distrusted, and it was doubtful whether they actually recognised and identified her as a drongo. It's possible they thought she was some other kind of bird, and it puzzled them that she looked, sounded and smelled like one of them. They fought amongst themselves, and were wary if she approached.

Then suddenly, as if working in concert, they began to attack and bully her, shouldering her out of the way of food, pecking, hissing, and treating her with disdain. Sam Ho was particularly vicious and treated Yat Ho with utter disdain, as if she were some kind of traitor to her kind.

She did nothing. True to Marcia's persona, she took everything they had to give her, and remained unmoved. The students were terribly excited by this, never having witnessed anything like it before in their golden days of learning. They could talk of nothing else but the drongos for the next six weeks, as Yat Ho continued to survive, simply by showing no reaction to the bullying—simply by *being*.

I must have been pretty boring too, as a date. My girlfriend, Xia, a Han Chinese from the north, is normally fairly tolerant of my enthusing, but I think those first few drongo weeks strained even her elastic patience.

Then something remarkable began to happen, which I should have expected, but which actually surprised me. The resilience of Yat Ho began to wear down the energy of the other two birds, especially Sam Ho, the main contender for bully of the season. She simply took what they had to offer in the way of violence, but when she remained seemingly unaffected by their aggressive behaviour, they gradually ceased to attack her. They still fought amongst themselves, but in their dealings with Yat Ho, they were almost nauseatingly friendly.

'They even bring her bits of food,' cried one Penny Lau, one of my students, 'and she takes the pieces as if she *deserves* them.'

It was true. They were courting her friendship, trying to get her to like them, forgive them for their earlier treatment of her. I was fascinated. What on earth was going on here? I couldn't get my notes on tape fast enough.

One evening, about the seventh week, I was sitting outside the aviary on my own, idly watching my three drongos. The students had all gone out for the evening. It was a holiday, Liberation Day, and they were out celebrating. Suddenly, something horrible occurred in that artificial world behind the glass screen.

Sam Ho was perched next to Yat Ho, their scapular feathers touching, when she turned and deliberately pecked through his right eye, into his brain. Sam Ho fell to the ground, fluttering and convulsing, but instead of flying off to some other part of the aviary, Yat Ho dropped on him like a hawk, and proceeded to peck the wounded bird to death. Yi Ho came up to find out what the fuss was all about, and Yat Ho fell on the second bird, who was killed even more quickly than the first. When she had finished her murders, Yat Ho calmly wiped her beak on the mossy branch of a tree, and took up her position on the original perch.

I was of course stunned and shocked by this behaviour. This was something quite out of the scope of my studies, even amongst aggression in carnivores. There was a cold feeling in the pit of my stomach. I could hardly believe that my bird was capable of such terrible violence. Black drongos might be aggressive, but they did not to my knowledge kill each other. The responsibility for those deaths resided with me. I had altered the normal relationship, by introducing unusual behaviour patterns into the equation.

It was only in the taxi, on the way home that another, more terrible thought still, came to mind: a nightmare in fact. There were another set of personalities in play, in a relationship that I had well-meaningly tampered with. That night I slept very little, and went through vast amounts of material, looking for reasons. I believed my concern was very real.

The following day I took a rain check on my lunch date with Xia, and instead went to the University canteen looking for Professor Chang Yip, the resident psychoanalyst. I sat down next to him and immediately launched into a description of the previous night's events, telling him what I had set out to do, at the commencement of the experiment, and what had been the final result. He stared at me throughout my explanation, a blank expression on his face, as if he was wondering why the hell I was telling him all this.

'My question to you, professor, concerns human behaviour. Is there a... a personality disorder that you are aware of, in which the subject is docile while under attack from an aggressive person, yet explodes in sudden violence when that aggression is no longer in evidence? I'm wondering whether, once the aggressor becomes docile himself and apparently vulnerable, the subject takes the opportunity to attack…?'

Professor Chang shook his head and looked down at his half-eaten fried noodles and prawns.

'I don't understand why you ask me this? What have birds got to do with the psychoanalysis of people?'

'It's just something I'm interested in,' I replied. 'It's not really relevant to my studies, but I would like to know.'

'Birds are not people,' were his final words, and then he got up and left, leaving the remainder of his lunch.

I should have guessed what would happen. In a university with no tenures the staff are suspicious of one another, and they like to keep things close to their chest. There are a lot of politics, always in the wind, and people are insecure. You can be indispensible to the faculty one term, and out on your ear the next. So if someone from another department comes to you with a request, suggestion, idea, *anything*, you listen, but give nothing whatsoever in return.

I remained very worried about the situation in the Philippines. Steve, once terribly aggressive, had been tamed by me. When he was in the scanner cubicle the night before he left with Marcia for the Philippines, I had superimposed the personality of a dove over his own. He was now, to my way of thinking, vulnerable. He had in effect been transformed from a drongo to a dove, and I wanted to make sure that everything was all right, for Marcia's sake as well as my brother's.

In the evening, I telephoned Steve. It took three attempts, but I finally had him on the line.

'How are you?' I asked, guardedly.

'Me? Couldn't be better, why?' he said in a pleasant voice. 'Anything happened?'

'Nothing, nothing really. I just hadn't heard from either of you, and… well, I heard something about rebels in the north.'

Steve laughed.

'There's always some trouble with the north, you know that. Look, I'm due to meet someone, Pete—business, you know. Was there something specific…?'

'No. Maybe I could have a word with Marcia, before I ring off. Is she there?'

'What about?'

'Mind your own goddamn business,' I said with mock aggression. He laughed again and the next voice that I heard was Marcia's.

'Hello?'

'Marcia, how—how do you feel?'

'I'm fine, thank you.'

'Good, good. How's Steve? How are you getting on with him over there?'

She said in that calm voice of hers, 'Well, the Philippines must be good for him. He's so nice to me. I can't believe it really…'

'You don't mind that?'

'Of course not,' still no real expression in the tone.

'You don't find it… irritating, or anything?'

There was a long pause, then, 'No. Look, Peter, I have to go. Steve's calling me from the lift. Bye.'

'Marcia…?'

She had hung up on me.

I bit my nails. Well, they sounded all right, I supposed. Steve was docile of course, but otherwise okay. And Marcia? I just didn't know. Yat Ho had exploded all at once, without warning. How could I tell? Marcia might wake up in the middle of the night and realise that this aggressive beast who had tormented her in the past was now at her mercy, look down at his eyes, vulnerable, exposed. She might get out of bed, find a pair of scissors, and plunge them… it just did not bear thinking about.

How could I tell her that it wasn't Steve I was worried about, but her—that there was a potential murderer, locked up in that sweet personality she showed the world? How could I explain she had a demon inside her, waiting for the moment when Steve no longer psychologically presented a frightening formidable monster to her, but instead revealed the pathetic creature underneath, the real Steven, who required reassurance, support, love. How could I tell her that there was a strong possibility she would then regard him as her victim?

Two months ago, when Steve introduced me to Marcia, I had formed an alliance with her. Steve was at that time heading for all sorts of trouble. He was up on an assault charge, for punching a toilet attendant in a hotel for splashing his trousers with water. There were complaints at his club about his behaviour after he had been drinking, and people were asking for him to be thrown out. There was some business about a scrape with a Porsche car, the owner maintaining that Steve had bumped him from the rear on purpose, presumably because he had overtaken Steve's Mercedes on the Waterloo Road.

All this reflected on me and my position at the university, and I hit on the idea of taming him, calming him down. Of course, I would never have got him to the doctor, and even if I had, he would have refused any treatment. So I hit on the idea of overlaying his persona with that of a dove's, which would encourage the exposure of his *real* butter-soft self underneath. I didn't want Steve suspecting anything, so I planned to get him into the laboratory by using Marcia as an excuse.

After my phone call with Steve and Marcia, I went back to the lab, where Yat Ho awaited me. I placed her under the scanner and removed the superimposed persona, then put her back in the aviary with two more drongos.

She quarrelled with them, fighting over perches and food, but there were no combats resulting in injury or death. I stayed there for twelve hours, studying the creatures, and in the end went home convinced that she had returned to her old self, a nasty bickering bird like all the other black drongos in the world, but with no desire to kill.

There was no change in the situation over the next two days, and I waited on hot bricks for my brother and Marcia to arrive back in Hong Kong.

The day arrived when they were due in from the Philippines and I drove down to Lantau airport to meet them with a churning stomach. Was Steve all right? Was Marcia still the sweet lovable woman she had been on leaving Hong Kong? Was I in fact being unnecessarily stupid in thinking that the behaviour of a bird might reflect the behaviour of a human being? Perhaps Yat Ho was just a strange drongo, given to bursts of violence anyway? Animals and birds have their mental problems too. My mind was like a maelstrom, spiralling the thoughts round and round, and dredging them back up again.

I waited at the bottom of the ramp in the airport concourse, for my brother and his girlfriend to appear. The airport was, as usual, monstrously crowded with thousands of Chinese milling around waiting for relatives and friends, amazingly managing to avoid touching each other—a personal contact they dislike intensely—though I would have had difficulty in sliding a piece of paper down the spaces between them. My heart was beating against my ribs, and for the first time in many years I was smoking again. I glanced at the labels on the suitcases, as passengers came down the ramp, for Philippine Airlines' labels, and soon they began filtering past me.

Then suddenly, there they were, amongst the sea of black heads, at the top of the ramp. The relief flooded through me, and I kicked myself for being so paranoid. What an idiot. To think that a sweet girl like Marcia was capable of killing someone! Now that they were home, safe and sound, the idea seemed ludicrous, even heinous. I vowed never to tell them of my fears.

I signalled, made myself visible to Steve, then went to take a place in the queue for taxis.

Steve reached me, just as I was coming to the head of the queue. Marcia was nowhere to be seen. I had assumed, because she was so small, she had been down below the crowd

We shook hands and I said, 'Didn't I see Marcia?'

Steve shrugged and smiled.

'She wanted to stay on for a few days, to see some relatives.'

That sounded reasonable. Her family were out on one of the many smaller islands, while she and Steve had been staying on the main island.

On the taxi drive to Steve's club, where he intended to leave his suitcase and have a meal, I studied my older brother. He seemed calm and relaxed, and in quite a good frame of mind considering he had been through the stress of travel.

Still, so long as there was no harm done, what did it matter now?

He seemed distracted, however, so I did not press him with questions, until we were actually sitting down to a meal in the club dining-room.

'How was the trip?' I asked.

'Oh, fine.'

He played with his table napkin as I spoke, rearranging it carefully on his lap, although this had been done once by the waiter.

'No problems, business-wise?'

'No, everything went according to plan.'

'And Marcia? She enjoyed the break?'

He nodded.

'She seemed to.'

The soup arrived at this point, and I ceased probing. He certainly looked well enough, but there was something about his manner which worried me. He was too distant, even for someone who was a little jet-lagged, and I wondered if his business had really gone well. Then a thought struck me. What if Marcia *had* attacked him, and he, being a strong male, had prevented her from injuring him? Perhaps my concern for his safety was justified after all, but he had successfully protected himself from the kind of deadly attack I had witnessed from my black drongo, Yat Ho.

I was about to say something, when three people walked through the door. One was a small olive-skinned man with a blunt chin and determined look. He was flanked by two uniformed Hong Kong policemen: an inspector and a sergeant. They spoke to a waiter, who pointed towards our table. The trio then made their way through the diners, to stand behind my brother.

The man in civilian clothes spoke, and I knew then that he was a Filipino.

'Mr Steven Bordas?'

Steve turned his head, wiping his chin with his napkin at the same time.

'Yes.'

'I am Sergeant Callita. You are under arrest…'

I must have heard any words that followed, but their memory is lost in the buzzing of shock that overcame me. Steve looked at me and gave me a tight smile, which said, *we both knew that one day I would do something like this*.

I grabbed the Filipino policeman's sleeve.

'It's not his fault, it's mine.'

It was so clear to me now, now it was too late. Yat Ho had not killed because of the change in the other two drongos, but because of the unnatural suppression of her own aggression. I had overlaid her real personality, with a placid one, effectively sealing it off. The drongo persona had bubbled underneath, unable to find a safety valve to relieve the pressure, and finally she had exploded. I should have been comparing Yat Ho with Steve, not with Marcia, having done the same thing to my brother's natural aggression.

He had murdered Marcia!

Steve was taken away and I called to him that I would get his lawyer on the phone. He waved his hand over his shoulder, as if he did not really care what I did.

I sat in the restaurant, stunned by what had happened. Poor Marcia, I thought. Poor sweet innocent Marcia. I had been instrumental in her death, as they say, by experimenting on my own brother. It was a terrible thing to do. I was determined that it should all come out at the trial. I would defend my brother with the truth. Poor Steve.

While these thoughts were running through my head, Marcia walked into the room, saw me and waved. She crossed the floor and took a chair opposite me.

'Something terrible's happened,' she said, as I sat there open-mouthed, staring at her. 'Steve told me to stay in Manila, but I caught the next flight out, after his. There are policemen after him...'

'I know,' I said in a shaky voice, 'they've arrested him. But what's he done?'

She told me then and though Steve was still in a lot of trouble, I heaved a sigh of relief. It was bad, but not as bad as I had first envisaged, thank God.

They had been in a waterfront bar and Steve had had too much to drink. Marcia went to phone a taxi, to take them back to the hotel. When she returned, all hell had been let loose. It appeared that Steve had suddenly exploded in a fit of violence and had proceeded to lay about him without warning. The clientele of that particular bar were no angels themselves and dockers, fishermen and wharf rats began to pile into the mad *gweilo* with boots, fists and one or two knives. Steve retaliated in kind, stepping up his attacks on the opposition, cracking heads and throwing the smaller Filipinos around like dolls.

Chairs were broken, jaws were broken, mirrors were broken. There were three unconscious bodies strewn about the floor and Steve was swinging a bottle at a fourth, just as Marcia entered. The barman had pulled out a revolver and was screaming to Marcia in Tagalog that she'd better get her boyfriend out of there, or he was going to blow the fucking madman's head off. Marcia managed to bundle Steve through the door and into the taxi, whereupon he collapsed in moody silence in the corner of the cab. The next morning they heard that the police were after him, for drunkenness, assault, and various other criminal charges.

'It's my fault,' I said to her. 'I've got to help him.'

STEVE STOOD TRIAL IN HONG Kong, there being a Far East Area Criminal Court in Kowloon. His lawyer picked off the various charges against him, but he still ended up with 'Assault with intent to cause grievous bodily harm'. He was sentenced to a year in the Far East Central Jail, of which he would serve about eight months the lawyer said.

SO NOW I SIT IN my cell, with three other convicted felons for company. I couldn't let Steve serve his sentence: I'm doing it in his place. While Steve was out on bail we extended our illegal activities to swapping psyches. I am now in Steve's body and he in mine. It's really only fair that I do his time for him, when the whole thing was my fault anyway. I'm tempted at this point to quote the words at the end of 'A Tale of Two Cities'—'It is a far better thing I do now…'—but I can't remember all the whole bit.

I've taken a year's sabbatical from the university and Steve has taken my body to Thailand with Marcia for a long holiday. She's was a little confused at first but doesn't seem to mind, so long as I don't care and Steve is happy. We've explained to her what we've done and have assured her that everything is fine with both of us.

Jail is quite interesting really, if you haven't got a lifetime to serve, but Far East prisons are tough places. You need to be a hard man to survive in here. Obviously Steve, the old Steve, would have been in his element being an instinctive bully. His aggressive attitude and pugnacious personality would have ensured he was left well alone.

However, Steve isn't in here—I am. I am fairly timid by nature and in these circumstances a natural victim. I doubt I could survive on my own. The oriental thugs in here would destroy a mild *gweilo* like me in very little time at all, these Chinese triads and Vietnamese gangsters. So I borrowed another personality before I came in: superimposed it upon my own. It seems to work. I can scrap with the best of them, steal their food before they rob me of mine, intimidate them, put them in their places, establish a pecking order with me at the top. They fear me for my inherently fierce nature, my vicious character, and either stay out of my way or suck up to me.

Why not? Someone's got to be the king pin, so why not me? With the help of an overlaid persona, of course—that of the most belligerent black drongo I could find, Yat Ho.

BONSAI TIGER

(Anyone who met Dylan Tom, my irascible house cat will know what sparked this story. Dylan would let you stroke him once, then he would turn and sink his teeth into your hand. He was not a bad cat. He just hated being fussed. Dylan lived 19 years, often sleeping in the open drawer of my desk while I worked. Strangely, I miss him.)

'BREAKING UP IS SO *hard to do.*'

My computer had come up with that when I had asked heaven that morning whether I would ever get over her.

It confessed it was a line from an old song, an *ancient* song, probably. Yet, like all simple, trite sayings, it was so true. Breaking up with Krystina was killing me. I was so depressed I wanted to murder her and the bloody new boyfriend. I hadn't even met him. When I tried to imagine the two of them together, he was like some phantom twerp in the shadows behind her, tall and weedy, good at nothing, cynical.

Krystina and I met for the last time in our favourite rice-wine bar on Reynold's Path, overlooking the river. I watched the water traffic skimming the wavelets on the other side of the smoked glass with moody eyes, hoping she was noticing how miserable she had made me.

She had noticed.

'Stop being so full of self-pity,' she said, coldly. 'It's history.'

'History is further back than two weeks,' I replied bitterly, though I added with some spirit, 'It's only history to you because I'm the one being dumped. When I suggested we split up last year you told me it made you feel sick to your stomach. You reminded me that we had both said it was Forever. Some short Forevers around here, that's all I can say.'

Her eyes were like those balls of light-blue ice barmen eject into drinks. 'Well, what did you ask me here for?'

I shrugged. 'I thought—I just wanted to talk it over. We're still friends, aren't we?'

'I don't think that's a good idea,' she said, fiddling with her shoulder strap. 'I think it's best we should break clean and not see one another again.'

'We always agreed that we'd stay friends,' I gasped. 'That we'd go on seeing each other, for lunch or whatever, even though we might have fallen out of love.'

'That was before I met Mendal. Now I don't think it's workable. I think you need to move on. I have. I've grown. I've gone beyond what we had together.'

'You bitch. Are you suggesting I was a stepping stone to something better?'

Her mouth twisted and I think she was about to say something really nasty, something that would have crushed my heart like a ripe plum thrown under the heel of a Spanish flamenco dancer, but then she changed her mind. Instead she offered a word of advice.

'Look, Dean, I don't want to say things that will hurt you. Have you thought of doing something to take your mind off things? What about going on holiday. The Far East? You've always liked Indo-China and jungles full of animals. Or better still, get yourself a pet. You can love that all you want and it won't leave you like one of us rotten bitches.' She said this tongue in cheek of course. 'What about one of those new bonsai pets? I'm sure it'll help. Now, I've got to meet Mendal at the theatre. You look after yourself, Dean, and...' I knew she was about to say 'keep in touch' but she thought better of it. '...you just hang on in there.'

She left me then. My heart was as black as sin. I felt ugly. I felt wasted. I felt destroyed. I paid for my coffee and then went out into the neon-jazzed night, to ride the flickering street back to my apartment. On the way I passed a hole-in-the-wall pet mart. What the hell, I thought, she could be right? Maybe a pet would help? At least it would give me something else to worry about, other than my pitiful self.

I went across to the mart outlet, thinking of a little puppy or a miniature kitten, and came away with a bonsai tiger.

It was in a secure cage, of course. I held it up under the pearl street lights. It was perfect. Diminutive, but perfect. About the size of a sewer rat it paced up and down the cage, stopping occasionally to stare out, not at me, but at some distant land beyond. It's stare went right through me. There was no expression in its face, nothing I could read in the tiny bright eyes like sequins buried in the black and yellow fur.

A marvel of genetic engineering, my bonsai tiger was a real wild beast from a far off place, an exotic half-shadow creature which could hunt and kill as well as any full-sized big cat, albeit its prey would be of proportions suitable to its own length, girth and breadth.

Under the opal light it yawned with its small mouth, revealing two rows of sharp white teeth and a little red tongue. My perfect little tiger then flopped down, cat-like, and curled its tail over its legs. It was beautiful. My new pet was beautiful—and already I was beginning to forget the horrible empty ache inside me.

'What was her name?' I joked with my pet, as we skimmed along. 'I don't remember, do you?'

Once at home I put my tiger on a shelf below the stacks of computer manuals. Actually, to be more accurate, it was a female, a tigress, but the world was swiftly erasing gender nouns, so tiger was fine.

'Sheba,' I said. 'A name fit for a queen. That's what you are, my Lilliputian Queen Sheba of Blackhill Street.'

Sheba looked up, as if acknowledging her new name.

'Excellent. We're going to be a cool couple. Krystina will be proud of me. I'll just look her in the eye when we meet, accidentally of course outside some bar or night club, and say, 'I'm living with Sheba now. She's great. We get on terrifically well,' and witness her surprise at how so together I am—how I still love her of course, evident only in my demeanour and the way I hold my head—but how I'm bravely getting on with life without her.'

My computer made a noise like a wet fart. They're not supposed to do that, but they do. They do lots of things they're not supposed to. I think it's the only way bored programmers get their rocks off.

Sheba, however, let out a tiny roar—I thought of approval.

The voice at the mart had said to feed her steak. I was having fillet of lamb for dinner. I cut off a small corner and pushed it through the steel bars of the cage. Sheba pounced on it and began to rip pieces off it with her teeth. It was fascinating. Nature in the raw. Those geneticists were geniuses. To be able to make tiny elephants, tigers, lions, panthers, crocodiles! Never again would there be endangered species. We had all the codes now, we could make the animal whenever we wanted it. Some of the extinct creatures had been revived. There were even miniature mammoths and dinosaurs on the way. Sabre-toothed tigers. Mini plesiosaurs and in aquarium tanks. Cycad jungles.

Jungles! Now there was an idea. Why not get a rainforest or a jungle for *my* pet? Why not indeed? I phoned Krystina. She was in a theatre lobby with people milling round her. As soon as she saw my face she said, 'I'm changing my number.'

I tried to catch a glimpse of the girl-stealing Mendal, but couldn't be sure which of the skinny males in the picture was him. Krystina had said he was 'sensitive' which meant he was a geek. She had implied she had gone up the evolutionary scale, the chain of being, from Neanderthal to Modern Man. It was my belief she'd found a codfish that talked.

'No, don't do that,' I said. 'I'm only ringing to say I'm fine with everything. I've...' but she had switched off. When I tried again the voice said, 'This number is unobtainable at present, please try again later.'

'Bollocks!' I shouted, taking it out on the synthesiser. 'Bloody bollocking bollocks.'

'*Testicles,*' said my computer smugly, programmed to answer definite questions or give the definitions of repeated words. '*Nonsense, a muddle, a mess. In American slang, to make a botch of.*'

Later I went to bed to dream of judgement days, but was kept awake by snuffling noises and the sound of straw being shuffled from one end of the cage to the other. The next morning Sheba's cage smelled a little high, so I changed the bedding. I lured her into a small compartment at one end of the cage with some raw liver, then changed the drawer containing her bed and faeces. It was all quite simple. I'd never had a pet before, but these bonsai animals were like having gerbils. There was little do except enjoy the ownership of a live creature.

Bonsai actually means 'bowl cultivation' in Japanese and of course originally referred to dwarf trees, but you know how words alter their meanings over time, especially when they come from another language. (*Sophisticated* originally meant 'artificial' but soon came to mean having the worldly wisdom characteristics of a fashionable life.) When the genetic labs starting producing tiny wild creatures for the commercial market they had to think of a marketable name. 'Shrunken beasts' didn't have the right ring to it, so they settled on 'bonsai pets'.

Naturally, the bonsai tiger only distracted me for a few days, then I descended into misery once again. I felt absolutely fucked up. And, of course, when you're fucked up, there's the extremely likely possibility of getting fucked up further, because you are so wrapped up in your own private hell you forget to do things that should definitely be remembered.

I forgot to feed Sheba.

Arriving back at the apartment after stalking Krystina and her Cro-Magnon (he wasn't that Modern after all and had threatened to smash my face in if I didn't stop following them) I found the cage on the floor. It had burst open. Three shelves had come down with it and there were computer manuals all over the floor plus a vase and my two soapstone carvings. My guess was that the tiger had become so hungry she had thrown herself at the bars of her cage in a frenzy and had brought the shelves down. The heavy manuals had crashed down on the cage and broken it open, allowing Sheba to escape.

'Shit!' I said. 'Shit, shit, shit.'

'*Faeces, excrement; the act of defecating; a contemptuous term for a person...*'

'Shut up, you stupid machine!'

'*...rubbish, nonsense; marijuana or heroin.*'

There was a pause before the computer spoke again, with a censure in its drone.

'*I hope you realise hard drugs are illegal and soft drugs do your brains in.*'

Bloody programmers. *They* ought to be made illegal.

The first thing I did was to glance around the room, to see if she was anywhere to be seen. She wasn't. Assessing the situation I came to the conclusion that the apartment was escape proof. There was no chimney, no open windows, and there weren't any chutes. There was no way she could get out.

I went into the kitchen and found the rubbish bin knocked over and its contents spilled all over the kitchen floor. Any edible scraps which had been in that bin had been devoured. At least she had probably assuaged her hunger. That was good, wasn't it? But where the hell was she?

'Sheba, Sheba, Sheba,' I called in a 'kitty-kitty' voice.

'*A biblical land corresponding to Sabaea in present-day Yemen, South West Arabia; an unbeaten racehorse during the first four years of this century; a Las Vegas drag queen whose lewd act included a live anaconda; a kind of sugared muffin made in Bhutan...*'

She didn't come of course. I went into the bathroom. A bar of soap lay half-eaten on the floor. Hell, when had I last fed her? I cleaned everything up then began a serious search of the four rooms. I couldn't find her anywhere. Maybe she *had* managed to get out somehow? There was nothing for it but to go to bed and have another look in the morning. Maybe she would be out looking for food. I started to think how I would catch her. Put some meat in her cage? That sounded right.

In the middle of the night there was a terrible fight in the living-room. I heard crashing and banging, then a thin high-pitched scream which hurt my ears filled the apartment for several minutes. When I got up the courage I went through the door and switched on the light. I almost threw up. There was blood all over the carpet, halfway up the cream-coloured curtains I had fought with Krystina over, smeared down one wall, and smudged on the sofa. In the middle of the room was a pile of putrid-smelling, smoking innards, draped across a broken lamp.

Right at my feet, in the doorway, was the severed head of a large rat.

'Jesus Christ! I cried out loud. 'I didn't know we had any rats in here! How did rats get into a modern building?'

'*Fact: rats are never farther than six yards away from a human, especially in a city.*'

'Thank you for that mind-boggling piece of information.'

'*You're welcome.*'

'Sheba!' I yelled. 'Come on out!'

Again I searched the apartment. Where the hell had she got to? Where could she be hiding? By the time I finished the kitchen, she had obviously been into the living-room again and eaten the rat's entrails, because they were gone. I cleaned up the blood and hair, finding a bald tail like a dead worm behind the sofa. It took me quite a while.

Then I went out and bought some raw hamburgers and a humane mouse trap. I was going to catch that she-cat if it took me all day. I set the trap in the living-room, where the action had taken place. Then I went out. I hoped to run into Krystina and her boyfriend by accident. If he attacked me again I was going to sue him for assault.

When I came home the mouse trap was all bent and twisted. Sheba had taken it apart from within. In despair I thought about getting a rat trap, but I guessed it was too late. She wouldn't go into another cage with sprung doors if I knew anything about wild creatures. I'd seen a programme about trapping animals. The trapper said you had to get the beast the first time, or you'd never see hide nor hair again.

Well, there was another way. Starve her out of her hiding place. There couldn't be too many rats in the apartment, surely?

I got rid of all the food I had, intending to eat out every night until she crawled out weak and submissive, begging to go into her cage.

During the next week Sheba gnawed just about everything soft and pliable in the apartment. It was costing me a fortune, but I was determined not to give in. Once I had her again, I was going to send her to Krystina as a goodbye present. That would serve both the bastards right. My bonsai tiger was a greater escapologist than Houdini. She would certainly stuff *those two* all right.

Saturday evening I went to bed early. I had a thick blanket ready by the bed to throw over Sheba. I felt she had to come out soon. She must have been absolutely starving by then. Poor *Panthera tigris*. All she had to do was come to papa. I'd promised her that very morning that if she came out I'd go and buy her some food immediately.

At three o'clock in the morning I was lying peacefully, partly-asleep, the distant sound of a police siren in my ears. Suddenly a terrible pain went shooting up my shin bone. I sat bolt upright, instantly, and screamed in agony. Ripping back the sheets I stared at my leg in the half-light coming from the neon signs outside. There was nothing to be seen, but I could feel a stickiness further down. Blinking away the tears of pain I called for the light, which flooded the room.

My right big toe was pumping blood. In fact, there was no toe. It had been bitten off at the root. Blood continued to pour out as I stared, holding my calf, the pain robbing me of any sense of what to do next. I got out of bed and immediately fell over, my sense of balance gone. Blood spurted onto the carpets. I was in shock and decided if I didn't get help soon I would bleed to death. This made my heart pump faster.

'Help!' I yelled. 'Somebody help me! Help! Help!'

'*Help. To aid or assist; to relieve the wants of; to provide or supply; to deal out; to remedy; to mitigate; to contribute…*'

The computer bumbled on.

'Call the paramedics!' I cried. 'Get me an ambulance.'

I heard the computer fast-dialling. At least help would soon be on the way. I stumbled forward, grabbed the sheet and wrapped it around my pulsing foot. Something flew out of the sheet, digging its claws into my throat. Sharp teeth sank into my lower jaw.

'Fuck!' I screamed, grabbing at her and trying to prise her from my face.

She was incredibly strong. She may have only been as big as a rat, but she was a pocket-sized block of ridged muscle. Sheba was a *tiger* after all, not some puny house cat. Fully-grown her jaws could crack the backbone of an ox. There was power in every limb, every twist and turn of the lithe torso. She scratched and tore like lightning with her claws, ripping skin and flesh from my chest. She bit deeply into my neck, sinking her small pointed teeth close to my jugular. When she turned her attention to my collar bone, and broke it with her jaws, I knew I was in very serious trouble and likely to be killed by this vicious little packet of muscle, fang and claw.

I fell on the floor, not screaming any more for that would have been a waste of energy. This was a deadly fight. I rolled over, my hands seeking something to hit her with. Looking down at her, as she ripped and slashed at my upper body, I could see her eyes were burning with fury. Her bloodlust was beyond control. She wanted to tear me to pieces. In desperation I threw myself front first at the chest-of-drawers, knocking one of my teeth out as my mouth struck a corner, but somehow dislodging the small killer which flew against the door.

Within a second she was back, a terrifying whirlwind of bloody claws, trying to get a grip on my groin. She succeeded in burying her fangs in my left hip. A bolt of pain went shooting up my body making me whimper. I gripped her body firmly with both hands and wrenched her from me. She took with her a mouthful of my flesh, baring my hip to the bone. I threw her on the far side of the room and scrambled and crawled into the living-room. This time she didn't chase after me. I heard her scrambling somewhere.

I was bleeding profusely from half a dozen places when I heard the opening bars to Carl Orff's *Carmina Burana*. Help had arrived. I yelled at the computer.

'OPEN THE DOOR!'

A moment later the paramedics rushed in and assessed the situation like the professionals they were. In no time at all they had staunched the blood from the worst of my wounds and had me on a stretcher. A drug-punch on my arm and the pain began to subside, ebbing away to some distant place, I didn't care where. I was on my way to hospital. They carried me out into the hall, towards the lift. One of them reached for the manual button to close the door.

'I don't care if anything gets stolen,' I yelled at her, 'Just leave the bloody door open.'

The paramedic shrugged and did as she was told.

'It's your apartment,' she said. 'Just don't blame us.'

The two weeks in hospital were a blissful rest. I was able to take stock of my life. Krystina, I came to the conclusion, was not worth all the tears. In fact, I had been on the point of dumping *her*, when she gave me the heave ho. It was only my pride which was hurt. Mendal was welcome to her. I had a bet with myself that he would get the same treatment within a year. Krystina was like that. Like me in fact. She went through partners like packets of crisps. We were two of a kind, she and I.

When I was sent home I had to use a stick. A new toe had been grafted on—not mine of course, one that came from the clone bank—but I was still not quite used to it. It didn't feel right. It was like a rubber toe, with no sensation in it. It was like walking around with a door-stopper screwed onto my foot. I hoped I would soon get to disregard it, just as I did all my other nine toes, instead of constantly being aware of its presence.

Stepping out of the lift I saw at once that my door had been closed. I knew that had been done the day after I went into hospital. I guessed by that time Sheba would have escaped from the apartment. If she hadn't she would be so weak from hunger by now she wouldn't be able to put up a fight and I could beat her to death with my walking stick. I wanted to. I had an intense desire to see her brains on my living-room carpet. The she-devil had nearly killed me. I bore her great malice.

Opening the apartment door I hobbled inside.

'*Welcome home!*'

'Welcome home, yourself, you heap of wires and chips.'

'*There's a package for you.*'

'Where?' I looked round.

'*In the kitchen.*'

I shuffled into the kitchen, wondering why the computer sounded so self-satisfied. There on the kitchen floor was a large box. There was a note on top.

'Dean,' it read, '*I'm sorry I was so rotten to you. I'm still with Mendal, but I'm feeling guilty for hurting you so badly. I decide to follow up my advice to you and get you a parting gift. It's something you'll like, I know, because you're always watching those wildlife programmes with savage beasts either bonking or eating each other. Anyway, this is new, this is special, and I hope he's a companion to you, on these lonely evenings. Sorry about how things turned out. It's probably all for the best, you know. Krystina.*'

The note was dated a week ago.

I stared down at the box. On one side of it, it said DANNY'S ANIMAL KINGDOM: BONSAI PETS. Underneath these words was a warning. THIS WAY UP. Well it wasn't that way up. It was on its side, obviously. I quickly upended it, so that it was right and proper.

It was then that I saw the hole that had been ripped through the far side, the packaging flaring outwards. The word TRY was printed on that side. Try what? Try to be careful with this box? Further inspection revealed a cage that had obviously been mishandled in transit. The bars were bent, one of them seriously out of kilter. Moreover, it was empty.

The conclusion was obvious: whatever had been inside the carrier had squeezed through the damaged bars and then torn its way through the plastic box. It was now on the outside. The box was a big one, holding a big cage. Much larger than the one which had contained Sheba. Then I realised that it didn't say TRY at all. These three letters were part of a longer word which had been ripped in half.

What they actually read was TYR

Quickly, nervously, I scanned the kitchen.

Something lizardy skipped rapidly across the doorway on two legs.

Garry Kilworth

ATTACK OF THE CHARLIE CHAPLINS

(This came from all sorts of directions.)

WHEN WE FIRST STARTED GETTING reports out of Nebraska that the state was under attack from heavily armed men dressed as Charlie Chaplin, the first thought was that a right wing group of anti-federal rebels was involved, and that they were using irony on top of force to make some kind of point. After all, Charlie was eventually ostracised to Switzerland for having communist sympathies. As more accurate reports came in however, it became apparent that these were not just men *dressed* as Charlie Chaplin, they were the real McCoy—they were *he*, so to speak.

'It's clear,' said Colonel Cartwright, of Covert Operations Policy and now acting as my ADC, 'that these are aliens. What we have here, General, is your actual alien invasion of Earth. Naturally they chose to conquer the United States first, because we are the most powerful nation on the planet.'

'Why Nebraska, Colonel?' I asked. I am General Oliver JJ Klipperman, by the way, and I was at the time on a secret underground army base in South Dakota. 'Nebraska isn't exactly the most powerful state in the union. Why not New York or Washington?'

Cartwright smiled grimly. 'Look at the map, General. Nebraska is slap bang in the middle of this great country of ours. It has one of the smallest populations. You get more people on Fifth Avenue on Christmas Eve than live in Nebraska. You simply have to wipe out a small population and you control this country's central state. Expand from there, outwards in all directions, and you have America. Once you have America, you have the world. It's as easy as that.'

I nodded. It all made sense. Nebraska was the key to the control of the US of A. The aliens had seen that straight away. 'What do we know about these creatures?' I asked next. 'The President will expect me to sort out this unholy mess and I want to know who I'm killing when I go in with my boys.'

The colonel gave me another tight smile. 'These creatures, as such?—nothing, General. Zilch. But we have a trump card. We've been preparing for such an invasion for many, many years and our *general* information is voluminous.'

'It is?' I said. 'How come?'

'Hollywood,' said the colonel, emphatically. 'We've been making films of alien invasions since the movie camera was first invented. We've covered every contingency, every type of attack, from your sneaky Fifth Column stuff such as in *Invasion of the Body Snatchers* to outright blatant frontal war, such as *Independence Day*. We know what to do, General, because we've done it so many times before, on the silver screen. We know every move the shifty shape-changing bastards can make, because we've done it in many films, sometimes twice—sometimes so many times it's become a cliché. *Alien, War of the Worlds, The Day the Earth Stood Still, Close Encounters of the Third Kind*, you name it, we've covered it. On film.'

'Weren't they friendly aliens in *Close Encounters*?'

'No such thing, General. What about those poor guys, those pilots they beamed up from the Bermuda Triangle in WWII? Eh? They kept them in limbo until their families were all dead and gone, *then* let 'em come back. Is that a *friendly* thing to do?'

'I guess not. So, Colonel, we've had all these exercises, albeit on celluloid, but what have we learned? What do we do with them? What do you suggest is our approach?'

'Blast them to hell, General, begging your pardon. If there's one thing we've learned it's that if you give 'em an inch, they'll take a planet. They've got Nebraska. That's almost an inch. We need to smash them before they go any further. Blow them to smithereens before they take Kansas, Iowa or Wyoming, or God forbid, Dakota.'

I always err on the side of caution, that's why I'm still a one-star general I guess.

'But what do we actually *know* about these creatures. I mean, why come down here looking like Charlie Chaplin?'

The colonel's eyes brightened and he looked eager.

'Ah,' he said, 'I have a theory about that, sir. You see, we send crap out into space all the time. I don't mean your hardware, I mean broadcasts. They must have picked up some of our television signals. What if their reception had been so poor that the only thing they picked up was an old Charlie Chaplin movie? Eh? What if it was one of those movies in which he appears on his own—just a clip—and, and here's the crunch, they, *they* thought we *all* looked like that?'

The colonel stepped back and nodded.

'You mean,' I said, 'they think the Charlie Chaplin character is representative of the whole human race.'

'Exactly, sir. You've got it. We all look alike to them. They came down as Fifth Columnists, intending to infiltrate our country unnoticed, but of course even most Nebraskans know Charlie Chaplin is dead, and that there was only one of him. The

Nebraskan dirt farmers see a thousand look-alikes and straight away they go, "Uh-huh, somethin's wrong here, Zach..."

'So, they did what any self-respecting mid-western American would do—they went indoors and got their guns and started shooting these funny-walking little guys carrying canes and wearing bowler hats. I mean, what would you do?'

'I see what you mean, Colonel. They're not from around here, so they must be bad guys?'

'Right.'

'Blow holes in them and ask questions later?'

'If you can understand that alien gibberish, which nobody can.'

'I meant, ask questions of yourself—questions on whether you've done the right and moral thing.'

'Gotcha, General.'

I pondered on the colonel's words. Colonel Cartwright was an intelligent man—or at least what passes for intelligence in the Army—which was why he was a senior officer in COP. He had obviously thought this thing through very thoroughly and I had to accept his conclusions. I asked him if he was sure we were doing the right thing by counter-attacking the aliens and blowing them to oblivion. Had they really exterminated the whole population of Nebraska?

'Every last mother's son,' answered the colonel, sadly. 'There's not a chicken farmer left.'

'And we can't get through to the President for orders?'

'All lines are down, radio communications are being jammed.'

'The Air Force?' I asked, hopefully.

'Shot down as it crossed the state line. There's smoking wrecks lying all over Nebraska. Same with missiles. We were willing to wipe out Nebraska, geographically speaking, but these creatures have superior weapons. We're the nearest unit, the last line of defence, General. It's up to us to stop them.'

'How many men have we got, Colonel?'

'A brigade—you're only a brigadier-general, General.'

'That's true. Still, we ought to stand a chance with four to five thousand men. They—they destroyed our whole Air Force, you say?'

The colonel sneered. 'The Air Force are a bunch of Marys, sir. You can't trust a force that's only a century old. The Army and the Navy, now they've been around for several thousand years.'

'Are we up to strength?'

'No, sir, with sickness and furlough we're down to 2,000.'

'OK,' I said. 'We go in with two thousand, armour, field guns and God on our side.'

'You betcha!'

A corporal came into the room without knocking.

'Yes, Corporal?' I said, icily. 'I'm busy.'

'I thought you ought to see this, sir. It's a message—just come through.'

She handed it to me. 'From Washington?' I asked, hopefully.

'No, sir, from the alien.'

'The *alien*?' I repeated, snatching the signal. 'You afraid of plurals, soldier?'

'No, sir, if you'll read the message, sir, you'll see there's only one of him—or her.'

The message read: YOU AND ME, OLIVER, DOWN BY THE PLATTE.

'Looks like he's been watching John Wayne movies, too,' I said, handing Cartwright the piece of paper. 'Or maybe Clint Eastwood?'

The colonel read the message. 'How do we know there's only one?' he asked, sensibly. 'It could be a trick.'

'Our radar confirms it, sir,' the corporal said. 'He's pretty fast though. It only looks like there's multiples of him. He seems to be everywhere at once. He's wiped out the whole population of Nebraska single handed.'

'Shit,' I said. 'What the hell chance do I stand against an alien that moves so fast he becomes a horde?'

'Fifty percent of Nebraska was asleep when they got it,' said the colonel, 'and the other half weren't awake.'

'What's the difference?'

'Some of 'em actually do wake up a little during daylight hours.'

'Gotcha. So, you think I stand a chance?'

The colonel grinned. 'We'll fix you up with some tricky hardware, sir. He'll never know what hit him.'

'But can I trust him to keep his word? About being just one of him? What if he comes at me in legions?'

'No sweat, General,' said the colonel. 'This baby,' and here he produced a shiny-looking hair-drier, 'is called a *shredder*. Newest weapon off the bench. One squeeze of this trigger and it fires a zillion coiled razor-sharp metal threads. Strip a herd of cattle to the bone faster than a shoal of piranha. The spread is one mile every foot after leaving the muzzle. You only have to get within ten feet of the bastard and you can annihilate him even if he becomes a whole corp.'

'Can I hide it under my greatcoat?'

'Nothing easier, sir. And we'll wire you with a transmitter. He's only jamming long-distance stuff. You can tell us your life story. Oh, and one more very important thing.'

'What's that?'

'We have to give him a nickname, General.'

I stared at the colonel. 'Why?' I said at last.

'Because that's what we're good at. We always give the enemy a nickname. It demeans them. Makes them feel self-conscious and inferior. It's our way of telling them that they're low forms of human life.'

'Or in this, case, alien life.'

'Right, General. So, we have to give him a humiliating nickname—like Kraut, Slopehead, Raghead, Fritz, Dink or Charlie…'

'We can't nickname him Charlie, he's already called Charlie.'

'OK, I take that on board. Now, his name's Charlie, as you say, so how about we call him *Chuck*?'

'Doesn't sound very demeaning to me. My brother was called Chuck.'

'Depends on how you say it, General. If we're talking about your brother, we sort of say "Chuck" in a warm kind of tone. But if we're talking about *Chuck*, we use a sort of fat chickeny sound—*Chuck*—like that.'

'I think I understand, Colonel. Well, let's get me armed and wired. It's time I taught *Chuck* a lesson.'

So that, as you know, Colonel, is how I come to be walking down to the Platte river at three in the morning. Are you listening back there in the base? The moon is gleaming on my path as I reach the banks. Here in the humid Nebraskan night I wait for my adversary. Single combat. *Mano a mano*. The old way of settling differences in the American west.

Hell, what am I saying, we didn't invent it. The *old*, old way. The chivalric code of the knights. A tourney. A duel. An affair of honour. Rapiers at dawn. Pistols for two, coffee for one.

And I am ready. You didn't send me out unprimed, did you, Colonel? You made me submit to *brainstorming*—masses of data has been blasted into my brain in the form of an electron blizzard. Every alien invasion movie ever filmed is now lodged somewhere inside my cerebrum, waiting to be tapped. Any move this creature makes, I'll have it covered. Hollywood has foreseen every eventuality, every type of otherworlder intent on invading and subduing us earthlings. They're all in my head.

Chuck's coming up over the ridge, thousands of him doing that silly walk with the cane and twitching his ratty moustache. *Don't let him get to you with the pathetic routine*, you warned me, didn't you, Colonel? '*You know how Chuck can melt the strongest heart with that schmaltzy hangdog expression. Don't look at him when he puts his hands in his pockets, purses his lips, and wriggles from side to side.*' Well, don't worry, I *hate* Charlie Chaplin. That pathos act makes me want to puke, always did. If he tries that stuff I'll shred him before he can blink.

He's getting closer now and he's suddenly become only one, a single Charlie Chaplin.

My fingers are closing around the butt of the shredder. I'm ready to draw in an instant. The bastard won't stand a chance. Wait, he's changing shape again. Now he's *Buster Keaton*. I never liked Buster Keaton. And yet again. Fatty Arbuckle this time. I detest Fatty Arbuckle. Someone I don't recognise. Now Abbot and Costello. The Marx Brothers.

Shit, he's only eleven feet away, he's suddenly changed again. He's gone all fuzzy. He's solidifying. Oh. Oh, no. Oh my golly gosh. God almighty. It's—it's dear old Stan Laurel.

'Hello, Olly.'

Did you hear that, Colonel? Just like the original. He—he's beaming at me now, the way Laurel always beams at Hardy, and I—I can't do it. I can't shoot. Of all the comic actors to choose. I *loved* Stan Laurel. I mean, how can you shoot Stan Laurel when he's beaming at you. It's like crushing a kitten underneath the heel of your boot. I can't do it. The flesh may be steel but the spirit's runny butter.

Whaaa! Oh God, he's shot me—right through gut—with some weapon of strange foreign design—not Japanese though—it's like nothing I've ever seen before—but deadly. It's—it's left a hole in my belly you could drive a tank through. He even had the gall to blow away none existent smoke from the weapon's muzzle. I'm dying, Colonel. I'm a dead man.

Wait, he's standing over me. I think he's going to speak. Listen to this. Are you listening, Colonel?

'You're supposed to say, "Another fine mess you've gotten me into, Stanley," and play with your tie.'

Hollywood, damn them.

Hollywood covered every contingency except one. In all the alien invasion movies they ever made the attacking monsters are always as grim as Michigan in January. As I lay here dying, the joke is on you and me, Colonel. There's one type of extraterrestrial they *didn't* plan on coming—an offworlder soldier just like our own soldiers—

—an alien with a sense of humour.

WHEN THE MUSIC STOPPED

by Christian Lehmann and Garry Kilworth

This story was a long time coming. Christian Lehmann is a life-long friend, who's highly regarded in his native France as a writer of off-the-wall fiction. We found out early that we both love jazz – *St James' Infirmary* especially – and the movie *Casablanca* and often talked about winding these two disparate pieces of art into a collaborated story. Eventually we did and the story was published in *Other Edens III*, an anthology edited by Christopher Evans and Robert Holdstock.

WHEN THE MUSIC STOPPED, HE alone would remain on the record, an audience of one applauding a non-existent performance. The old 78, scratched and marked by decades of overuse, would contain only the sounds of a small boy's clapping. Unless—unless he were to die first of course, to leave Chuck to the solitude of his haunting piano playing.

HE REMEMBERED THE DAY WHEN the first of them had died. The record was playing, but something nibbled at the edges of his mind. Something was not quite right with the playing. Something was *missing*. It took him several plays of the record to realise what it was.

At first he had put it down to weariness: the kind of mental exhaustion that came from having to live with a perception disability. He remembered thinking: *the music sounds a little hollow, a little lacking in background strength. The clarinet? No, that was there. He could hear the syncopating rhythm of Peanuts Baker quite clearly now that he was listening for it. What? What then?*

Then it had come to him. The trombone. There was no trombone.

He played the 78 through again, immediately afterwards, then looked at the sleeve. There was a blank where the trombonist's name should be on the list of players. Miles Teegarten! *Jesus, Miles Teegarten was dead!*

All the jazz musicians on that platter were personal to him. He had been present at that recorded jam session in Chicago, January 27, 1933. It had been a birthday treat from his uncle the day he had reached eight years of age. The clapping in the background: he was part of that sound. (And Uncle Pete too, until he died.)

What a night that had been for a young boy: the atmosphere full of cigarette smoke; the beer flowing, some of it onto the floor; the chatter and informality of great men. Louis Armstrong had actually spoken to him: wished him a happy birthday. There was much laughter when the trumpeter, his round face creased in smiles, announced, 'We have an old man in the audience. Eight years today. Man, that's a heavy burden, eight years. Let's all say happy birthday to Sebastian there, hiding behind that big glass of lemonade pop…'

Everyone had called out to him, some of the musicians trotting out a fanfare on their instruments. Then they had played it, *St James Infirmary*. Some might call it a morbid song but from that moment Sebastian was hooked on the blues and *St James Infirmary* gave him much pleasure whenever he heard it after that night. Until the musicians began to disappear, as he knew they would. *Then* the sadness and bitterness came.

He put the record on now, while he ate his breakfast, and since the vocals and most of the instruments—the players (even Satchmo himself)—had gone, he sang along with it, providing the lyrics himself.

'Went down to St James infirmary—saw my baby there—stretched out on a long white table—so cold, so still, so fair. Let her go, Let her go, God bless her…'

The tears streamed down his face as he tried to drink his coffee. All those gaps. All those fine people. Even the audience had gone. Just one lone player, Chuck Davis, on the piano. And a single, solitary clapper at the end. A childish, unrhythmic sound that he knew to be his own small eight-year-old hands— enthusiastic but lacking coordination.

The record finished and he left it, hissing round and round, on the turntable, while he finished his coffee and wiped the tears from his cheeks with a table napkin. Such pain. Such heartfelt *pain.*

He left the house and began to walk to work, along the avenue covered with a crisp layer of dry leaves. There was an autumnal nip to the air which made him turn up his coat collar and retreat into himself, like a turtle drawing its neck into its shell. Sebastian needed these small barriers between him and the world, especially on days like today. He knew his boss was going to offer him promotion again and he was not looking forward to it. The refusal, as it always did, would leave his boss looking frustrated and puzzled. Sebastian was a postal clerk.

'I like my work as a sorter,' he would explain. 'I enjoy the shift work—the varied hours. It gives me time to do things… things I wouldn't have time for if I worked nine to five. Really.'

The excuse was feeble but the real reason would lose him even his present job. If they promoted him to the records section he would be lost. Many of those records contained files on dead people, had been written by people who had since died, and to Sabastian they would be just blank pieces of paper. Of course, from time to time a letter came in written by a person since deceased, but these were rare and he could get away with putting the plain envelope back into one of the racks for the next shift to find. If one was addressed to someone who was dead, only the name would be missing, the destination would be there.

He passed the cinema and glanced at the billboard. Some of the names of the stars were missing. He could see the obvious spaces. He averted his eyes. So many reminders. There had been a time when, spurred by the talk of others, he turned to a classical programme on the radio but all he could hear was the scraping of chairs and some fools coughing and farting. He wondered why he could hear *St James Infirmary* when its creator, Primrose, was no doubt dead, but he guessed it was because of the spontaneous nature of jazz. Each performance was immediate and differed so much from the original that the connection was broken with its composer. Who knew, really? Sabastian's psychological disability was weird enough without searching for the reasons for aberrations from a standard.

His paranormal impediment (as he called it) was to a certain extent selective. It never entered the third dimension. Buildings did not disappear because their architects were dead, for instance. It just made him so miserable sometimes, this distorted perception. Some people might have felt special, but not Sabastian. He longed to be ordinary.

At the corner of the avenue was a newsstand and he bought a daily paper.

'Mornin',' he said to the woman as he passed his money to her.

As usual she was dressed in clothes that must have belonged to a man twice her size, probably thirty years ago, judging from the stains and frayed trouser cuffs. He was better off than some people, he reminded himself. At least he wasn't down at heel. He could afford to feed and clothe himself properly. More than that poor woman could do.

He enjoyed the newspaper because most of the articles and photographs were still visible to him. Books were different. There was something shocking about picking up a book and finding it blank. All those white pages. It still took his breath away for one horrible moment if he had not prepared himself for it. It drained his soul. *Hemingway, where are you now?* Hemingway had been one of Sabastian's favourite authors until, in 1967, he had been reading *The Sun Also Rises* when the words started to blur before his eyes. He had not needed to put on the news to find out for whom the bell tolled.

All those books to which he would never have access! At school they had thought him retarded, gave up on him when he reached a certain age. But he could read, all right, though he had hidden it from his teachers. The post office had to hire a certain percentage of invalids and misfits and he had begun as a van driver, later to graduate to sorter when they had forgotten he was supposed to be semi-literate.

He opened the newspaper as he walked along. The centre pages were devoted to the J.F. Kennedy assassination, recently revived due to further evidence suggesting a Cuban-Mafia involvement. There were many blanks on the pages but a photograph of the Oswald killing held his attention. Lee Harvey was missing, but Jack Ruby was still there, in that half-crouched position, leaning forward, pointing the murder weapon at the spot where Kennedy's supposed assassin would have been to a person with a normal perception.

Jack Ruby should *not* have been in the picture.

He was supposed to have died of cancer in 1976 or thereabouts. So what was he doing here? There was a huge conspiracy at work somewhere, which Sabastian would dearly have loved to reveal to the world—but who would believe a postal clerk who announced that Jack Ruby was still alive because he had not disappeared from a photograph? They would put him away, no doubt about that whatsoever. Sabastian had a gift that was not a gift: it was an affliction, a burden.

Someone greeted him from the far side of the road—one of his fellow workers—and he waved back. The day's work had begun.

Sure enough, his boss offered him the promotion he sought to avoid, and as usual his reluctance brought the expected reaction: the shaking of the head and the resigned expression. Some of his workmates were a little jealous of his rapport with the boss. They showed it by their silence when he returned to the office. However, by lunchtime he was back in his place on the sorter's desk and they realised that once again he had refused promotion. It made him, perversely, something of a hero amongst them. They bought him beers in the pub where they had their lunch.

Then one of them had to go and play a few records on the juke box, some of which he heard and some not. He recalled, morosely, the time he had reached fourteen and Herbie Lund, the sax player, had disappeared from his favourite record. It was the first time he realised the full personal scope of his disability, the first time it struck home. Uncle Pete had been there that night and had come up to his room to comfort him while he sobbed. He remembered the knock on the bedroom door, and Uncle Pete coming in, silently. He tried to recall his uncle's expression, but the man was gone now and the features had faded from Sabastian's memory. Most of the conversation too, was forgotten, but he recalled the sentence, '...Herbie's gone, but his music's still there, Seb. His music hasn't gone with him. It goes on.'

But for Sabastian the music did not go on, and he had nearly blurted out the whole of his secret to Uncle Pete—the secret that was to cause so much emotional pain throughout his life. He had held back, letting his uncle think he had read of the death in the newspaper, not wanting to hurt the old man of whom he was so fond. Sabastian was the only member of the family to share Uncle Pete's love of jazz and if his disability were known it would have caused his uncle a lot of sorrow. To be without jazz was death itself to Pete.

At four o'clock the shift finished and the evening sorters came on duty. Sabastian was on evening shift the next day, so he had quite a few hours to fill until then. He kicked at the leaves as he strolled home, feeling just a little better than he had done on leaving the house that morning. The autumn sun was a huge ball of orange behind the changing street trees. A woman passed him with two laughing children. He wondered what it would be like to live a family life with loved ones filling the silence of the rooms with happy talk and warm feelings. He had always been too shy to approach girls and now that time was long past. Who wants a man in his late fifties with nothing to offer but a bizarre viewpoint on death?

He often thought of phoning one of the marriage bureaux to see if he could find a companion with whom to spend his last few years of life. At least he didn't drink heavily, or smoke, or anything like that. *Boring,* he thought, suddenly. I live a boring life. Tomorrow. Tomorrow he would contact one of the agencies—find someone who needed him. There, the decision was made. He *would* go through with it. There was surely a woman understanding enough to allow him his deviant perception without becoming frightened of it?

He picked up a bunch of leaves and threw them into the air like confetti, watching them float slowly to the ground. Suddenly, he was aware he was being observed and saw a woman hastily turn the key in the lock of her door, then disappear with a quick glance over her shoulder. He felt uncomfortable for a moment, then laughed it off. Hell, she was probably one of those old crones who peeked from behind curtains at the world outside and found it all a bit distasteful, a despicable place inhabited by odd men who threw leaves into the air and allowed them to settle on their shoulders and hair while wearing silly smiles. He wasn't going to let a woman like that put him off. It was people like her that took all the romance, all the magic out of the air, and left a dry insipid place with no hope for the future. Let her grumble into her cup of coffee and reduce her own world to ashes and dust. She wasn't going to affect *his*.

He came to his own house, entered, made himself a cup of hot milk then had a bath. Filling the time was a bit of a problem, but of course all that would change when he found himself someone to share his life. They would be able to talk, well into the night, exchanging experiences. Maybe he could find a woman with a disability of some kind, so they had something in common? It would not be like *his* problem of course, he was pretty sure he was unique, but something, some missing thing with which he could sympathise. That would make a change: to feel sorry for someone else, instead of feeling sorry for himself.

He started.

This won't do at all, he thought. No, no. He shook his head sadly. Instead of thinking about sharing happiness, he had been indulging in thoughts of exchanging feelings of *pity*. Perhaps he had lost the ability for happiness?

As the evening wore on he became a little morose again. Finally, he switched on the TV for the late night movie. It was the wrong thing to do. Late night films are almost always old ones and it turned out to be an umpteenth reshowing of *Casablanca*.

Like *St James Infirmary* the movie *Casablanca* had got to him from the first time he had seen it in 1945. There was a powerful haunting quality to the film. It spoke to him of almost-forgotten memories, good times that had gone by, friends now lost. Maybe it was the way the theme song *As Time Goes By* had triggered the opening of old wounds.

He sat and watched the film, waiting for *her*.

She was all he had left now. Bogart had gone early, around '57, and so had Peter Lorre and Claude Rains. The German heavy, Conrad something or other, had died just after the film's release, and Sabastian had never seen him, which hadn't helped his comprehension any. Up until three years previously, every time he watched *Casablanca* he would make bets with himself whether the refuge would still be there; the old guy who had been the only surviving character in the film's first twenty minutes, who turned to an invisible actor to deliver that incredible line, 'We hear very little and we understand even less.' Every time he saw him, Sabastian cheered the old geezer's appearance on the screen. *Hang on in there, buddy*, he would say. Then one evening… he sighed, remembering.

He watched the empty background streets, scenes, waiting for her: his beloved survivor.

INGRID BERGMAN GLIDED INTO RICK'S Café Américain, moving around the screen like a beautiful ghost in the silent empty room. There were drinks on the tables, smouldering cigarettes in the ashtrays, and not a single person in sight. Doors opened and closed for her, chairs were pushed back as she moved along, lovely and remote, warm and mysterious, the unattainable woman in an impossible romance.

She roamed through the dead marketplace, where Persian rugs and embroidered curtains rippled and displayed themselves, craving attention. His heart went out to her, wherever she was on this earth. If he had been a poet he would have imagined her as an angel, walking with courage amongst the ruins of this dying, forgotten world. But he was a simple man, one of the strays of life, and when she spoke her lines into thin air he filled in the blanks, as she waited for the non-existent replies from the unseen Bogart.

'We'll leave Casablanca together, Ingrid,' he said out loud.

'You're the only woman I have ever loved,' he murmured, as she embraced empty space.

They were lovers in an ancient game, far from the prying eyes of the crowd. It was the only time his disability became a boon. To be alone with her, Ingrid-Ilsa, in the moonlight sequences in Paris, to kiss her one last time... no, there wasn't any need for that... he wasn't Bogey, he didn't have to be left behind. Every time he boarded the plane with her on that rain-swept airfield, just before the car's doors opened of their own volition for dead German soldiers who would never, now, stop the lovers. In fact it even seemed to him once that the slamming car doors was an applause for their escape.

The image of that plane leaving Casablanca, carrying his lover with him, would keep him company well into the night. He anticipated it eagerly as, luminous, she turned towards him (Bogey?) and, with that heartbreakingly beautiful look on her face, told him, 'I said I would never leave you.'

Something was wrong with the television set...

Ingrid smiled faintly and then her face began to blur.

Sabastian sat upright on the sofa. Christ! That damn TV set. Not now!

She came back, one last time, a solitary tear running down her cheek. Then she was gone. She had disappeared from the film.

There was nothing wrong with the set. Ilsa had gone. Ingrid Bergman was dead.

It was such a shock that Sabastian sank back into the sofa, his heart like a crumpled paper bag. She was gone, dead, forever. His Ingrid.

Bogart, the real Bogart, had her now. Had taken her away from Sabastian in the end, as if he had been mocking him from the grave, all along. *When I want her, I'll just click my fingers, sweetheart.* No, that wasn't Bogey. Bogey was hard on the outside but tender underneath. Death was the one to blame.

Such a feeling of sorrow choked him, coming out like the sound of a baby's gargle. His head developed a pain which threatened to split it from brow to the base of his neck. Death. Was it a nothingness? Was he privy to the afterworld, where there were not even shadows of the living? Just blank spaces where people had once been? Someone once glowing with animation? Was this the promise of the hereafter?

He switched off the set and sat staring at the grey screen, nursing his aching head in his hands. Tomorrow. He had to do something tomorrow. He couldn't live with this horrible knowledge alone any longer. He had to have someone to share the terrible secret with him.

He pulled open a drawer which had been closed for years and wrenched out a photo album, tearing through the pages in a kind of frenzied excitement. His father, his mother? Uncle Pete? Where? Cards with background scenes, but no people. Portrait photographs with no faces, just studio background curtains. Where was Uncle Pete? He wanted to see him again. Study those kind old features. Nothing. An old school photo was there. Rows of chairs, only half of them occupied. All those empty seats. Nothing people who had led nothing lives and now blanks in the nothingness of death. He ripped the picture to pieces, ranting at the same time, scattering the shreds. He snarled and turned on the frame with the white card which, before 1973, had been a print of Picasso's *Bathers Playing Ball*. He took hold of it and smashed it over the back of a chair.

The shards of glass crunched under his feet as he moved around the room destroying things. His head was a ball of raging pain. It spurred him on to greater demolition. He wrenched the wires of the TV out of the socket with a savage yell of rage and sorrow.

When he had worked himself into a state of exhaustion, he crawled up the stairs. In the bathroom cabinet was a bottle of painkillers. Sabastian swallowed two, then three, then began cramming them into his mouth, washing them down with water, until he had finished the whole bottle. For a while he just leant against the white tiles, feeling their coolness behind his agony, then the pain began to recede.

He stumbled, almost fell downstairs, and moved over to the record player, putting on his favourite disc. Then over to the sofa, in front of the blank television screen.

...she can look this whole wide world all over—she'll never find another man like me. Drifting. Drifting... *a boxback coat and a Stetson hat*. Into the night. Long into the night. Sleep. *And the boys will know I died, standing pat*.

The piano. He could hear nothing but the piano. No clapping. At first it was faint, but then it built in volume, until Satchmo's voice growled from the platter and all the instruments began to come in, one by one.

The television was right in front of his eyes. Misty pictures began to appear on the grey screen. They seemed muddled at first, slightly distorted, coming from far away, then near. People.

What's happening? he wanted to say, but had difficulty in even just thinking the words.

The man in the white smoking jacket and bow tie turned towards the black man. He spoke with a faint lisp.

'He hasn't got it yet. Look at him,' and he nodded out at Sabastian from the screen, smiling that lopsided smile.

'You know what he wants to hear,' said the beautiful woman, coming up behind the two men. 'You played it for me, now play it for him. Play it again. It's his day…'

The black man's face fractured into a grin, as lifting his trumpet to his lips, he said, 'Man, all those years. That's a heavy burden.'

The sounds of the trumpet filled the air and suddenly the screen began to get very crowded. Then the man in the white jacket turned and leaned out of the group. He cocked his thumb and pointed his finger.

There was a tremendous final bolt of pain in Sabastian's chest. Playing to an empty room, the piano was the last survivor.

Christian Lehmann and Garry Kilworth

CHERUB

(There are two kinds of cherub. One is the medieval cherub: the naked chubby infant with wings. The other is your actual biblical cherub: a terrifying monster. The following story makes only passing reference to the first kind.)

HARRY MEEKER STOOD SHIVERING IN the cold wind which swept around the corner of the Royal Festival Hall. His raincoat sagged deeply on one side. In the left pocket was the gun, which he had hardly touched since it had been given to him by John-the-Butcher. Harry didn't want to touch the gun. He hated the feel of the weight and the way it knocked against his thigh every time he moved.

Harry stared out moodily over the River Thames, watching the occasional boat drift up or down, sometimes studded with coloured lights, sometimes blacked out except for the mandatory port and starboard lamps. The first were usually full of noisy people, the second silent and mysterious. Harry wished he were on any one of them, heading for an unknown destination, somewhere where he couldn't be found.

Suddenly, doors flew open and the building began to disgorge its patrons. People came out, some in evening dress, some not, to fill the precinct outside the hall. Harry went rigid with tension and peered into the chattering crowds as they swept past him, looking for Chas McFey. Harry hoped he wouldn't see him, though he knew the consequences of failure. It didn't bear thinking about: someone waiting in the shadows to blow *his* brains all over his coat collar.

At that moment he caught sight of Chas, all spruced up in black tie gear, walking with his wife on his arm. Harry's cold but sweaty hand closed around the butt of the gun in his pocket. His legs started shaking. He couldn't do it here, of course, in front of all these witnesses. It would be necessary to follow Chas and do it in some quiet street. Chas lived only walking distance from the South Bank: there would be no car or cab.

Somehow, Harry got his legs to move, and he followed the couple down a series of steps, to the streets below. Chas and his wife turned into York Road at the bottom, and along, and then finally into Leake Street, a small quiet area. Harry tried to pull out the gun, but it caught on the lining of his pocket, and it took him at least a minute to untangle it. When he managed to free it, Chas was almost at his house. Harry ran forward, his hand trembling violently, and pointed the gun.

'Chas!' he croaked.

Both Chas and his wife turned and stared, wide-eyed, into Harry's face. For some reason they didn't look at the gun and he wondered if they had even seen it. Harry knew that he would have to kill both of them. He tried to pull the trigger, but his finger was somehow locked. His heart was pounding so fast he wondered if he were going to have a heart attack. He felt sick and faint, wanting to vomit.

'Harry?' Chas said, finally looking down at the gun.

Harry's arm hurt where the muscles were cramping with the tension. There was no way he could pull that trigger. Wincing with the pain, he gradually lowered the weapon.

'I can't do it,' he moaned. 'I just can't do it.'

And still Chas and his wife were no help. They stood there, looking shocked. Then suddenly Chas's wife started screaming— screams that would have penetrated Hitler's bunker—and Harry started running.

He ran all the way back down to the river, stood for a moment on the walk, then threw the gun into the water.

Then he started walking, his hands buried deep in his pockets, towards Blackfriars Bridge.

'I've bloody had it now,' he kept telling himself. 'I'm in the shit right up to my neck now.'

John-the-Butcher had ordered Harry to top Chas McFey, had thrust the gun into his hand and said, 'Get rid of the bastard, Harry, and we'll forget what you owe.' Harry did indeed owe the Butcher a substantial amount, for Harry was a gambler with an extraordinary talent for losing. Harry could bet on a fixed race and the horse would fall over and break its neck right before the finish line. That was how good Harry was at losing.

But Harry was *just* a gambler. He didn't steal, commit violent acts, or kill people. The Butcher did all those things. All Harry ever did was lose on the races and borrow more money. That wasn't an offence against anyone, not society, not even Butcher John. What *was* a crime was not paying his debts on time and though the law of the land was fairly lenient in such cases, the Butcher saw it as a crime of the most heinous nature. Raping the Butcher's grandmother was not as serious as failing to pay him what you owed.

So John-the-Butcher wasn't *asking* Harry to kill Chas McFey. He was *telling* him. Now Harry would be lucky if the Butcher didn't top *him*, for not doing what he was told. At the very least the Butcher's boys Dave and Phil would put Harry's legs over a kerb and jump on them, several times, until the bones were in splinters. Harry's stomach churned at the thought. Harry sweated. Harry's brain buzzed with fear.

As he walked through Blackfriars, after crossing the bridge, Harry came across a small chapel. The doors were open. On impulse he went inside and sat down in a pew. Not being a religious man he didn't know what to do at first, but gradually he managed to start praying. He prayed for all sorts of things, from John-the-Butcher getting a cardiac arrest, to God providing him, Harry, with a guardian angel.

'I think I've earned it, Lord,' whispered Harry. 'I saved a man's life tonight... at the expense of my own. I mean, doesn't it say somewhere, something about its the greatest thing you can do, give up your life for your friend? I did that tonight. You owe me, Lord...' this sounded a little impertinent, so Harry added, 'in a manner of speaking. In return, I promise to be Good, always.'

After his 'Amen' Harry waited around to see if anything was going to happen, then sighed and left. He had never had much faith in mumbo-jumbo but it was worth a try. As a child he had been sent to Sunday School to get him out of his mother's hair for a morning. In those days he had been pretty impressed with things like miracles. Now there was only the reality of the Butcher and Harry's own vivid imagination.

'I did let Chas live though,' he murmured, 'and I'm glad.'

He saw no point in hiding. The Butcher would eventually find him. So Harry went straight back to his flat in Camden.

As he put the key in the lock, Harry could smell burning.

'Must have left the gas hob on,' he muttered.

When he entered the hallway, it felt very warm. He frowned. There was a kind of roaring sound, coming from the living-room. Surely the Butcher's men hadn't been round already? It was too soon for them to have heard. Yet it seemed that his living-room was on fire.

Harry went forward cautiously. The living-room door was partly ajar and he pushed it open and peered inside. The next second he jumped back, slamming against the hall wall, his eyes starting from his head.

'JESUS CHRIST!' he screamed.

His breath came out in quick gasps, robbing him of oxygen. His heart was stuck somewhere in his windpipe, choking him. Fear was like a flood sweeping through him.

There was a monster in the corner of his living-room, breathing fire.

Harry stared at the creature, which did not move.

The *thing* was crouched there, but if it had stood up Harry guessed it would be about twelve feet tall. It was indeed monstrous, with a huge body covered in eyes and tiny wings. There was a semblance of human shape about it, though it seemed more head than anything else. Its beak-like mouth was cavernous and its enormous claw-feet spread out across the carpet. The whole creature was grotesque, like something that had stepped out of a nightmare, and it was *alive*.

'Oh, Jesus…' groaned Harry.

The creature's head turned at this word and it seemed to be staring at Harry with quite a few of its eyes.

It was not exactly *breathing* fire, as Harry had first thought, but was flailing the air with a fiery sword. It never stopped. It was like a demonstration by an Oriental juggler spinning flaming brands, very skilfully, in order to create a circle of fire. Harry could feel the heat of the sword and hear the roar of its burning. Yet it seemed not to start any secondary fires in the room.

Even through his terror, it struck Harry that if John-the-Butcher's men came to the flat, they would have to deal with this monster, as well as Harry himself. Harry was inclined to think that the monster would not be easily subdued. It appeared to be the kind of creature which might put up a bit of a fight, get a little angry, if someone annoyed it. This gave Harry a modicum of comfort. Gradually, as it became apparent that the creature was not going to attack him, a calmness of spirit crept over Harry and he began to relax.

Exhausted, both by the night's events and by the heat, Harry slid down the wall to the hallway floor, where he lay in a pool of sweat and drifted off into a fitful sleep, the catherine wheel of fire still flashing and roaring before his eyes.

When he woke, at five in the morning, the monster was still there, still swishing about him with his flaming sword, still creating wonderful fire patterns in the air. Its grotesque crouched form filled a good third of Harry's small room

'Mornin',' croaked Harry, his throat parched. 'Haven't you got the cramps yet?'

When the monster didn't answer, Harry went to the bathroom, had a drink of water, stripped, took a shower, and came out feeling refreshed. He went to his bedroom and dressed in clean clothes, lit a cigarette, then picked up the phone and dialled.

'Cynthia? Yes, I know what time it is, but you haven't seen what I've got here... no, I'm not being coarse—I mean in my living-room. It's a sodding great monster—well, I'm sorry, I know you don't like swearing but there's no other way to describe it. It's—it's—well, I really *can't* describe it—alright, I will...' and he told her what the thing looked like, what it was carrying, and what it was doing with it.

'You see why I'm ringing you? It seems harmless enough but I need you to find out what it is. Can you come over? Bring a couple of books. We'll go through them together. Okay, see you in a bit. Sorry about waking you—yeah, okay. Bye.'

Harry put down the phone. Cynthia was his occasional girlfriend and a school teacher. If she couldn't find out what the thing was, nobody could. Cynthia was bright.

Harry went into the living-room and sat in a chair and stared at the creature. The creature stood, waved its flaming sword, and stared at Harry. It was a woefully uneven contest.

Cynthia naturally went into hysterics at first, saying she thought Harry had been hallucinating, or had the dee-tees, or something normal, but she never expected to see a definite, real, honest-to-God monster in his living-room. Harry told her he had got used to the creature now and just wanted to know what the hell it was, so he could decide what to do about it.

Cynthia had brought some books with her, thinking she might have to humour him, so when she had calmed down, about an hour later, they went through them together. The books she had brought were full of mythological and fabulous beasts, like the basilisk, the gryphon, the senmurv, dragons, Tengu, Garuda...

'That's a bit like him, that Garuda thing,' said Harry.

Cynthia studied the creature in Harry's living-room corner and then the picture of Garuda, the Indonesian god.

'Nothing like it,' she said. 'You should be wearing your glasses.'

She continued to search through the books, while Harry made her a cup of tea, then she suddenly shrieked.

He came running into the living-room thinking the beast was devouring or ravishing her, only to find her holding up a picture with the word 'CHERUB' beneath it.

'A *cherub*?' Harry cried, amazed. 'I thought cherubs were plump little babies with wings?'

'That's how renaissance artists depicted them, but this is drawn from a description in the bible.'

'Read me what it says underneath,' said Harry, squinting at the monster.

Cynthia read. '*A cherub is a divine being that belongs to the ranks of angels, a multi-eyed, multi-winged giant. One of the functions of the cherubim is to serve as guardians. Their weapon is the ever-turning flaming sword. See Genesis 3:24.*'

'A guardian angel?' cried Harry.

Cynthia nodded. 'You've got it.'

'That's it then,' breathed Harry. 'I prayed for a guardian angel and I got one. Why doesn't that sword thing set light to my curtains?'

'It's probably *holy* fire,' explained Cynthia, practically. 'Not ordinary fire.'

'Oh,' replied Harry, still just as confused. 'You mean it's sort of different.'

'It probably burns demons and evil things, but not ordinary mundane stuff.'

'Oh,' said Harry again.

He went up as close as he dared to the cherub and stared at it in wonder. It stared back at him, many many times over, and its beak opened a fraction, its hundreds of small wings fluttered, its feet moved a fraction. Even though it continued to twirl its sword, Harry believed it had responded in some way, had acknowledged Harry's presence.

'This is my angel,' he murmured. 'I was sort of expecting the traditional type—you know, Cynth, the ones with feathery wings and white shifts? I thought if one came it would protect me against bullets and stuff, stepping in and snatching them out of the air, that sort of thing. But this,' he paused again to look the cherub up and down, as it twirled its roaring sword like a juggler, 'this will probably *eat* the Butcher whole.'

'What about taking me to breakfast somewhere?' said Cynthia. 'After all, you got me up early.'

'Right,' said Harry. 'Let's go.' He took her arm and steered her towards the door. The cherub lumbered after them, filling the hallway, still swishing its sword around, knocking lamp shades and chipping a hat rack.

'Be careful with that thing,' warned Harry, half-turning, 'the landlady will have my guts if you damage anything.'

They all stepped outside the front door, one after another. The cherub stretched to its full height and looked extremely formidable. Dogs ran on sight of it. Cats arched and spat. Birds looked as if they felt inadequate.

It was now eight o'clock in the morning. They wandered along the grey street, Harry and Cynthia holding hands and the cherub walking massively three steps behind them, slicing bits off the overhanging branches of trees. People on their way to work stopped and stared, and pointed. Children on their way to school shrieked and pointed. A police car stopped alongside. The cop in the passenger seat wound down his window carefully, first staring fixedly at the cherub, and then at Harry and Cynthia. He pointed.

'You can't bring your friend along here, squire,' said the copper. 'Not while he's waving that thing.'

'Nothing to do with me,' lied Harry, uncomfortably.

'Why's he following you two then?' asked the other policeman at the wheel of the car.

'We weren't aware that he was,' said Cynthia. 'I—I think it's someone dressed up for an advertisement—like the Burger Turkey. You know, advertising fast food.'

Harry walked on quickly, with Cynthia trotting at his side, the cherub kept pace with them. The two policemen tried to have a word with the cherub but were ignored. They barked into their radio mike and started the siren.

Harry and Cynthia ducked down a tube station. The cherub was right behind them. It crashed through the turnstile after them and onto the crowded platform. People made a space for them. When the train arrived there was a crush inside. Harry and Cynthia managed to squeeze in, making two more. The cherub miraculously made it three. People were instantly squashed into unfriendly packs, cheek to jowl, lip to shoulder.

The whirling sword was given flailing space, ignored only by the skinhead buried in the tabloid, whose knees were spread wide and whose elbows demanded both seat rests. Not one person spoke or made eye contact, except for the carriage's one token schizoid who glowered and muttered defiantly at the cherub and everyone else, daring someone to meet to his glare. The majority of the passengers suffered as always in silence, a story under their belts for when they reached the sanctity of the office.

'You'll never guess what some bloke brought on the tube this morning—bloody great thing with a flaming sword yea long...'

Harry and Cynthia left the tube, went up to street level, and found a restaurant serving breakfast. The cherub stumped after them, ducking to get through the door. Its myriad wings fluttered, its manifold eyes took in every nook and cranny of the room. Harry had to give the cherub its due: it was more effective than a gross of secret service agents when it came to protecting its charge.

Fresh coffee aroma had a calming effect on Harry's nerves.

When they sat at a corner table, the cherub stood nearby, as if ready to assist the chef with any flambé dishes. A waiter's eyes bulged and he called the manager. The room began to get warm and people left, right in the middle of their breakfasts. The manager came and remonstrated with Harry.

'A restaurant is not the place for circus freaks,' said the manager.

'We could have you up for that,' replied Cynthia. 'That's prejudice, that is, and it's not politically correct.'

'I don't care whether it's politically *insane*—you're ruining my trade,' hissed the manager.

'I don't think you can refuse to serve us, just because our—our companion is vertically disadvantaged.'

'He's not just too *tall*,' growled the manager, 'he's a bloody mutant—get him out of here.'

The two of them left the restaurant with the guardian angel in tow, but it was the same everywhere. People scattered and screamed, left in dread, or stared curiously with open mouths. No restaurant would serve the couple with the monstrous figure trailing them like a nightmarish fire wielder. The managers began ringing each other up, warning of an approach.

In the street, no one would come near the trio, except for a lone drunk who staggered up to the cherub and asked for a light for his cigarette.

The police eventually caught up with them, but could do nothing with the creature. When one of the cops tried to arrest Harry, the cherub leapt forward with alarming alacrity and seemed about to take off the policeman's head, so the law decided to call in the army. An anti-terrorist squad eventually arrived, while the police kept the trio ringed on a bench in a private park belonging to London University. The squad commander assessed the situation then told the police if they wanted someone killed, his men would do it cleanly and efficiently, but the case did not seem to warrant such drastic action.

The police eventually agreed and all the officials left after giving Harry a severe warning.

'If that thing starts wandering about the streets again,' said a police chief, 'I'm holding you responsible...'

'I'm off home,' said Cynthia. 'I'm starving. I'll be back later, Harry. Would you like a picnic?'

'Yes, that would be nice,' Harry said, distantly.

Harry was left sitting on the park bench with the cherub standing by, entertaining a crowd of spectators on the other side of the fence with its flaming sword. Eventually this showy but rather repetitive exhibition began to bore the crowd who yelled for 'some more tricks' which were never forthcoming.

They too finally drifted away.

Harry remained alone amongst the trees of the park. The day wore on and Harry began to get really hungry. Also there was a horse running in the 3.30 at Epsom, which he was certain would solve all his financial problems. Still, he stayed where he was because if he started walking, the whole business would erupt again, with the police and the army. If he remained in the park there seemed to be an unspoken agreement that the law would leave him alone. He hoped Cynthia would return later with a sandwich and a flask of tea, and maybe the *Racing Times*.

While he was sitting there, John-the-Butcher arrived with two heavies, one at each shoulder.

'A little bird told me you was here. You've been a naughty boy, Harry,' said Butcher John, hunching his shoulders inside his overcoat. 'You better tell your mate here to scarper, while we talk business.' The Butcher stared at the cherub for a minute, then shivered. 'Ugly looking bastard, ain't he? Get rid of 'im, before Dave and Phil have to sort him out.'

'No,' said Harry, defiantly, staring at Dave and Phil, the Butcher's two henchmen. 'My guardian stays where it is.'

Dave and Phil flexed inside their windcheaters, then came forward, their fists bunched. The cherub stepped in front of Harry and seemed prepared to protect him. The two men stopped in their tracks. Phil ran his hand over his shaven scalp. Dave sniffed noisily.

'Like that is it?' said Phil, raising his right-wing eyebrows. An iron rod slipped down out of his coat sleeve neatly into his right hand.

Dave sniggered and reached inside his jacket, producing a butcher's knife.

'Wanna change your mind, Harry?' asked Butcher John.

'No,' said Harry.

Dave and Phil came forward again, Dave slicing the air with the knife, Phil whirling the iron bar round his head. They seemed to be competing with the cherub. The cherub skipped forward as agile as a Thai dancer and, with a spectacular flourish which would have delighted its erstwhile audience, ran Dave through the chest with the flaming sword. Dave dropped to the ground with a little sigh, dead as Smithfield pork.

Phil cried, 'You done for my mate, you bastard…'

Then he too was impaled on the flaming sword with no less an impressive swish and thrust of the weapon. The blade went through him like a hot skewer through lard. Phil gave a surprised little shudder and fell beside his mate.

On the cherub the multitudinous wings fluttered with each killing stroke. The cherub's ten-thousand eyes seemed to close simultaneously in a half-smile. This was obviously its *raison d'être*. All its training had been channelled towards these needle-point moments when the ever-turning sword was put to efficient and piercing use.

Harry pondered on the fact that if JFK's bodyguards had been just one tenth as well-trained as the cherub, the great President would probably be alive and still fornicating today.

Despite his horror, Harry was interested to see sort of neat little burn holes, still flaming, in the middle of the hoodlums' chests. Then the bodies swiftly shrivelled into crisp burned wads that flaked off and blew away on the breeze. Soon there was nothing left but a stain on the grass.

John-the-Butcher's eyes were starting out of his head.

'You sod,' he whispered. 'Why couldn't you have done that to Chas McFey and his Mrs?'

'*I* didn't do it,' said Harry. 'It was my guardian angel. Dave and Phil attacked him. It was only defending itself.'

'I thought angels had wings and stuff like that?'

'It's got wings,' protested Harry. 'Lots of them.'

'Not little sparrow jobs—two big ones in the proper place on its back.'

'Not this kind. This is a cherub—I know you thought cherubs were sweet little babes…'

'Not a bit of it, pal. The wife calls her nephews "cherubs" and they're nasty little bastards. They'd destroy a Churchill tank if you took your eyes off 'em for a second.'

John-the-Butcher moved cautiously forward, peering hard at the cherub.

'Be careful,' said Harry.

'I ain't goin' to do you, I'm just getting a closer look at this thing. Where did you get it from? What did you say it was? A cherub?'

'That's right,' replied Harry.

The Butcher said, 'Do they all look like him?'

Harry thought about the books he had seen earlier.

'Well, the next biggest size up is a seraph. They've only got six wings but they're quite a lot meatier. They don't have flaming swords, but they do have these terrible feet…'

'A seraph sounds more my mark,' said John-the-Butcher, moving even closer to peer at the cherub's muscles. 'I'm not struck on the flaming sword stuff. It's a bit conspicuous and what's more bloody unnecessary with a bloke this size, ain't it? I mean, all that ruddy twirlin'…'

'Don't get too close!' warned Harry. 'That's *holy* fire. You're an evil bugger, John. You'll go up in…'

But it was too late. The sword touched John-the-Butcher's hair and he immediately exploded in a ball of flame with a loud *whumph*. The heat from the burning Butcher singed Harry's eyebrows. In two seconds flat there was nothing but ashes on the ground. The ashes blew away on the wind. Harry wondered whether the police would arrest him, as an accomplice to murder, but he subsequently realised no one had seen, and there was nothing left of the three crooks to prove they had been there at all. Certainly they would not be missed.

A short time later Cynthia came to the park with a flask of coffee and some roast chicken sandwiches.

'Hi,' she said. 'It's still with you then?'

The cherub was doing a deft underarm pass with its sword at that moment.

'Yes,' replied Harry, a little gloomily.

Cynthia said, 'Why so glum? At least it's protecting you from John-the-Butcher.'

'Erm, I don't think I need a guardian angel any more—the Butcher's gone away.'

'Oh,' said Cynthia surprised. 'Where?'

'Somewhere warm—look, how am I going to get rid of this thing, Cynth? I've tried praying. That doesn't work.'

'I've been thinking about that. The trouble is, you're basically a *good* person, Harry. Guardian angels look after good people. You've got to become wicked if you want it to go.'

'What sort of wicked?'

'Well let's take the Ten Commandments—you need to break some of the rules.'

'Thou shalt not kill? That sort of thing? Well I'm not killing anyone, so that's out. I'm not married and I don't know any married women, so adultery's out too. I certainly don't wish to dishonour my father and my mother, so what else is there? I don't want to steal anything either, that's not just one of the Ten Commandments, it's also a crime. No point in getting rid of the cherub if I'm just going to end up in jail.'

'Um, Graven images? No, bit old fashioned. Thou shalt not bear false witness?'

'I dunno what that means, really. Sounds a bit like fixing a gee-gee and then telling everyone else to bet on it, to make the odds on the second favourite go up. I can't do that. It's against my professional ethics.'

'What about coveting?'

Harry shrugged. 'I thought that had to do with wanting next door's wife. She's 75, and frankly Cynth, even the thought turns my stomach. I couldn't even fake it.'

The whirling flaming sword was distracting him, flaring through the evening air above his head. The cherub was a liability and with all those eyes it didn't miss a trick. Harry couldn't even touch Cynthia, without it blinked and stared with at least a few hundred of them. It was most disconcerting and certainly not conducive to a good sex life.

'Well, there's also menservants, oxen, asses, anything that's your neighbour's.'

'Don't really want any of those either,' said Harry, feeling depressed. 'I wouldn't mind his red Porsche, but that's not the same thing, is it?'

'Do you really, really, *really*, envy him his car?'

'Of course I do—who wouldn't? I sometimes imagine it's mine and... and...'

'And what, Harry?' asked Cynthia, huskily.

'And—you know, I told you—you and me, on the back seat—it's leather upholstery you know.'

Harry went all hot as he thought about it, and when he looked up, the cherub had gone.

'Blimey,' he said, surprised. 'Is it that easy?'

'It is for *you*,' smiled Cynthia. 'You're such a nice man, Harry. It doesn't take much for you to be wicked. Here, I've brought you the *Racing Times*. There's a horse running in the two o'clock tomorrow at Haymarket called Guardian Angel.'

'Really?' Harry took the paper eagerly.

'But Harry…'

He looked up. 'Yes?'

'Don't bet more than you can afford and stick to the tote.'

Harry sighed and nodded. 'Right, Cynth.'

Later, as they boarded the tube train, a man got in after them with a seven-foot demon at his heels. He was a small, mild-looking man, with round glasses and a little wispy moustache. He looked very miserable. They all travelled in silence for a while, the demon seemingly happy to study a group of skinheads who had suddenly gone very quiet.

Harry glanced at the ferocious-looking demon, then at the mild, little man, and said, 'Boy, are you in trouble.'

'I know,' sighed the little man.

'It's much harder to *keep* the Ten Commandments, than *break* them.'

'I know, I know,' sighed the little man.

The demon just grinned and kept his peace.

THE COUNCIL OF BEASTS

(The Cornelis Saftleven painting, mentioned in the story, is where this idea came from. It is one of those paintings which, when you first glance at it, looks rather humorous. Then on subsequent inspections grows darker and more chilling with every study.)

THE DOG GESTURED TO ME from across the tavern and finally I got up and went to his table. Dressed in a tweed suit, a plain shirt and tasteful tie, he was some kind of terrier. He opened his jaws in the semblance of a human grin, but rather than put me at my ease it chilled me to the marrow. I had never seen anything so terrifying. I tried to smile back.

'Pull up a stool,' he said. What made it worse was, he didn't growl. He spoke with clear diction. 'Sit down. You look as if you need a friend.'

I didn't ask the dog its name. I'd already made that mistake once and been beaten for it. They told me that in this city the animals had no given names. It was humans who gave creatures personal names and to the animals here having a name was a symbol of slavery.

It was three weeks since I had arrived in the City of the Beasts. I was weary with walking, ragged of mind. Naked and filthy, I'd slept in cobbled alleys, eaten rubbish from the gutter, tried to beg from passing sedan chairs containing arrogant creatures of all kinds: beasts wearing silk coats and dresses. Goats, cats, dogs and foxes mostly.

The larger animals, like horses, could not of course be carried. They tended to live on the pale of the city in hovels with stable doors. I once saw a donkey sitting on the town hall steps smoking a pipe, but that was an unusual sight.

'Can you help me?' I croaked. 'No one will help me. I don't know what I'm doing here. I don't know how I came to be here. Please, can you help me?'

'Calm down, calm down,' he said, glancing around him. 'You're attracting attention. Sit.'

I did as he bid now, taking the stool. He signalled to the cat in the faded dress, the serving feline, and she brought two jugs of ale to the table. As always I was fascinated by the way she carried the tray and lifted the jugs. She was dexterous where she should not be. One of the reasons humans evolved into tool-makers and ruled the world was because of their prehensile hands. The opposing thumb. The secret was supposed to be in the thumb. Yet she managed to carry the tray, lift the jugs, place them on the oak table.

'I think I can help you,' said the dog in undertones. 'Have you spoken to anyone else?'

The tavern was becoming riotous now, with drunken beasts slopping ale on the floor, some talking so loudly they were shouting, others displaying obnoxious behaviour. Two dogs in shirtsleeves were fighting in the corner, using their paws like fists, punching each other, kicking, but not using their teeth. A badger was encouraging them in their violence, hissing first at one to go in, then the other, delighted when blood was drawn.

'I've attempted to talk to other—other beasts,' I replied in despair, 'but no one seems to want to answer my questions. When I first arrived I tried to walk out of the city, but I kept finding myself back in the streets again.'

The dog put a paw on the back of my hands and I felt the rough cloth of his jacket against my bare skin.

'Don't do that,' he whispered. 'Never do that. It's dangerous. You're in your own mind. If you try to go out of your mind, you'll end up insane. That's what it is, isn't it, insanity? Being out of your mind?'

'Yes,' I replied bleakly, 'but I don't understand.'

'Don't worry. Look, I can get you in to see the Council of Beasts. They're the only ones who can really help you. What do you say? Would you like me to do that?'

The dog's brown eyes glittered in the lamplight. He stared into my face, his hot musty breath overpowering me. There was sweat dripping from his tongue onto my left leg, soiling my skin. I wanted to scream at him, hit him over the head with my ale jug, smash that look off his features, but I couldn't. He would have had me beaten into insensibility by those around us. They did that, when you angered them. They were basically savage creatures, who reacted instinctively.

When I had earlier seen a goat put on his hat, I knew I should have laughed—it was so absurd—but I gagged with horror, causing the goat to say, 'What are you looking at?' in vicious accents, before shouldering past me.

I said to the dog, 'Why? Why are you doing this?'

He drew back from me a little, looked a somewhat hurt, and then replied, 'I want to be your best friend.'

If only there were other humans here, I should have someone with whom to talk this over. Just one other would have been enough. Perhaps between the two of us we could have worked out some reason for it all? But so far as I knew, I was the only member of *Homo sapiens* in the city.

It was not so much that I was hunted down, or even openly reviled, but I was *here*. Yes, I had been treated with contempt, forced to eat from the gutter, made to sleep in filthy corners, but this was more a matter of neglect than open hostility. No one cared about me. They lived their lives around me, their indifference to my suffering hurtful, but there was no positive attempt to degrade or physically harm me.

'Do you want to come home with me for the night?' asked the dog. 'I can find you a place to sleep.'

I nodded, all my pride gone.

When we left the tavern, I went out first, and two footpads carrying cudgels—dogs by the look of them under the lamplight—crossed the street towards me. However, when they saw my terrier they dropped their eyes and changed the direction of their walk. Soon they had gone, down one of the slick black alleys which led to the river, where they could ply their trade in the fog.

'You see,' said the terrier, patting a bulge in his waistcoat pocket. 'You have me to thank for your safety. Or rather my position as a Constable of the Watch. Did I not mention that to you? Well then, we have known each other for such a short period of time.'

He led me to a modest town house in the area of the prison and unlocked the door with a huge iron key. Inside the rooms were not unfriendly but sparsely furnished. I wondered what I had let myself in for, but the terrier did not seem overly interested in me except to see me bedded down in a corner of the kitchen, just behind the stove, on warm flags.

I pulled the ragged blanket over my head, hoping as always when I fell asleep, that I should awake in a morning where the nightmare had gone. It was a hope which was never fulfilled, but

I still nurtured it. This city, peopled by beasts in clothes, was a horrible dream. It seemed to me as if there were something I had to remember, which would be the key to my escape but since I did not have an inkling of what it was I could do no more than pray some revelation would come to me.

The dog had mentioned the Council of Beasts.

Perhaps they could help me?

'It's funny,' said the terrier, as he left the kitchen with a lighted candle, 'we used to be under your domination. Now you look to me for sustenance, shelter, comfort. Our roles have been reversed. I find that funny, don't you?'

'Yes,' I said. 'Most peculiar.'

'And funny,' he said, leaving me.

The next day he took me to the town hall, in the cobbled square. It was a Gothic building, with round turrets, spires and narrow windows. Shadows lurked in the corners of its deep sills and arches. The windows were filthy. A trail of dung led from the great doorway, out into the square, where it filled the cracks between the cobbles. On a hot day this square stank of drying straw and animal droppings. There was a pile of steaming hay in the hallway as we entered, whose damp heart must surely have been about to combust.

'Up the stairs,' said the terrier. 'Our appointment is for noon.'

That could have meant just about any time between 8 o'clock in the morning and mid-afternoon. Since there were no clocks here it was immaterial. The beasts only had four times— midnight, dawn, noon and dusk. They had no need of exacting seconds, minutes or hours. Midnight was the most flexible, since there was nothing to mark it except perhaps a vague knowledge of where the moon and stars should be at such a time.

We sat on a long wooden bench outside a set of tall narrow doors which rose to three times my height. On the bench there was a goat, three pigs all in open-necked shirts with dirty collars, a fox and several rats. It seemed they were all waiting to get in to see the council.

I sat next to the goat in the torn cloak who was chewing a wad of hay the whole time, occasionally spitting the juice across the corridor at the wall opposite, where it dribbled down to the skirting beneath. Once or twice he inclined his head to stare at me curiously, but said nothing.

The pigs were talking in low, urgent voices together, as if they were concocting some story on which they had to be consistent and word perfect. Occasionally their mumblings were audible, so that I caught a partial sentence.

'...so then *you* say,' murmured the saddleback hog, '"I have no need of a third of a whole acre..."'

The rats remained nervously quiet, not looking at each other, scratching themselves impatiently.

Suddenly the doors to the council chamber flew open and a small dog appeared.

'The visitor!' he called.

The terrier nudged me and I got to my feet. On the bench there was some shuffling of hooves and paws, and mutterings about jumping the queue. These I ignored as I entered the large council room. On the way across the bare floor I passed a dejected-looking poodle who gave me such a look of disgust I felt that whatever his petition had been, he blamed me for its failure. Since he no doubt had to blame *someone* I was as good a choice as any. The doors were closed behind him.

I was invited to sit in a wheel-backed chair before a great mahogany desk. I stared around the room. It looked much like the council chamber in my own town hall, back in the real world. Behind the desk, piled with papers and books, ink and quills, was a goat in a stiff, high collar and a cat in a creased blue dress. They were attended by two dogs in black suits. There seemed to be much conferring between the dogs as they put various papers before the two judges, but none between the goat and cat themselves. Eventually the cat looked up over the top of her metal-rimmed spectacles.

'You wish to return to your own city?' she said. 'Is that correct?'

'Yes, er, ma'am,' I mumbled.

'Cat, not *ma'am*,' she corrected me.

'Yes, cat. This dog here…'

She stared at the terrier in an unblinking fashion.

'Your counsel, yes. Have you come to an arrangement for his services?'

I felt the flutterings of uncertainty in my breast.

'Arrangement?'

'Yes, has he made his terms known to you?'

The terrier said, 'No—not yet.' He turned to me and said, 'You must take care of one of my kind, my breed, when you go back.'

'Anything,' I said, desperate to be home again.

'It doesn't have to be you. Just make sure a terrier gets a good home. Do you agree?'

It seemed simple enough. 'Yes.'

'Good,' said the goat, speaking for the first time. 'Now, you were brought here for… hmmmmm,' he studied a piece of paper in his hoof. 'Yes, the assassination.' He stared at me hard. 'You must promise, you see, to kill someone when we allow you to go back.'

'Kill someone?' I faltered, horrified.

'Yes,' said the cat. 'There is a man who has been responsible for a lot of cruelty—animals have suffered terribly under his hand. He is called…' and she gave me the name of a well-known pharmaceuticals manufacturer about whom I had read in the newspapers. His laboratories had been in the newspapers regarding animal experiments.

'I have to shoot him?' I queried, my mind spinning with the thought.'

'Shoot him, stab him, suffocate him, poison him—we do not care. The method of the murder is left up to you. What must happen is the man must die by your hand. Otherwise, you will remain here for the rest of your days.'

'There are no other choices?' I cried, in despair.

'None.'

'I see,' I said, looking down.

'You will of course,' remarked the goat in rather ponderous tones, 'receive the city's highest reward possible—once the deed has been performed to our satisfaction.'

'What is the nature of the reward?'

'It will be your action which will decide *that*,' said the cat. 'You will determine your own reward.'

Finally, I agreed to their terms, and the next morning found myself back in the real world.

Now when one has undergone such an experience, one is naturally shaken at first. One wakes, in one's own sweaty bed, thankful the nightmare is at an end. One looks back on the horrible events in one's dream and makes resolutions.

'I shall be a better person in the future. I shall be careful of making judgements on my fellow creatures. I shall not be hasty in my actions.'

Trembling and physically exhausted from the night's happenings, I rose and made a cup of tea. I sat in the bleak grey rays of dawn and drank the same, wondering if I would keep my promise to the terrier in my dream. In the end it made sense that I should, if only for my own peace of mind. There was a nephew who had requested a dog. I would purchase him the self-same breed as the hound which had acted for me in the matter concerning the Council of Beasts.

This I did, but also visited a psychiatrist, who gave me due warning of what was to come. His name was given me by a friend, a politician whose acquaintance I had recently made by chance. This man recommended the doctor as being one of the foremost authorities on displaced states of mind.

'He won't laugh at me?' I said.

'Not at all,' said my political friend. 'He is thoroughly professional concerning such matters and treats them with all proper seriousness.'

Fortunately, the doctor lived in the district. It was a short walk from the politician's house to the psychiatrist's door. In my anxious state my steps were quick and eager. On being admitted I fairly flew through the hallway and into the office dominated by a brown leather couch. I lay on this item of furniture, conscious of it once having been a bull.

'These things usually come in threes,' said the doctor, on hearing my confession. 'I don't know why, something to do with the brain's obsession with that number. You will no doubt return to this strange kingdom of the mind, where beasts rule over mankind, and there have to account for yourself again.'

I had told him nothing about the man I was supposed to kill, only that the beasts had also demanded kindness and consideration from me in future years as further payment for my escape.

'Is there nothing you can give me, which will forestall such a return to that state?'

'I can give you medication, drugs, but these will only work in the short term. Once you stop taking them, you will experience the illness again—probably. I'm not saying it's certain. Nothing is certain in this business. However, I would be very surprised if you went back to this dream world of yours. Perhaps another, but not the same one.'

I agreed not to take any medication, though I was very frightened of having another breakdown. On the way out of the doctor's office I walked more slowly than when I had entered. In this more casual frame of mind I noticed a print on the hallway wall. It said it was 'From a painting by Cornelis Saftleven (1607-1681) called *The Council of Beasts* (Prague Museum of Art).' It had strangely clothed animals standing or sitting in groups—a goat, standing upper centre-left side, a cat sitting lower right side, both attended by dogs.

I went straight back into his office, almost hysterical, and demanded to know why he had not mentioned this picture to me. The doctor looked acutely surprised and told me he had forgotten he had it. 'It's been on the wall for so long, perhaps thirty years. I've stopped looking at it. I didn't even recall its content when we were talking about your dream. You know, it's like the wallpaper, after a while it blends into the wall itself, becomes a blank in your mind, even when you spend eight or nine hours a day in its company. Do you understand?'

I tried to recall the wall-covering on the living-room of my grandparents' house—and failed—even though I had been raised in that house.

'Tell me one thing?' I asked. 'Have I been here before?'

The doctor put his thumbs in his waistcoat and stared at me hard in the face.

'Not that I recall. Your name is not on my register. But I have been practising for three decades and have not always been as careful with my paperwork as I must be these days. Can *you* ever remember coming to see me?'

'No,' I croaked. 'I have no such recollection.'

'Then let us say this was your first visit.'

I begged the doctor's forgiveness and left the premises. On my way past the picture, I averted my face, not wishing to be reminded of my terrible ordeal.

Three months passed before I once again found myself in the City of Beasts. The terrier was waiting for me. He led me to the council room. This time I noticed that although the beasts walked upright and talked like humans, they wore no clothes. They did not smoke pipes, nor play flutes, nor drink ale. They were closer to beasts than they had been on my first incarceration.

'Have you killed him yet?' bleated the goat.

'No,' I admitted. 'I didn't think you were real—I thought you were all from a dream.'

'Don't make that mistake again,' hissed the cat, and she drew a set of claws across my forearm, scratching me deeply.

This time, when I returned to my own world, I found myself on a park bench. It occurred to me that I had dozed off in the warm sun. I immediately inspected my arm and found blood. The skin was scored where something or someone had scratched me. It took me half an hour to run all the way to my psychiatrist.

'Are you sure you haven't come into contact with a local cat?' he asked, as his receptionist dressed my wound. 'What about a stray in the park? Some feral animal that might have attacked you while you slept? Or perhaps it's not a cat scratch at all? Maybe you caught yourself on some barbed wire...?'

This time he was not so convincing. It was as if my stories were changing *his* beliefs. He asked me questions about the City of Beasts in a way that made it seem as if he were satisfying his own curiosity, about an exotic land he would never be able to visit, like tenth century Africa, or medieval Japan. Far from attempting to assure me that I was merely ill, and could be cured, he seemed intrigued by my adventures.

'What am I to do?' I asked him. 'You told me I wouldn't return to that place.'

'I said I'd be surprised if you did—and I am.'

When I left his office I glanced up at the picture in the hallway. It had been changed. There was now an innocuous woodland scene—a shady path through a rough avenue of trees at the end of which was a shining lake. At least, it seemed innocent enough until I studied it more closely, and then it seemed to me that some of the shadows formed faces, and bodies, and were in fact animals hiding amongst the trees, waiting for someone to pass by the spot. Where they about to ambush a victim? That's what it looked like to my eye.

This time I did not return to the office to confront the doctor, but hurried away, anxious to get home and amongst familiar surroundings. That night the wound on my arm pulsed and throbbed. I hoped it would not make me sick and put me into a fever. I was afraid of what might happen if my mind were in a febrile state. While my head was clear and open, I could deal with this terrible ordeal, but I did not trust myself to remain sane were I to go into the drugged half-sleep that fever brings.

Another month passed, during which I did little but wait anxiously for any sign of the animals. In that time I went through the motions of researching my potential victim, just in case I was being watched. I discovered his whereabouts, his family circumstances and his habits.

He was a relatively young married man, with two small children. He lived in Shooter's Hill and actually walked to work each day across Eltham Common to his company's head office on Rochester Way. His morning walk was early—he began it at seven-thirty—and I saw possibilities in this walk should I ever have to carry out the deed.

Of course, I never expected to do that, but just when I thought I was rid of the nightmare, I once again found myself amongst those grotesque creatures in their city. This time they were not only without clothes, but on all fours. When I stood before the council, they were in a bare room, without furniture, and stood before me like a domestic farmyard group.

'Have you killed him yet?' whine the cat.

'No,' I moaned. 'I cannot.'

'You *must*,' she screeched.

I found myself in a department store, walking around as if in a dream, staring at leather coats and handbags. An assistant asked me if I was all right. She took me to a staff room where they gave me a cup of tea and a biscuit. Eventually I made my way back to the street, but I felt sick inside.

This time I did not go to the psychiatrist. It had occurred to me that the attacks were becoming less surreal. That is to say the animal world was becoming more like the actual world with every visit. In the City of Beasts they now looked like animals and walked like animals. It was only in their speech that they became preternatural and even that was changing. I decided that the next time I visited them they would be in some meadow, surrounded by wildflowers and hedgerows, making animal noises. I felt no desperate urge to carry out their command, since here I could not be touched. All I had to do was keep making promises until they went away.

That was before I visited my nephew.

Peter, fourteen years of age, met me at the station and carried my bags to the taxi.

'I'm glad you came to us, uncle,' he said. 'Mother was beginning to remark on how down you have sounded on the phone lately.'

His mother was my sister Alice.

'How's Toby?' I asked, enquiring after the terrier I had bought him. 'Still boisterous?'

'Oh yes, you know how silly terriers can get, uncle.'

Toby met us at the garden gate and leapt up and down in the excited way that terriers do. I threw a chewed tennis ball for him, already sodden with saliva, mentally grimacing and wanting to wash my hands immediately. He brought it back instantly, putting it in front of me and looking up eagerly, yapping when I ignored the offer to continue the game.

Alice fed me and I went to bed early. I woke the next morning feeling remarkably refreshed. Alice and Peter had to go into town, to get Peter some shoes, and I was left sitting in a deck chair in the garden, soaking in the country ambience. I guessed Toby would be bothersome, but I actually did not see him until he came sidling round the corner of the cottage close to noon. He came round to the front of me and sat on the lawn, his head on one side, his mouth partly open. He was panting as if he had been running from a distant place.

I felt it best to ignore him and continued reading the paper which had been delivered shortly before.

After a while he was so quiet I thought he had gone away, but when I slowly lowered the newspaper, he was still there, staring up at me. There was such a look of malevolence on his canine features I started backwards and let out a little cry. He continued to glare at me, ferociously. Then just as Alice and Peter came into view, walking up the lane, he spoke.

'When are you going to kill him?' he growled, quietly.

My nightmare was beginning to materialise. The beasts were able to get at me in the real world. They were penetrating what I believed to be a safe haven—sanctuary—and I knew then that I would never be let alone until I did as I had been ordered to do. It was true, I had no choice. The council had known that from the start and had told me so.

That weekend, in the peaceful atmosphere of the cottage, I devised a scheme to murder the pharmaceutical manufacturer. I have always been a meticulous planner and I doubt anyone could have faulted my detail. I was to follow him one morning from his home to his office and on the way push him under a bus. It was a simple but I hoped effective plan.

A week later, in the early dawn, I stalked the victim from his house, tracking him across the common. While he was waiting to cross Rochester Way, busy even at that time of the morning, I bent down as if pretending to tie a loose shoelace and butted him hard in the back with my head. The blow sent him flying out into the traffic. He was hit first by one car, then another from the opposite direction.

Tossed into the air like a run-over rabbit, he landed almost at my feet again. His bloody face stared up at me with surprise on his features. It was certain he was dead.

I hurried away from the scene, hoping my part in his death had not been noticed. My suitcase was ready in a locker at the train station and I went there immediately. I caught a train to my sister's house. Toby was there, waiting at the gate for me when I arrived at dusk. I looked him directly in the eye.

'It's done,' I said.

He did not reply, but merely seemed eager for me to throw his damned ball for him. I did it to get rid of him while I entered the garden, actually feeling less revulsion for his toy than I had the first time. Later I caught him staring at me, as I moved around the house, in a quiet, understanding way.

Nothing happened for a few days. Then at dusk one evening I was trying to watch television, but was experiencing difficulty in focusing. I could hear the words plainly enough though and I recognised the voice of my politician friend. It seemed that he had been for a long time an executive on the board of a pharmaceuticals company. He was holding forth to the correspondent on the terrible circumstances of the death of the firm's late chairman. My acquaintance said he was preparing to leave politics to become the new chairman of that company, to fill the void which the tragedy had left.

'What a remarkable coincidence,' I said to Toby. 'I had no idea of a connection there—had you?'

Toby refrained from answering me, possibly because there were other humans in the house, but I knew what he was thinking.

'I expect,' I said, 'we might have to do something about the *new* chairman, too? And we mustn't forget the psychiatrist. My sessions with him are supposed to be all strictly confidential, but really, he knows far too much…'

At midnight, just after the church clock had struck ten, I discovered the nature of my reward from the Council of Beasts. As I took off my shoes and socks I noticed that my feet had begun to shrink and harden. I stood up quickly and stared into the dressing-table mirror. The pupils of my eyes were no longer round, but were vertical ellipses. On top of my head two small bumps were beginning to poke through my scalp.

I turned to Toby, sitting in the doorway.

'Maaaahhhh,' I said to him. 'Maaaaaaaahhhhhhhhhh…'

Toby smiled.

THE FROG CHAUFFEUR

(I share David Attenborough's love of frogs, toads and natterjacks. In this age of genetic engineering I have written several versions of the following story, but this is the one I like best.)

ISABEL FAIRFAX WOKE BY THE large pond in her garden to find a beautiful young man asleep beside her. He was dandelion-haired and handsome, and completely naked. She marvelled at the way the droplets of water on his skin glistened with rainbow colours in the sunlight. Skin that was pale to the eye and firm to the touch. Beneath it were tight muscles, smooth as stepping stones across a stream. He had small hips, a flat stomach, slim strong shoulders and hard rounded buttocks with a shallow dimple in each.

Isabel wished she were twenty instead of forty as she carefully picked a piece of green pond weed from behind the youth's ear and threw it back where it belonged.

'Wake up, sleepy head,' she said drowsily. 'You've wandered into the wrong garden. You're lying on my book of Tennyson's poems and dampening the pages.'

It was surprising that the young man had decided to go swimming in her pond, in the nude, on this bright Sunday afternoon in June, but Isabel was broad-minded when it suited her. She was a spinster (a word she detested for its connotations of age) and almost a virgin (a word she rather liked for its undertones of youth) having only once yielded to a man who had loved her passionately for at least several minutes following a New Year's Eve party. That was a long time ago, twenty years, but remained a treasured souvenir from that other country of which LP Hartley spoke.

Despite her best efforts to wake him the youth remained dozing in the late afternoon sun. Isabel remained with him on the lawn, dressed in her old-fashioned shirt-waister and broad-brimmed hat. She tried studying the wide pond's yellow flags, waving in the breeze, then her quite grand 16th Century cottage at the end of the sweeping lawns, restored to a former ambiguity now that the beams had been stripped of black paint, but each time her eyes were drawn back to the wonderful creature whose drying arm rested on her lap.

Finally he woke, and smiled at her, stretching his arms and legs, revealing webs of skin between his fingers and toes. She rather liked this imperfection, which only reached as far as the lower finger joints in any case. It made him more human to her, less of a sun god. His eyes, she noted, were of the deepest green, the colour of a temperate ocean. He reached out to touch her cheek and she drew back.

'Why, whatever is the matter?' he asked her. 'Do you not want me now that you see me?'

'Want you?' she asked, faintly. 'For what?'

'Why, for your lover, your man, your husband.'

She looked around her then, suspecting a joke. Some of her friends were perhaps teasing her? Or some television programme was happily making a fool out of an innocent woman in her own garden?

'Where are you from?' she asked, since she could think of nothing else to say. 'Are you visiting the village?'

'From there,' he waved a hand generally over the garden, 'and I want to live with you always.'

'Do you have a name?' she said, smiling at this game.

'No, but you can give me one.'

'We'll think of one later. In the meantime, why not come up to the house for tea?'

And so they went into the cottage. She found for him a pair of shorts which Special-Friend Frank had left there on one of his occasional visits, and a T-shirt with SAVE THE TIGERS on the front. Then she made them Lapsang Souchong tea, with scones, blackcurrant jam and cream. Sometime before the flush of twilight had left the face of the sky, she found herself in bed with him.

His aromatic hair smelt of hay left baking in the sun as he gently entered her. Gradually he eased his hard pole into the crevice in the soft mossy bank between her thighs. She kissed his shoulders, licked his textured skin, which tasted faintly muddy. Later he used his own tongue, that long beautiful tongue, in a variety of wonderful ways which had her biting the pillow to prevent herself from screaming. Never had Isabel experienced such physical joy and she cared not whether it lasted an afternoon or an eternity.

He remained at the house, seemingly happy just to be in her company. If they ever did go out, it was in her little green car, which she taught him to drive. They would simply cruise the byways of the countryside, staying clear of towns, with him perched happily behind the wheel. She sat in the back, navigating for him, giving him instructions. He became, as well as her lover, her most reliable chauffeur.

Special-Friend Frank, who had never shown the slightest sexual interest in Isabel, suddenly after many years of sporadic stays, began brushing against her in the greenhouse, and accidentally pressing his elbow against one of her breasts while he read 'Lochinvar' to her. True to the contrary nature of men, now that someone else wanted her, Frank wanted her too. She might have lived to be a hundred and Special-Friend Frank would still have been visiting the cottage only to prune her plum trees and do her accounts.

'Marry me?' Frank murmured one day. 'I'm an accountant—I earn lots of money.'

'No,' she replied, flatly.

'Why?' he asked, angrily. 'Because of him? Because of that *boy*? Who is he anyway? Where did he come from? He doesn't even have a name. I've been coming here for years, helping you with your tax returns, sorting out your plumbing, digging over the difficult bits of your garden. He's done nothing for you.'

'I don't care,' she said, lifting her chin defiantly. 'He's lovely. He's loving. He's *love*. He spends too long in the bathroom, but nobody's perfect. I want *him*.'

Thus Isabel married the golden youth, who smiled all the way through the ceremony. The wedding took place at the little 11th Century minster, built by the Viking King Knut, on the hill above the river. The choir and altar boys wore scarlet cassocks, because it was a church connected with royalty. When it came to the part where the youth needed a name, he turned to Isabel.

'I shall take *your* name and be known as Fairfax!'

'And the given name?' asked the vicar with a little cough.

'Prince,' said the youth without hesitation. 'Prince Fairfax.'

'No, that won't do at all,' Isabel chided, this offending her sense of taste. 'You're not a pop star, after all, you will be my husband. Some simple name would be best—John—John Fairfax.'

And so they were wed in the season of the daffodils. Isabel was viciously happy, snatching at every precious moment with her young sun prince and swallowing it whole. She had one, two, three children, just like that—two boys and a girl—and they were all very pretty babies. They sat in a row in the back of the car, while their father drove around the country lanes and their mother murmured instructions.

They lived, self-contained and blissfully happy, in the Tudor cottage. She would read to him poems under the lamplight and he would sit enwrapped by her low voice spilling out the words, staring up at the standard lamp. When she asked him why he was always looking at the lamp he told her that to him it was a kind of totem whose deistic duty it was to miraculously attract creatures like damselflies, or dragonflies, or even multi-hued moths.

'Why, what a lovely thought, dear,' she said. 'But would you like to see such creatures flying in your room?'

'Of course, they are the closest thing we have to pretty newts,' he replied, enigmatically, 'swimming around one's head in the deepest part of the pond.'

It was in their fifth year that Isabel first discovered things were going wrong. She entered the dining-room of the cottage one day to find John with his face close to the bulls-eye window panes. She watched, fascinated, as he studied a fly while it buzzed, infuriated, in the corners of the window, wondering why there was this invisible wall in front of it. Then to her horror out shot John's tongue and the insect was gone, down his throat. Afterwards he straightened and made a strange sound not unlike a burp.

'John?' she said, faintly. 'Whatever are you doing?'

'What?' he spun round, looking guilty. 'Why nothing, Isabel. Nothing at all. I was simply—peering through the glass, trying to see out into the garden.'

'You ate that bluebottle!'

'No, no, you're mistaken, Isabel. Why should I do a thing like that?'

He sounded so sincere that she thought that perhaps she had been mistaken in what she had seen, that perhaps she had perceived something which had not actually taken place. It was in her nature to blame herself before others, for any error of judgement or observations. She stopped taking the ginseng tea, believing it responsible.

Yet, three weeks later, as they were walking around the garden after a shower of rain and she was chatting about how lovely the lilac smelled, John absently reached out picked a small snail from the leaf of a shrub. He popped it in his mouth, crunched and swallowed it, still lost in some reverie. She said nothing to him this time, but later while sitting in the summer house on her own, she began to recall the several strange habits of her husband.

There were those times when she had found him squatting in the corner of the room, apparently asleep. There was his obsession with cold baths. There was the eerie delight he took in drawing water lilies for their children, as if they were some kind of icon for future happiness. There was his dread of herons, his phobia of grass snakes, his intense dislike of French restaurants. Finally, there were those condemning webbed toes and fingers.

It was true he still liked to drive the car, but she was sure that came from some other hidden lake of his personality, some other well of his psyche.

Afraid, but wanting to know the truth, she found an encyclopaedia and read all it had to say about frogs. Everything was there, even the snails, which formed a part of the common frog's diet. With increasing anxiety she decided to give John one last test. In order to put him off his guard one evening, she read him Andrew Marvell's 'The Garden', knowing he loved the lines:

'Annihilating all that's made

'To a green thought in a green shade.'

When he was safely locked in that dream world into which he slipped at times, she placed before him a dish of live garden slugs and earth worms. He ate them absently with apparent relish, not pausing to consider what kind of fare she had given him, and whether it was seemly for a youth to gobble such creatures. She knew then that he was from the pond, beside which she had first found him, damp and weed-strewn.

'Never mind,' Isabel told herself. 'He's my husband now and we can still live a good life.'

Nevertheless she read a version of *The Frog Prince* from a red book of Grimms' tales published by Grosset & Dunlap of New York, one of a boxed set of two volumes, the other a green book of Anderson's stories.

It told how the frog changed into a prince not with a kiss, but when the princess threw the frog violently against her bedroom wall, and how the faithful servant Henry had his heart bound with three iron bands to stop it breaking when his master had become an amphibian, and how those bands snapped as his heart swelled with joy when the princess married the handsome returned prince.

Isabel looked up from her reading under the pale light of the lamp.

Not a kiss then, as the romantics would have it, but a sudden sharp shock! What if the frog had been out of the pond that day, hopping by Isabel's sleeping form, when she suddenly thrashed in her dreams, struck out and hit the passing frog a blow, causing it to change into John?

But where would a frog have come from, in the first place, which had a human form locked inside it?

Isabel was no slouch when it came to puzzles. She had intelligence, she had the patience. Slowly she unravelled the mystery to her own satisfaction.

What if the frog who turned into the prince, all those centuries ago, had been with another frog before his transfiguration? What if the female he had held in amplexus in the pond in the palace garden, had spawned her three-thousand eggs and he had fertilised them all? There would be, even after his elevation to kingship, thousands of frogs with the genetic code of a human being locked in their DNA, awaiting a sudden sharp shock to release it.

And those frogs would mate with other frogs, the females spawning the males fertilising, thus over the centuries laying millions of little hopping, swimming time bombs ready to burst into mortal form at any moment.

It was an amazing and breathtaking thought that all you had to do was go down to the pond in the garden, pick up a few dozen frogs, and throw them at the nearest hard surface to produce a youth or maiden. It would be like looking for pearls in oysters. Loneliness would become obsolete, for each Jack would find a Jill, and every Sheila a Bruce. Even better, collect a jar of tadpoles, put them in the blender and hand out children to childless couples, to be loved and cherished and grow into beautiful people.

Yet—that agonising *yet*—Isabel had discovered that of course after so many centuries the frog and human were too closely melded to ever separate completely. The man had been inside the frog, yet the frog would always be part of the man. It came out at the oddest times. Impossible to protect against. Perhaps a shock—a near traffic miss crossing the street, stepping on a garden rake—might have the reverse effect, with the man changing back into the frog?

Isabel shuddered. 'I must warn my John about what might happen to him,' she told herself, closing the book of fairy tales. 'I must tell him what he is, where he came from, and caution him against any possible scare.'

That evening, in the privacy of their bedroom, while the children were asleep, she told him the dreadful news.

'But I will keep you safe, my darling,' she said to him. 'You have really nothing to fear.'

He lay there in the dark, staring at the ceiling, and just before she fell asleep she heard him murmur, 'So that's why I like water so much...'

The following morning, a bright spring day, she awoke to find the bed empty beside her. Fearing the worst she put on her silk dressing gown and combed the house for her husband John. Not finding him there she went out into the garage to see if he was sitting in the car. He was not. Finally, with a sinking heart, she ran down to the pond.

There he was, her dear heart, floating face down in the water, the pond weed caressing his naked body, stroking it lovingly as if welcoming home a lost son. When she turned him over, on his face was a look of serenity, as if he had found the way to Marvell's green shaded place where he could think cool green thoughts for ever.

The funeral was simple. She had him buried in the garden, by the pond. Special-Friend Frank came down to see her through her time of sorrow, but she didn't need him. She had her children, who were beginning to blossom in splendid ways. They still loved going out in the car and she was pleased to drive them.

It was while she was thus engaged that she realised why her husband had been fascinated by the car, felt comfortable inside it. Being in the car, looking through the glass at grass and overhead trees, was like being under a pond looking out through the watery surface at the green world beyond.

And two of her children are now famous.

You must remember Yvonne Fairfax, the Olympic long jumper, whose extraordinary standing-jump style won her the hearts and minds of the people of Munich? And Arthur Fairfax, who swam his way to a gold in the Games at Montreal? Two brilliant sporting children, who had inherited intrinsic skills passed on to them by their deceased father.

And the third child?

Why he has a love of poetry that excels even that of his mother, whose traits he bears with vocal pride.

HAMELIN, NEBRASKA

(As a child I was always fascinated by the fact that many American towns were named after European ones. The Paris of France and Texas. The Boston of Lincolnshire and Massachusetts. The Sierra Nevada Mountains of Spain and USA. It is natural for me to think they may be linked in spirit as well as in name.)

MIDNIGHT IN THE SMALL TOWN of Hamelin, Nebraska.

Hamelin was one of those places which seemed uniquely American. Just another sleepy hollow where people minded their own business but knew everyone else's just the same. It boasted a doctor, and a lawyer, a school teacher, and a mayor. It also had a nasty stain on its history, like most small towns anywhere, but this had nothing to do with bigotry or hatred of strangers. No innocent Japanese immigrants had been shot to death after the attack on Pearl Harbour. No black citizens had been lynched in the heat of the night. Hamelin's blemish occurred through positive negligence, a turning of the back against responsibility, a washing of the hands.

Hamelin's shame, like most shame, had been born out of fear.

Sheriff Phil Watkins had sent his Deputy home and was preparing to lock up his office and make tracks for his own bed, where his wife Matty was lying awake, expectantly. Saturday night was their night of the week, since Sunday was a lazy day when neither of them had to rise early. They would have a couple of drinks in bed, watch some television on the portable set propped up by their feet, then they would turn to each other and enjoy safe middle-aged sex.

Hat in hand, Phil Watkins turned off the light, went through the open doorway into the warm night, then locked up, rattling the door to make sure it was secure. He had just removed the key, when something struck him on the head, behind the left ear, causing him to reel backwards in intense pain. He blinked rapidly, reaching up to feel a warm sticky wetness in his salt-white hair.

'Hey...!' he cried, then looked down where the object had bounced on the porch boards, and saw a heavy rock. It was smeared with his own blood. 'What the hell?' He turned, dizzily, just as another rock struck him in the chest, immediately above the heart.

'Jesus!' he wheezed. Then angrily, 'Who's out there, goddamit? If that's you Eb Shaffer, I'm...'

He got no further because a third hunk of stone hit him in the mouth, knocking out three teeth. Phil Watkins staggered backwards, drawing his gun, but it was only halfway out of its holster when the rocks began to come at him in numbers, catapulting out of the darkness with considerable force behind them.

Within a few minutes he had been stoned to death.

THREE PEOPLE DIED THAT SATURDAY night. One of them was the mayor and the town's banker, Stan Fredericks, who was first silenced with a piece of fruit.

Stan lived alone and like most fat men, slept with his mouth wide open, to draw in enough oxygen to feed his massive bulk. Someone had plugged that airhole with a large apple. Thus muzzled he was then dragged bodily from his bed and drowned in his own swimming pool. Whoever had killed him left red marks around his neck where presumably they had held his head under water. His body was still on the edge of the pool, belly-up, while his head lolled back in the water.

Some of the poorer folk from the edge of town, who had at various times been threatened with foreclosure of the mortgages Stan Fredericks held on their homes and smallholdings, could not help but feel that perhaps there was some kind of divine punishment involved.

Furthermore, Mayor Fredericks had given the seal of approval to several buildings erected out of public funds, like the new town library, while Banker Fredericks provided loans to the construction companies that were awarded the contracts. The bank's interest rates were surprisingly high, though Stan Fredericks maintained this was necessary to protect his clients. When the town saw him lying next to his pool barbecue, looking like a bloated suckling pig, the apple still jammed between his jaws, many of them nodded sagely.

THE THIRD DEATH, BY SUFFOCATION, had been administered to Wincy Jacobs, the lady who delivered the mail. She had been smothered by her own rose-scented pillow, the slip and cover of which she tore through with her teeth in her death throes, as she tried to gnaw her way to fresh air. There were down feathers caught in her throat, trapped in her nostrils. Her nails had splinters under them, where she had clawed at the bedhead, presumably blindly trying to find the eyes of her attackers.

'What we have here,' said Deputy Dan Starkly, in his ponderous fashion to a gathering of the town's most influential citizens, 'is a multie murderer. Hamelin–' (he pronounced it 'Hammerlen') '–has a killer who just likes to kill…'

David Werner, the town's young lawyer, interrupted.

'We don't know that. We don't know anything at this time. All we know is we've got three dead bodies.'

'We know they was killed,' snapped someone from behind him. 'They didn't just roll over and die.'

David turned in his chair and addressed the person directly.

'Yes, we know that much, but no more. Dan talked about *a* multiple murderer. How do we know it was just one person? It could have been a dozen. Maybe some sort of gang passed through here in the night and are halfway across South Dakota by now? Let's not make emphatic statements, Dan. Let's look at what we've got and then make some *assumptions*.'

'Okay, okay,' muttered Dan, 'let's look at them *assumptions*. Three violent killings, no weapons involved, less you count rocks, apples and pillys as weapons. I don't. A gun's a weapon. A knife's a weapon. They don't just come to hand. The instruments used here, was just things that came to hand, on the spur of the moment so to speak. Am I right Dave?' He looked to the lawyer for approval.

'These were opportunist tools, as you say, Dan.'

'Fair 'nough. So I *assume* that what we got here is a person, or *persons* unknown, goin' out not looking to murder, but taking it as it comes. Nothin' was stole. There don't seem to be no motive at all. Less someone had a special grudge against these three folk, which I personally can't see any connection, we got to worry about the rest of us. When you get down to it, you got to figure Dave's right, that there's more'n one. Have to be a pretty strong man to drag the mayor from his bed, him weighing what he did.'

The meeting broke up shortly after that little speech, with Dan warning the townspeople that perhaps the killers would not stop at an odd number, but go on to round it up, maybe into double figures. David Werner was convinced they were looking for a Manson type gang. The state police had been alerted of course, but until the town elected a new mayor and sheriff, they had only Dan to look after them. Dan Starkly was a good solid youth who could hit things he aimed at with his thirty-eight, but as an investigative detective he would make a good short order cook.

Some people, naturally scared, were asking if the FBI could be brought in, but there was an incident in the town's past, an *ugly* moment in its near history, of which others were ashamed and had no wish to reveal to outsiders. The FBI were good at uncovering such skeletons, so it was better to keep out the feds until someone absolutely insisted they be involved.

Dan Starkly and David Werner went through the clues together, retraced possible movements of the victims, tried to come up with some conclusions, but by the end of that day were no nearer to any answers. The two men had a beer together, then went home to lock their doors and windows, securely, for the first time in many years.

THE NEXT MORNING THEY FOUND Eb Shaffer, the town troublemaker, decorated with pointed sticks. He was lying in the middle of the bridge, over the ravine at the back of town, looking like a porcupine. The bridge was one of those preserved timber affairs, with strengthened supports to take the weight of modern vehicles, of which small towns like Hamelin were proud. It gave them a sense of history.

The sticks bristling from the anatomy of Eb Shaffer weren't much more than twigs, maybe nine inches long at the most. They had been sharpened, it seemed, on sandstone rock. Just like the twigs Eagle Scouts fashioned to spear their sausages before cooking them over a campfire. About sixty of these barbecue skewers protruded from the soft parts of Eb's body: his throat, stomach, eyes, and his groin. Dan said the sight made him sick to his stomach, and kept subconsciously touching himself between the legs. Doc Skimmer remarked that Eb Shaffer must have been attacked somewhere out in the hills, and had staggered, blinded by two of the sharp sticks, to the bridge to die.

'You can see the marks in the dust,' he said, pointing with his pipe stem at the weaving tracks. 'Poor bastard must've been in terrible pain. My guess is he was wanting the ravine, to kill himself quick, but God bein' a contrary old goat, guided his feet to the bridge.'

'Don't cuss,' said Dan, looking around the ravine nervously, 'we don't know how this is happenin' yet.'

'You think God's got a hand in this?' cried Doc Skimmer, contemptuously. 'This is more like the work of some crazy people, out looking for vengeance. You know what I mean,' and he took a puff on his pipe and nodded, his eyes narrowed.

David Werner took this up immediately.

'You're saying... by Jesus, you may be right. It makes sense. Revenge killings.' He turned to Dan Starkly. 'Get on to the state police. Check out the family who came through here last fall. The Williamsons, they were called.'

Dan's thickset shoulders dropped, like they always did when he was asked to do something for which he had no taste.

'What'll I tell them? I have to tell them somethin'. They'll want to know *why* the Williamsons have got a grudge against the town. You know how folks feel about that incident now. If it got into the national papers, why, we'd be sneered at by every son of a bitch from the Atlantic Ocean to the Pacific.'

David Werner knew that Dan was right. Most people in the town would not approve of bringing in outside help if it meant opening a cupboard full of bones.

Several years ago a family—no one even knew where they came from—drove into the town. They had three children in the backseat of their truck, all of them sick. Doc Skimmer was unable to diagnose the fever but it appeared to be serious. He prepared some beds in the back of his surgery. Being a small town the word spread quickly, and soon a deputation of frightened citizens called on Sheriff Watkins. The sheriff then paid a visit to the doctor, telling him the family, named Williamson, had to go on to Alliance, where they had a hospital which could deal with such things.

'Hamelin's not equipped for highly infectious diseases, you know that Doc. Say we're sorry, but there's some supplies been placed by the vehicle, an' they got to go.'

Doc had argued that Alliance was nearly two hundred miles away and that the children were very weak. The day was hot and dusty.

'You know what you're asking? I've done what I can for the moment, but they'll dehydrate on the journey.'

Sheriff Watkins was no man to do battle with, once he had made up his mind on something. Doc Skimmer was not a native of the town, having come there from Lincoln when Doc Albertson died fifteen years previously. He was an outsider who had to be taught his place.

'Get 'em on the road Doc,' said the sheriff firmly, 'or start looking for another town, someplace else.'

Doc Skimmer was old, and weary—too old to go looking for another practice elsewhere. Watkins would throw him out on his neck and still send the Williamsons to hell.

To his eternal shame, the doctor did as he was told, and had regretted it bitterly ever since. Mr Williamson had begged him to let his children stay, to treat them as best he could, but Watkins had dragged the man out to his truck and sat him behind the wheel. The wife had been more aggressive and had attacked both Doc and the Sheriff, first with her small fists, and when this failed, with her tongue.

'You filthy bastards,' she shrieked at them, 'if anything happens to my kids I'll come back here and tear your eyes out, I swear. How can you *do* this? You're supposed to be civilised people. You're nothing but animals.'

Doc, knowing this was true, told lies to himself and tried to pacify the woman.

'The children need to get to a hospital. One that can deal with advanced states of fever. We can't treat them here. This is a small town, and I'm just a general practitioner. I fix broken bones and give advice for measles, but I'm not equipped to deal with major diseases. Any responsible doctor would do what I'm doing.'

Sometimes, now, he woke in the middle of the night, sweating with guilt. He hoped the rest of the town did the same, for two of the children died on the way to Alliance, and though the rest of the family survived and went on to California, those two little souls stayed to haunt the streets of Hamelin, Nebraska, for as long as memories of the dead lived in the minds of men.

'Right,' said David Werner, briskly, 'this is what we do then. Tonight the whole town stays awake. If the Williamsons are doing this, we'll get them, we'll catch them red handed...' he looked significantly at the other two, but they were in no mood for jokes, so he continued, '...we'll catch them ourselves. All right, we did wrong once, but I guess four deaths more than pays for that mistake. I think we're owed, don't you?'

Dan nodded, his eyes glittering and his hand went automatically to his gun butt. 'Damn right,' he said. Here was something he knew how to deal with: direct action against a known enemy. 'I'll get people organised,' he said.

Doc Skimmer remained at the bridge with the body. Looking down on it thoughtfully and shaking his head. Finally he took the pipe out of his mouth, refilled it slowly, tamping the tobacco down with a medical spatula he kept in his pocket for the purpose, and said to the corpse:

'Ain't you glad you're out of it?'

JUST BEFORE MIDNIGHT THEY CAPTURED seven of them coming over the bridge. They caught them with a fine mesh net that Eb Shaffer had once used to trap small wild birds.

They were just children—hard eyed and not at all innocent-looking—but kids just the same. They were all naked, but not the least bit self-conscious about it. When David Werner got them to the town hall under the bright lights, an uncomfortable pricking sensation accompanied his close inspection of them. He felt as if beetles were crawling over his skin, under his shirt, and kept scratching himself, almost unconsciously.

'Where the hell do they come from?' he whispered to Doc Skimmer.

It was their faces that fascinated the townspeople, all of whom had gathered in the hall at the sounding of the church bell. Their faces were smooth and shiny, like the pebbles of streams, polished by time and motion over millennia. Their eyes were like flints, glittering from deep sockets. Though small, the *creatures*—David Werner could think of no other word—were very strong. They now stood in a sullen group, hemmed in by citizens wielding various sharp instruments, shotguns and hunting rifles.

One of the creatures said something in thick guttural accents.

'What kind of language is that?' cried David Werner, the hairs on his neck rising. 'Sounds like something that might come out of the Devil's mouth.'

Alice Maurer, the librarian, spoke quietly from the back.

'It's German,' she said.

'German?' cried Brunnel, the school teacher. 'I know German and I can't understand what *he's* saying.'

Alice said, 'It's Old German, and I think there's a heavy dialect there. I studied Old German at university. I can't catch all of it, but I recognise some of the words.'

'How old's old?' asked Doc.

'Maybe twelfth, fourteenth century. Somewhere thereabouts.'

David Werner said to Alice, 'Can you interpret for us? Can you tell us what that—that creature is saying to us?'

'I caught the gist of it,' she replied. 'It was something like "the Pied Piper is gone" or "dead". I think it was *dead*.'

There was a stunned silence in the large hall after this remark, as each person in the room, not counting the speaker and those whose words had been translated, stood and pondered on the meaning of this remarkable if incomprehensible piece of information.

Finally, David Werner spoke again.

'What the hell is that supposed to mean?'

'The Pied Piper of Hamelin. He led the children away, into another place, beyond this world.'

'I know the goddamn *story*,' cried David Werner, 'Jesus Christ, this *is* Hamelin. Some of the folks here are descendants of settlers who came from the original town in Germany. What I want to know is what the fuck it has to do with us, and why these mountain dwarfs are going around killing our people because this guy has died?'

The librarian spoke haltingly to the strange little people, with many repetitions and gestures. Finally there was a terse reply. David Werner could see something in those flinty eyes as the replies were flung back. It was a kind of timelessness, but weary, as if death could not be too soon in coming. These creatures were old, he realised. No, not old, *ancient*. They had seen the coming and going of centuries. It was this realisation that paved the way for the next: he suddenly had an inkling as to what they were—*who* they were—and the thought chilled him through to his heart.

The immigrant translated what he had been told.

'The Piper died in his sleep not long ago, though they have a strange way of expressing time, so I have to guess at several days. They miss him, because his music was like a drug to them. They have difficulty in going on without it. All the good feelings they ever had are now gone, replaced by a bitterness as cold and hard as a German winter.

'They say they are the original children of Hamelin, that time in the Piper's land is different from here, which is why they still look young. They will never grow old, but they will eventually die, like the Piper—not in the way we do here. Not for many hundreds of our years.'

Again, there was silence. Then someone laughed. Dan Starkly said something like, 'Heck, we're in fairyland,' and grinned at David Werner, looking for approval.

Doc stopped the sneering.

He said to David Werner, 'Do they look human to you?'

The lawyer shook his head. There *was* something supernatural about these creatures. He could sense it, deep down. It stirred up all the unease of childhood nightmares, brought it to the surface like scum. He had often criticised, when he watched movies, how easily the victims unquestionably accepted paranormal events. Now he was assailed by the same sort of feelings. There was no need for logic. This came from the part of the brain, perhaps the soul, where reason did not intervene. It came from a warning system that had been in primitive man, in the human race since the beginning of time: an intuitive, instinctive knowledge.

'No.'

'Nor me either. They look like something out of hell. This may be funny to some of you, but four of us are dead, and I've a feeling more will follow, even if we lock these creatures away. You can see they're different. You can *smell* they're different. I wouldn't want to bet we've heard the last of this. They're out to get us for some reason. You can see it in their eyes. They hate our goddamn guts.'

Someone shouted, 'Ask 'em what the hell they want here? This is America. What're they murderin' decent Americans for?'

David Werner nodded to Alice and she went into another long seemingly-tortured conversation. Someone went out for coffee, beer and cokes, while this was going on. Dan Starkly asked Bill Smith to fetch him a burger-no-onions from Gus's place, forgetting that Gus was in the hall with everyone else. A dozen other people ordered sandwiches or burgers, and Gus sent Sly Broder his short order cook, with Bill Smith to fill the orders, seeing no reason to turn down a little business.

The drinks and food were in the hall before Alice felt able to pass on her information.

'As far as I can make out, they think this is Hamelin—the original Hamelin, I mean—and they say that over the years they've come to hate us. They say we never went looking for them and we should have paid the Piper in the first place. We broke our promise to him.

'The Piper's land is somewhere out there, in the clouds or the mists they keep telling me. I don't know what that means. It's not in *this* world. I suppose they're trying to tell us that it's in another dimension, or something. It's a beautiful land, with green hills, clear streams and rich forests, but without the Piper's music, it seems barren. And it's getting colder. The seasons run in millennia. There was never any snow except on the mountain peaks. The children arrived there in the middle of a thousand year summer. Now the frosts are beginning to come, the leaves are falling, and they realise that winter will eventually freeze over the land.' She paused and then added, 'That's about as much as I can get out of them.'

Someone cried, 'That still don't explain why *here*, in Hamelin, Nebraska. Why don't they go back to the old town, in Germany? It's them they want, not us. We never saw no Piper—we ain't done wrong.'

Doc said, 'Don't bet on it,' and puffed hard on his pipe.

The lawyer studied the nearest child. Its skin was like obsidian, yet the child itself, a girl, looked vulnerable. *If you picked her up and dropped her*, he thought, *she would smash like porcelain*. He caught her staring back at him, with eyes of lapis lazuli, and he looked away quickly, embarrassed because she was around thirteen years of age, a girl, and nude. He felt as though he had been caught peeking into someone's bedroom through a crack in the curtains.

When he looked back at her, she had turned away slightly, as if trying to distance herself from him. Once again, looking at the skin over her smooth shoulders, her buttocks, she reminded him of things from the earth: marble, quartz, malachite. Her fingernails shone as if polished by wind-blown dust. Even the highlights on her cheeks were the deep red of garnet, not of apples or anything that had once had life. There was no bloom on her, no natural softness anywhere.

Doc's right,' said David Werner, 'I'll tell you what it is. This town. These *children* are taking their revenge on the adults of Hamelin for stealing their childhood from them, for allowing the Piper to take them from their homes and families. Hate has replaced the love that was in their hearts when they were young.'

Dan said, 'But this *ain't* Hamelin—not *their* Hamelin.'

'No, it's not,' said the lawyer, 'but they found their way here to the ancestors of their parents. The original Hamelin is a big thriving town now—with a much larger population than it had in the fourteenth century. Hamelin, Nebraska, now that's about the right size, the right population. And there's this stink of guilt in the air—something to do with betrayal—something to do with sending children away to a place from which they can never return. You understand what I'm saying here? The Williamsons?

'This is not geography, this is *sensing*, this is following an emotion through from some other dimension, somewhere beyond our imaginations. I think these little guys mean to get even with their parents, and since their parents are long gone, they'll settle for us, the adult inhabitants of Hamelin, Nebraska, the people who couldn't give a damn whether kids live or die, so long as they're safe themselves.'

'What do you think we ought to do, Dan?' asked another citizen, ignoring the young lawyer.

The deputy replied, 'Hold 'em here. They got more friends out there, that's for sure. We'll get 'em all in one night, when they come for these gremlins.'

'I don't think that's a good idea, Dan,' remarked David Werner. 'Call in the state police. Let them deal with it. This is getting out of hand.'

Dan Starkly shook his head emphatically.

'Hamelin settles its own troubles. Anybody tries somethin' tonight, they get what's coming to them. People have been killed here. The mayor, the sheriff. When I get all the perpetrators in custody, *then* I might think about callin' in some help. I want those little guys to myself for a while.'

There was no changing the deputy's mind, even when Doc got behind the lawyer and supported his advice. While they were arguing one of the creatures made a run for the door, would have made it to the outside, when a nervous farmer let loose with his twelve gauge, deafening everyone in the room. The heavy shot took away the back of a rattan chair and almost cut the child in half.

Doc Skimmer walked over and inspected the body.

'Hell,' said Doc. 'Nothin' I can do for this little fellah, that's for sure.'

David Werner crossed the room and stared down on the corpse. It had not shattered into a thousand pieces. It was not china or glass: it was flesh and blood. There was a boy-child on the floor, and it was dead. *He* was dead. Looking back, sharply at the other children, David thought he detected smiles on their marble features. Not smiles of satisfaction, knowing smiles that said *you'll pay for that soon enough*. A chill went through the lawyer during this observation. These strange kids had a secret which they hadn't divulged, weren't about to either.

He shook his head, slowly, and then turned to Dan Starkly.

'I think we've dug ourselves a pit here. They're going to come for us now—the rest of them.'

'Shit,' said Dan, 'they're only children.'

David Werner nodded, a darkness coming to his eyes.

'Yeah. Only children.'

They waited out the night, nervously, sitting in natural groups—the farmers here, the businessmen there, the professionals in a corner away from everyone else—until the dawn began to creep through the cracks in the shutters. Occasionally one of the lost children would stir and adult heads would turn, stare anxiously, until the rustling ceased.

Along with the crowing of a lonely rooster, came another sound from outside. Distant it seemed. A high-pitched noise that was painful on the ears, though you couldn't call it loud.

'What the hell's *that*?' said Dan Starkly, as if this were the last straw.

'I'll go and look,' answered David Werner, who made his way to the spiral staircase that led to the top of the clocktower.

He took the wooden steps three at a time.

Once at the top he stared out, into the dim light.

He could see the lost children coming, a long line across the landscape, roughly in the shape of a crescent, but what held his attention more was the ground before them, around them, behind them. It seemed to be moving, the whole surface of the earth, rippling towards the edge of town. David Werner leaned out over the rail of the balcony, trying to penetrate the gloom with his eyes. Then he drew back sharply with a swift intake of breath.

Suddenly, he knew what it was.

'Shit. Forgot about them.'

The smell of tobacco smoke hit his nostrils. Doc was behind him, puffing away on his weed. David Werner pointed to the waves approaching Hamelin as a grey tide slides over a wide, gradually-sloping beach.

'What is it?' asked Doc, straining his elderly eyes to see what the young lawyer was trying to show him.

'*The first shall be last*,' quoted David Werner. 'What else did the Piper take with him into his hidden land? Before he took the children?'

Doc's jaw dropped.

'The *rats*,' he finally replied.

'Right. The rats. And here they come. Millions of them. Like the children, I guess they have the gift of longevity—I guess very few of them have died. Unlike the children, though, they've been breeding all this time. Rats do that, pretty efficiently I understand. There's probably close on a billion rats out there, heading towards us.'

'Can we run?' asked the doctor.

The lawyer shook his head.

'We'd never make it.'

There was nothing to say after that.

The two men descended to the hall below.

'They're coming,' said David Werner to the citizens of Hamelin, Nebraska. 'Anybody brought any explosives with them?'

A farmer coughed.

'Got a couple of sticks of dynamite,' he replied. 'In my truck out back. Gonna blow out a stump on my way home.'

'Right, you take the women and kids. Run for the ravine. Run like hell. When you're over the bridge, blow it behind you. Quick now. You may stand a chance, I don't know. It depends on how long we can hold them, keep them busy.'

'What's this?' said Dan, but Doc waved him quiet. The farmer left with the with the women and all the children under fifteen years of age.

'Now we'd better get to the windows,' said David Werner. 'Those with scatterguns take the best positions.'

'How many of 'em?' asked Dan, and Doc just gave him a mirthless grin.

'You got a spare handgun, boy.' said the elderly practitioner. 'Give it to me.'

'Sure,' replied the deputy, pulling a Colt from his waistband. 'Didn't know you was a gun man, Doc?'

'I'm not. Couldn't hit a barn door holding the handle. This is for me. When they get inside, I'm taking the easy way out.'

Dan Starkly gaped, his lack of understanding evident in his expression.

He said, 'Just kids...'

'Not any more,' replied David Werner.

The young lawyer crossed to the window and stared outside. He did not speak for a long time, but when he did, it was a low voice, the tone of a man who has given up hope.

'I think I've been right, in my assessment of the situation,' he said. 'I'm sure I have. Those of you who want to see what we're up against, come over here and look. Scream if you want to. It won't make any difference.'

Then he took an automatic out of his pocket and simply pointed into the thick mass of scrambling bodies coming through the picket fence, firing rapidly, one random shot after the other, hitting something every time.

A few seconds later the enemy began pouring through the doors and windows, and the carnage began.

HUNTER'S HALL

(This is one of two stories in this volume originally written for kids [the other being 'The Megowl']. I think it stands well enough beside the tales for grown-ups.)

THERE HAD BEEN A MOMENT when the sky darkened and the snow-covered forest became still. A moment when the shadows merged, the light fled, and there was utter silence. One second the distant church bells had been ringing their Christmas message through the icicles on the trees—and the next, stillness. The hunter had never known such a silence. He imagined it was like being buried deep in snow. Not a single thing, over the whole earth, moved or made a sound. It struck fear in his heart: a terror which was like a cold shadow itself.

Then came the terrible pain in his chest, followed by the sound of the shot. He thought it was funny, feeling the bullet hit him first, then hearing the sound of the rifle, but then he remembered that a bullet travelled faster than sound. He had often seen the puff of smoke from a far-off rifle, before the sound of the shot reached his ears.

The pain in his chest was over with quickly. Lying there in the snow, his body numb, he wanted to say to his fellow hunters, 'I know it was an accident, so don't blame yourselves.' But he could not open his mouth, or move his lips.

Then, miraculously, he felt fine again. He got to his feet, brushed the snow from his hunting jacket, and turned to say to his comrades, 'I'm still alive.' But he found himself alone. All his companions had gone. Strangely, there were not even any marks in the snow, where they had been standing. Nothing. Though there were noises now, of birds and animals, the distant Christmas bells were still silent. The trees looked the same, yet seemed different. The whole scene had a curious atmosphere.

He began to call out, 'Hey, where have you all gone? Jan? Albert? Peter? Wait for me!' Because the fear was back with him again.

There was no answer. So, he began to walk.

As he battled through the deep snow, he saw an incredible number of animal tracks on the forest floor. Among others he recognised hare, deer and fox. There were also prints which looked like those of a wolf, but he told himself that wolves had not been in the region for at least a hundred years, so decided it must be some sort of dog. Then he came across the tracks of a wild boar. He was absolutely certain about the boar, being an expert on such creatures. The hunter became very excited and unslung his rifle from his shoulder. What a terrific thing it would be to shoot the last wild boar!

He followed the boar's trail until he reached a clearing in the forest.

As he approached the clearing, he remembered his earlier foolishness. To be afraid of shadows! How ridiculous! Yet the memory of that terrible moment came back again and suddenly he wanted nothing more than to step out of the forest and into the full light of day. A dramatic change had come over him and over the woodland. The hunter was the same man, the trees the same trees—yet everything was, somehow, different.

The broad oaks and beeches, the great hornbeams, the tall stately ash trees were now seen by the hunter in great detail. He was aware, without close study, of every knot and whorl in their trunks, every twist of their boughs, and the very course of their sap was interesting. He found himself admiring their shapes and lines. The firs and pines, laden with heavy snow, had all looked the same before. Now they were like individual people to him, all quite different.

Yet there was something frightening about these sudden changes and new ways of looking at things. This fear made the hands holding his rifle tremble, just as the icicles on the wych elms were trembling. He had a new insight into nature's secrets, yet with this power had come a strange dread. He wondered if it had anything to do with shooting the badger, earlier in the day, but he had always taken such opportunities when they presented themselves. He killed such creatures by instinct. The badger had died because it was a wild animal and the hunter was an excellent shot. It was as simple as that and nothing more.

When he stepped into the clearing and felt the breeze on his face, the hunter felt himself relax. Switching on the safety catch of his rifle, he swung the weapon onto his shoulder, using the strap to carry it by. Then he surveyed his surroundings and was pleasantly surprised, if not amazed.

Before him stretched a broad lake, frozen silver in the weak evening sun, with patches of reed tucked away in shallow corners. Around the lake was grassland, sparkling with frost where it poked through the thin layer of snow. Enclosing the meadows and the lake was the woodland in which he had been hunting that day, with its oaks and elms, its pines and firs.

It was the sight on the far side of the lake that astonished him, however, for on that shore stood a magnificent building. A low, rambling, timber lodge covering some four or five acres rose out of the snow-covered grassland. It appeared so natural it might have grown from the landscape.

The hunter took out his binoculars out of their fur pouch wiped the misted lenses. Then he studied this strange dwelling.

From various points on the thatched roof of the lodge sprang tall, twisted, redbrick chimney stacks, smoking lazily into the evening sky. The hunter could see narrow windows of leaded glass, dozens of them, scattered along the walls of the lodge. Two thirds from the east end, though it was difficult to make out where the corners were, stood two great arched double-doors with decorative hinges of solid brass. Snow-decked ivy curled about the wavering eves, that dipped and ran with wooden gutters, and dropped down to rain barrels at various unlikely intervals.

The hunter, who was fond of wooden buildings, thought the lodge magnificent. Its presence in this setting took his breath away and he found himself hoping it was some kind of hotel or inn, at which he could spend the night.

'Better than bivouacking in the woods,' he muttered to himself, for that was what he would have had to do. 'Too cold for that kind of thing at this time of year.'

The hunter made his way around the west shore of the lake, not daring to trust the ice to hold his weight. He passed some holes in the ice on the side near to the dwelling, as if someone had been fishing. Finally, he came upon the massive double-doors, the entrance to the great lodge. Above the doorway was a simple sign in German, burned into a slice of oak, which said: *Jaegerhalle*.

'Hunter's Hall,' he said to himself. 'Perhaps it is a place to spend the night?'

He opened one of the doors and entered.

If the magnificent outside of the lodge had not astounded him, certainly the scene within would have done. The whole lodge seemed to consist of a single enormous room, the roof held up by magnificent pillars of oak. There were stone hearths scattered over the wooden floors. The light from the narrow windows did not go far into the vast room, making shafts of dying sunlight around the edge. Even though the log fires and lamps lit the centre, it was difficult for the hunter to see the far side. The atmosphere was thick with the scent of pine planks and woodsmoke, human sweat and animal skins, mead, ale and cooking meat.

'Wonderful,' whispered the hunter.

Around the blazing hearths sat men, mostly men, and a sprinkling of women, dressed in various modes of hunting gear, some quite modern, but others clearly historical. There were plain green breechclouts, cracked leather jackets shiny with use and fur mittens and gloves. There were deerstalker hats, rough tweed coats, high calfskin boots. There were waxed-skin waterproofs with many pockets, and thick winter shirts, and camouflaged overalls such as the hunter himself was wearing.

Those sitting or sprawled around the fires were either talking in low voices, or cleaning and polishing their weapons, or both. And such weapons! Guns, bows, spears and all manner of hunting tools. And the guns were not simply modern high-powered rifles or shotguns, but barrel-loading flintlocks, single shot breechloaders and various other oldfashioned firearms.

At the feet of many of the room's occupants sat gun and hunting dogs of all description, from retrievers to springer spaniels to pointers to Irish setters. Like most hunting hounds, they were as quiet and docile in the indoors, as they were active and sharp in the outdoors.

In the centre of the great lodge was the largest of the fires and hanging from a chain, over its flames, was the biggest cauldron the hunter had ever seen. It was from this huge black iron pot that the wonderful odour of cooking meat and potatoes was issuing forth and filling the room.

The hunter stood for a long while, taking in this scene, which affected him to his very soul. It was the kind of place a weekend hunter dreams of, while he works at his job in the city, or travels on a jet to a business meeting with people he has no time for outside making money. This was clearly a gathering of huntsmen, like himself, in a perfect setting.

Feeling a little humble, the hunter walked across to the nearest fire and spoke to a man sitting there, cleaning a long old-fashioned rifle.

'Excuse me, sir. May I sit by you?'

The man answered him, but in French, which he did not understand at all. The hunter walked away from him, feeling bewildered. However, a second man, on the other side of the hearth, called to him.

'Sit by me. I speak your language. We can talk together about tomorrow's tracking or today's success. We can discuss the Christmas day feast and the New Year hunt. We can speak about the lore of the forest, the run of the game.'

Now this was the kind of conversation in which the hunter loved to participate. Gratefully he crossed the hearth and took the place indicated by the speaker, sitting on a deerskin close to the burning logs.

The man was large, with a moon-shaped pleasant face, and skin the colour of weathered mahogany. His black hair was long, hanging over the collar of his leather jacket, and his eyes were deep brown and clear. At the man's feet lay a black Labrador retriever, staring into the flames.

In his hands the man held a breechloading rifle, the barrel of which he was subjecting to a vigorous pulling-through with a cleaning cloth. He offered the hunter a look down the barrel, at the shining spirals of rifling, as the hunter sat down beside him.

'Good,' said the hunter. 'Not a spot of rust.'

'As it should be,' said the man, in a satisfied tone.

The hunter pointed to the retriever, who was now watching him with a movement of the eyes only.

'Fine water dogs, those,' he said.

The man patted the dog on the head and received a lick on the hand as acknowledgement.

'Yes, wonderful beasts. This one has been with me for a long time now, haven't you old girl? She doesn't like the winter months though. Not enough for her to do.'

The dog nuzzled his hand.

The hunter said, 'What is this place?' he gestured with a sweep of his hand, taking in the lodge. 'Who are these people? Is this some sort of Christmas Eve gathering?'

The man raised his eyebrows and looked a little sad.

'Ah, you are new? Then you may be in for a little shock, I think, unless you've guessed already.'

'Guessed what?' asked the hunter, who hated puzzles.

'These people, as you call them, were all great huntsmen or huntresses when they were alive. As you must have been yourself, for here you are, in *Jaegerhalle*. The place we are in is of course the lodge where we now reside, sleeping around our fires, preparing for the next day's hunt...'

The hunter smiled.

'You're making fun of me,' he said.

The man stared at him with serious eyes.

'No, I do not joke. You are dead my friend and in the hall of the great hunters. No one here can remember what they were called in life. Do you have a name?'

The man then concentrated on cleaning his gun, seemingly allowing the hunter time to think about what he had said.

The hunter tried desperately to recall his own name. How could he forget such a thing? Yet there was nothing there, not even a hint of who he was, or what he was called. His mind remained a complete blank on that aspect. He knew *what* he was, but not *who* he was, nor who his parents were. All he got from a searching of his memory was a feeling of frustration.

Wait a minute, he thought triumphantly, I can feel my own heart beating in my chest! Or was that illusion? Was he breathing, or simply going through the motions of breathing? Surely he was being made fun of, the object of hunters' humour, an initiation ceremony on first entering the lodge? Yet there were no others within earshot, to enjoy the joke. Only his darkhaired companion, intent on servicing his rifle.

The man was looking at him again, with quizzical eyes.

'What,' said the dark-haired man, 'is the last thing you remember, before the sky darkened and the stillness came?'

This question shocked the hunter dreadfully.

It meant the man knew about the incident in the forest. How could that be, when the man had not been there? Perhaps the man had been hiding behind a tree? Surely he would have come to the hunter's assistance if he had? And in any case, something had happened *inside* the hunter, as well as outside.

'What do I remember?' he repeated, and received a nod from his companion.

What did he remember? Why, he and his friends had been tracking a stag, an animal with magnificent antlers. His first shot had struck the beast in the flank, wounding but not crippling. The stag had run, of course, a ragged route through the trees, and the hunters had followed the trail of blood, and then the tracks in the snow when the blood had dried on the wound.

Then what? There was a sort of dark area in his memory after that, between tracking the stag and the moment when the sky closed and the silence fell. It was as if his mind was a shade in which a memory was hidden. The memory wouldn't come out. So he had to concentrate, to try to understand its shape, though it attempted to remain vague. As he focused intensely on that dark area, the memory began to emerge, gradually. The reason it had remained hidden was because the nature of it was harrowing and the hunter had subconsciously thrust it away, not wanting to remember something so appalling.

Yet, here it came, out of the murk.

Why, yes, he had been standing between two pines, when the stag appeared again, to his left. He recalled trying to swing the rifle round, but the strap had caught on something, a branch, a bush, hampering his aim. Then… the stag had come on, at speed, its antlers lowered in a charge. Someone else, one of the others, had then aimed and fired.

A sudden flush of fear. Terrible pain. Blood coming out of his chest and mouth in gouts. Then the darkening, the silence. These were his last memories.

Dead? he thought. *Am I dead?*

The thought must have shown in his eyes, for the other man said, 'I'm sorry.'

'I'm still not convinced,' said the hunter. 'But I'll go along with it for now.'

His new acquaintance shrugged.

The hunter then stared around the lodge, at the other hunters. Indeed, they were a strange mixture of men and women, the majority of them with the appearance of being from the past. The Hall of the Hunters? How wonderful if it were.

He said to the other man.

'What happens then? To us… dead?'

'What happens?' the man smiled broadly. 'Why, what happens is you *hunt*. The lakes and streams outside are stocked with every kind of fish: carp, salmon, trout, even minnow. The forest around the lodge has wild boar, deer, hares… you see that woman over there?' he pointed to a slim huntress who was waxing the string of her bow. 'She can hit a hare on the run, pinning it to the earth with a single arrow. Pheasants, quail, wildfowl of every description, you name it, it's here.

'Yes, the hunting here is good. The best. And everything we kill during the day goes into that pot you see, making the best stew you have ever tasted. Here of an evening, in the great lodge, we feast. We eat, we drink, we enjoy our stories, and the next day, why it happens all over again. Those creatures we killed the day before, they rise again out of the woodland mosses, out of the lake mud, out of the bark of trees. I have shot the same boar, seven times now, and still he runs the forest tracks.

'Tomorrow of course is the greatest banquet of the whole year—the Christmas Day Feast.'

If this is death, thought the hunter, it is better than life.

'Is this heaven?' he asked his companion.

'I should say so, though it can be hell too.'

Hell? That sounded ugly. But the hunter was not curious enough at that moment to ask about the dark side of death. He was content only to bask in the comradeship of fellow hunters and enjoy what had been his reward. The Hall of the Hunters! How he had dreamed of such a place.

'If that is so,' he asked of the man, 'where are the really *great* hunters of the world. For instance, I see no pygmies here. Where are the Efe of Zaire? Where are those small dark hunters who excite their hunting dogs with cries and songs, to flush the quarry? Where are those renowned little archers?'

The man shrugged, a gesture which seemed typical of him.

'There are a few hunters from other parts of the world, here in this lodge, but mostly they prefer their own type of hunting grounds, the ones they were used to in life. Those two men over there are Australian Aboriginals, and in the far corner behind the great hearth you will see a group of Iban Indians. There are others. We join together, for feasts from time to time, and try each other's hunting grounds.

'There are great hunts in which we all become involved together, and afterwards we exchange stories, talk about our different skills. Here in Hunter's Hall you will see mainly those who have been touched by the mysticism and legends of our own land, by the beliefs of our forefathers... those who hunted in the bush during life, or in the jungle, or across the snowy tundra, usually want the same landscapes after death. The Inuit do not want to hunt in our forest all the time, nor we on their icy wastes. But there is nothing to stop you doing so, if you wish. You can hunt in any landscape you like, or on the sea. It's your choice.'

'I think I understand.'

There was silence between them now. All that could be heard was a murmuring, around the room, as hunters told hunters their tales of the hunt. It was their one source of entertainment, for the long lazy evening hours, when the dying sun shone through the tall windows, into the dimness of the great room. The hunter breathed the scent of burning hickory chips and sighed in contentment.

The darkhaired man then engaged his attention once more.

'Tell me,' said the man, 'the *best* hunt you ever had in your life.'

The best hunt? A surge of excitement went through the hunter's breast. Oh yes, the very best of hunts. But could he tell this man about that time, on so short an acquaintance? He decided he could not. Instead, he recounted the time he had tracked and killed the wolves.

'...they were the last wolves left in Scandinavia, an old pair but still potentially dangerous. And tricky. They threw me off the trail several times, I can tell you. I tracked them over the snow and shot them outside a cave. The whole thing took many weeks. It was a great experience.'

A frown had appeared on the brow of the other man.

He said, 'Did you not eat the flesh? Or did you need the pelts to keep from dying of the cold? Or perhaps the wolves attacked and killed a child...?'

The hunter, puzzled by his companion's questions, shook his head vigorously.

'No, none of those. You don't understand. I killed them for sport. For the *thrill* of the hunt.'

'Then,' said the man, 'I cannot understand why you are here, in this lodge. Here we have only huntsmen who killed out of necessity, or to protect themselves or their families. This is the mark of the true hunter, the real hunter, who kills to feed or clothe himself, but not simply to see blood.'

For a moment the darkhaired man's words stunned him, but then he shrugged and said, 'I am here.'

Suddenly the hunter had a great desire to shock this man, to whom he was beginning to take a dislike. He decided to tell his self-righteous companion the story of the greatest of all hunts, the greatest of all prey which he himself had once hunted. If the darkhaired man did not like it, there were others to talk to in the room.

'I once stalked the most cunning creature on this planet,' said the hunter. 'I pursued him, tracked him down, and killed him where he stood. Never has anything equalled the moment when I squeezed the trigger and saw him jerk backwards to lie in the dust, a bullet from this very rifle in his heart.'

The man stroked his dog, not looking at the hunter now, and asked, 'What quarry would that be?'

'A man,' said the hunter.

Now the brown eyes flicked to his face and he felt satisfaction, knowing he had disturbed the owner of those eyes.

'Yes,' he told the other, 'a manhunt. One night we captured... it doesn't matter who or what he was, except that he was a human being, a man. We let him go, into the wood, then we went in after him. It was my shot that killed him.'

There was a long silence between them, until finally the man stopped stroking his dog and looked up. His eyes were full of sorrow and pity.

'You killed a fellow creature,' he said, 'one of your own kind—for *sport*. Now I understand why you are here. This will be your only night in the lodge, to give you the opportunity to witness and experience what you *might* have had, what you have thrown away. Tomorrow you go into the forest.'

The hunter felt a certain fear at the other man's words, but he said quickly, 'As you will, yourself.'

'But I go as a hunter,' said the man. 'You will be the prey.'

The newest hunter felt a bolt of terror go through him, at these words, and he looked about him, his mind in a turmoil. He glanced at the other hunters, cleaning their weapons, at the soft rugs on which they would sleep that night, and finally his eyes rested on the cauldron, the great stew that would be eaten before retiring.

A feeling of faint triumph trickled through his mind, bringing with it hope. Something was wrong with the logic of his fireside companion. There were surely errors in the rules, the laws of this place. Perhaps the dead told lies and the truth was still to be revealed? Maybe the mistake was not yet his? Possibly these things were not set in stone, but could be changed by clever argument? He would not accept what had been said to him without further dispute.

'Ah,' he said to his disapproving companion, 'but there's something wrong here. You told me a moment ago that what the true hunter kills, must be eaten. That means if I am to be the prey, and you kill me, you must eat me. Are you then cannibals? 'Even if I am changed into a beast, to be hunted and killed, over and over again, for all eternity, I am still in my soul, a *man*. I may not keep a man's body, but I will always have his spirit, which can't be altered because it is *me*.

'Do you hunters, you *great* hunters, do you eat the flesh of your fellow men? Do you gnaw on the bones of your comrades? Do you drink the blood of your own kind? Are you then going to hunt and kill me, then *eat me*?'

The black-haired man looked deep into his eyes.

'No, of course we won't eat you,' he said, 'but we have to feed our dogs.'

SOMETHING'S WRONG WITH THE SOFA

(Believe me, this is the future of soft furnishings and sex.)

WE SHOULD NEVER HAVE INVITED Starkey to the party.

Starkey is wutheringly wild and still youthfully coded, possibly because at three-hundred-something, he's the youngest and rawest of our friends. You can't expect someone who hasn't reached their millennium to act in a rational and decipherable manner, especially at a weekend squall. But then, as Jakoe pointed out to my partner Mica the other week, Starkey had just lost his wife and his vents were blocked. We had to try to open him up a little, let some joy inside.

Don't get me wrong, it was a storm of a party.

It's just that, well, the soft furnishings are *new* and though I didn't want to change our old flops, Mica likes to be up-to-the-hour fashionable, and she insisted. Hell, it was her money to do with as she liked, so who was I to stand on top of the Zugspitze, dispensing consumer wisdom? Now the strafing sofa's ruined and we suspect, in fact we as good as know, that it's all Starkey's fault. Who else could it have been? He's the one who slept on it.

Let's go back to before the any of this ever happened, when we first installed our new soft furnishings. Jakoe came round to discuss plans for the party and he was one of the first to try them out. Already sitting on one of the chairs when Jakoe came into the room, I was nestled down onto silk-covered flesh, having my neck massaged by a soft pair of hands. The arms of the chair were, I guess, originally the thighs, but once a person has been resculptured its difficult to tell which body parts are where, though obviously some of them are recognisable for what they are.

Jakoe winced as he watched me being stroked.

'You're not worried about getting strangled then?' he said. 'Like that old woman in the high-rise apartment.'

'Nobody ever proved that case,' I answered. 'It was mostly supposition. Sit down.'

Jakoe did as he was told, but nervously, as if he didn't trust my new armchair one bit. He was actually sitting in the *best* chair, the one which had been fed on butter-milk to make it more pneumatic, softer on the buttocks. Some people are never comfortable with live furniture though.

'I heard a jack came in drunk and beat up his wardrobe the other night,' Jakoe informed me, squirming on the edge of his seat. 'Left bruises all over the doors.'

'What did he do that for?'

Jakoe shrugged. 'Just one of those aggressive types. They've banned him from owning any live furniture now.'

'I should think so,' I said. 'That's strafing disgusting. I can't understand where these jacks come from. Is he out of the caves?'

'It wasn't as if the wardrobe could run away—not like a table or something with legs—it just had to stand there and take it.'

I relaxed into my own seat, feeling it close around me, warming me with its body heat. I couldn't understand people like the slab Jakoe was talking about. What satisfaction could they possibly get out of attacking a human being that can't even answer back, let alone defend itself? That was sick.

Jakoe and I discussed the party, then he made an excuse to go, and left me still comfortably ensconced. It was so quiet after he'd left I could hear the furniture around me delicately breathing, one or the other of them occasionally letting out a barely audible sigh. I was glad we'd bought one of the more expensive suites of flops, with internal waste disposal units, so we didn't have to worry about the carpet.

Not that *any* of them aren't, well, *housetrained.*

They all have some kind of built-in protection, but there are some units you can actually hear working, like softly-gurgling stomachs, and Mica decided that any reminder of what they had once been capable of would display a lack of taste. I think I agree with her.

That got me thinking. *What they had once been?* People, of course, but what had made them put themselves up for resculpturing? What was in their minds at the point when they submitted passively to becoming pieces of soft furniture? I suppose if I could answer that, I would know the secret of apathy—why it ever struck at all, when we have everything.

What do you do when your interest in life is drained to the last drop?

We've banished death, but we've never managed to conquer boredom.

Oh, yes, we all say that it'll never happen to us, that we'll always be able to pierce boredom to reach passion, that we're different, that bright becks of consciousness course around our curves.

Some of us think to fend off apathy with a spectacular hobby, but apathy comes to us all, sooner or later—usually later rather than sooner.

So what do you do when you have no ergs left to move or think, let alone work or play? Go into a torpor and stay that way, soliciting spider's webs, waiting for the day, the hour, the minute that will never come?

There are those however, who still have a strong work ethic and genetic resculpturing has been a cleanser to those of us who want to *do* something after apathy sets in.

What could be more useful too, my work ethic friend, than being reshaped as a chair, or table, and thus becoming an object in a friend's or stranger's lodge? A born-again bedside lamp? A footstool, thus satisfying a long-felt masochistic craving? A chest full of perfumed flimsies? A bookshelf containing all your favourite zip stories? A standing mobile, hands and feet gently waving in the draught when the front door is opened to admit visitors?

As a user I can recommend human furniture to any one of you cave dwellers. It's soft and comfortable, being fleshy, but durable, having a fine, solid frame of human bones. Your new chair, table, bed or sofa won't talk or walk, or give you the skits you in the middle of the night, yet it will conform to your personal contours, adjust itself once you sit or lie on it, and its gentle breathing is soporific rather than disturbing, especially if you keep the automatic drip-feed tuned.

I wouldn't have anything else in the lodge.

It was Mica who persuaded me.

'I'm always right,' she said. 'That's why you live with me— you love being wrong about things.'

However, there's always the flipside.

There's a deeper, more philosophical aspect that strikes us people who like to be wrong. Something which penetrated me instantly, but passed Mica by. It's this. Once we'd bought flops I couldn't help wondering about what sort of people the furniture had been, before they had volunteered themselves for resculpture.

I held conversations with Mica about it.

'The table, for instance,' I said. 'Maybe it was a politician? Or a deep-sea-bed walker? Or some famous zip story author?'

'Or your great-great-great grandmother,' retorted Mica. 'What does it matter? I'd rather think of it as just a table—*my* table—I couldn't care less what it was once.'

'*Who* it once was, not what,' I argued 'And how can you say that? You might be eating your dinner off the back of the woman who invented the matter shifter, or the self-building house, or the person who discovered the fourth primary colour.'

'The person who found the new colour was a *man*. Our table's definitely feminine.'

'All right, but you know what I mean. We could have a whole clutch of acubrains here—people who quaked the world with their inventions, or their poetry, or their acting, or their songs? Doesn't that make you stop and think?'

Mica said it didn't stop her and didn't make her think.

Sitting on the sofa, my favourite out of all the flops we had bought, even if it was strafing expensive, I tried at times to imagine how *I* would feel, if I were one of them. What would I be? I decided I wasn't joyed about being sat on, not unless there was a choice of owner. I might be sold to some massively overweight, flatulent, sweaty jack not inclined to wash too often… well, it just doesn't bear thinking about.

At first I thought I might like to be a writing desk, an antique of course, but with special features.

My hands might be left free to hold spare stylos; my feet turned into secret drawers to harbour illicit love-notes; my tongue wet and ready to lick envelopes and stamps.

I abandoned that idea and decided I could be a spinet, or harpsichord, or piano, providing they could fracture me out with strings and keys. A resonant, vibrant smiley box, an antique bash-and-cry. I imagined being stroked by the party egotist, persuaded against his will to charm the guests. Then I remembered there were still kids around, treble-sixers with tacky pincers, brimming with discord, and gave up that idea.

I finally decided on a small Korean tansu, where one might display hologram jars of the early dead. A low, delicate piece of furniture, with simple key designs on the drawers: a centrepiece for someone's looking-room.

In my recesses would be kept mementos of unfinished affaires—a vaccy glass containing a preserved rosebud, a slot to the opera, a natural chunk of china from a far-off beach—small treasured objects from the past. There would be tinsies on one end of my surface, perhaps a porcelain bowl containing flutes at the other end, or a pearl-handled nail trimmer, a dish of geoids fashioned from semi-precious stones, a twitch-watch belonging to a many-greats grandfather?

Yes, a tansu.

But how would I *feel*? What would be my thoughts, if any, as people came and went, touching my surface occasionally, but more often than not ignoring my presence? After all, I would be a *thing*, not a person. There would be no need for people to acknowledge my appearance, attractive as I might be, for I would not be expected to react in any way. I think I should resent their altitude, albeit I had lost interest in all that went on around me. The fact is, I can only imagine myself as a piece of furniture in my present state of mind, not what it might become, *will* undoubtedly become, in future centuries.

And what if one day I were rejected by some new owner, a fresh tenant to an apartment, and cast upon the gash pile, at the mercy of spiders, rats, mice, and all the other ghastly indignities heaped upon discarded objects?

Surely that would be too much to pack, wouldn't it?

Jakoe came to see me after the party was over and this time he was so agitated he sat down on one of my chairs without even thinking.

'I'm sorry about Starkey,' he said. 'I shouldn't have brought him.'

Jakoe didn't look at the sofa when he spoke, but he was aware the thin silk covering had been damaged, torn away from the back and arm.

'It wasn't your fault,' I lied. 'You weren't to know.'

'But I feel responsible.'

He went on like this for at least an hour, until I was becoming impatient with him. Mica was due home and Jakoe was not one of her favourite persons at the moment, any more than was Starkey. In the end I told Jakoe he would have to leave and he tried to stand.

'Hey,' he said, softly. 'This chair's gripping me—it won't let me get up.'

'What?' I said. 'They're not supposed to do that.'

'It's—it's *squeezing* me,' he wheezed. 'I think it's trying to crush me.'

He had gone very white, with red blotches on his cheeks, and his eyes looked scared. I felt he was exaggerating things, but it was useless to remonstrate with him. Getting out of my own chair was easy and I gripped his arm and gave him a tug.

'Come on, Jakoe, use a bit of effort,' I said, finding he was *really* stuck. 'I think it's you—you should go on a diet or something.'

'It's-not-me,' he croaked. 'This strafing chair's squashing the breath out of me. Oh Christ, help me man.'

At that moment Mica came into the room. I shouted at her that Jakoe was in real trouble, that she was to come to my aid. To give Mica her due she immediately dropped her outwear and assisted me by getting hold of Jakoe's other arm and pulling with me. There was a moment when I thought we weren't going to extract him from the chair, but finally he shot out as the chair let him go, giving an almighty yell as he did so.

'It bit me!' he cried, rubbing his thigh. 'The strafing chair bit me!'

'They're not supposed to do that,' I said.

Mica added, 'I expect it was upset over the sofa—after all, Jakoe, you're the one who brought Starkey to the party. It was you who insisted we invite him—against our better judgement. I'm really not surprised the chair bit you.'

'I might sue,' he said, in an aggrieved tone, as he limped from the room. 'It wasn't my fault—it was Starkey's.'

Starkey—yes, poor Starkey—but not *blameless* Starkey. I must explain that his wife, the woman he has loved since he reached two-hundred years of age, has become a piece of furniture. She was older than Starkey of course—much, much older—though as beautiful as a mountain rill in early spring. She glistered, she was clear and unclute, she bubbled forth her love for Starkey until one day she simply seared her canals, became a bed of arid dust, and finally volunteered herself for resculpturing, without telling him.

No one, not even Starkey knows what kind of furniture she is now. It must be strafing hell for him, staring at this friend's table, or that stranger's chair, wondering if it's *her*. It's driven him to a distraction, I know, because the weekend of the squall he was half out of his hat, depressed yet manic, and he put away dylan knows how many stims in his endeavours to escape thoughts of her, dreams of her, memories of her.

All this does not excuse Starkey's behaviour.

At the end of the party he didn't even want to go back to their apartment, so he stayed over with us, sleeping on the sofa.

Our sofa.

My favourite soft furnishing.

What Starkey did was not only inexcusable, illmannered and downright unpolitic—I believe it may also be illegal. That young wuthering wilder has ruined Mica's most expensive item of furniture and expects to get away with it.

You see, there's a smooth bulge down at one end, right on the place where I normally find it most comfortable to sit.

Something's wrong with my sofa.

I think it's pregnant.

EXPLODING SPARROWS

(When I was in the RAF I worked some of the time for Communications Intelligence.)

IT'S DANGEROUS OUT THERE. IT'S not even safe to step outside the doorway. Not since they started exploding like flying grenades. Not since our volatile feathered friends became feathered bombs. Not since cock robin was killed and they exchanged their little bows and arrows for internally detonated devices that can take a man's head clean off his shoulders.

The reports have been coming in thick and fast, from other cities, from other parts of this city. I haven't been out since they first said it was the sparrows. I don't want to, though I may have no choice in the matter. There are heroes enough, without me. I mean, the last time I was outside, I heard the explosions, saw the mess afterwards, but I didn't actually *see* any of them go off.

Now I know it's the sparrows, I can see how suicidal it would be to go outside. I mean, there are thousands of them out there. They're on the limbs of the statues in the yard. They're clustered on the concrete. They decorate the overhead wires, the signposts, the lamp posts. They're on the pavement, in the gutter. They're everywhere. When are they not? You don't even notice them, normally. You take them for granted, consciously, even subliminally, ignore them.

They're there every day, but today is different, today they are what they are. Any one of them could be. Potentially potent. The *it* among the *they* could blow you to kingdom come and go, so they tell us. It's been on the news, in the news, everywhere, word of mouth, word of print. I don't know which of them are, and which aren't. How can you tell? Looking at them they all look the same: they all look innocent and deadly.

You have to sit well away from the window, just in case one of them lands on the sill. I've heard, they've told me on the comm, that slivers of glass fly in like knives shot from a gun, to strip you to the bone. That's what I've heard. So you stay away from windows, keep the curtains closed, maybe even wire-net the inside.

Why me? This was the first, possibly very selfish, thought that crossed my brain when I got the call. Why me? Others have got the gift of *insight*, so why not them? Why not that dickhead Williams, or Danny Pugerchov? How come I was chosen to do the investigation. Who have I upset in the last few years? Who wants me out of the way for good? Unless the other agents are already dead? Unless they already have a hole in their torsos through which you could pass a football? Unless their heads are already decorating the town centre and suburbs as biltong and bone shards.

If I had any time, these questions themselves would be investigated. If I live through this, I will certainly seek out my enemies, and nail the bastards to the wall. In the meantime, I have to stay with it, stay on it, stay alive.

The first part of any investigation is of course easy. Pure research. Books can't hurt you, at least in your own living-room. You don't have to protect your eyes from splinters of bone and beak when reading a book, because books don't explode, not yet anyhow. Maybe books will one day be the most dangerous articles in the office, but today at least they are innocuous. I have a substantial library in my office, which is where I live, eat, sleep and breathe. I don't have to go out on the streets and risk getting my head blow off zipadee-doo-da-there's-a-brown-bird-on-my-shoulder style.

'*Sparrow* (spærou) *noun.* a member of *Passer,* fam. *Fringillidae* (*FINCH) esp. the house sparrow [O.E. *spearwa*].'

Good enough. So much for the dictionary. I always like to start with the definition. I mean, did you know the sparrow was a finch? Maybe you did, but a lot of people don't. Me for one. I thought a sparrow was a sparrow.

'*SPARROW.* Though probably the most often seen of British birds, sparrows are not the most numerous; they are outnumbered by chaffinches and blackbirds. Sparrows appear numerous because they live in close association with man, building untidy nests in holes, in thatch and walls and in hedges. There are two species of British sparrow: the tree sparrow and the house sparrow.'

Hedges? *Tree* sparrows? Walls and flagstones. Bricks and mortar. *Concrete* sparrows.

Seed eaters, it goes on to say. That was *then*. Now of course, there is no seed. No seed, no hedges, no trees. Not outside the greenhouses. Only concrete. Now they get what they can, where they can. They peck away at anything. It used to be the waste food in the trash: vegetable matter, offal, fat, gristle. Now even that is denied them, since the recycling of all edible rubbish, for domestic stock.

Enough of the encyclopaedia. There is more to say that is unwritten. That is, there are millions of the little bastards, swarming around the cities. They like us, or rather, they like the food we give them. They are worldwide. Sometimes so numerous as to be a hazard. Mao Tse Tung listed them as one of the 'Four Pests' and ordered their extermination in China. The year after the slaughter the country was invaded by insects.

The comm.

'Hello?'

'Listen, we need an answer soon. How close are you to an answer?'

'I only just got started.'

'We have to know. Is it the government? Is it anarchists or terrorists? Is it the big corporations or financial houses? It has to be one of these three groups.'

'I'll get back to you.'

The comm falls silent. Of course it has to be one of the big three. As a loner you poison a jar of baby food and demand a ransom. That's cheap and easy. You plant a bomb in a supermarket for fun, because you have a warped mind and you are an individual. You shoot fourteen, fifteen people with an automatic weapon because you are a sociopath or you do a string of serial murders as a psychopath. These don't cost a great deal, no big layout.

But to produce genetically-detonated little flying bombs—that costs money. Big money. You need to be a billionaire several times over for that kind of thing.

An explosive random killer. Not a BIG bang, of course, but bigger than a feathered ball full of plastic explosive. What about nuclear fission, on a small scale? Is that possible? Can you control a chain reaction: limit it to pocketsized boom? I don't know too much about the science, but I know nuclear bombs need heavy elements to produce those enormous releases of energy. I know that much. Maybe the sparrows contain lighter elements? The explosion is large enough to rip apart a good sized room. If you're inside with one when it goes off, so I'm told, they need a finely-sharpened razor to scrape you off the walls.

Something coming down the mail chute.

What's this? Nobody writes letters any more. A parcel?

A live creature flies out of the tube and into the room and I instinctively dive for the space behind the desk.

After a second or two I see it's not a sparrow, but a canary.

It's got to be a joke. One, or some of the boys in another department in the building, trying to get me going, now that I've been put on the job. It's probably that sicko, Jameson, in Dispatches. What the hell though, canaries may have started interbreeding with sparrows. Maybe it's in the chromosomes and they pass it on, the deadly little sperm carrying the genetic code? A billion to one but who the hell wants to risk it? The heartbeat is rapid, pattering in the tiny chest. Shit, maybe this is the fuse? A time bomb. Not *tick-tock-tick-tock*, but *pat-pat-pat-pat-pat*, and on the eight-thousandth heartbeat, the detonation, the explosion? A room full of bits of feather and flesh, bird and man mingling on the wallpaper, on the ceiling, on the floor tiles.

Using my *insight* I check out the canary, find nothing.

I call Jameson.

'Hey, Jameson? Did you send me a bird...? Oh, for my birthday? It's not my birthday for five months. Remind me to do something nasty to you when I see you next.'

Now, what to do about the bird?

First I catch it, in the wastepaper basket.

Now, do I blow its head off? Shoot the thing? What with, a .45? Overkill. Stifle it then? Wait. If I kill it violently, maybe there's a genetic device, a failsafe primer hidden in the DNA, like a trembler on a conventional bomb? Maybe if I stop the heart, dead, it will go up automatically? Best to stop it slowly. Put it in the freeze compartment of the refrigerator, slow the heart beat down gradually, turn the poor little bastard to ice. This is survival after all. You can't afford to be squeamish when you're threatened with a nasty form of extinction.

I make another call, to the boss.

'Are you sure this is real? I mean, have you actually heard one, seen a sparrow go off?'

'There are people who have.'

'Yeah, but apocryphal tales and all that shit? Everyone knows someone who knows someone who has, but no one has actually seen it for themselves. I mean, truth or myth? Is it really serious, or is it just rumour?'

'It's serious, believe me. Get on it.'

'What about catching some, in a net, and looking at them under controlled conditions.'

'We've done that. Pugerchov's had a look at a whole room full of them.'

'And?'

'Zilch. Someone has to look at them in the wild, that's to say, in their own environment.'

'The concrete jungle?'

'Okay, the only environment they've got left. *Outside*. Whatever you like to call it. Nothing shows up when they're in captivity. It's up to you.'

'Why me?' I ask the question at last.

'You know why. You're the man.'

'One of them.'

'One of those.'

I am proof that the Theory of Punctuated Evolution, which states that evolution is not gradual and regular, but punctuated by drastic leaps to meet extraordinary circumstances, is no longer simply a theory. I'm one of those: a drastic leap. One of the few who can read the *inscape* of other people, read their emotions like a map, feel their intentions, discover their design. Survival. I find the terrorist in a crowd. I find the psychopath, the sociopath, when I get close enough to smell the desire for death, feel the absence of emotions. The human race has need of me, in this overdeveloped world, full of neuroses, madness, violence. I read them, and all other creatures, any and every living thing.

But there are quite a few others who can do the same. I'm not unique. I am no freak, you understand.

'What's happened to the others? What are they doing right now? Where's Williams?'

'You're the investigator on this one.'

'I might get blown to pieces and then I'll be nothing. How about a protective suit, or even a flak jacket and helmet?'

'Wear what you want. Protect yourself. But get out there. It's your job.'

It's my job. They know that. Others know that. Did Jameson really send me the bird? Was that his voice on the comm or a clever copy? What do I know? Nothing. I can't use *insight* at a distance, through walls. I have to get close to my subject to see inside it, understand it.

I look inside the canary again, carefully study its *inscape*. It feels innocent enough. Nothing registers. Maybe they've got it screened in some way. You evolve the gift of *insight* and then someone comes up with a screen to prevent it. That's progress. Only thing that stands between unstoppable attack and ultimate defence is *time*. You get one, the other follows naturally, as night follows day, only in unknowable hours.

Into the freezer with the canary.

Sparrows. Just the right size. Not too big, not too small. All over the goddamn place. Random. Millions of the little fuckers. Flying bombs. Hiding on the ledges, the rooftops, in the eves, in the drains. Not hiding at all, but hopping along pavements, roads, pathways. Scattered in the squares, looking harmless. How the hell are we going to find out? What do we do when we do find out? Gas them all overnight? Maybe someone will come up with a device for killing them. A freeze gun? You point the thing, squeeze the trigger, and a dozen sparrows fall out of the sky. *Thunk, thunk, thunk*. Little balls of solid ice.

Wait a minute. Maybe the gun has already been invented? Maybe it was invented before the sparrows became biological experiments? The gun had no use, so then the inventor invented a use? Perhaps the sparrows are here because the gun needs to be marketed, sold in all the retail stores, for the inventors to get their money back? First the freeze gun, then the sparrows? I would buy one. Who wouldn't? Even if the truth got out, you would still want a weapon, and if that was the most effective, then purchase and be damned, regardless of moral distaste.

How many of these have there been, in recent years? The cure without the disease, so then discover the disease, let it loose, get rich curing it?

Could be the big corporations.

Back to the research.

The Ornithologist's Guide: 'Sparrows do not migrate.'

They're local then. You can contain the experiment, within a given area. This is more like government, testing out its new weaponry. 'Don't worry boss, it won't get out of hand. We'll just test it out on a few people. No one will know. Nobody will ever find out. Nothing can go wrong.' Famous last sentences, rearrangeable syntax. Myxomatosis wiped out sixty million rabbits in this country alone and it wasn't even started here. They started it on the other side of the world. It *always* gets out of hand, always *goes wrong*. Sixty million. That's the total British population, of people, right now.

Governments are good at hiding things, covering up their insane blunders, losing documents. Yet they never stop their experiments, on people, on animals, on nature. Wonderful methods of destruction: defoliants, napalm, nuclear weapons. They move too fast when starting things, and move too slowly to stop them. God has always made the big disasters, and now governments too. The disasters get bigger all the time. Government equals God now. Disasters at nuclear power stations. Windscale, Three Mile Island, Chernobyl, over a period of thirty years. Random disasters, flying around in history by the hundred million, too few in a lifetime to alarm, but in geological time, too many.

The comm again.

I am impatient with them.

'What?'

'Go outside and look around.'

'Fuck you. You go outside.'

A voice charged with quiet panic.

'You can be replaced.'

'So replace me.'

'You can be punished.'

'Yeah? Who's going to come round to smack me?'

Click.

So what about the third possibility?

Terrorists don't do things for nothing. They want something. Prisoners released. Land returned. Ideologies destroyed and other ideologies put into place. An end to war, a start to war. Not *nothing*. Something. What do they want then?

How about the Mafia? They want money and power. No money and power to be had with random terror.

Strike out terrorists and criminals.

Maybe anarchists? Any government is a bad government, no government is a good government. I'll go along with that. So why kill the ordinary people? The population? Does that upset the government? Not really. They do it themselves, in various ways.

Sparrows. What if they increase in number, the bomb-sparrows as opposed to the non-bomb-sparrows? Maybe there's say, one in a thousand at the moment, but with breeding? What if it's a dominant gene? A dominant gene and a season to pass it on, before the ticker reaches the required number and takes out the wall of a house.

Comm. Me again.

'Fuck it, I'm going outside. I'm going crazy in here. There are no answers to be found indoors.'

'About time.'

'I'll get back to you.'

'Leave the line open, so we can hear.'

'Hear what?'

No answer.

Someone singing in my head: *My sweet ex-pend-able you...*

After putting on a flak jacket and helmet I prepare myself, psychologically, for going outside. There's no point in wearing anything over the whole of my head, like a diver's helmet, because that would interfere with my *insight*. Anyway, it's just a gesture. When you get that close to a bomb, the concussion turns your brains to porridge, whatever you've got on in the way of protective clothing. There are other more important considerations to worry about.

What if it's not a time bomb? What if it's some kind of heat-trigger that sets it off? You walk close to a sparrow and Goodbye Columbus. Or maybe some kind of beam from their eyes and you break the circuit? Perhaps the exploding birds have funny laser eyes, that blow you to hell?

I have plenty of questions.

'I think it's nature,' I say into the comm, 'not governments, terrorists or corporations. They're big noises to us, but mere hiccups in time to nature, to history. Just little glitches, little pops and fizzes, like seedpods exploding under the sun. What if it's the way they reproduce now, spread their egg-seeds over a wide area like exploding pods, grow sparrow-blooms that break off in the spring and fly away?'

'Have you been outside and taken a look?'

'That must be it. Nature. It's something we've done to the atmosphere, with our radio waves, our space junk, our deodorant sprays. We've polluted the sky and the earth, letting in things through the ozone layer. The sparrows are just freaks, but natural freaks, so not freaks at all. I mean, if they've altered naturally, overnight, then they're not mutants, but simply quick-change artists of evolution, like me. Humans the unfortunates that get in their way? Wham-bam, evolutionary spam.'

'Listen, have you been outside?'

'I'd like to go, but there's death out there. On the streets, in the air. I used to be scared of motorways and skin cancer, but now it's sparrows that obsess me. I *will* go out, but not today, not till I get used to them, take them for granted, like bombs in the blitz.'

'If you don't go out soon, we may never get to know, we might not be given the chance.'

'That's true. Do we need to? I mean, do we have to know the *why* of everything? Can't we leave just one question unanswered, one puzzle unsolved? Why do we have to classify all the shapes on the earth, label them in Latin, count their bones, their heartbeats, witness their sexual antics, watch them eating each other? I mean, these are the first exploding sparrows, so they don't fit into any group, type, family or species. Or if you really can't bear for it not to have a scientific label, then how about *Passer bombicus*? That'll do, won't it? Why do we need to explain everything?'

'It's your job.'

'What, to understand the whole universe?'

'No, to find out what this is.'

'Well, let's leave this one, eh? Why not? Let's just have a wonder we don't know anything about. A deadly wonder. We've killed enough cobras and dissected them. We've hunted enough sharks and measured their jaws, numbered their teeth. Let's have one very dangerous thing we don't know anything about and let it keep its secrets? The cryptic sparrow, with its weird unknown biological reaction to God knows what. Here we have what used to be the common house sparrow, ladies and gentlemen, which suddenly turned into a kamikaze killer, for no logical reason. Reach out with your emotions, and feel what you feel: hate, admiration, fear. Marvel but don't analyse. Empathise, but don't try to understand, or you'll destroy the wonder of the thing. What do you say? I'm going to hang up now, and I don't want to hear from you again.'

It's driving me nuts, not knowing, and they're right, it *is* my job. *My* job. It's what they pay me for. I just like to do it in my own time. I need to psyche myself up first.

I go outside.

Outside it's peaceful, but I don't like it. The sparrows chatter in the street. I'm only human, still flesh and blood, despite the gift I have. I still experience fear, an instinct to survive.

Maybe it's a virus, that will spread to humans?

Next on the Extinction List, exploding people?

One of the sparrows hops over to my foot. I look inside it, finding nothing. Others come. They too, do not register anything more than *sparrow*. Tweet. Harmless. What about screens? Not all of them. Too many. Millions. It's just paranoia, that's what it just is, surely to God?

An explosion down the street.

Something—a feral cat?—staggers, blood pouring from its headless corpse, falls in the gutter, twitches.

The sparrows descend. They pick at the bits of flesh, blood and bone that have rained on the lawns.

Punctuated evolution. The sparrows have leapt.

They're all round my feet now, dozens of them, maybe hundreds. I can see nothing, feel nothing, but I think I've got the answer.

What if the actual punctuated leap itself triggers the explosion?

No *insight* would show that up, not beforehand.

This ability to detonate themselves, to leap evolution, is deliberate and voluntary. One of them, sacrificing itself for the good of the many, not by intelligent choice, simply by instinct— but still a choice.

You have to evolve to survive.

The sparrows have leapt at a way to feed themselves.

Is this the answer I've been looking for? It feels right, righter than anything else.

Their innocence is too absolute. Nobody, nothing, is that innocent. There is no such thing as the perfect creature, without a blemish on its spirit. There is no such thing as purity. The robin has a savage heart, its terrible beak poised ready to spear any creature of spearable size. If I were smaller, or he bigger, he would spear me without compunction. The sparrows cannot be so innocent, beside such a bird. They must have *some* bad in them, however slight. Yet I cannot see it, feel it, when I reach out with my gift.

I look towards my escape.

It is a long long way away. Several steps. Further than an instant. Almost infinity.

'Are you going to give me a chance?' I say. 'Or what? Do I get just a try at it?'

There is no intelligence there, no way to reason. They do not even look at me, as they peck around at the cracks in the concrete, searching for grubs and insects. They are carnivores, trained on cooked meat but long since graduated to raw flesh, when it's available, when they can *make* it available.

I turn and run.

DEATH OF THE MOCKING MAN

(I've been hooked on Medieval China ever since I first saw *The Water Margin* when it was on television. Stories grow out of fascination.)

MAI SONG WAS TWELVE YEARS of age when the mocking man first appeared at her side. 'You are the daughter of an impoverished war lord,' he sneered. 'You will never amount to anything.'

'I am not concerned about riches or fame,' she replied, 'so long as I find happiness.'

The mocking man laughed in a particularly offensive manner.

'That too will be beyond your grasp, if I have anything to do with it.'

Mai song was an accomplished archer. She could hit a knotted clout at a hundred paces with the bow her father had given her. However, her next shot missed the target. The mocking man laughed and jeered.

Thereafter the mocking man was always there, at crucial times, to denigrate her. He jeered at her efforts to paint beautiful watercolours of the firs clinging to the crags of Guilin's hills, telling her that mud splashed on walls by the wheels of ox-carts was more artistic. He called her horse, the beast she loved, a shambling monster. He said she rode it like a frog rode a lump of driftwood floating on a scummy pond. Her efforts at Chinese characters, the lovely picture-language of her nation, he said were pathetic and corrupt, and therefore meaningless. Everything and anything she did was ridiculed by the mocking man, until the princess felt she was totally unworthy. She might have been utterly and hopelessly miserable if she had not a companion, a talking crane which landed in the courtyard of the garden on the odd frosty morning, and who told her she was estimable.

'Do not listen to the mocking man,' the white crane told her, as it took fish from the lily pond, 'he is trying to break your spirit.'

It upset Mai Song's father to lose his precious goldfishes, but Mai song told her father cranes had to eat just as people did. Moreover, when the white crane was in evidence, the mocking man stayed away. Just the presence of the white crane seemed to deter the mocking man from appearing.

Mai Song's home was alive with mosquitoes and bog rats, snakes and leeches. Mai Song lived in a bamboo castle on the edge of the marsh country over which her father ruled. The war lord's subjects were mostly poor fishermen who scraped a living from the shallow waters of the swamp, or hunters of small birds and game in the bogs and fens. These people lived for the best part in rickety houses on stilts, though some had to use their small fishing rafts as their places of rest. They gave no money to their lord because they had none. He and his small contingent of soldiers provided protection for these people from the bandits who were the scourge of the water margin. The war lord was paid in kind: fish and fowl mostly, but sometimes with manual labour. In this way he maintained his bamboo castle and fed himself and his daughter, his wife being long dead from swamp fever.

Sometimes there would pass by her father's castle the troops and retinues of rich and powerful war lords. She would glimpse silk banners in the distance, fluttering like trapped birds on the tips of tall lances. Then knights in bright metal would appear under them, as they reached the crest of rising ground. They would be riding magnificent chargers: black, white and dappled, dripping with curtains of flank armour, their brown eyes peering through dark holes in satin hoods. Behind the cavalry the foot soldiers would come, their heads high, green plumes spouting from their helmets like fountains of liquid jade, *chinking* and *clinking* as they marched over the soft marshy earth.

In the centre of this long lizard of metalled military rode a large arrogant man, sitting tall on his goatskin saddle, his eyes like flint arrowheads. This was the war lord himself, surrounded by strolling figures in silk robes: scribes, overseers, body-servants, grooms, cup-bearers, and sometimes, a sorcerer. Following the war lord was often a brocade-covered litter, behind which sat the war lord's wife or daughter. This person sometimes drew back the rich folds of the litter's drapes to peer out at Mai Song who stood on the battlements of her father's wooden fort watching the carnival go by. The eyes of these women and girls were full of disdain for the young child behind the bamboo spikes. When she grew older they glanced at her close-cropped hair and often mistook her for a kitchen boy, dismissing her at once in a single indifferent glance.

But sometimes a sorcerer!

Yes, it must have been a sorcerer, accompanying a war lord, who was responsible for the mocking man. Just before her twelfth birthday Mai Song had been standing on the battlements as she usually did, watching a parade of soldiers go by, when she happened to stare at a young man of some fourteen winters who had eyes like a snake. He stared back, it seemed belligerently, as if he were offended by her interest in him. When her eyes did not waver this youthful wizard wafted the air with his right hand, no doubt leaving a curse on the child.

The mocking man was not real of course, being simply an image in the likeness of a young man. Though the mocking man's features were not at all clear, being shrouded in a misty darkness which clung to his form, Mai Song got the impression that he was not more than eighteen years of age, a petulant youth with a crescent red mouth that curved up on either side of a lean nose. His hair was long and lank, hanging down to his waist. He wore a silk gown covered in strange symbols and leather sandals with gold buckles on his feet.

The mocking man was invisible and silent to all but Mai Song. The war lord thought his daughter was quietly mad, but did not blame his child for that, given the environment in which she had been raised.

One day when she had grown into a woman Mai Song was playing mah jong (which is called *mah jeuk* in the local dialect) when a prince rode by the castle. This prince had no bodyguard of shining soldiers, no litter, no feng shui man or sorcerer accompanying him. He was entirely alone, the prey of bandits and rogue war lords along the water margin. This prince called up to Mai Song and asked her if he might spend the night at the castle. She replied that she would have to ask her father, who was the war lord, but thought the answer would be yes.

That evening the prince dined with the Mai Song and the war lord. The prince's name was Pang Yau (which means 'friend') and his father was the King of Gwongdong, one of the most wealthy and powerful regions in all China. Mai Song felt instinctively that though his father had the reputation of being a tyrant, Prince Pang Yau was a good man.

The prince radiated goodness from his face, his hands, his feet. He smiled at her all the time, his hazel eyes twinkling, and once during the meal he 'accidentally' touched her hand with his fingertips. A dramatic thrill went through Mai Song.

The mocking man appeared and on seeing her expression, laughed at her.

'Do you honestly think you could capture the heart of a man like this? A woman whose hands are rough with washing dishes because her father cannot afford a scullery maid? A sweeper of floors? Why this is a young fine prince from a wealthy family. He would not look twice at you if you were not the only woman for a hundred miles.'

She thought this was probably true. Mai Song knew that men who went into regions where females were scarce, thought the first woman they saw on returning to their homeland was beautiful.

Before he left in the morning, Prince Pang Yau asked the war lord's permission to return once his visit to a far country was over.

'I shall tell you my reason,' said the prince. 'I have fallen in love with your daughter, Mai Song.'

The war lord was dubious about this match. 'Mai Song is pretty, I grant you—but not beautiful. You are still a very young man. You may yet see other women in this far country who appeal to you more.'

The prince shook his head solemnly. 'I am not as fickle as you believe me to be. I have seen many beautiful women. My father's palace is full of them. My father gathers them in droves from his kingdom and parades them before me. Mai Song *is* pretty, but that is not why I have fallen in love with her. I have fortunately—though sometimes it is a curse—been born with insight—and she has the most gentle and lovely spirit I have ever encountered in any woman. It is *her* I love, not her looks, though I am grateful for her pleasant features too.'

When Mai Song heard what the young prince had said her heart soared. She ran to the prince and proclaimed her love for him. She was gratified to see he was bursting with happiness at this news. They strolled outside the castle walls, holding hands, along the banks of the marsh. For the first time she saw beauty in the still waters of the swamp: dragonflies hovered like chips of lapis lazuli above the surface; reed warblers swayed on the rushes and sang high sweet notes to her; emerald lizards and small marsh frogs flashed their green in the sun.

Once the prince had left her side Mai Song took her turn to sneer back at the mocking man.

'Not fit for a prince? Perhaps. But this prince looks beyond my menial surroundings, my poor upbringing. He sees someone who could love him better than any other. You shall not put me down in this matter. When Pang Yau returns, I shall marry him.'

'*If* he returns,' derided the mocking man, his mouth curved downwards for once. 'Perhaps I can do something about that!'

Fear for the prince's well-being struck Mai Song deep in the heart like a sword. She said nothing more to the mocking man, for she remembered that he was in effect a sorcerer's image. She had no doubt that all that went on inside the bamboo castle was known to the sorcerer himself. Running to the battlements she managed to shout a warning to the prince, as he rode away, but her words were lost on the wind. He turned in his saddle and waved back at her, no doubt thinking she was wishing him a good journey and a safe return to her side.

For many months Mai Song waited for her prince to come. He had promised to return within two, but six, then eight months passed by. No letter came. No messenger arrived. The mocking man crowed.

Finally, the terrible news came with a passing pedlar. Prince Pang Yau had been captured and imprisoned by a powerful wizard in the north of China. The prince was being held in a high tower in a castle with only a single door and no windows. The prince's father had sent his own sorcerer with an army to attempt to free the youth, but all the soldiers in the world could not get inside the impregnable fortress, and the king's sorcerer failed in his bid to force an opening. It was said that the wizard inside the castle was feeding on the goodness of the prince and growing stronger for it.

'Prince Pang Yau is like some tethered cow, which is bled and milked each day for its nourishment. The prince's spirit regenerates, just as do blood and milk. So the wicked sorcerer need never go outside, need never seek food elsewhere. However, since he now lives in darkness, the sorcerer has become part of the darkness itself. Should he ever be subject to the light of day he might vanish in its brightness.'

'Why not just knock down the walls?' asked the war lord, grieving along with his daughter. 'Why not smash it to pieces?'

The pedlar shrugged, as he wrapped his pots and pans in oiled rags, and fitted them to the frame which he carried on his back.

'Why not indeed? But the castle is immensely strong. Such a feat is not possible. The blocks of stone of which the walls are made are each as large as a house. There is no machine known to man which could breach such walls. And even if one could, how would you ensure the survival of the prince? If but one should fall on the prince, he would be crushed. I have no doubt the sorcerer moves the prince around, within the walls, so that those on the outside never know exactly where the young man is located. It is a grave problem, which has all the wise men in the kingdom pacing the floor of nights.'

'And the door?'

'The door too, is made of huge grey slabs of slate, with a great iron lock the intricate works of which have defeated even the most superb locksmith. They say the key itself weighs more than a man, and is of such complex design that craftsmen of the first order could not even imagine the amazing twists and turns it takes. No, no, I am afraid the prince has been incarcerated until he dies. It is a sad and shocking story.'

Of course, Mai Song wept. The mocking man made much of this, saying she could sob until the swallows stayed for the winter, she would not see her prince again. Once she had cried enough, however, she sat down and thought about the problem. If the King of Gwongdong's wizard had not been able to release Pang Yau then Mai Song saw little point in appealing to sorcerers. Wizards worked for money, power or position, not for love, and the king had presumably offered the first three in order to have his son released. There had to be another way. The next time she saw the white crane, she asked the creature if he could help.

'I don't envy your situation,' said the crane, spearing one of her favourite goldfish, 'but I do have some advice. This is a very powerful sorcerer who has your young man in captivity. I can understand why it is difficult to find another wizard to go against him. However, you can go in search of your own magic, young woman. If you do break into the sorcerer's castle, do so during the day, when he will be rendered helpless.'

Mai Song thanked the white crane for his advice, but asked, 'Where will I find such magic?'

'Everyone knows,' said the crane, 'that magic can be found in the bones of dragons. All the dragons are now gone, but their skeletons remain, hidden in various crevices. Dragons are born of fire, in the hearts of volcanoes, and there they go to die. Their bones turn to glass in the great heat and the glass has magical properties. I know of at least one volcano not a thousand miles from here which secretes the bones of a dragon…'

And the white crane told her the name of the volcano and where she might find the glass bones of a dead dragon.

Mai Song went to her father.

'The white crane said *everyone* knew about dragon's bones, but I didn't.'

'Neither did I, daughter, but then we live on the edge of nowhere and though everyone *else* might know, we are ignorant of such commonly recognised facts.'

Mai Song then told her father she wished to go on a quest to find the bones of a dragon.

The war lord was dreadfully unhappy. 'How can I let my only daughter, an innocent child, go out into the wilderness? You have hardly been outside the walls of the castle, except to take part in the peasant festivals and harvest blessings. There are vicious bandits out there, and giants, and lone monsters who would eat you whole at one swallow. I must go myself.'

'No,' replied Mai Song, 'you must not. I must go. I love Pang Yau and it must be me who saves him from death in the hands of the dark sorcerer.'

The mocking man instantly appeared by her side. 'You?' he scoffed. 'You are but a mere girl, a piece of pink ribbon, an empty-headed female. How could you even imagine you are strong or wise enough to save this prince?'

'Go away,' said Mai Song, coldly. 'You are nothing to me any longer. Once you were the only companion I had, but now I have someone I love, and who loves me, and you are unnecessary.'

The mocking man gave her an angry look before vanishing.

'Who are you talking to, daughter?' asked the war lord. 'This business has turned your mind. Let me go instead, I beg of you? I am a man, used to bearing arms and fighting with the forces of evil. You are but a young woman. I do not want to lose you, daughter. You are all I have left of your mother, whom I loved dearly.'

But Mai Song would not hear of her father taking her place. Instead she asked to borrow his black-and-gold armour, which he wore when he went to battle against the enemies of the marsh people. Her father gladly loaned it to her, along with his sword and his charger. Mai Song needed to pad her limbs and torso, to make the armour fit. Once she was accoutred she set forth on the charger, heading north towards the great volcano the crane had told her about.

Her first night out in the open was not easy. She was unused to raw weather and became damp and cold in the exposed conditions. Mai Song soon learned however, and thereafter sought the shelter of rock overhangs, or gullies, or copses. She found soft mossy banks on which to rest, taught herself how to construct bivouacs and soon became proficient at making fires. She had never lacked hunting skills and had always been good around the marshes of the castle with her little bow. Small mammals were her main fare, and plump birds, supplemented by wild vegetables. There were herbs and spices growing free in the wilderness, which made her meals that much more appetising and nourishing. Gradually, over the days, her physical condition hardened and her mind quickened.

Her father's armour was heavy and chafed her elbows, neck and knees, but she told herself she must get used to that. If she were to be confronted by a foe, she would need to look fearsome, and so had to wear the metal except when sleeping. Her horse was the most important thing in the world to her and she made sure it was fed and watered, groomed and blanketed, even before taking care of herself. This was not just because she had a love of the beasts, but was wise husbandry. Without her horse she would doubtless not survive for very long.

Mai Song's first enemy was a giant who lived in a limestone cave she hoped to use as a night shelter.

The giant was tall and naked, wearing only a gigantic helmet on his head, his body being covered in long hair. His nose was a snout, much like that of a pig's, and his feet were huge and spreading. He came out of the cave at a rush, roaring obscenities and threats.

The mocking man appeared for a few moments.

'Now you're for it,' he crowed. 'You'll be spitted on that monster's teeth before long.'

Mai Song ignored the mocking man, speaking instead to the onrushing giant.

'What are you getting in a fuss about?' she enquired. 'I only wish to share your cave for the night.'

The giant skidded to a halt and stared, then said in thick husky accents, 'You have the voice of a young woman.'

'That's because I am a young woman.'

The giant smiled lasciviously at this having little enough sense or guile to keep his face clean of his thoughts.

'Why, then you can certainly share my cave with me.'

Mai Song made a fire in the cave, since the giant had never known how to work such common wonders. Later, while he stared at her across the flames, she took two of the broken boughs she was using for logs and sharpened the ends with her sword.

'What are you doing?' asked the giant.

'These?' she laughed. 'Don't you know that wood burns better when one end of the log has been cut to a point? We shall need these to start the fire again from its embers, tomorrow morning.'

'I knew that,' muttered the giant with a scowl, 'I just wanted to make sure you did.'

Mai Song slept fitfully in her armour, keeping her sword by her side, while the giant lay awake, his milky eyes on her form. In the early hours she was woken by the giant shaking her shoulders. Sitting up she saw that her sword was on the other side of the cave.

'Wake up,' growled the giant, his voice thick with lust, 'I find that I want you.'

'Oh *that*,' she laughed. 'Just a minute while I put some more wood on the fire. We don't want to be cold, do we?'

She went to the wood pile and picked up the two sharpened stakes. 'Oh,' she then said, with the two stakes poised above the glowing charcoal, 'the fire's a bit low. Can you blow on the embers?'

The giant went down on all fours and started to blow on the coals.

Mai Song quickly rammed the stakes down on the giant's two spread hands, pinning them to the earth. The giant screamed in agony. Mai Song then leaped to snatch up her sword and swiftly decapitated the giant before he could wrench the stakes free.

The giant's head rolled into the fire, his mouth still cursing her. His filthy wild hair was soon in flames, the scorched smell driving her from the cave. Mai Song mounted her charger and sped away, through a low valley. She rode hard and long, but could still hear the giant's severed head shrieking at her from more than a league away.

This was only her first encounter with a problem. In the next few weeks she had to outwit a man-eating tiger which picked her scent, by laying false trails for the creature to follow. She fought and killed a monster snake, which had wrapped its coils around her steed during the night hours. She had wide raging rivers to cross, chasms to negotiate, wandering hordes to avoid. There were villages where the people were kind to her, and gave her food and shelter, and there were villagers who drove her out with stones and shouts the minute she entered their community. Once she unwisely stayed amongst the bone-urns of a graveyard and someone's ancestor rose up and in hollow accents ordered her to be gone from that sacred place before she was forced to stay there permanently.

There were chill and unfriendly mornings when the isolated shrines to wayfarers' gods were sparkling with frost crystals. There were days when the snow lightly covered the bridges across gullies and hid them from her searching eyes. There were nights when the rain came down in silver torrents from an indifferent moon.

Finally, not long after her encounter with the phantom, Mai Song came in sight of the volcano she sought. But before she could begin to scale its heights she was attacked by a group of bandits, coming out of the east, their banners flying from tall black lances. They wore the red armour of men of the south lands and their steeds were stocky ponies with hairy ankles: sturdy little creatures that could cover rough terrain without injury. The riders were short men, with wide shoulders. The bandits hemmed Mai Song in with spear points, until she called them cowards, thieves and murderers, keeping her voice low and masculine this time.

'We are no thieves,' said their chief, furiously. 'We are the dispossessed. Once my family had land until a mandarin from the south stole it from us. We are no murderers. We always give our victims a chance to defend themselves against equal odds. We are certainly no cowards, as I shall prove to you in single combat.'

With these words the man who led the bandits prepared himself for battle.

The mocking man appeared before Mai Song.

'You easily overcame that oaf of an ogre in the cave because he was stupid, but this youth has brains as well as brawn. I think this time, missy, you have met your match. I shall enjoy seeing your entrails decorate the lance of this bandit chief.'

Once again, Mai Song simply ignored the mocking man as if he were not there, and he fumed and fretted, accusing her of incivility and bad manners, before vanishing in a cloud of petulance.

Ringed by the bandits, Mai Song's lack of experience with a blade in battle soon became evident. The bandit chief at first attacked her armour with vigour, causing many dents to appear. But when he saw how inexperienced she was at combat, her wild blows easy to avoid, he was puzzled. What was, quite evidently, a callow youth doing wearing a war lord's armour, wandering around in bandit country? The bandit chief simply began defending himself against the uncontrolled blows she tried to rain down on him in her enthusiasm.

Finally, becoming bored, he disarmed her.

'Let me see the features of one who wears the armour of war lord, but fights like the boy who brings in the kindling,' cried the bandit chief. 'Let me see your face.'

'Let me see yours,' retorted Mai Song, snatching her bow from the saddle of her horse. 'Don't think because I'm not good at sword play that I can't hit a running rat at fifty paces with this bow.'

The bandit chief removed his helmet to reveal the handsome rugged features of a young man.

'I am Chang, of the clan On, whose home was in the far south until his father was killed, his mother raped and murdered, and his home taken from him. Now let us see the stripling behind that armour. Does your father know you are out?'

Mai Song put down her weapon and removed her helmet. 'Yes, he does,' she replied, furiously, 'and he approves.'

On Chang had the good grace to gasp on seeing the face of a woman appear, while his men burst out laughing.

Mai Song spent the night with the bandits, sitting talking around a fire. They said they would have offered to help her in her quest, but they could not because the King of Gwongdong was their sworn enemy. He was the one who robbed them of their heritage. 'This prince you wish to marry,' said On Chang. 'He is not a good man. He cannot be, since he is the son of a very bad man.'

'A son does not have to be like his father,' replied Mai Song, in defence of her lover. 'Pang Yau is all goodness—a pacifist. You would know if you met him. Forgive me for my bluntness, but the following is true. You have been forced into the ways of a nomadic warrior: you are a rough man, not used to finer feelings. That is not your fault, but Pang Yau will teach me about art, writing, and philosophy—things you could not understand, with your way of life—having to kill and loot to make a living.'

'Well,' replied On Chang, generously, 'if you believe him to be this—this demi-god of gentleness, then perhaps he is. Maybe we will help you anyway, even though he is the son of a pig.'

But Mai Song said she wanted no help. She wished to complete the mission on her own. The next morning she left her horse and armour with the bandits and climbed the volcano. It was sweltering on the volcano, as Mai Song approached the rim, for the cone was still active. Not far down inside the lava bubbled and spat. Huge gobbets of molten rock leapt and fell, splattering on the stormy surface of the boiling lake. Liquid stone spurted ribbons of fire across the top of the crater. Mai Song tried to shield her vulnerable eyes from the heat, as she sought the crevice in which the glass bones of the dragon lay.

Finally, she found what she was looking for, but there was very little of the skeleton left. Only three ribs remained. These she gathered in her arms and went back down the slopes of the volcano.

The bandits were intrigued with her discovery. One man among them had been apprentice to a sorcerer, before he was dispossessed. Mai Chang questioned him about the properties of the three ribs.

The man inspected them carefully. 'These two bones are from the upper part of the skeleton,' he announced, 'close to the shoulders. If struck, one of them will shatter all glass within a region of a thousand miles. Similarly, if struck, the note from the second rib will open all locks within a hundred miles. The last rib, the smallest, I recognise immediately. It is the rib from which sprouted the dragon's right wing. If this glass rib is struck, its note will summon the winged horse of Tang. She is the fastest steed in all China and will carry you anywhere you wish to go with the greatest of speed...'

'But,' said Mai Song, 'how will I know which of the two large ribs will open the lock to my lover's prison? If I strike the wrong rib, the other, being made of glass, will shatter.'

The sorcerer's apprentice shrugged in sympathy. 'I do not know how you will accomplish your task. The ribs are identical. There is no way you can tell by looking at them, which is the one to shatter glass, and which to open locks. I can't help you. I'm sorry.'

On Chang sat with her and pored over the two glass ribs, trying to find some mark or symbol which would give her a clue as to the identity of the magic contained within. After three hours they had exhausted every possibility. Mai Song thanked On Chang for his help. She then struck the small rib with her sword. A high note rang out and the rib immediately shattered into a million fragments.

A whinnying sound was heard on the wind, then suddenly a magnificent horse appeared in the sky, flying down towards the bandit camp. The golden mare with a blonde mane and tail had huge feathered wings on its flanks. The wonderful beast shone in the sun as it swooped to land nearby. Once on the ground it folded its beautiful wings and stood waiting, pawing the ground gently, for its mistress.

Mai Song said goodbye to the bandits. She left them her father's charger, armour and sword, requesting that they be delivered when the bandits next swept by her father's castle on their way to pillaging Gwongdong. On Chang said he would hand them to her father personally. Mai Song then wished the bandits well in their fight to regain the clan's lands and castle, after which she mounted the great horse of Tang. In her belt were the two glass bones of the dragon, like curved swords one on either hip. Her face was set and purposeful.

Into the air she went, her hair flowing behind her as a stream of jet. High above the plains and fields the flying horse took her, until the world was spread below her. She could see fine brown rivers wriggling like long worms across the land. There were green squares which were the paddy fields of rice plants, and white-tipped mountains in the distance, and rugged wasteland around the water margin. It became colder the closer she went to the sun, which seemed a strange thing to her.

Finally, after a long flight, the mare began to descend. It landed near a dark building made of huge blocks of granite. It was without any windows and there was only one door made of heavy grey slabs of slate. There were no hinges on the door. A flat iron girder halfway down the door, its ends buried in the granite either side of the doorway, held the slate monstrosity in place. There was a massive lock in the middle of this girder, cryptic in design and no doubt in operation.

Mai Song alighted from the horse of Tang. She stood before the sorcerer's castle, with its single high tower, and pondered on her problem. There was no white crane to help her now. Her lover's fate was in her hands and if she failed Pang Yau would remain a prisoner forever, his soul feeding the damned. Mai Song prayed to her gods, especially Wong Tai Sin, the goatboy whose visions had helped many lost spirits. This time however, Wong Tai Sin did not answer the orisons. It might be that he knew the woman already had the answer, if only she could find it deep within her keen brain, recognise it, bring it out into the light.

'You will never find the key,' murmured a silky voice near to her ear. 'You are a silly woman. Give up now. Go home, live in obscurity, before you make a fool of yourself once more.'

She knew the mocking man had appeared again, by her side, but she steadfastly refused to acknowledge his presence. Instead she concentrated on her problem. As she was thinking, she kicked idly at a stone, which shot from her foot and struck another stone. The two rocks cracked together, to fly off in different directions. At that moment Mai Song had the answer and turned to laugh in the mocking man's misty face. 'You are the fool,' she said. 'You spend your whole time trying to destroy me with your bitterness and hate. Well this is the last time I want to see you. Do you understand? To appear before me again would be quite useless. I will never look at you again, nor will I hear your foul tongue. You are dead to me.'

The mocking man wailed and rippled away rapidly into the middle distance where he waited to see what would happen.

Mai Song took the two glass ribs from her belt and struck them both together, thus producing a note simultaneously from each rib. Both ribs shattered immediately, but at the same time a loud *CLANK!* came from the keyhole set in the iron bar. The knitted lock had unravelled itself. The great slate door fell forward with a crash, into the dust, leaving the way from Pang Yau's prison wide open. Pang Yau came walking through the doorway to freedom, just as the whole castle began collapsing. It seemed that the slate door had also been the keystone to the ugly construction. It was soon no more than a jumble of blocks lying scattered in the dirt. Mai Song hoped that the sorcerer himself was buried under their weight.

'My darling,' said the prince, taking her in his arms, 'you passed all the tests with flying colours!'

Mai Song was confused. She pushed Pang Yau out to arm's length. Studying him, he did not look like someone who had been incarcerated in total darkness, within cold stone walls, for many months. He was smiling gently at her, his mouth a curved crescent below his narrow nose. She compared him with the pathetic mocking man, who still stood whining some distance away. The darkness had now blown away from the creature who had tormented her since she was twelve years of age.

The two figures could have been twin brothers, they were so much alike.

'A test?' said Mai Song, in a disbelieving tone. 'A *test*? Where is the dark sorcerer who imprisoned you? Are you trying to tell me there is no such person? Was all this engineered by you and your father's wizard? I don't understand, Pang Yau.'

The prince was too full of himself to notice the dramatic change in her voice and expression.

'I see you have been comparing me with myself!' he said, nodding towards the mocking man. 'Yes, I have been with you all along, since I first saw you leaning over the battlements of your father's castle. I fell in love with you then, but there was a problem. My father would not consent to a marriage to a lowly marsh lord's daughter. Only when I agreed to put you through a series of tests did my father agree to even consider the match.

'First I had to try to destroy your will. My father's wizard fashioned an image of me for this purpose, an engine of sorcery which you call the mocking man. It was the mocking man's task to bend you, to try to break your spirit, though I always knew you would win through. We even sent "hope" in the form of the white crane, for there must always be a tiny fragment of hope around to make the torture complete. Those without hope simply fall into apathy and listlessness. There is no victory for a mocking man in forcing a state of indifference.

'Yet, still you did not succumb to the torment. You battled through as I knew you surely would. I am so proud of you. This last great test, to free me from a sorcerer's power, has lifted you up even higher in my eyes. Not only are you virtuous, but full of courage and ability. You are truly worthy to be the wife of one of the most powerful princes in all China. How could my father have ever doubted you? I certainly did not.'

'I don't know,' Mai Song replied, in a quiet determined voice, 'but I do know this. I was wrong in my earlier judgement. So very wrong. It is sad, but I find you are your father's son after all.'

And with those final words to her erstwhile lover, Mai Chang mounted the great horse of Tang. She left Pang Yau standing on the windy plains. The vestiges of the mocking man moved to clutch at his raiment as swirling mist clings to the bark of trees. Mai Song flew off towards the camp of On Chang the bandit.

It has been the report of those who claim to have seen her since, that the daughter of the war lord joined the bandits in their fight against the King of Gwongdong. It has been said that she ruthlessly slew the king's son in savage battle on the wilderness beyond the water margin. There are those who say she found love and are ready to swear that the demi-god Wong Tai Sin was a witness at her wedding to On Chang of the bandits.

I am inclined to believe these matters.

WAYANG KULIT

(I was fascinated by a *wayang kulit* hanging in Gwyneth Jones' house in 1986 and so jumped at the chance to see a shadow-puppet show in Bali three years later. This is an attempt at a monochrome story.)

1

SHE CLOSED THE DOOR GENTLY and was gone, and her leaving made little difference to the ambience of the room.

I lay on the rough-hewn bed, with its carved end posts, for another hour, just staring at the ceiling. Then I got up and went out onto the balcony. It was five-thirty in the evening and the sun was setting on the Balinese rice terraces. A beautiful, light-green landscape surrounded the hut, the tiers dropping away to the front and rising above behind. The hut seemed to be floating like some forgotten gazebo in an emperor's garden. Beyond the fields, in the far distance, was Gunung Agung, one of the many dominating active volcanoes.

The duck herders were calling in their flocks on the rice terraces. The herders carried bamboo staves, twice the height of a man, which slimmed out to whip thin at the top and were arched, weighted by a coloured rag. They stuck this in the ground and their ducks gathered around it. When they finally left, the ducks following, the tall crooks made the herders appear stately, like princes in the midst of a gabbling rabble.

I sat in the rickety bamboo chair and drank some cold tea.

It was the forest at the back of the town that had frightened her. The mosquitoes, even the cockroaches and snakes, didn't bother her as much as they did me, but the forest had troubled her. We had been out walking and I insisted we follow a path through the undergrowth. She would have none of it, saying she didn't like the shafts of light, lancing the lacework canopy. They worried her, especially when there was a breeze, stirring the branches, causing the patterns on the ground to change.

What are you afraid of? I had asked her.

Of getting lost, she replied.

But there's a path through to the other side, I said.

Not that kind of lost, she had answered—*lost forever*.

This answer was incomprehensible to me and I gave way to my temper, shouting at her, calling her an idiot. It was, I saw now, inexcusable of me, but the damage had been done. I was not forgiven. Later she told me she was leaving.

We had been thrown together in a vernacular hut in the middle of rice fields and I guess it had put a strain on the relationship. Maybe it wasn't the forest? Maybe it was us—or just me? Maybe she'd discovered, after seven days together, seven nights together, she just didn't like me? Or that our cultures were too different? Hell, I didn't know.

Anyway, I sure as heck wasn't going to stay on Bali now and thought I might go to the coast tomorrow, to find a ferry.

I went indoors again and had an all-over wash in the mandi at the back. A kind of concrete bath with a saucepan for splashing water over oneself, the mandi substituted for a shower in the cheaper accommodation. I was on a backpacking holiday, using the Lonely Planet Guide. It meant I was free to do as I wished, go anywhere I pleased, and pick up whatever accommodation was available. Nyoman, a local woman, had attached herself to me several weeks ago, and I had begun to think we were in love with each other, but those feelings had evaporated.

I dressed in shirt and slacks, and remembering the mosquitoes, thick socks. Then with torch in pocket I took the raised narrow paths down to the town, which happened to be Ubud, the place of the artists and carvers. Everywhere there were paintings for sale, and textiles, and wood carvings. I had already bought a root carving of a lizard emerging from its hole, and a painting of Garuda surrounded by villagers. Nyoman had persuaded me to buy both the carving and the picture.

Nyoman was fashioned in the fay mould of the Balinese. She had dainty limbs and a light step. She had the shy smile and quiet demeanour. I was beginning to miss her already.

As I walked down the main street, pieces of paper were thrust into my hands by hopeful touts. There was one inviting me to an 'old ritual dance—*sanghyang*—a trance dance in which Rama sets out to rescue Sita from the clutches of the Demon King assisted by a huge army of monkeys'. The flier wasn't clear whether the monkeys were with Rama, or with the Demon King, but knowing the local monkeys it was probably the latter. One had bitten Nyoman on the ankle when I wasn't looking.

There were the usual Barong and Kris dances, a dedari dance and a jaran dance, but the one that took my attention immediately was an invitation to a *wayang kulit*.

I had read a good deal about the shadow puppet plays and I knew that tourists did not often get invited. The *wayang kulit* had religious significance and was actually performed mostly in temples during the day: was for some reason necessary to the temple rituals. The *dalang*, or puppet master, was a consecrated priest, a mystic, and was regarded with some awe.

I went back to the man who had given me the *wayang kulit* flier.

'I can go to this?' I asked.

'Yes mister.'

'How much?'

He named me a figure in rupees, which seemed reasonable. One might bargain for a bemo taxi, or a carving, but not for a ticket to a shadow play.

'I'll take one,' I said.

'Two?' he asked, seemingly puzzled

He had obviously seen me with Nyoman.

'No, *one*,' I replied, firmly.

He nodded and then looked me in the eyes. 'You want for someone to come with you?'

I stared at him for a moment, then said, 'You mean *you*?'

He smiled disarmingly. 'I can tell you about the shadow puppets. It will mean nothing otherwise.'

I nodded. He was right. Although I knew a good deal already the *wayang kulit* was immensely complicated and complex, full of heroes and heroines, demons and ogres, and a cast of hundreds. I might enjoy the spectacle, but I would have only a vague idea what was going on. The stories were from sacred classical literature, written originally on palm-leaf manuscripts, and brought to life mythic beings from both the natural and supernatural worlds. It would help to have someone with an inherent knowledge of the art.

'You're hired,' I said. 'How much?'

He shook his head, smiling. 'You pay my ticket.'

All he wanted was to get to see the show himself. That was fair enough. He knew I would probably tip him too, but that wasn't an essential, only a possible extra.

'What's your name?' I asked.

'Ketut,' he replied, and I remembered that Balinese have only four first names—Wayan, Made, Nyoman and Ketut—which they give to their children in that order. After Ketut, the sequence is begun again. My companion was his parent's fourth, or eighth, or twelfth child.

I left Ketut, promising to meet him outside the Frog Pond Inn at seven. The shadow puppet show was in a village just outside Klungkung, the centre of an old Balinese kingdom. It was some thirty kilometres away and would take us at least an hour on the poor back roads, past endless Hindu temples and lily ponds, banana plantations and wayside shrines.

Walking towards the Frog Pond Inn, where I intended to eat, I strolled past the open shops and looked round suddenly, half-expecting to see Nyoman behind me. She had followed me around in life for so long I now took her presence for granted. A very quiet woman with little to say, happy to be with someone without imposing her personality upon them, much of the time you almost forgot she was there. It was only when you noticed some change, perhaps in the light, that you remembered she was accompanying you. These were not conditions I would have wished on her, or anyone, but were a fact of her existence. I used to tease her, saying she must be a closet Carmelite nun, and had taken a vow of silence.

It was not just me who saw her in this way. In a crowd, at a party, she was hardly noticed. Even if someone took the trouble to speak to her, they did so self-consciously, as if they were afraid they might be accused of talking to themselves.

The street was empty behind me and I continued my stroll.

Ketut met me at the arranged time and we boarded a rickety bus full of German tourists bound for Klungkung. Just over an hour later I was sitting with a bottle of Fanta in my hand, in a palm-leafed long hut, lit only by a single 25-watt bulb which dangled, bare of any shade, from the central rafter. Around me were several Germans, one or two Australians and New Zealanders, and half a dozen British tourists.

The rest of the room was jam-packed with locals, children and adults. The Balinese are a small, dusky, ethereal people— self-effacing and diffident—with a lightness of form which made me feel like a pantomime oaf. They seemed so much closer to the living earth on their volcanic island, a garden land of blooms and lush greenery, volatile yet with a deep, delicate beauty.

In front of me was a make-shift raised booth. I had already walked around this object. There was a white cotton screen illuminated by a coconut oil lamp, whose light was soft and evocative. Under the lamp, cross-legged, inside the booth, sat the *dalang*, the puppet master. He was meditating when I passed by him: preparing himself for the performance during which he would exceed the bounds of reality, for himself and his audience, if not in actuality.

The *pusaka*, or puppet chest, passed down through families as an heirloom, stood at the end of the booth.

Within arm's reach, down either side of the booth, were the shadow puppets, made of buffalo hide. They were flat, intricate cut-outs of gods, heroes and heroines, painted and chiselled according to precise traditional requirements.

'First tonight is a Hindu myth,' whispered Ketut. '*Kala Purana*. In this the demon-god Kala wishes to devour twin brothers born in the week of Tumpek Wayang. The *dalang* Empu Lègèr conquers him by shadow play and purifying...'

'You mean ritual exorcism? A shadow play within a shadow play, eh?' I wanted to show that I had taken the trouble to read some of the background myths. 'Is this the one where Kresna smashes the demon king's head to pieces?'

'No,' replied Ketut. 'That is *Bomantaka*.'

I could hear by the reverent tone he used that he regarded the shadow theatre with intense seriousness.

'You believe this is very holy?' I asked him.

He nodded, slowly. 'The wayang has hidden secret wisdom concerning the meaning of life.'

'You said *first*—are there two shows tonight?'

'Yes. Second comes *Bima Suci*, where the Pandawa brother Prince Bima is sent into the forest by a false priest to fetch holy water. Bima is attacked by ogre but he slits its throat with his long fingernail, *waspenek...*' Ketut showed me one of his own long nails and drew it across his neck. 'The ogre's soul becomes the god, Indra. Bima takes the head of the ogre back to the Brahmana priest who sent him into the forest and the priest then confesses the holy water is in the middle of the ocean.

'Bima meets large snakes there and cuts off their heads, but he dies in the water. When he is dead he asks the god Tunggal three questions: why does man have to die? why does man dream? what is the purest thing on earth? Tunggal says man dies when the gods leave his body, man dreams to let his soul out to wander and nothing on the earth is flawless, even flowers, though the god of love, Semara, is the purest in heaven.

'When Tunggal answers the questions, he opens his legs and the Prince Bima goes into his body through his phallus. In heaven Bima finds the holy water in a gold casket on a five-tiered shrine. He takes this and goes home, to rejoice with his family. The lying priest is punished.'

He had obviously memorised this passage of English translation from a guidebook of some kind, but before I could comment the electric light went out and a hushed atmosphere seized the spectators in this monochromatic drama.

The lamplight was even more subtle now, illuminating the screen with a deep yellow glow. It might have been the moon behind that cotton divider. The musicians in the small orchestra began playing on percussion instruments and the Tree of Life appeared in shadow form on the screen. Then characters began to enter, the epic unfolded, while the *dalang* recited the story at the same time as manipulating his puppets.

Very soon I was lost in the enthralling play on the screen before me. The puppets were handled with such rapidity, such skill and deftness, that after a while the rhythms of the shadows became a mesmerising sequence of dexterous movements before my eyes, hypnotising me. It did not matter that I did not fully understand the plot, or that many of the characters were anonymous to me, it was the vibrant shadows creating dramatic stimuli that held me spellbound, commanded absolutely my attention. I drowned in the performance.

Arrows flew across the screen, sword fights were enacted, and surely, surely, there were at least a dozen characters, a dozen voices, at any one time in the thick of great battles, while the *dalang* only had one mouth, one pair of hands? How were these wonders achieved, if not by mysticism and magic? This holy man behind the screen was himself a puppet of the gods, his mind wholly engaged by them, his hands assisted by theirs. There was a kind of wizardry in force, in which the priest was but the master, and we the audience were his neophytes.

The music was insistent, adding to the mesmeric voice, the hypnotic movements. At times it was monotonous, dulling my senses to the point of utter receptivity; at other times it was sweet and beguiling, persuading me to open my perceptions; and lastly it could be almost cacophonic, loudly demanding my attention and my submission.

We were participants too, in the frenetic activity being played out on the screen, this battle involving men and gods, demons and monsters. Our hearts were black shadows awaiting the deadly dagger; our eyes perceived threats to our personal safety; our hands itched to wield weapons.

These were not simply dark images, icons flitting across a screen: they were immediately true.

We were drawn into new ways of comprehending reality, sitting in that room.

The battles on the screen became more frantic, more intense, until the villains were vanquished and the heroes victorious.

The two performances had taken almost five hours during which many of the tourists had left quietly and gone home. I guessed that many of them had got bored, especially since they could not take flash photographs, the curse of the modern traveller.

I staggered outside the long hut to get some air, grateful for the perfume of the frangipani blossoms after the closeness of so many bodies with their unavoidable human smells. Then just as the bus was about to leave, I realised my watch had gone from my wrist. Using my torch I searched the immediate area, but couldn't see it anywhere.

'Hold the bus,' I said to Ketut, and went back inside the hut to look around where I had been sitting.

I couldn't find the light switch, so I used my torch to search the floor.

While I had my head down, there was a sudden *clack* from the platform above. It sounded as if someone was still there. When I looked I saw that the lamp was still on at the back of the booth. It was quiet and still in the hut now: a kind of hushed hallowed silence had descended upon the place in the absence of the *dalang*. Then the *clack* came again.

I switched the torch off and tip-toed up the steps to the platform and stared in the booth, the temple of this priest-wizard with the magic hands.

Surprisingly, it was empty except for the shadow puppets, still in their sockets ranged along both sides of the booth. Had one of them slipped and made the sound I had heard? Their strange cut-out heads and bodies looked sinister in the flickering yellow glow. There was fat Merdah, and Tualèn, and big-bellied Sangut, the great hero Kresna, and the kakayonan, the tree of life and sacred centre of the universe.

Their colours—the ochres, cobalt blues, blacks, Chinese yellows, whites, pinks—all glistened attractively in the lamplight. Their stillness made them appear strangely menacing after the frenetic activity they had shown during the performance. It was as if they were awaiting a signal to leap into violent action, like a cat that appears not to be paying attention to a bird, until the bird hops within reach of its instant spring.

I stared at the flat, cut-out puppets, fascinated by the elaborate filigree work upon their decorative forms. Narrowed eyes stared back at me, steadily, unmoving. It was difficult not to think of these pieces of leather as animate in the smoky atmosphere from the lamp. Which one of them had moved in its socket? They were all at a slight angle, none of them poker straight in their holders.

I could smell strong fragrance of the coconut oil burning, trapped inside the booth. There was also a residue stink of sweat and activity, and underlying smells of hardwood and buffalo hide. This heady mixture of scents made me feel a little giddy.

For some reason I felt impelled to enter the booth, and did so, my heart beating faster than usual. I gazed at the lamp which hung from the rafters. In the original palm-leaf manuscript of the myth *Sigwagama*, the lamp was played by Brahma himself, while Iswara was the *dalang* and Wisnu the musical instruments. That Brahma was light and could create shadows made him the most powerful of the three, even though the manipulator was Iswara and Wisnu played with the senses.

I happened to glance behind me as I was crawling into the central space and saw my own shadow on the cotton sheet. I suddenly thought, *what am I doing here? I might be guilty of desecrating some holy place*. If the *dalang* returned, or one of his assistants, I might be in serious trouble.

Yet I did not turn and go. I was transfixed by my own dark shape on the sheet, where so recently the myths had been re-enacted. My silhouette now stood frozen where gods had played, where heroes had run, where ogres had danced. There was a strange sensation of looking into another world, of standing alone on the threshold of a mythical kingdom. I was like some shambling giant, lurking at the gates, waiting to be told that I might enter and take my place amongst the lower shadow forms.

At that moment, while I stared at my foreshortened silhouette on the screen, the door opened at the back of the hut. One of the puppets moved in the breeze from the outside, dropped forward, with a *clack*, so that its shadow fell across my shadow. Staring, I saw that it was the puppet of Kala, Lord of the Demons, which had slipped in its holder. His frightening outline had closed with mine on the white screen.

A chill went through me.

'Are you there, mister?' said Ketut, softly.

I scrambled out from behind the booth, feeling shocked. Ketut's eyes opened wide when he saw me. I tried to explain that I thought perhaps one of the musicians might have picked up my watch and left it there, but I don't think he believed me for one moment. He looked at my hands, probably expecting to see I had stolen a puppet, but when he saw this was not so, he murmured that we should be catching the bus.

What he did see, however, and this surprised me as much as it did him, was that my watch was still on my wrist.

We were mostly quiet with one another on the way back. The bus was being jolted this way and that, by an uneven road full of potholes. I couldn't understand why I thought my watch had been missing, when it had been on my wrist all the time. Had I been hypnotised in some way, during the performance? It was the only explanation I could give for such a mistake.

With the constant jarring I began to develop a pain in my shoulders, which began to make me feel ill.

I did manage to ask Ketut, 'What is the main function of Kala? What does he do?'

Ketut replied, 'He eats men.'

By the time we reached Ubud I was in agony. Ketut kept looking at me: sidelong glances which told me that my appearance was not good. When the bus stopped, he hurried off, thanking me over his shoulder for buying his ticket. I made my way to the rice terraces, where my path lay.

I didn't need my torch. It was a full moon. The peaked houses, their rooftops sweeping upwards to horned points in the Indonesian manner, were casting shadows on the ground. Clustered together as the houses were, the shadows tended to be complex criss-crossings of shade. There were latticework fences too, which overlaid these designs on the ground. I tried to avoid their dark networks, since they reminded me of the shapes of puppets cast on a cotton screen.

I reached the forest in front of the rice terraces and again the shadows locked and interlocked: this time they were moving, as the treetops of the canopy were blown by the wind. They formed and reformed figures on the forest floor, and this time I *had* to walk through them, since I could reach the rice terraces no other way. As I hurried through them, they seemed to gather to one single giant shape, which stalked my own shadow.

I began to run. It was as if I were being pursued through the trees, by some predator, and my heart was banging against my ribs, though I didn't dare look behind in case I saw something unreal. I was absolutely convinced now that I had been hypnotised and I was not going to allow the art of the hypnotist to fill my eyes as well as my head with fictitious horrors.

I emerged onto the terrace paths, feeling safer out in the open fields, with no trees to cast shadows.

How was I going to shake this fantasy that gripped my conscious? Someone was having a very cruel joke at my expense. I was sure that once I was in my hut, with the artificial light on, I could break the mood and shed these terrible feelings.

As I hurried along I saw a man coming towards me, a duck herder, probably on his way home from a friend's house.

Since the path was narrow, with room for only one person, I stopped so that we could step around one another carefully.

The man obviously did not notice me until the very last second, when he almost ran into me, and then his eyes went white around the edges. He stared at me for a second, as if peering into a dark hole, then muttered what sounded like a prayer or chant, before stepping into the paddy water and hurrying on. He looked back once, before he reached the drop to the next tier.

Watching him I had the terrible feeling that he had hardly been able to see me, yet it was extremely bright under that great moon. The deleterious pain in my shoulder began again.

I looked around me and saw that I was standing under a duck herder's crook, left sticking in the mud. The rag on the top fluttered in the breeze, casting a changing shadow near my own dark shape. There, in the light of the full moon, I saw that the rag's shadow had formed itself into the puppet shape of Kala, the devourer of men.

Kala's form was eating my shadow.

Already much of my shadow had been consumed, in the streets, in the forest, and now under the staff's rag. There were great chunks missing from around the shoulders and the back. My neck was now a gander's neck, with a huge grotesque head perched on top, where the shadow had been eaten away.

I recoiled quickly in horror, only to see Kala's black form dart forward and begin feasting again, as the wind increased in strength and bent the duck herder's pole.

The pain was excruciating now.

I laughed out loud, hysterically, the sound echoing over the rice terraces. Surely, surely this was just some trick of the light? This was no Brahman lamp, this moon, and I was no *wayang kulit*, no shadow puppet.

Yet, on the other hand, it occurred to me that in any shadow world the shadows must be the main characters, and the objects that cast them subordinate to the shadows' needs and desires.

I was in their world at the moment, the world in which they held sway. I had entered through the dimension of the *wayang kulit*, which had seduced my mind into passing through the gate, and the power was in the hands of the shadows.

My own weak shadow was now a ragged thing as the ravenous Kala moved over it, devouring it ferociously, like a starving wolf consumes its kill.

I turned and ran, heading for my hut, desperate to get out of the light of the moon before my shadow was totally destroyed, for the man who casts no shadow is not there. He no longer exists in this world.

When I reached the hut the voracious Kala, using the waving palms around the hut to cast his shape, began feasting once again. Weak now, I fell on the steps of the hut, unable to shake off the dark creature on my shadow's back. By the time I was able to crawl through the doorway, little was left except a few wisps of me. I felt ravaged, tattered, my shadow a weathered black banner that had been through many battles, many seasons.

I lay in the safety of the darkness feeling shaken and terrified. Awake for several hours my mind ran away in a panic, knowing that the sun would rise the next morning, and most likely the moon at night. I was trapped inside this hut, unable to turn on the light. Kala must have been laughing, knowing I would have to come out some time. So long as he was patient, I would be delivered to him eventually.

The next morning it was bright, sunny day and I cowered in the corner of my hut, afraid to be caught in any of the beams that cut through the gaps in the curtains. At three o'clock however, the sky clouded over and a tropical storm threatened. It was soon dark enough for me to leave the hut without casting a shadow.

I hurried out to find Ketut.

At first he tried he ignore me, but when he saw how distressed I had become, he motioned for me to step off the street into the house of his parents.

'You must help me,' I cried, watching the distant lightning on the horizon getting closer by the minute.

Ketut listened to my story and then told me we had to find the *dalang* quickly. He took me by the hand and led to me to a temple at the end of Monkey Forest Road. By this time it was raining hard—a torrential monsoon downpour that could drown a cat if it didn't find shelter—and I had no fear of shadows. The pressure of the rain caused palms to genuflect, turned dirt streets to muddy rivers, and lowered visibility to zero.

Once in the gloom of the temple's recesses, with the rain thundering on the metal roof, Ketut went off to find the *dalang*. He reappeared a little later.

'Come,' he said, beckoning me towards a small room. 'The *dalang* will help you.'

I entered the room in which the same *dalang* sat cross-legged in the centre of a large palm-leaf mat. A small, wiry man with dark eyes, the *dalang* motioned for me to sit down on the mat. I did as I was told, knowing I was in his hands completely.

Ketut said, 'He wants you to turn sideways.'

A profile. Right. Once I was in the correct position, the *dalang* took out a wad of dirty cloth and unrolled it. In it were a row of small chisels and knives, which glinted in the dull light from the doorway. He began cutting and shaping a piece of stiff hide, scraping out hollows, chiselling holes, perforating the tough leather, working swiftly. I realised what was happening, of course. He was making a *wayang kulit* from my silhouette.

I was to be a shadow puppet.

While the *dalang* was working, Ketut left me alone with him for a while, returning after a few minutes.

Once the form was cut, it was painted and hung up to dry.

Ketut said, 'Later the *dalang* will add the sticks. You must now go back to the darkness of your room. Tonight the *dalang* will use your puppet in the story of *Bomantaka*.'

'What will happen? How will that help me?' I asked.

Ketut said seriously, 'Your shadow must kill the shadow of Kala, king of the demons, to free yourself of him.'

A chill went through me. I didn't dare ask what would happen if my shadow failed. What if Kala killed *me* instead, then ate my puppet's shadow? Would that mean the end of me too? *The man without a shadow is not there.* I knew it would probably mean my death too, as well as that of my shadow.

I went back to my hut on the rice terraces to find Nyoman had returned. The shutters to the hut were still closed and it was hot inside. She was lying on the bed in the darkness. She patted the bed beside her.

'Come,' she said, 'you must lie with me. Ketut called me on the phone and told me what has happened.'

There were no more words needed. I lay down beside her and waited. She held my hand. I think I fell asleep just as the ducks were being called in for the night.

2

I AM BEHIND A ROCK near the trunk of the Tree of Life. Sooner or later all things must pass by the Tree. It is a huge growth, reaching halfway to the clouds, and spreads its canopy massively over a third of the world. Here and there a great branch dips to the earth, then rises again as a mighty river of bark. In its flourishing vast network of leafy branches, more numerous than the blades of grass in the true world, are all manner of creatures, real and unreal: birds and beasts, mythological beings and monsters. Their forms proliferate. Spots, stripes, dark and light, but no colour, for this is the land of shadows. They decorate its foliage. They are part of the tree, growing with it, from it, in it. They are its fruit, its nuts, its buds and blossoms.

As well as growing and nourishing every known creature, except man, the arboreal god is a provider of real fruits: figs, oranges, grapefruits, limes, lemons, walnuts, hazelnuts, coconuts, grapes, bananas and every fruit known to humankind as well as those fictitious delicacies which adorn the mosaic walls in forgotten temples deep inside the last jungles.

There are greys within greys, shade upon shade: there are as many delicate monochromatic tones as the colours of the real world in the Tree of Life, hiding some things, revealing others, constantly unfolding new wonders, endlessly concealing old ones. It is life, uncurling like a fern, twisting in agony like a wounded creature, cryptically opening a flower of stunning shadowed beauty here, secretly closing a faded bloom there.

This is the wonder under which I wait, a long curved dagger in my right hand, my heart beating madly with fear. What if I fail? What if the great Kala swallows my shadow, my soul? Shall I then be *nothing* in the universe?

Lone warriors have passed me by, armed to the teeth with an extraordinary arsenal of weapons—spiked objects, deadly pointed missiles, strange ropes and leathers—some of which I can only guess at the use. Bands of brigands, monsters, ogres, fairies and giants, all have wandered past, some clearly looking for war, others avoiding it.

Armies too have marched by the enormous trunk, their feet and horses' hooves thundering on the hard dark earth, their generals magnificently arrayed in dull armour.

Sometimes these armies meet on the plain to fight and the air sings with arrows, wails with spears, clatters with the blades of swords. Thousands fall, their blood mingling with the dust, and heroes rise out of the dead, silvery heroes shining with pure brilliance, their sword in one hand, the Ring of Truth in the other. Their followers rally, inspired by the magnificent spectacle of light-rising-from-darkness, to clash again with the foe, to send them fleeing north, west, east and south, over the fading edges of the world, into the void which surrounds the land of shadows.

Around me the lone and level plain falls away on all sides, disappears at the edges into misty regions of the unknown, where perhaps lurk even more grisly creatures—perhaps some that would stop a man's heart dead just by their mere appearance?

I hear a sound behind me! Out of a cave-hole in the ground a giant, horned serpent has appeared. Sparks fly from its eyes. Its foul breath has the stink of brimstone and flames hiss from its nostrils. Its tail, when it appears, is a club of spikes, each tipped with some terrible toxin whose drips instantly wither the leaves on shrubs. Bat-wings unfold with leathery cracklings. As it moves towards me, scales drop from its skin, razor sharp, to slice and bury themselves into the earth like skimmed metal shields.

It opens its mouth to reveal not just two, but rows of fangs each as long as the curved knife I hold in my hand. It prepares to strike, rearing back, and I have only my dagger to protect me. As the beast's head descends, jaws open wide, I fling the dagger down its throat with all my strength. The creature screams in agony, writhing away from me, thrashing its loathsome coils in the dust beneath the Tree of Life. It squirms and convulses, tying itself in knots, until finally it disappears back down the dark tunnel from whence it first emerged.

At that moment Kala appears on the horizon, taller than six ordinary men, his great feet pounding the earth. He roars, triumphantly and I now know it was he who sent the serpent, to wrest my weapon from me. Kala, the great evil one, king of the demons, devourer of men, comes thundering over the plain. His face is a cruel mask of savagery. There is no mercy in his lustful eyes, only DEATH and GREED, both of which are his rulers. His arms have the strength of mighty apes, his legs the power of stallions. From his chest armour and shoulder straps dangle a thousand shrunken skulls—eaten men—and from his hips and thighs dried gristle and rattling bones. A belt of human hair supports the scabbard of his terrible scimitar.

Kala, humpbacked, thick-chested and starey-eyed, a dwarf figure fleshed into a giant, has magic in those hands that can bend the strongest metal. There is sorcery in those feet that can crush rocks to powder. He believes he is invincible, but he has been destroyed, many times, by a great hero. He wants my flesh, my bones, my soul. He wants to devour me. He has tasted of my shadow and is now obsessed with the tang of me on his palate. He must have me to gratify his insatiable appetite for the bodies and souls of men.

I am helpless against his onslaught. My dagger has gone, tricked from me by the demon-king. There is nowhere to run to, for the world is too small to hide from Kala. I stand and wait in terror as his ferocious form pounds towards me.

In the suspended moment before I am snatched up into his brutal jaws a figure leaps from behind the trunk of the Tree of Life. It is Nyoman armed with two bright swords. Nyoman, sheathed from head to foot in black leather armour. Nyoman, light as a dancer on her feet, dextrous as a juggler with her weapons. She stands before Kala, challenging him with her stance, her bright blades swishing the air before his eyes, slicing away the darkness he has trailed with him across the plains.

'Nyoman!' I shout.

Kala lunges at her with a heavy arm, but Nyoman skips out of the way, slashing the hand. Dark blood spurts forth from the wound and Kala screams in agony and rage. He stamps with his horny heel, trying to squash this little warrior, only to receive yet another deep wound in the tender bridge of his foot.

Kala clutches at a branch on the Tree of Life as he staggers back, his foot gushing blood. The branch is unable to support his great weight and snaps away. He falls, crashing to the dust, and the world shakes as in an earthquake. Nyoman leaps onto his chest and begins stabbing this way and that, at the throat, in the shoulder joints, at the eyes. Kala is blinded. In his terrible sightless fury he grips the small figure on his breast, but his fingers slide from the oiled leather armour. She is a slippery lizard, unable to be grasped, dancing the dance of death on Kala's form.

'Quickly,' she calls to me, 'it must be you who delivers the mortal stroke.'

Nearby is the branch which was torn from the Tree of Life. Where it has broken away the torn end is sharp, like the jagged point of a stake. I snatch this weapon, jump onto Kala's chest, and plunge the stake into his heart. There is a flood, a fountain of blood shoots forth, high as a cedar. Kala lets out a loud, hollow moan, which fills every crevice in the land of shadows, and echoes back and forth through the distant mountains and valleys on the edge of the world.

Kala quivers and shimmers like a black poplar in the wind, his protruding eyes full of the terror of DEATH, the GREED in them shrinking rapidly as the light fades, and his armour rattles, shaking me from his breast. His pupils dwindle to the size of black gnats and his limbs wither. His teeth rot and crumble in his mouth. Down between the massive thighs, his once huge phallus shrivels until it resembles a tiny root. His scrotum bag deflates like a dead puffball and splits open: a dusty powder spills out and blows away on the warm night breezes, seeding the grasses with impotent evil.

Kala is dead.

'Thank you, Nyoman,' I say, 'I owe you my whole existence.'

'I am yours and you are mine,' she says, then she walks away, over the lone and level plains.

I stare at the giant Kala and shudder. Even in death he is a terrible sight. Then the wonderful Kresna, comes out of the east, his blue-black form shining with holy beauty. His tall, handsome figure comes to stand beside me and I feel the glow of his Goodness, and Righteous Wickedness, filling my heart. His hand is on my shoulder, as he tells me, 'Someone has done my work for me...'

3

I AWOKE FROM MY DREAM in the safety of the darkness and found myself on the bed. I remembered someone shared the other half.

'Nyoman?' I whispered. 'Is that you?'

'Yes,' she replied in her quiet voice. 'Don't worry, my darling.'

She folded her wraith-like form around me, holding me in the nothingness of her touch.

'A terrible thing has happened,' I cried, my voice seeming to fade a little. 'A frightening thing.'

I clung to her in my distress, needing comfort, needing her sympathy and companionship.

'I know,' she said, running her light fingers through my hair, 'Now we're the same and we can be happy together. You do feel happy, don't you, darling? You do want to be with me?'

I knew I was safe now, even in the moonglow, safe from Kala, as Nyoman opened the shutters and we saw the tattered remains of my shadow next to the ragged shade she herself cast. I had not noticed until now, that her dark twin was such a shabby creature: a stray mongrel amongst shadows, thin and wasted: a shadow that had been ravaged, yet one that had, eventually, emerged victorious from the struggle of life over death.

It was true that though I myself had a certain substance, my form was a nebulous thing, undefined and indefinite. I was now that forgotten person in the crowd, unnoticed, to be disregarded by my fellow creatures. I was myself as evanescent as a shade, as elusive as Nyoman, and my reply choked in my throat as I tried to express my utter and eternal love for her.

INSIDE THE WALLED CITY

(Hong Kong, again. I was taken into Kowloon City [the Walled City of the Manchus] in 1991, shortly before it was razed. It was a unique shanty town of individual shacks built into a single unit: a higgledy-piggledy block of misfitting walls, floors, roofs and tunnels. Few *gweilos* have been inside. Few would want to go inside. The number of rats exceeded the number of illegal immigrants who spent their lives within its walls, protected by this quirk of politics, this square mile of Chinese territory deep within British Hong Kong.)

THEY HAD BEEN LOUD-HAILING the place for days, and it certainly looked empty, but John said you can't knock down a building that size without being absolutely sure that some terrified Chinese child wasn't trapped in one of the myriad of rooms, or that an abandoned old lady wasn't caught in some blocked passageway, unable to find her way out. There had been elderly people who had set up home in the centre of this huge rotten cheese, and around whom the rest of the slum was raised over the years. Such people would have forgotten there was an outside world, let alone be able to find their way to it.

'You ready?' he asked me, and I nodded.

It was John Speakman's job as a Hong Kong Police inspector, to go into the empty shell of the giant slum to make sure everyone was out, so that the demolition could begin. He had a guide of course, and an armed escort of two locally born policemen, and was accompanied by a newspaper reporter—me. I'm a freelance whose articles appear mainly in the *South China Morning Post*.

You could say the Walled City was many dwellings, as many as seven thousand, but you would be equally right to call it a single structure. It consisted of one solid block of crudely built homes, all fused together. No thought or planning had gone into each tacked-on dwelling, beyond that of providing shelter for a family. The whole building covered the approximate area of a football stadium. There was no quadrangle at its centre, nor inner courtyard, no space within the ground it occupied. Every single piece of the ramshackle mass, apart from the occasional fetid airshaft, had been used to build, up to twelve stories high. Beneath the ground, and through every part of this monstrous shanty, ran a warren of tunnels and passageways. Above and within it, there were walkways, ladders, catwalks, streets and alleys, all welded together as if some junk artist like the man who built the Watts Towers had decided to try his hand at architecture.

Once you got more than ten feet inside, there was no natural light. Those within used to have to send messages to those on the edges to find out if it was day or night, fine or wet. The homemade brick and plaster was apt to rot and crumble in the airless confines inside and had to be constantly patched and shored up. In a land of high temperatures and humidity, fungus grew thick on the walls and in the cracks the rats and cockroaches built their own colonies. The stink was unbelievable. When it was occupied, more than fifty thousand people existed within its walls.

John called his two local cops to his side, and we all slipped into the dark slit in the side of the Walled City. Sang Lau the guide going first. Two gweilos—whites—and three Chinese, entering the forbidden place, perhaps for the last time. Even Sang Lau, who knew the building as well as any, seemed anxious to get the job over and done with. The son of an illegal immigrant, he had been raised in this block of hovels, in the muck and darkness of its intestines. His stunted little body was evidence of that fact, and he had only volunteered to show us the way in exchange for a right to Hong Kong citizenship for members of his family still without Hong Kong citizenship. He and his immediate family had taken advantage of the amnesty that had served to empty the city of its inhabitants. They had come out, some of them half-blind through lack of light, some of them sick and crippled from the disease and bad air, and now Sang Lau had been asked to return for one last time. I guessed how he would be feeling: slightly nostalgic (for it was his birthplace), yet wanting to get it over with, so that the many other unsavoury remembrances might be razed along with the structure.

The passage inside was narrow, constantly twisting, turning, dipping, and climbing, apparently at random. Its walls ran with slick water and it smelled musty, with pockets of stale food stink, and worse. Then there were writhing coils of hose and cable that tangled our feet if we were not careful: plastic water pipes ran alongside wires that had once carried stolen electricity. When the rotten cables were live and water ran through the leaking hoses, these passages must have been death traps. Now and again the beam from the lamp in my helmet transfixed a pointed face, with whiskers and small eyes, then it would scuttle away, into the maze of tunnels.

Every so often, we paused at one of the many junctions or shafts, and one of the Chinese policemen, the stocky, square-faced one, would yell through a megaphone. The sound smacked dully into the walls, or echoed along corridors of plasterboard. The atmosphere was leaden, though strangely aware. This massive structure with all its holes, its pits and shafts, was like a beast at the end of its life, waiting for the final breath. It was a shell, but one that had been soaked in the feverish activity of fifty thousand souls. It was once a holy city, but it had been bled, sweated, urinated, and spat on not only by the poor and the destitute, but also by mobsters, hoodlums, renegades, felons, runaways, refugees, and fugitives, until no part of it remained consecrated. It pressed in on us on all sides, as if it wanted to crush us, but lacked the final strength needed to collapse itself. It was a brooding, moody place and terribly alien to a gweilo like myself. I could sense spirits clustering in the corners: spirits from a culture that no Westerner has ever fully understood. More than once, as I stumbled along behind the others, I said to myself. What am I doing here? This is no place for me, in this hole.

The stocky policeman seemed startled by his own voice, blaring from the megaphone: he visibly twitched every time he had to make his announcement. From his build I guessed his family originally came from the north, from somewhere around the Great Wall. His features and heavy torso were Mongol rather than Cantonese, the southerners having a tendency toward small, delicate statures and moon-shaped faces. He probably made a tough policeman out on the streets, where his build would be of use in knocking heads together, but in here his northern superstitions and obsessive fear of spirits made him a liability. Not for the first time I wondered at John Speakman's judgment in assessing human character.

After about an hour of walking, and sometimes crawling, along tunnels the size of a sewer pipe, John suggested we rest for a while.

I said, 'You're not going to eat sandwiches in here, are you?'

It was supposed to be a joke, but I was so tense, it came out quite flat, and John growled, 'No, of course not.'

We sat crossed-legged in a circle, in what used to be an apartment: It was a hardboard box about ten-by-ten feet.

'Where are we?' I asked the torch-lit faces. 'I mean in relation to the outside.' The reply could have been 'the bowels of the earth' and I would have believed it. It was gloomy, damp, fetid, and reeked of prawn paste, which has an odour reminiscent of dredged sludge.

Sang Lau replied, 'Somewhere near east corner. We move soon, into middle.'

His reply made me uneasy.

'Somewhere near? Don't you know exactly?'

John snapped, 'Don't be silly, Peter. How can he know exactly? The important thing is he knows the way out. This isn't an exercise in specific location.'

'Right,' I said, giving him a mock salute, and he tipped his peaked cap back on his head, a sure sign he was annoyed. If he'd been standing, I don't doubt his hands would have been on his hips in the classic 'gweilo giving orders' stance.

John hadn't been altogether happy about taking a 'civilian' along, despite the fact that I was a close friend. He had a very poor opinion of those who did not wear a uniform of some kind. According to his philosophy, the human race was split into two: There were the protectors (police, army, medical profession, firemen, et al.) and those who needed protection (the rest of the population). Since I apparently came under the second category, I needed looking after. John was one of those crusty bachelors you find in the last outposts of faded empires: a living reminder of the beginning of the century. Sheena, my wife, called him 'the fossil', even to his face. I think they both regarded it as a term of endearment.

However, he said he wanted to do me a favour, since he knew that my job was getting tough. Things were getting tight in the freelance business, especially since Australia had just woken up to the fact that Hong Kong, a thriving place of business where money was to be made hand over fist, was right on its doorstep. The British and American expatriates equalled each other for the top slot, numerically speaking, but Aussie professionals were beginning to enter, if not in droves, in small herds. With them they brought their own parasites, the freelancers, and for the first time I had a lot of competition. It meant I had to consolidate friendships and use contacts that had previously been mostly friendships and use contacts that had previously been mostly social.

Sheena and I were going through a bit of a rough time too, and one thing she would not put up with was a tame writer who earned less than a poorly paid local clerk. I could sense the words 'proper job' hanging in the air, waiting to condense.

Even the darkness in there seemed to have substance. I could see the other young policeman, the thin, sharp Cantonese youth, was uncomfortable too. He kept looking up, into the blackness, smiling nervously. He and his companion cop whispered to each other, and I heard 'Bruce Lee' mentioned just before they fell into silence again, their grins fixed. Perhaps they were trying to use the memory of the fabled martial-arts actor to bolster their courage? Possibly the only one of us who was completely oblivious, or perhaps indifferent, to the spiritual ambience of the place was John himself. He was too thick-skinned, too much the old warrior expat, to be affected by spooky atmospheres, I thought he might reassure his men though, since we both knew that when Chinese smiled under circumstances such as these, it meant they were hiding either acute embarrassment or abject terror. They had nothing to be embarrassed about, so I was left with only one assumption.

John, however, chose to ignore their fears.

'Right, let's go,' he said, climbing to his feet.

We continued along the passageways, stumbling after Sang Lau, whose power over us was absolute in this place, since without him we would certainly be lost. It was possible that a search party might find us, but then again, we could wander the interior of this vast wormery for weeks without finding or being found.

A subtle change seemed to come over the place. Its resistance seemed to have evaporated, and it was almost as if it were gently drawing us on. The tunnels were getting wider, more accessible, and there were fewer obstacles to negotiate. I have an active imagination, especially in places of darkness, notorious places that are steeped in recent histories of blood and founded on terror. Far from making me feel better, this alteration in the atmosphere made my stomach knot, but what could I say to John? I wanted to go back? I had no choice but to follow where his guide led us, and hope for an early opportunity to duck out if we saw daylight at any time.

Although I am sensitive to such phrases, I'm not usually a coward. Old churches and ancient houses bother me, but I normally shrug and put up with any feeling of spiritual discomfort. Here, however, the oppressive atmosphere was so threatening and the feeling of dread so strong, I wanted to run from the building and to hell with the article and the money I needed so much. The closer we got to the centre, the more acute became my emotional stress, until I wondered whether I was going to hyperventilate. Finally, I shouted, 'John!'

He swung round with an irritated 'What is it?'

'I've—I've got to go back...'

One of the policemen grabbed my arm in the dark, and squeezed it. I believed it to be a sign of encouragement. He too wanted to turn round, but he was more terrified of his boss than of any ghost. From the strength of the grip I guessed the owner of the fingers was the Mongol.

'Impossible,' John snapped. 'What's the matter with you?'

'A pain,' I said. 'I have a pain in my chest.'

He pushed past the other men and pulled me roughly to one side.

'I knew I shouldn't have brought you. I only did it for Sheena—she seemed to think there was still something left in you. Now pull yourself together. I know what's the matter with you, you're getting the jitters. It's claustrophobia, nothing else. Fight it, man. You're scaring my boys with your stupid funk.'

'I have a pain,' I repeated, but he wasn't buying it.

'Crap. Sheena would be disgusted with you. God knows what she ever saw in you in the first place.'

For a moment all fear was driven out of me by an intense fury that flooded my veins. How dare this thick-skinned, arrogant cop assume knowledge of my wife's regard for me! It was true that her feelings were not now what they had been in the beginning, but she had once fully loved me, and only a rottenness bred by superficial life in the colony had eaten away that love. The mannequins, the people with plaster faces, had served to corrode us. Sheena had once been a happy woman, full of energy, enthusiasms, colour. Now she was pinched and bitter, as I was myself: made so by the shallow gweilos we consorted with and had become ourselves. Money, affairs and bugger-thy-neighbour were the priorities in life.

'You leave Sheena's name out of this,' I said, my voice catching with the anger that stuck in my throat. 'What the hell do you know about our beginnings?'

Speakman merely gave me a look of contempt and took up his position in the front once more, with the hunchbacked Lau indicating which way he should go when we came to one of the many junctions and crossroads. Occasionally, the thin one, who now had the megaphone, would call out in Cantonese, the sound quickly swallowed by the denseness of the structure around us. Added to my anxiety problem was now a feeling of misery. I had shown my inner nature to a man who was increasingly becoming detestable to me. Something was nagging at the edge of my brain too, which gradually ate its way inward, toward an area of comprehension.

God knows what she ever saw in you in the first place.

When it came, the full implication of these words stunned me. At first I was too taken aback to do anything more than keep turning the idea over in my mind, in an obsessive way, until it drove out any other thought. I kept going over his words, trying to find another way of interpreting them, but came up with the same answer every time.

Finally, I could keep quiet no longer. I had to get it out. It was beginning to fester. I stopped in my tracks, and despite the presence of the other men, shouted, 'You bastard, Speakman, you're having an affair with her, aren't you?'

He turned and regarded me, silently.

'You bastard,' I said again. I could hardly get it out, it was choking me. 'You're supposed to be a friend.'

There was utter contempt in his voice.

'I was never your friend.'

'You wanted me to know, didn't you? You wanted to tell me in here.'

He knew that in this place I would be less than confident of myself. The advantages were all with him. I was out of my environment and less able to handle things than he was. In the past few months he had been in here several times, was more familiar with the darkness and the tight, airless zones of the Walled City's interior. We were in an underworld that terrified me and left him unperturbed.

'You men go on,' he ordered the others, not taking his eyes off me. 'We'll follow in a moment.'

They did as they were told. John Speakman was not a man to be brooked by his Asiatic subordinates. When they were out of earshot, he said, 'Yes, Sheena and I had some time together.'

In the light of my helmet lamp I saw his lips twitch, and I wanted to smash him in the mouth.

'Had? You mean it's over?'

'Not completely. But there's still you. You're in the way. Sheena, being the woman she is, still retains some sort of loyalty toward you. Can't see it myself, but there it is.'

'We'll sort this out later,' I said, 'between the three of us.'

I made a move to get past him, but he blocked the way. Then a second, more shocking realisation hit me, and again I was not ready for it. He must have seen it in my face, because his lips tightened this time.

I said calmly now, 'You're going to lose me in here, aren't you? Sheena said she wouldn't leave me, and you're going to make sure I stay behind.'

'Your imagination is running away with you again,' he snapped back. 'Try to be a little more level-headed, old chap,'

'I am being level-headed.'

His hands were on his hips now, in the gweilo stance I knew so well. Once of them rested on the butt of his revolver. Being a policeman, he of course carried a gun, which I did not. There was little point in my trying force anyway. He was a good four inches taller than I and weighed two stone more, most of it muscle. We stood there, confronting one another. Then we heard that terrible scream that turned my guts to milk.

The ear-piercing cry was followed by a scrabbling sound, and eventually one of the two policemen appeared in the light of our lamps.

'Sir, come quick,' he gasped. 'The guide.'

Our quarrel put aside for the moment, we hurried along the tunnel to where the other policeman stood. In front of him, perhaps five yards away, was the guide. His helmet light was out, and he seemed to be standing on tiptoe for some reason, arms hanging loosely by his sides. John stepped forward, and I found myself going with him. He might have wanted me out of the way, but I was going to stick closely to him.

What I saw in the light of our lamps made me retch and step backward quickly.

It would seem that a beam had swung down from the ceiling, as the guide had passed beneath it. This had smashed his helmet lamp. Had that been all, the guide might have got away with a broken nose, or black eye, but it was not. In the end of the beam, now holding him off his feet, was a curved nail-spike. It had gone through his right eye, and was no doubt deeply embedded in the poor man's brain. He dangled from this support loosely, blood running down the side of his nose and dripping onto his white tennis shoes.

'Jesus Christ!' I said at last. It wasn't a profanity, a blasphemy. It was a prayer. I prayed for us, who were now lost in a dark, hostile world, and I prayed for Sang Lau. Poor little Sang Lau. Just when he had begun to make it in life, just when he had escaped the Walled City, the bricks and mortar and timber had reached out petulantly for its former child and brained it. Sang Lau had been one of the quiet millions who struggle out of the mire, who evolve from terrible beginnings to a place in the world of light. All in vain, apparently.

John Speakman lifted the man away from the instrument that had impaled his brain, and laid the body on the floor. He went through the formality of feeling for a pulse, and then shook his head. To give him his due, his voice remained remarkably firm, as if he were still in control of things.

'We'll have to carry him out,' he said to his two men.

'Take one end each.'

There was a reluctant shuffling of feet, as the men moved forward to do as they were told. The smaller of the two was trembling so badly he dropped the legs straight away, and had to retrieve them quickly under Speakman's glare.

I said, 'And I suppose you know which way to go?'

'We're near the heart of the place, old chap. It doesn't really matter in which direction we go, as long as we keep going straight.'

That, I knew, was easier said than done. When passageways curve and turn, run into each other, go up and down, meet new forks and crossroads and junctions with choices, how the hell do you keep in a straight line? I said nothing for once. I didn't want the two policemen to panic. If we were to get out, we had to stay calm. And those on the outside wouldn't leave us here. They would send in a search party, once nightfall came.

Nightfall.

I suppressed a chill as we moved into the heart of the beast.

Seven months ago Britain agreed with China that Hong Kong would return to its landlord country in 1997. It was then at last decided to clean up and clean out the Walled City, to pull it down and re-house the inhabitants. There were plans to build a park on the ground then covered by this ancient city within a city, for the use of the occupants of the surrounding tenement buildings.

It stood in the middle of Kowloon on the mainland. Once upon a time there was a wall around it, when it was the home of the Manchus, but Japanese invaders robbed it of its ancient stones to build elsewhere. The area on which it stood was still known as the Walled City. When the Manchus were there, they used it as a fort against the British. Then the British were leased the peninsula, and it became an enclave for China's officials, whose duty it was to report on gweilo activities in the area to

Peking. Finally, it became an architectural nightmare, a giant slum. An area not recognised by the British, who refused to police it, and abandoned by Peking, it was a lawless labyrinth, sometimes called the Forbidden Place. It was here that unlicensed doctors and dentists practised, and every kind of vice flourished. It was ruled by gangs of youths, the Triads, who covered its inner walls with blood. It is a place of death, the home of ten thousand ghosts.

For the next two hours we struggled through the rank-smelling tunnels, crawling over filth and across piles of trash, until we were all exhausted. I had cuts on my knees, and my hair felt teeming with insects. I knew there were spiders, possibly even snakes, in these passageways. There were certainly lice, horseflies, mosquitoes and a dozen other nasty biters. Not only that, but there seemed to be projections everywhere: sharp bits of metal, cables hanging like vines from the ceiling and rusty nails. The little Cantonese policeman had trodden on a nail, which had completely pierced his foot. He was now limping and whining in a small voice. He knew that if he did not get treatment soon, blood poisoning would be the least of his troubles. I felt sorry for the young man, who in the normal run of things probably dealt with the tide of human affairs very competently within his range of duties. He was an official of the law in the most densely populated area of the world, and I had seen his type deal cleanly and (more often than not) peacefully with potentially ugly situations daily. In here, however, he was over his head. The situation could not be handled by efficient traffic signals or negotiation, or even prudent use of a weapon. There was something about this man that was familiar. There were scars on his face: shiny patches that might have been the result of plastic surgery. I tried to recall where I had seen the Cantonese policeman before, but my mind was soggy with recent events.

We took turns carrying the body of the guide. Once I had touched him and got over my squeamishness, that part of it didn't bother me too much. What did was the weight of the corpse. I never believed a dead man could be so heavy. After ten minutes my arms were nearly coming out of their sockets. I began by carrying the legs, and quickly decided the man at the head, carrying the torso, had the best part of the deal. I suggested a change round, which was effected, only to find that the other end of the man was twice as heavy. I began to hate him, this leaden corpse.

AFTER FOUR HOURS I HAD had enough.

'I'm not humping him around anymore,' I stated bluntly to the cop who was trying to take my wife from me. 'You want him outside, you carry him by yourselves. You're the bloody boss man. It's your damn show.'

'I see,' John said. 'Laying down some ground rules, are we?'

'Shove it up your arse,' I replied. 'I've had you up to here. I can't prove, you planned to dump me in here, but I know, pal, and when we get out of this place, you and I are going to have a little talk.'

'If we get out,' he muttered.

He was sitting away from me, in the darkness, where my lamplight couldn't reach him. I could not see his expression.

'If?'

'Exactly,' he sighed. 'We don't seem to be getting very far, do we? It's almost as if this place were trying to keep us. I swear it's turning us in on ourselves. We should have reached the outside long ago.'

'But they'll send someone in after us,' I said.

And one of the policemen added, 'Yes. Someone come.'

''Fraid not. No one knows we're here.' It came out almost as if he were pleased with himself. I saw now that I had been right.

It had been his intention to drop me off in the middle of this godforsaken building, knowing I would never find my own way out. I wondered only briefly what he planned to do with the two men and the guide. I don't doubt they could be bribed. The Hong Kong Police Force has at times been notorious for its corruption. Maybe they were chosen because they could be bought.

'How long have we got?' I asked, trying to stick to practical issues.

'About five more hours. Then the demolition starts. They begin knocking it down at six AM.'

Just then, the smaller of the Chinese made a horrific gargling sound, and we all shone our lights on him instinctively. At first I couldn't understand what was wrong with him, though I could see he was convulsing. He was in a sitting position, and his body kept jerking and flopping. John Speakman bent over him, then straightened, saying,

'Christ, not another one…'

'Six-inch nail. It's gone in behind his ear. How the hell? I don't understand how he managed to lean all the way back on it.'

'Unless the nail came out of the wood?' I said.

'What are you saying?'

'I don't know. All I know is two men have been injured in accidents that seem too freakish to believe. What do you think? Why can't we get out of this place? Shit, it's only the area of a football stadium. We've been in here hours.'

The other policeman was looking at his colleague with wide, disbelieving eyes. He grabbed John Speakman by the collar, blurting, 'We go now. We go outside now,' and then a babble of that tonal language, some of which John might have understood. I certainly didn't.

Speakman peeled the man's stubby fingers from his collar and turned away from him, toward the dead cop, as if the incident

247

had not taken place. 'He was a good policeman,' he said. 'Jimmy Wong. You know he saved a boy from a fire last year? Dragged the child out with his teeth, hauling the body along the floor and down the stairs because his hands were burned too badly to clutch the kid. You remember. You covered the story.'

I remembered him now. Jimmy Wong. The governor had presented him with a medal. He had saluted proudly, with heavily bandaged hands. Today he was not a hero. Today he was a number. The second victim.

John Speakman said, 'Goodbye, Jimmy.'

Then he ignored him, saying to me, 'We can't carry both bodies out. We'll have to leave them. I...' but I heard no more. There was a quick tearing sound, and I was suddenly falling. My heart dropped out of me. I landed heavily on my back. Something entered between my shoulder blades, something sharp and painful, and I had to struggle hard to get free. When I managed to get to my feet and reached down and felt along the floor, I touched a slim projection, probably a large nail. It was sticky with my blood. A voice from above said, 'Are you all right?'

'I—I think so. A nail...'

'What?'

My light had gone out, and I was feeling disorientated. I must have fallen about fourteen feet, judging from the distance of the lamps above me. I reached down my back with my hand. It felt wet and warm, but apart from the pain I wasn't gasping for air or anything. Obviously, it had missed my lungs and other vital organs, or I would be squirming in the dust, coughing my guts up.

I heard John say, 'We'll try to reach you,' and then the voice and the lights drifted away.

'No!' I shouted. 'Don't leave me! Give me your arm.' I reached upward. 'Help me up!'

But my hand remained empty. They had gone, leaving the blackness behind them. I lay still for a long time, afraid to move. There were nails everywhere. My heart was racing. I was sure that I was going to die. The Walled City had us in its grip, and we were not going to get out. Once, it had been teeming with life, but we had robbed it of its soul, the people had crowded within its walls. Now even the shell was threatened with destruction. And we were the men responsible. We represented the authority who had ordered its death, and it was determined to take us with it. Nothing likes to die alone. Nothing wants to leave this world without, at the very least, obtaining satisfaction in the way of revenge. The ancient black heart of the Walled City of the Manchus, surrounded by the body it had been given by later outcasts from society, had enough life left in it to slaughter these five puny mortals from the other side, the lawful side. It had tasted gweilo blood, and it would have more.

My wound was beginning to ache, and I climbed stiffly and carefully to my feet. I felt slowly along the walls, taking each step cautiously. Things scuttled over my feet, whispered over my face, but I ignored them. A sudden move and I would find myself impaled on some projection. The stink of death was in the stale air, filling my nostrils. It was trying to drive fear into me. The only way I was going to survive was by remaining calm. Once I panicked, it would all be over. I had the feeling that the building could kill me at any time, but I was savouring the moment, allowing it to be my mistake. It wanted me to dive headlong into insanity, it wanted to experience my terror, then it would deliver the *coup de grace*.

I moved this way along the tunnels for about an hour: neither of us, it seemed, was short of patience. The Walled City had seen centuries, so what was an hour or two? The legacy of death left by the Manchus and the Triads existed without reference to time. Ancient evils and modern iniquity had joined forces against the foreigner, the gweilo, and the malodorous darkness smiled at any attempt to thwart its intention to suck the life from my body.

At one point my forward foot did not touch the ground. There was a space, a hole, in front of me.

'Nice try,' I whispered, 'but not yet.'

As I prepared to edge around it, hoping for a small ledge or something, I felt ahead of me, and touched the thing. It was dangling over the hole, like plumb-line weight. I pushed it, and it swung slowly.

By leaning over and feeling carefully, I ascertained it to be the remaining local policeman, the muscled northerner. I knew him by his Sam Browne shoulder strap. I felt up by the corpse's throat and found the skin bulging over some tight electrical cords. The building had hanged him.

Used to death now, I gripped the corpse around the waist and used it as a swing to get myself across the gap. The cords held, and I touched ground. A second later, the body must have dropped, because I heard a crash below.

I continued my journey through the endless tunnels, my throat very parched now. I was thirsty as hell. Eventually, I could stand it no longer and licked some of the moisture that ran down the walls. It tasted like wine. At one point I tongued up a cockroach, cracked it between my teeth, and spit it out in disgust. Really, I no longer cared. All I wanted to do was get out alive. I didn't even care whether John and Sheena told me to go away. I would be happy to do so. There wasn't much left, in any case. Anything I had felt had shrivelled away during this ordeal. I just wanted to live. Nothing more, nothing less.

At one point a stake or something plunged downward from the roof and passed through several floors, missing me by an inch. I think I actually laughed. A little while later, I found an airshaft with a rope hanging in it. Trusting that the building would not let me fall, I climbed down this narrow chimney to get to the bottom. I had some idea that if I could reach ground level, I might find a way to get through the walls. Some of them were no thicker than cardboard.

After reaching the ground safely, I began to feel my way along the corridors and alleys, until I saw a light. I gasped with relief, thinking at first it was daylight, but had to swallow a certain amount of disappointment in finding it was only a helmet with its lamp still on. The owner was nowhere to be seen. I guessed it was John's: he was the only one left, apart from me.

Not long after this, I heard John Speakman's voice for the last time. It seemed to come from very far below me, in the depths of the underground passages that worm-holed beneath the Walled City. It was a faint pathetic cry for help. Immediately following this distant shout was the sound of falling masonry. And then, silence. I shuddered, involuntarily, guessing what had happened. The building had lured him into its underworld, its maze below the earth, and had then blocked the exits. John Speakman had been buried alive, immured by the city that held him in contempt.

Now there was only me.

I MOVED THROUGH AN INNER darkness, the beam of the remaining helmet lamp having faded to a dim glow. I was Theseus in the Labyrinth, except that I had no Ariadne to help me find the way through it. I stumbled through long tunnels where the air was so thick and damp I might have been in a steam bath. I crawled along passages no taller or wider than a cupboard under a kitchen sink, shared them with spiders and rats and came out the other end choking on dust, spitting out cobwebs. I knocked my way through walls so thin and rotten a single blow with my fist was enough to hole them. I climbed over fallen girders, rubble and piles of filthy rags, collecting unwanted passengers and abrasions on the way.

And all the while I knew the building was laughing at me.

It was leading me round in circles, playing with me like a rat in a maze. I could hear it moving, creaking and shifting as it readjusted itself, changed its inner structure to keep me from finding an outside wall. Once, I trod on something soft. It could have been a hand—John's hand—quickly withdrawn. Or it might have been a creature of the Walled City, a rat or a snake. Whatever it was, it had been live.

There were times when I became so despondent I wanted to lie down and just fade into death, the way a primitive tribesman will give up all hope and turn his face to the wall. There were times when I became angry, and screeched at the structure that had me trapped in its belly, remonstrating with it until my voice was hoarse. Sometimes I was driven to useless violence and picked up the nearest object to smash at my tormentor, even if my actions brought the place down around my ears.

Once, I even whispered to the darkness:

'I'll be your slave. Tell me what to do—any evil thing—and I'll do it. If you let me go, I promise to follow your wishes. Tell me what to do...'

And still it laughed at me, until I knew I was going insane.

Finally, I began singing to myself, not to keep up my spirits like brave men are supposed to, but because I was beginning to slip into that crazy world that rejects reality in favour of fantasy. I thought I was home, in my own house, making coffee. I found myself going through the actions of putting on the kettle, and preparing the coffee, milk and sugar, humming a pleasant tune to myself all the while. One part of me recognised that domestic scene was make-believe, but the other was convinced that I could not possibly be trapped by a malevolent entity and about to die in the dark corridors of its multi-sectioned shell.

Then something happened, to jerk me into sanity.

THE SEQUENCE OF EVENTS COVERING the next few minutes or so are lost to me. Only by concentrating very hard and surmising can I recall what might have happened. Certainly, I believe I remember those first few moments, when a sound deafened me, and the whole building rocked and trembled as if in an earthquake. Then I think I fell to the floor and had the presence of mind to jam the helmet on my head. There followed a second (what I now know to be) explosion. Pieces of building rained around me: bricks were striking my shoulders and bouncing off my hard hat. I think the only reason none of them injured me badly was because the builders, being poor, had used the cheapest materials they could find. These were bricks fashioned out of crushed coke, which are luckily light and airy.

A hole appeared, through which I could see blinding daylight. I was on my feet in an instant, and racing toward it. Nails appeared out of the woodwork, up from the floor, and ripped and tore at my flesh like sharp fangs. Metal posts crashed across my path, struck me on my limbs. I was attacked from all sides by chunks of masonry and debris, until I was bruised and raw, bleeding from dozens of cuts and penetrations.

When I reached the hole in the wall, I threw myself at it, and landed outside the dust. There, the demolition people saw me, and one risked his life to dash forward and pull me clear of the collapsing building. I was then rushed to hospital. I was found to have a broken arm and multiple lacerations, some of them quite deep.

Mostly, I don't remember what happened at the end. I'm going by what I've been told, and what flashes on and off in my nightmares, and using these have pieced together the above account of my escape from the Walled City. It seems as though it might be reasonably accurate.

I have not, of course, told the true story of what happened inside those walls, except in this account, which will go into a

253

safe place until after my death. Such a tale would only have people clucking their tongues and saying, 'It's the shock, you know—the trauma of such an experience,' and sending for the psychiatrist. I tried to tell Sheena once, but I could see that it was disturbing her, so I mumbled something about, 'Of course, I can see that one's imagination can work overtime in a place like that,' and never mentioned it to her again.

I did manage to tell the demolition crew about John. I told them he might still be alive, under all that rubble. They stopped their operations immediately and sent in search parties, but though they found the bodies of the guide and policemen, John was never seen again. The search parties all managed to get out safely, which has me wondering whether perhaps there is something wrong with my head—except that I have the wounds, and there are the corpses of my travelling companions. I don't know. I can only say now what I think happened. I told the police (and stuck rigidly to my story) that I was separated from the others before any deaths occurred. How was I to explain two deaths by sharp instruments, and a subsequent hanging? I let them try to figure it out. All I told them was that I heard John's final cry, and that was the truth. I don't even care whether or not they believe me. I'm outside that damn hellhole, and that's all that concerns me.

And Sheena? It is seven months since the incident. And it was only yesterday that I confronted and accused her or having an affair with John, and she looked so shocked and distressed and denied it so vehemently that I have to admit I believe that nothing of the kind happened between them. I was about to tell her that John had admitted to it, but had second thoughts. I mean, had he? Maybe I had filled in the gaps with my own jealous fears? To tell you the truth, I can't honestly remember, and the guilt is going to be hard to live with. You see, when they asked me for the location of John's cry for help, I indicated a spot… well, I think I told them to dig—I said… anyway, they didn't find him, which wasn't surprising, since, well, perhaps this is not the place for full confessions.

John is still under there somewhere, God help him. I have the awful feeling that the underground ruins of the Walled City might keep him alive in some way, with rejected water, and food in the form of rats and cockroaches. A starving man will eat dirt, if it fills his stomach. Perhaps he is still below, in some pocket created by that underworld? Such a slow, terrible torture, keeping a man barely alive in his own grave, would be consistent with that devious, nefarious entity I know as the Walled City of the Manchus.

Some nights when I am feeling especially brave, I go to the park and listen—listen for small cries from a subterranean prison—listen for the faint pleas for help from an oubliette far below the ground.

Sometimes I think I hear them.

MY LADY LYGIA

(This is an indulgence which grew out of my love of the stories of Nathanial Hawthorne and Edgar Allen Poe. Other lovers of their tales may enjoy the references herein, which are many, if a little obscure in places.)

I DO NOT REMEMBER PRECISELY where it was that Hawthorne and I held our meeting, nor do I recall the exact means by which I travelled there. That it was some central landlocked country on a continent with an extensive history is within the limits of possibility, and certainly the climate was inclement, inclining towards low temperatures and high winds, for I have vague memories of heavy figures promenading along slippery cobbled streets, their thick tall-collared coats casting shadows on the mean little bull's-eye windows of myopic houses.

That it was north of the Tropic of Cancer, is beyond doubt, for there were long grey hours of twilight in which the shade of thin church spires invaded narrow alleys, and most assuredly it was not above the Arctic Circle for the period of daylight matched the darkness almost to perfection.

Although the name of the city has now slipped beyond recall, when my concentration is at its most powerful, which is not frequent in these days of increasing age and poor health, there is an ill-defined impression of a certain species of fungus growing between the pitted bricks of a high garden wall. This particular type of mushroom is used in the recipes of a soup found only in a principality west of the region where two transcontinental rivers have their confluence. The actual rendezvous point however is indelibly printed on my memory and took place at the Café M-----, a pavement restaurant on the east side of the city in the vicinity of the graveyards, where it is said several poor souls have been immured while still drawing shallow but life-sustaining breath, the scratch marks of desperate fingers having been discovered on the inside of certain coffin lids.

Although he was heavily disguised I recognised my enemy, the despicable Mr Hawthorne, by the venomous-looking purple bloom he wore in his lapel buttonhole, and by the strange strawberry birthmark that marred his otherwise flawless complexion. These two marks of identification he had communicated to me before our meeting, so that I should not make the mistake of approaching the wrong person. I, in turn, had warned him to look for a man whose throat bore the scar of a razor, from ear to ear. There were similar cicatrices to be found on my chest, caused by another honed instrument, somewhat larger than a barber's razor, but these striations were of course hidden beneath my shirtfront.

To be absolutely certain of each other we immediately exchanged tokens. Out of sight of prying eyes I passed Hawthorne a small gilded cockroach. I received in its stead the most delicate of model insects, possibly a tiger moth, which fluttered in my cupped palm until I applied pressure and the beautiful tinsel creature was crushed. On seeing what I had done, Hawthorne contemptuously flicked my golden bug down a nearby sewer. We glared at each other, knowing the artefacts had taken infinite patience, and not a little skill, to construct. Finally, to be triply certain we were each dealing with the person who professed to be, in his case, Hawthorne, and in mine, Poe, there were prearranged passwords, or rather pass-phrases in the jargon of real estate agents (under which guise we were both travelling) to be voiced for the benefit of the public. We referred to each other by agreed pseudonyms, arranged previously by correspondence.

'The market is not good, M. du Mirror,' I said, so that others might hear and not suspect. 'Prices of houses are coming down. Why only the other day a client of mine, a Mr. U-----, the owner of an old manse, remarked upon how his property was falling...'

'Quite so, Mr Wilson,' interrupted Hawthorne, 'and clock-towers too, for there are those that possess such edifices, are quite unstable in the current economic climate.'

Thus we established our credentials and sat at separate tables, able to converse in whispers over our shoulders, while others in tall hats and long coats passed us, never guessing the true nature or purpose of our presence in the city. It may seem to the casual observer that our precautions with regard to one another's identity might be regarded as over-elaborate, but such enquiries were entirely necessary, as will be revealed in the course of this narrative.

'How was your journey?' he sneered. 'Did you experience any difficulties on your voyage to this remote corner of the civilised world?'

'Uneventful,' I said, staring coldly ahead, 'apart from the descent into maelstrom, but that was no fault of the ship's captain. And you? What of your travels across land?'

'Likewise,' he said, 'though some narrow-minded folk took exception to my presence in a southern town and sent me on my way suitably attired in hot pitch adorned with the feathers of an eiderduck. Hardly distressing to one such as myself, who has frequently entered nightmare situations and come through mentally unscarred.'

'Let us be about our business then,' I said, finishing my glass, and received a murmur of assent from my enemy. 'You have, in your custody a person most dear to me. My lady, Lygia. The hate I bear you for abducting my wife is beyond all reason...'

'Matched only,' he interrupted with barely suppressed passion, 'by the hate I have held for you these past three decades...'

I should perhaps explain at this point that Hawthorne and myself are secret agents for two separate central European States of differing ideologies. We are rival spies who have thwarted each other time and time again, though our methods are the antithesis of each other, his inclining towards dark elaborate plots, and mine favouring straight-forward action. Over the years whilst each of us has pursued out nocturnal and clandestine careers we have countered and counter-countered each other's moves like expert chess players, so that until this time every game has ended in stalemate and the principality to which I owed my allegiance was no further in gaining superiority over the Duchy to which Hawthorne had pledged his loyalty, nor vice versa. We had repeatedly blocked and stifled each other's attempts at subterfuge.

There was however one marked difference between us. I treated such rivalry as a natural part of any espionage activity, while Hawthorne took my interface personally and had always vowed that he would destroy me. Several attempts had been made on my life but I am a difficult man to assassinate. Now the agent Hawthorne had stooped to kidnapping, one who is dear to me, possibly to lure me into some devious trap. My darling Lygia, whose history is as mysterious as my espionage activities, was in the hands of this foul creature. I had come with the purpose of wresting her from his clutches and restoring her to my bosom.

'One hour,' he said, swallowing the last of his coffee. 'We will meet at the W----- Inn.'

'One hour,' I agreed, draining my own cup to the less.

We separated, following our different paths to the same destination, an inn which lay beyond the dreary houses and gloomy shops with their gabled windows, down by the river where the mists rose through iron gratings to invade the foul passageways of the harbour wharves. At first my footsteps echoed in the cobbled alleys, but once in open streets the creaking of shop signs on rusty hinges disguised the sound of my progress through the night. Exactly an hour later the masts of ships hove in sight through the fog, their dark crosstrees like thin gallows, and I knew I had reached my journey's end when a river rat made his passage across the toe of my shoe on his way from a basement window to the dirty waters.

On arrival at the W----- Inn, I made my way to the public bar, where I knew my enemy would be waiting, his being the shorter route. Indeed, he saw me as I was removing my muffler, and smiled into the froth, which crowned his tankard of ale. It was a pathetic sight and one I tried to ignore in case pity should drive me from my purpose.

It was then I saw my Lygia, pale but lovely, sitting at his side. I paused in mid-stride, hardly able to contain my overwhelming emotion, resisting the urge to rush forward and take her into my arms. There was no smile upon her face, and her eyes revealed a blankness which frightened me. The hue upon her cheek was blood red, as if a fever had overtaken her and was at the apex of its trajectory. There were demons at work within her, not of her own making.

Gathering all my reserves of strength I stepped forward.

'Good evening, Hawthorne,' I murmured, 'we meet again.'

He looked about him nervously, the smile instantly gone.

'Please,' he whispered. 'Remember our agreement! I am travelling incognito. Please refer to me as M. du Mirror…'

'Ah,' I replied, 'your usual alias. How well it has served you over the years.'

My purpose achieved I sat down and removed my gloves, calling to the landlord for more ale for my companion 'M. du Mirror', and brandy for myself.

'And a new candle,' I cried, 'for monsieur and I have much to discuss. The night hours are long, but friendship such as ours needs no sleep.'

I heard a faint groan of annoyance escape monsieur's lips. I knew he detested bonhomie from one such as I, but his breeding and gentlemanly manners would no more allow him to refute my words, than would the stomach of a starving urchin permit the child to reject the discarded entrails of a slaughtered pig.

I studied the hollow visage of my fellow reveller. His earlier disguise of the well-fed estate agent had been discarded. He had pared his appearance down to reality and was indeed much thinner and paler than when we had last encountered one another at a way-station some several miles from N-----k on the eastern seaboard. His eyes were ringed with dark aureoles and lacked the lustre of a person in good health. There were about his lips the dry cracks of one whose surface moisture has been drained by long hours of raving speech. There was something new about his expression and it took me some minutes to decide that the twitch in his left eyelid had not been there at our last meeting.

It was now necessary to begin the game of delving into each other's recent activities, to see which of us could reveal the least and lie the most successfully. We were both past masters at devious and wily conversation.

'So,' I begin, 'what stories have you for me today? Please, do not repeat those twice-told tales you forever foist upon my ears, for you know I am fully aware of their content, though the manner in which you expound each romance differs with every new telling. Perhaps you would favour my ear with any fresh yarns you may have invented since our last meeting?'

He gave a kind of gasping sound and clutched his tankard so hard his knuckles went visibly white. For one awful moment I believed he was going to refuse, to decline outright to pass the information I so desperately desired. Instead, what came was merely in the form of a mild protest.

'Sir,' he croaked, 'since you have already heard all my stories, several times, perhaps we should both drain our glasses and leave this establishment?'

'No more games,' I cried. 'I must know what you have done to my dear wife, who has been prisoner for close to three days now. Not once has she cast a fond look in my direction, but sits by your side like a dead creature, robbed of any reason to smile, bereft of speech, empty of thought. She whose countenance was divine has the features of a corpse and the eyes of an inmate of Bedlam.'

A triumphant smile at last found its way to the corners of his mouth as I tried to attract the attention of my darling Lygia, to signal in our special eyelid code, that she was ready to make good her escape. I received a blank stare in acknowledgement. There appeared no spark of recognition in her eyes, no welcome there, no sign of relief. There was simply… nothing.

What have you done to her?' I hissed again.

Du Mirror sniggered.

'She does not remember you, Wilson,' he sneered. 'She will never know you again. I have administered a drug: one which erodes the memory, destroys it for good…'

I sat back in my chair with a start. Such news was of course horrifying. My own dear Lygia, my beloved wife, did not know me. This lady without whom life was an emptiness to be compared only with the void of space, had no knowledge of my existence. Indeed, she stared upon me now with the cold politeness of a stranger. That she was kind and good, generous and loving, was evident only in her unblemished complexion, her sweet demeanour, not in her eyes. There was no warmth in them for me.

'You are an evil man du Mirror,' I said, 'but you have calculated wrongly this time. If it takes me the rest of my life I will win again the love of my dear wife and restore myself to the rightful place in her heart.'

Turning to the lady in question I said, 'Madam, allow me to introduce myself…'

I was interrupted by a startling cackle, ejaculated from the mouth of my enemy. His eyes were feverishly bright, as if he were in the last days of some consumptive disease, and his thin red lips were cruelly twisted in a gesture of mockery. The lank dark hair that fell about his brow seemed infused with every essence of nefariousness. He was iniquity itself, but he was not yet finished with his wickedness.

'You poor fool,' he said, 'do you not realise the extent of my scheme? You have taken the drug, not but an hour ago at the Café M-----. The third waiter there is my man. At last, I have you William Wilson!'

I recoiled in horror at the words, but I too had something to impart to my enemy, which would have him reeling before my eyes. I am not a man to be treated with contempt, regarded as a mere nothing in the eyes of foreign agents, looked upon with disdain. I am a man of action: I do where others have not yet done. I spoke to him then, in the accents of the victorious.

'You, sir, are an even poorer fool. The third waiter at the Café M----- is obviously a double agent, for he is also my man, and the potion he slipped into your Turkish coffee should be taking effect within just a few moments from now.' I stared at him grimly, then, added, 'The difference between our methods ends at last the deadlock we have found ourselves in these past thirty years. You are an elaborate showster, sir, while I am a practical artificer. I have no desire to fool around with vials of liquid that induce amnesia. The fluid that went into your coffee was plain and simple strychnine. Enough to kill a razor-wielding orangutan, let alone a worn out husk of a middle European with Gothic pretensions. You are a dead man, du Mirror!'

There was silence between us then, for several seconds. The candle burned, the mists seeped under the ill-fitting door from the river, and the landlord coughed from his stool by the cellar door.

It was then that Hawthorne, alias M. du Mirror, fell forward across the table, foam bubbling from his lips.

'Curse you, Poe,' he whispered with laboured breath, 'my one solace is that you will never again recognise your own wife, the lady Lygia...'

'The lady who?' I said, pulling on my gloves, but received no reply, for he laughed an insane laugh before gargling his final breath.

I rose from the table intending to take my leave, but not forgetting to bow briefly but politely to the dying man's female companion, a lady of unquestionable beauty though uncertain age.

'Madam,' I said, 'your escort appears to be intoxicated. I suggest you call for a cab and transport him to his lodgings without delay. A very good evening to you. I have been glad to make your acquaintance but I must go to... go to...' I searched my mind but finding nothing, left the table in as little confusion as possible. Somewhat puzzled by my elusive thoughts I made my way to the street and strode out in the direction of... Before I had gone about a quarter of a mile, I heard police whistles piercing the stillness of the night, and hurrying footsteps behind me. The woman from the inn passed me at a rapid pace, closely followed by the landlord. It seemed that some terrible deed had been perpetrated of which I had no knowledge. I returned to the inn and offered my assistance to the inspector whose task it was to solve the crime, the murder if an unknown patron of the ale house. Through weeks of diligent detective work I was able to establish that the man had been poisoned, not in the place where the body was found, but by the third waiter in a café on the other side of the city. The guilty fellow was duly tried and executed according to the law. The identity of the corpse however was never discovered and police files remain closed in that particular respect.

All this was a long time ago. It is a peculiarity of the drug which Hawthorne administered that a reversal takes place in later years. Whereas one would normally expect to experience a decline into senile dementia, as one grows older, I in fact have noticed a sudden improvement in the machinations of my faculties. Certain areas of lost events have returned with a clarity never previously possessed. I have recently managed to communicate with my dear wife Lygia, who has also recovered much of the memory of her previous life. Hawthorne, on the other hand, has made no such happy discovery regarding the poison I had delivered to his lips. He has experienced no resurrection; has not leapt from the grave thoroughly invigorated; has not cast off his shroud and danced upon his own tomb. This indeed proves the value of the practical over the absurd. Hawthorne remains, firmly and securely, as dead as a nail.

ORACLE BONES

(Lectures at Hong Kong's *Royal Asiatic Society* sometimes sparked off ideas. 'Oracle Bones' was one of them. 'China Coast Pidgin' was another. I haven't written that one yet and I've forgotten much of the pidgin I used, though one phrase will remain with me forever: 'piano' in CC pidgin was 'toothy-face, bashy-in, cry'.)

WHEN THE YOUTH REACHED THE hill village, the elders were in the Happy Hut, locked in a debate concerning the nature of heavenly bodies and their effect on regional game. The old men were of course smoking opium in order to keep their heads clear during the argument and to increase their skill at presentation. There was nothing the tribes-people enjoyed more than a lively contest of words. It was at the height of this serious discussion that the runner arrived, bristling with urgency. He was told to wait.

One shrivelled husk with a hollow, rattling chest stated emphatically that each time a bird was caught in a snare, or a squirrel was shot with a musket, a new star appeared in the night sky. There was an impatient murmur of agreement. This fact was not in dispute. That a tally of the hunters' kills was maintained by the gods was a truism. In the time of the first ancestors, far back, the heavens had been black and almost empty. The point that was contested was whether each star was a permanent replacement for each separate kill, because certainly the game had decreased dramatically in number over the centuries. It was a fact that wild pigs had all but disappeared. The deer, once as numerous as the termites, were now impossible to find.

The young messenger, who was from the same tribe but from a different village, waited outside the Happy Hut in frustrated silence for the debate to finish. Though the women had immediately taken care of his thirst, his bare feet were hot from the three-day run, and he longed to bathe in the cool stream. He sighed and scratched his insect bites, his heart full of things other than the carrying of urgent messages.

The boy's own people lived three valleys away in the direction of the sun and his long run was not yet over. There was the return journey to make. When he had been asked to deliver the message he had been halfway through a careful but hasty erection of his bridal hut. Sixteen years old, he had been wed just over seven days, but had yet to consummate the marriage. The living-hut, which he had inherited from his father was not a fit place for the sexual act, since the spirits of his ancestors hovered around the corners and flickered on the support poles, and they would be shocked if he and his bride performed in their view. So, like all young men, he had to build a separate little bridal hut of bamboo roofed with banana leaves. This post-nuptial dwelling had to be at least a body-length from the living-hut. There, he and his new wife could reveal themselves to each other, away from the eyes of family ghosts. He had to build carefully since it had to be strong enough to withstand youthful athletics, yet swiftly because he was eager to experiment with procreation.

The youth looked up at the sky and sighed again. Dark clouds were buffeting each other across invisible terraces. He could make out the shapes of dogs amongst them, and wondered what that meant. A rain-wind was coming in low, through the treetops. He could see the shape of this broad wind running like a river over the foliage. Perhaps that was all it was? Rain coming?

Amongst the creased and withered elders, who puffed on their clay pipes creating a dense fug in the debating hut, was a man of great standing. He was the most ancient of any of the tribal dignitaries, having survived disease, accident and the rigours of opium for an unprecedented half century, though a recent respiratory problem indicated that it was doubtful he would make his fifty-first birthday. Though, this particular village was one of the poorest of a poor nation, this man was their most powerful shaman. It was to him that the youth had come running.

The village was on a tall place, the peak of a long ridge, and the youth hopped from one foot to the other, staring out over the hardwood forests below thinking of the beauty of his bride. She was plump and round-faced, with large dark eyes, and when he had first taken her to the courting garden and offered to push her on the swing made of vines, she had accepted without hesitation. There had been problems with her father of course, who had not approved of the youth as a suitable husband, but the boy had obtained a magic egg and had enticed the girl into the jungle. Once they had cooked and eaten the egg together, without interruption, the father naturally had to consent to the marriage. The egg had cost the youth two piglets, but she was worth it. Her cheeks were like ripe fruits and she had strong fat thighs. The youth's feet itched when he thought about those thighs.

Finally, though the debate was not yet at an end, the elders left the hut to perform their individual toilets. Clearly the exercise and fresh air was not good for them, because as soon as they were on their feet and out of the smoke they began to stagger.

The messenger went immediately to the shaman, who was leaning on a portal attempting to catch his breath.

'Great one', cried the boy, 'messengers have come from the big river to warn us of a coming!'

Red-veined eyes regarded the youth with little interest.

'Coming?' wheezed the old man. 'Who is coming?'

'Men. Men clad in clothes stained brown and green, and they have weapons, which shoot musket balls in great showers. They are as numerous as marching ants, and some of them come from the sky in whirling things, which fire thunderbolts. We are afraid they are coming to kill us all.'

'What do you want me to do?' whispered the shaman, coughing red flecks into the palm of his hand.

'You must tell us what course of action to take. The headman of my village has sent me here to ask your advice. This is an evil which threatens our whole nation and you, as our greatest shaman, have been given the authority to consult the oracle bones.'

A light came into the shaman's red-rimmed eyes.

'The oracle bones?' he breathed. 'Aaahhh!'

The elders were recalled from their functions in the forest and told of the news. It was universally agreed that the shaman should consult the oracle bones and a woman was despatched to fetch the last two bulls owned by the village headman. The corral where the cattle were kept was much closer than the village from which the young man had made his run, and the domestic beasts were in the hands of the shaman by nightfall. A ritual killing took place, then, the flesh was stripped from the bulls and roasted over log fires. The old men put aside their pipes and feasted on the meat, which since the bulls had been slaughtered by the shaman in a secret ceremony, was sacred and could therefore only pass the lips of an elder. All this was only right and proper.

The smell of the roasted bulls drove the young man mad and he went off into the forest to sleep. There under the moon-green roof of the world, he lay and dreamed of his fourteen-year-old bride. He had seen some of the girls in this village, as he had passed the spring where they filled their gourds, and none of them was as pretty as his own puff-cheeked wife. They had giggled as he ran swiftly past them, a stranger in their midst. It was true that there were probably several in the courting gardens that evening, waiting to see if he would appear, for there is no one more likely to cause turmoil in the hearts of local maidens than a youth from foreign climes. In his own village he might cause little excitement amongst the girls he had grown up with (his beloved being the one exception), but here he was a slim young god from exotic regions. There would be much speculation amongst older married women of seventeen or more about what his loincloth shielded, and concerning the tight roundness of his buttocks. The thoughts of the maidens, less direct, would be dwelling on his sinewy arms and thighs, and on the clarity of his eyes. Altogether, there would be little of his anatomy left untouched by the minds of the female population of this high village.

He slept fitfully, bothered less by the bark beetles and the spiders than by his own mental agitation. He went once to the spring for water, and interrupted an illicit meeting between a couple, married, but not to each other. The sounds of the elders feasting were disturbing the whole community, and there were few people in their beds. At dawn the women rose and began to pound the rice with foot-worked beam-hammers, and even the demons deep in the earth had their teeth rattled. The young man went and performed his ablutions, passing cleansed under the gate with the dogs' skulls and wooden figures that guarded the village. Elders had told him that once he was old enough to smoke opium and be privy to the true nature of the universe, he would see those wooden figures dance on the ends of their poles. The young man was not certain he was looking forward to this privilege.

The elders rose at noon and found their instructions for scraping clean the bulls' sternums had been duly carried out. A charcoal oven, which, had been built beyond the village perimeter was consecrated, and two large bones were heated in this makeshift kiln. The young man knew that the shaman would retrieve the bones, once they had been allowed to cool, and inspect the cracks caused by the intense heat. Reading these symbols, sent by the gods through the fire into the bones, the shaman could divine the future. One sternum bone represented peace and the other war, and by this method would he know how the tribe should treat with the hordes now crossing the big river.

The youth waited in an agony of loneliness and homesickness while this ceremony took place. He wondered what his beloved was thinking right at that moment, as she worked out in the fields under the blazing sun. Was she dreaming of him? Of course, she must be. And the hut, still only half finished! Perhaps if he made it smaller, it might be nearer completion, but then they had little enough room in which to romp as it was. Like most youths he wanted it large enough for her to be able to hold herself temporarily aloof, so that the eventual coming together would be that much sweeter. They needed to find each other in the darkness, not too soon, or the pleasure would be common and earthly. He anticipated going out on his first hunt, after their first union, and bringing home a tree squirrel or a fish for the pot. How her delighted cheeks would shine for him! He had been told by the elders that the pleasure of satisfying boy-girl desires was secondary to the wonders of the pipe, which he would be allowed to discover after his twenty-fifth birthday, but he could not believe such a tale. That was old men's talk, for those whose loins had since dried like seedpods under the sun. That was talk from those who could enjoy only dreams, whose passion had moved to their heads.

The following day he was summoned to the hut of the elders and the shaman gave him double-edged news.

The oracle bones had emerged from the charcoal without a crack on either of them. Such a thing had never happened before in the history of the tribe.

'It means,' said the shaman, 'either the tribe has no future to record on the bones, or the invaders will pass over us without disturbing us.'

'Should we risk it? Why don't we all hide?' said the youth. 'Why don't we run up into higher country still, where I have heard there are caves? We could stay there until these invaders have left our country, and then return and rebuild our villages. They would never find us up there.'

The shaman pursed his lips.

'Would you have us defy the gods?' he said.

'Is it possible,' asked the youth, 'that the fire was not hot enough? Or the bones too fresh? I have seen hotter fires, bones that were drier.'

'Leave us,' said the shaman. 'Go back to your village.'

The youth left readily enough and ran for three days, pausing only to drink from some broad-leafed plants that had formed basins for the rainwater during the last downpour. He arrived back at his home just as news reached his own elders that a village further down the valleys was already in flames. The elders took the youth's message and fell immediately into grave debate, while the young people crowded round the youth and asked questions of one that had travelled the world outside, had journeyed to the unknown regions of another village.

The boy ate then slept after that and awoke to the sound of rapid gunfire. He snatched his own long-barrelled musket, powder and ball, and ran outside. His young bride was running towards him, having raced from the fields. Her round face was bright with fear

'The enemy are coming,' she gasped. 'They are shooting and burning.'

The youth waited no longer. He grabbed her by the wrist and led her towards the first ridge. He would take her to the next village and try to persuade the elders that they should take action, prepare to resist the foe, or escape into the mountains. As he ran, pulling his frightened bride behind him, he called to his brothers, sisters and cousins to join him, but they merely stopped and stared as if he were mad, then turned their bemused eyes in the direction of the forest, from which plumes of flames emerged with crackling roars. The sound of whirling clatter came from the distant sky.

This time the youth took four days to reach the village where the great shaman lived, due to the weariness of his own body and the slowness of his new wife. On the way he stopped to shoot a domestic pig with his long rifle. The pig had not belonged to him but the young man argued with his bride that now the end of the world had come, private property had become public.

When the pair had arrived at the great shaman's village they found that the elders had just emerged from a long debate concerning the blankness on the oracle bones. These grave and pious elders took their duties extremely seriously. The opium was their link with their ancestors and it was the work of the elders to extract opinions from their hallowed forebears and impart it to their fellow debatees. Unfortunately, there were as many divine dead as there were men to question them. The fact that the old men could hardly stand when they left the Happy Hut, and frequently toppled over, indicated how long and hard the discussion had been.

They finally came to the conclusion that 'blank bones' meant the tribe had no future. The invaders, said the elders, would kill every man, woman and child in the tribe.

'That's true, that's true,' cried the excited young man, 'they have already destroyed my village. Look, you can see the smoke from here...' and pointed to the black vertical column which rose from beyond the southern ridges. There were other dark pillars of cloud visible further back.

The great shaman ignored the youth. The old man's face was full of light and wisdom. He lifted his ancient hand, extended a bony finger and pointed dramatically towards the smoke in the south.

'It was when we saw that sign from the gods,' he told his people, 'that we knew the tribe had no future.'

The young man nodded vigorously, and was about to remonstrate with the elders, to spur them to some kind of action, when they retired to the debating hut once more to decide whether their particular village had no future because of the presence of the invaders—who might indeed be satisfied with their conquest of the lower villages and come no further—or because the elders had killed its last two bulls and could not survive without breeding stock.

The youth was disgusted with the old people. He and his young wife set out for the caves in the distant mountains, he explaining to her that there was no need for a bridal hut now, because their ancestors had been left back there in the village of their birth. She, not without a little pique, was explaining to him that if he loved her as much as he said he did, he would not forego her traditional rights just because they had been forced away from their roots. He was supposed to build her a pretty hut of bamboo poles and banana leaves. If he loved her, he would still do this little thing.

A healthy discussion ensued, as they hurried onwards.

When they reached a mountain pass, they came across more of the enemy emerging from huts with whirling arms that had come down from the gathering of rain-clouds. The green and brown warriors carried guns the boy had never seen before and looked more like wooden figures from a sacred gate come to life than they did flesh and blood men. Clearly the enemy were not interested in debate, for they swooped on the village in a silence interrupted only by the roar of their weapons.

The youth and his bride hid in a cave and they stayed there for two days before venturing out again. He went down to the ruined village to see if anyone was left alive. Unhappily they were all dead.

At the time of the attack the great shaman had been caught in the middle of some wonderful rhetoric, for his blackened jaw was still wide open. When the youth sorted through his smouldering bones, in the haze of a smoky afternoon, he found they were cracked in many places. Although he had never smoked opium, the boy was able to read these divine messages easily, and predict the future of the tribe.

In the evening, it rained, sizzling upon the hot earth.

PAPER MOON

(Travel the world, meet interesting people and fill in endless forms for no particular reason. Bureaucracy, the bane of any traveller's life. Also a dangerous weapon of control.)

'THEY'RE NOT SUPPOSED TO DISCRIMINATE,' said the angular man to my left, 'but they do. Yes sir…' His voice trailed off in bitter resentment. There were three of us, humans, sitting together—the idiotic herd instinct. Moreover, we had been together for nine units, and I knew the whole orchestral range of his indignation, from the low whine to the high, heated complaints. I was sweating. The temperature of the room was very uncomfortable. You had to admit those Spicans had it all weighed up. This was acceptable heat for most races. Not for us, though, and that was the main reason for it being set so high.

The woman said, 'Discriminate? I've been here thirteen times.'

Here was the location of the only Spican bureau in the Affiliation—the moon of a remote planet that circled Algol.

'But I'll get past them,' she muttered, tight-lipped. She was thin and brittle and, I guessed, touching seventy Earth years.

'They won't keep me out. I've been to all sorts of places they've not even heard of.'

I stared at the oval doorway through which I would pass within the next few units. Inside that chamber was a Spican. Not many people have seen a live Spican, let alone talked to one. They were humanoids, a lot like us... or maybe not. Physically Earthmen and Spicans were compatible. That was the main source of their dislike for us. Our physical compatibility. Mentally, spiritually, we were galaxies apart. The clerks in the outer chambers were all Alterians, Spican employees with a flair for petty bureaucracy. My God, did they have a gift for that little game! They could drive a man up the concave walls and halfway to insanity with their endless cards, disks, tapes, and *I'm afraids*.

'I'm afraid you haven't the required seal on your application, sir. You'll need to have this reprocessed.'

'I'm afraid the clerk you spoke to previously has now left our employ. Could you begin again?'

Greasy, oil-blue excuse me for a smile. The snapper showing a band of hard bone.

Lost cards. Lost tapes. Lost identity. Signatures from inaccessible officials. Excessive quarantine periods. Stringent medicals. Monetary investigations. Family history. The works.

The salesman stood up, his rumpled, soiled clothes at variance with the expensive luggage. He walked over to a free window and impatiently rapped on the screen. Behind the screen the clerk stood up and, without giving any indication of having heard or seen, moved out of our range of vision. The salesman loosened his collar, shrugged, and dropped down heavily onto the purposely hard, lumpy benches that were so low to the floor that an average Terran's knees almost dislocated his jaw when he used them.

'See what I mean?' he said. 'Bastards. Ignorant as hell. Make a fuss and they're all over you with their slimy apologies. But you still don't get anything done faster.'

'Patience, pal,' I said

'Patience, shit!' he shouted. 'I've just about had enough! Anybody else says patience to me, I'll punch a few noses—or whatever,' he snarled, glaring round at the other members of the Affiliation. A Miran coughed in the silence that followed.

'Settle down, chum,' I said softly. 'You're frightening the lady.'

'Like hell he is,' the lady in question cackled. 'I just wanna see him break a few things.'

I said quickly, 'None of us will get to Spica's worlds that way. We'll all get canned.'

'That's just what these guys want, right?' said the salesman, now taking my advice and calming down. 'Well, they're not gonna get it—not from me. I'll get past immigration if it kills me.'

'Dead ones don't get in any quicker than live ones,' muttered the old lady. The salesman took no notice of this advice.

'Get in,' he said, 'that's all they told me at head office. "Get in there and sell," they said.' He looked at me with stricken eyes, and I suddenly pitied him.

'How the hell can I sell when they keep me away from my customers?'

I nodded. He was right. He would never get to a Spica world. But I would. The infinite delaying tactics employed by the Spicans couldn't stop Alex Clay. I was no grit-eyed salesman or kitsch-loving tourist sponging up ethnic origins and alien cultures in order to drench my penurious relatives. The machine wasn't built that didn't grind to a halt when my spanner landed in its guts. G-time was seventeen units. I stood up and strode toward the oval doorway leading to the inner chamber. I heard the salesman behind me say, 'Now where the hell does he think...?' An Alterian stepped in my path. He wasn't a full head shorter than I.

'You can't—' he began.

'Oh but I can. You see, I've waited ten units. I'm entitled.'

His eye glanced around nervously.

'No violence,' he said flatly.

I smiled. 'Of course, no violence. I'm merely telling you the law. We're on Spican soil—here in this immigration office—and I've waited ten units. I am now entitled to an audience, under Spican law,' I finished softly. His snapper came open involuntarily, and he closed it, using his claw. He stared for a while, then said, 'Wait here,' and passed into the oval.

A short time later he was back, and under the incredulous stares of my erstwhile companions, I entered the inner chamber.

'You quote Spican law to me?'

A tall, elegant creature was standing with his back to me, gazing through the transparent wall over the silent landscape of the moon. It was dusk outside and still. The only light, a purple glow from a cluster of house-high rocks nearby.

'I do,' I replied quietly.

He turned to face me then. We were about the same height, and I am tall for a Terran, but his build was better proportioned than my own. He was also very handsome.

'And who are you?'

'Alex Clay. I'm a Terran engineer.'

'I'm aware of your planet of origin—only two races that answer to the pattern of the human form, and you are no Spican. I believe that's what you call us?' His accent was a peculiar mixture of rounded vowels and clipped word endings.

'You know very well what we call you,' I replied. I laid my identisc on a polished slate table before him. He made no move toward it, his hands clasped behind the multifold cloak.

'How do you know of our laws?'

I glanced around the chamber. It was tastefully decorated with bright metallic centripetals that covered the walls and ceiling. 'Nice place.'

'Answer my questions,' he said.

I snapped, 'I don't have to answer questions of that nature. I won't be intimidated by some petty official.'

He flushed at this and seemed about to palm an eyeswitch.

'And calling your minions won't help you this time,' I anticipated. 'I've had enough of their brand of intimidation, too.'

He hesitated, and finally his hand fell back to his side. 'I am asking you now, as a polite inquiry. How did you know that under Spican law an official must admit a suppliant to his presence after ten units?'

'I was told,' I replied. 'Now that I'm here, I shall inform you in your official capacity that I intend to emigrate to a Spican world.'

'Which one?' He sounded sure of himself. Sure that no matter what passed between us, I would never make it.

'Alca-s.' I pronounced it perfectly, softly hissing the end of the word.

He winced. 'You'll have to do something with that after-s,' he replied, destroying my illusions. 'It grates.' He continued, 'We don't have much call for engineers. In fact I think we are fully employed.'

'How the hell do you know?' I replied quickly, sitting down on the cushion. 'You don't know my discipline.'

'Starship maintenance?' He looked away from my eyes. 'Well, you didn't think I'd see you without looking at your personal file, did you?'

'I'd have been disappointed had it been otherwise,' I answered. 'Do they have any trees on Alca-s?' This time I didn't attempt a correct pronunciation.

'Trees?' He looked offended at the word.

'Yes, tall organic structures composed of wood.'

His voice, turned cold. 'I don't see the connection–'

I interrupted. 'It's a protest on my part,' I said. 'Forested planets produce an administrative mechanism based on paper. Even after the paper's gone, the administrative blocking techniques live on. Paper is manufactured from wood,' I explained.

'I know about paper,' he nodded seriously. 'I still don't see.'

'The Alterian worlds are forested. That's why they suit your purposes—why you use Alterians as clerks in your immigration offices.' His eyes began to register intelligence. The irises were a soft mushroom grey. 'It's a sickness, really—Terra has it, always will have. The bogging bureaucrats.'

He nodded and I could see he was following my argument.

'You use it to keep us out,' I said. 'You need the Affiliation for the security of its economy, for the trade. But under Affiliation law you have to accept immigrants as part of the package deal. The right of free passage for all member worlds. Yes?'

'Yes,' he said. He walked to the far side of the chamber and washed his hands in a moonshaped dish. Symbolic?

'Do you work for the government. Clay?'

'The Affiliation of Worlds?' I said.

'You know what I mean. The government of Terra. Your own government.'

'I used to, once upon a time,' I said, aware of what was in my personal history—the recorded part, that is. 'I was an engineer on their solar freighters as a young man. Later I graduated to starships and left Earth for good. I haven't been back in... nearly five megaunits.'

He rubbed his hands into each other. He said. 'You're suddenly being very cooperative. Why the change of tactics?'

'Perhaps I wasn't getting anywhere?'

'You had me on the run.'

'You turned and faced me.'

He smiled then, for the first time.

'I like you, Clay. You're much the same as me, in personality, thinking.'

'But not physically,' I said, contradicting the truth. We were alike superficially, but he was a Greek god and I was fashioned more on the lines of a galley slave.

'No, not such a...'

'Magnificent specimen?' I finished for him, using an old cliché.

He laughed openly at that and said something in his own tongue.

'What?' I asked.

'Nothing. It doesn't translate perfectly. It loses.' I nodded.

'Anyway, now that we're friends,' I said frivolously, 'how about my application?'

A frown appeared on his face, and he pulled the cloak firmly around his body before settling on a nearby cushion.

'Let me tell you something about this place you wish to live in. Alca-s.' His tongue seemed to savour the word. 'My own world, incidentally. It's one of the three inhabited Spican planets. The temperate one. A pleasant overall climate, discounting the equator and the poles. The other two worlds, Alca-ns and Alca-cs, have extreme climates, even in the so-called temperate zones. One too hot, the other too cold.' I nodded. I knew it all anyway.

'Alca-s. The women are beautiful and the men are...'

'Beautiful,' I finished again. I couldn't resist it.

'Yes. True. They are, but more to the point, they are xenophobic. You would hate it there because they would hate you. None of us has ever emigrated because we... we can't live among strangers.'

'Not true,' I said. 'Official policy, maybe. But your ordinary people... I can't believe they hate those they have never met.'

'What do you know about my people?' he suddenly rapped into my face. 'I know my people.'

I replied simply, 'So do I.'

He jerked upright from his crouched position. 'What do you mean?' There was a thick atmosphere between us, and I could see by his taut expression that he was having difficulty in controlling his anger. I let him have the earthquake. The one I'd been saving for the right moment.

'I mean,' I said, 'I'm married to one.'

All the tension went out of his facial muscles, and the clenched fingers uncurled. I could smell the sweet oil on his palms.

'That's impossible,' he said at last. He spoke the words as if he were trying to convince himself rather than me.

'No,' I answered.

'You mean... you mean you're actually married to one of my race? We don't marry—not in the same way.' It was a desperate argument.

'You're clutching at straws,' I said. 'I married her—our way. A Terran wedding.'

'Ah! You wouldn't last on our world. It wouldn't work.'

'I'll last. Besides, if your people are such racial purists, how come you let others in? How come it's just us you block?'

'Well, ah, I should have thought that was obvious. Bad blood.'

'Yes? Well, I'm going to tell you a story, friend—a love story.' He lifted his hand as if to protest, but I waved it down. 'You'll need to know, in your official capacity, so I'll tell you anyway. Listen. Once upon a time—we always start stories that way— once upon a time there was a starship carrying a group of Spican politicians home from a conference. The destination of the ship was Alca-cs.

'Suddenly, a long way between worlds, something goes wrong with the main drive. The ship halts—well, not exactly, but worse still, it keeps going, with no way of stopping. Runaway. The engineer onboard this small executive craft gets to work right away, but wouldn't you guess it, he gets a jolt from a naked power line and zang! he's busted, too. Bad deal! The ship keeps flashing through space. Pretty soon it'll hit something—a planet, a sun—and whammo, full stop… Say, is my frivolous delivery bothering you?' His eyes told me the truth, even though his expression remained blank. I was enjoying myself.

I continued, 'Anyway, out goes the distress call, and who should be the only listeners within striking distance but the bad-blooded old Terrans. Quick decision. Do you allow yourselves to be contaminated by the presence of untouchable Terrans? Or do you risk certain death? To hell with dying, you say, even though it means fumigating the ship afterward.

'Among the Terran engineers that intercept the runaway is a tall, handsome gentleman who has a way with the ladies—and who should be among the cabin staff, but this adorable creature from Alca-s, no names, no pack drill…'

'What?' he interrupted in a faraway voice. I ignored him. 'So these two wonderful creations of God brush past each other in a narrow gangway, quite by accident, of course, not by design of the gentleman, who is indeed an honourable and upright citizen of Earth, and zang, something busts inside the male.

'I will admit,' I said, 'the female winces. One of those disgusting Terrans has actually touched her sacred person. But! But, my friend, she has felt the zang, too, and mingled with her loathing is a certain something she's not sure of. And somehow she finds herself bringing drinks to the drive room and passing the time of day with the handsome Terran brute. Oh, you may roll your eyes, Spican, but women love taming the brute in a man, especially when it's not really evident—the product of propaganda. Here is an animal who is really quite a charming, elegant person—what's he like in bed? It took thirty prolonged units to repair that starship, and at the last moment the female Spican impetuously consented to secretly marry the male Terran...'

He spoke. 'Cabin staff? A low-intellect clan...' He curled his lower lip in scorn.

'I'll remind you that you're talking about my wife,' I said very quietly.

'I'm sorry.' He pulled himself together, the hands clasping again behind his back. He walked around the room while I envied the muscles in his magnificent legs. You note envied, not admired.

'How were you married?' he asked at last.

'By the captain of the repair ship. It's legal—and binding.'

'And how do I know you're not... making this up? How do I know you're not lying?'

'I have a document—one of those boring sidelines a bureaucracy creates,' I said maliciously. 'It's recorded at the Affiliated World Record Centre. You can call it forward now.' I pointed to a computer terminal at the far end of the chamber. 'The alphanumber's, uh, 504-72083LSGN. Document number 710328.'

He made no move toward the terminal. 'I've told you before we don't recognise marriage. Not in its Terran form. We mate people according to their genes.'

'Classical,' I said scathingly. 'However, I'll remind you of Affiliation law. As a partner to a female from another world, I am entitled—automatically—to citizenship of that world. She is equally entitled to the benefits of my world. I'm here to give you formal notice that I'm on my way to join my wife. What's more, the Affiliation authorities know it, so please, let's not have any roughhousing.' He stared at me as if I were the most despicable creature that God had caused to be born.

'We have always carried out our obligations according to the law,' he said with dignity in his voice.

'Bully for you, Jack. Then you know that a negative state, by the Affiliation rules, is overridden by a positive one. To wit: Terrans are entitled by their own law to be with their relatives. I take it you have no laws positively forbidding marriage?'

His voice was so low I could hardly hear the No.

'Great, then I'm on my way.' I stood up and turned toward the exit.

'Clay!' he said sharply.

I swung round. 'What? Make it quick.'

His eyes had the look of a panic-stricken beast in them. I was about to destroy his race as he knew it.

'It couldn't last forever,' I said. 'One of us had to beat the system sometime. You're not so foolish to believe you could keep us out forever?'

His shoulders collapsed and he moaned softly. 'Yes,' I nodded. 'I suppose you are that foolish. You are children.'

His eyes flashed again. 'Don't speak of children... you. You Terran humans! You spawn indiscriminately. No thought for the mind or the body that is the produce of the union, oh, no. Sate the lust...'

'Hey, hey,' I shouted, 'it's not quite like that, friend. We have affection, a fondness for our partners. Sometimes it's a pretty strong one.'

'Love?' He snorted. 'Tell me about this thing love that creates gross interbreeding between unmatched pairs and results in freaks, small people, tall ones, IQ variations, idiots and morons, people of all shades, humpbacked, fat, thin, ugly...'

'That's it, isn't it? That's the whole bit? You can't stand to see abnormality. Well, our idea of normal isn't so narrow, that's all. In fact, it's pretty broad. It covers all but the insane. But you... you have to be perfect. I know what your infant mortality rate is. What do you do? Bash their heads against a rock if they come out with a strawberry birthmark on their buttocks? We know why you keep us out—we're the only race that can mate with Spicans and produce offspring, and you're afraid... afraid that mixed marriages will result in less-than-perfect Spicans. Not imperfect—just not perfect. We had a name for your type once...'

'We let one of you in,' he said in despair, 'and we let you all in. All of you. You don't mate by the clan system—you mate with anyone. This long Terran ancestry.'

I nodded. 'Well, that's why you've kept us out. You know it; we know it. Funnily enough,' I said seriously, 'we did try the clan system once—it produced inbred idiots. Funny how one thing suits one race and not the other. Anyway, looking on the bright side, you may benefit from a cultural exchange, who knows?' I turned again and walked toward the exit. He was right behind me.

'It was the Terran government, wasn't it? They planned this—the girl was hypnotised—drugged. She couldn't—she wouldn't sell our perfection for...'

'For love?' I said, pausing. 'I very much doubt it. Maybe it's just good old-fashioned contrariness. Lila's got a bit of the rebel in her...'

'Lila—so that's her name. Clay?'

'What?'

'Don't let them in, Clay. Stay out. It's the thin end—your children will mate with pure bred Spicans—don't you see?' I walked away from those hot, grey eyes. I hate to see men, any kind of men, begging for something they can't have. He followed me into the outer waiting room.

I passed the salesman, and he stood up.

'Did you get in?' he said eagerly.

I smiled. 'You bet.'

As I was about to enter the connecting tunnel to the ships, a guard stepped in front of me. 'Exit visa, please.'

'Ah, yes. One moment,' I replied.

I went to the fourteenth window and showed the mandatory five documents necessary for an exit visa.

'I do not see your Certificate of Flight Worthiness, sir.'

'My what?'

'Your CFW—for the ship.'

'But I've never had to show that before.'

'It's a recent regulation, sir.'

A pricking sensation began at the back of my neck. They were trying to hustle me.

'How recent?' I was aware of the Spican's eyes on my back.

The salesman called out. 'Half a unit ago—while you were in there talking to what'sisname.'

'Why wasn't I informed?' I said.

'The, uhmm, information was broadcast, sir, over the speakers.' He pointed out the objects in question. I nodded.

'My CFW is on my ship. I'll go and get…'

The guard said, 'I'm afraid I can't let you let you go to your ship without an exit visa…'

I turned to the Alterian clerk. 'And I can't get a visa without a CFW.'

Oily smile. 'I'm afraid not, sir.'

I made a last, desperate bid. 'You realise that I'm a Spican by marriage—and this is Spican soil we're standing on.'

Now the guard was amused.

'Only in here—in this building. Once you step outside, you're on Alterian soil.'

'And this is an Alterian regulation?'

The guard nodded. 'I see,' I said.

This distance between me and my ship was about half a click. I turned to look at the Spican, and both of us knew what I was going to do. The Alterian guards were short and clumsy and did not carry weapons. There was really only one person who stood between me and my wife, and that was the Spican, the Apollo of outer space. I saw him brace those magnificent leg muscles and give me an arrogant stare.

'Okay, pal,' I said softly. 'Let's see if you're the real stuff, or just showy beach boy…' It was the old story: love against authority, love versus tradition, love takes on the world.

This time, love was going to win.

I hit the tunnel entrance going like a pro.

The Spican was right behind me.

STORE WARS

(Started off with the parody title and developed from there.)

No one really knows how the conflict started. The store was closed for business, it being the morning before the Turn of the Century Sale. The doors were to be opened precisely at noon, 1st January 2000.

Some of the customers had been there since the previous evening, braving the night air, the street frosts, armed only with vacuum flasks full of coffee, nips of brandy and thick sleeping bags. Time takes on a different meaning in such circumstances. They made the remarkable discovery that the night is not all darkness, but the twilight lingers long and comes again early. The globe actually turns quite slowly. It is people who move fast. They had entered a world of idle hours. Around them the streets were almost silent, the night winds turning scraps of paper into live creatures on strange urgent business elsewhere. Philosophies were formed, accepted, discarded. Old grudges shrank to insignificance and promises of reconciliation were born.

They found they had time to reflect on their lives, to make decisions on a change of direction, on marriage, on divorce, on leaving their job at the insurance office or bank and hitting the road. In the early hours of the morning, lifelong friendships were formed with people behind them in the queue. There were even affairs begun, and some ended. They found you could live more in a single night than in many years of ordinary time.

Then, as the noonday opening came within sight at last, they remembered why they were there.

There were always bargains to be had at Maccine's sales: washing machines for a fraction of the retail price, just-out-of-style dresses and suits, sports gear that had last year's colour on their motifs.

Within the building, all was not well however.

Animosity had been building up between floor and department managers at Maccine's, the world's largest store, for as long as people could remember. The company fostered rivalry between the managers, and consequently, the departments. Substantial prizes were given each year for the highest takings at the till. Maccine's believed in the reward system. They boasted jokingly that no employee had been flayed or hanged for close on a century.

Competition was fierce and bloody. Staff had, in the past, been known to sabotage rival departments. Some recall when the sprinkler system had been tampered with then deliberately activated one morning by persons unknown. It was at a time when there was a difference of opinion between Men's Tailoring and Hardware regarding the entitlement to sell workmen's coveralls. Men's Tailoring suffered a terribly when hydrochloric acid instead of water sprayed their stock and staff.

Then there was the incident when tiny needles tipped with neurotoxic poison were found fixed to the telephone earpieces of a new little corner department known as Ribbons and Bows, whom Haberdashery called the 'upstarts'. Three people spent seven months in hospital, seriously ill with nervous system disorders.

Managers had been known to have had fistfights in restaurants, when they came across deadly rivals unexpectedly while out with their wives. Junior staff formed departmental gangs outside the workplace and wore silk windcheaters with purple lettering such as Bedroom Furniture Dragons or Lions of Curtains and Draperies emblazoned on the back. These gangs fought pitched battles in the street, their members often getting arrested for carrying concealed weapons.

The inter-departmental messengers carried, in the main, sacks of hate mail between managers. Ex-Viet Cong immigrants were recruited and a booby trap called the 'bamboo bed' began to appear in dark corridors. This fiendish device was a spring-loaded trellis covered in spikes, which flew up from the floor when triggered by a foot. There was one famous booby trap, where a young woman from Clocks and Watches put a dozen assorted poisonous sea snakes, each just over twelve inches long, into the cistern of the Garden Equipment manager's toilet. A banded yellow-black bit him on the left cheek as he was in the middle of his morning ablutions.

Although people were reprimanded, no one actually lost their job in any of these incidents, and truth to tell the company actually encouraged inter-departmental conflict. They felt it showed keenness. Inefficiency was not tolerated. For incompetence of any nature you could be out on your ear within the hour. However, nobody ever actually got the sack for unruly behaviour in the cause of patriotism for one's department.

There were vast spy networks. People who had transferred from one department to another, but who still retained old loyalties, were constantly passing secret messages back and forth. One member of Glassware 'fell' in front of a train while on her way home from work and the store detectives, the only impartial group in the building, were convinced she was pushed. Glassware had apparently discovered she was an undercover agent for Porcelain and Pottery, having left the company and rejoined for the express purpose of feeding information to her old department.

There were religious differences it was true. Perfumeries, Electrical Goods and Hardware were one-hundred percent Catholic, and Protestants were in the high majority in Lingerie and Sporting Goods, but there were many other departments where the mix was thorough and the two Christian groups amicable. The Restaurant, Groceries, and the Coffee Shop on the 101st Floor had a strong Islamic element, while Pharmaceuticals and the Dispensary were almost entirely Hindu. There were occasional problems which might have been traced to extreme religious prejudice, but the only real fundamentalists were in the packing department, way down in the basement, and in no strategic position to assist an escalation of the fighting.

Much the same could be said about any racial disharmony: there was little evidence to suggest that people of different races at the store persecuted each other. Those who were discriminated against were minority departments like Men's Socks and Ties and Ladies' Fripperies. The staff in these small departments were bullied and hounded by all, and only rarely was there a token member of such sections invited on a quiz panel, or to form part of any sports team. They were of course continually campaigning for their 'rights' and occasionally, when a strong leader arose amongst them, there would be an assassination, usually carried out by some redneck from Sporting Goods.

Naturally every member of each department considered his or her floor to be superior to all others. The battles at the till were fierce and customers searching for an item which was not to be found in the department where they were enquiring after it would be quietly directed to a rival store further down the street, rather than to the floor in Maccine's that stocked the object. The majority of the counter staff were young and hot-blooded, and they carried their grievances on their shoulders. They might hate their department manager, but at least he or she was one of them, and not a stupid Nail bender (Hardware Department Assistant) or a dirty Glue-sniffer (Stationary Department Counter Clerk).

Feelings were running high on the day of the sale. There were big prizes to be won and only the night before DVDs had encountered Video Tapes at a seasonal dance. There was supposed to be a truce on, over the sale period, and both sides avoided contact for most of the evening. However, Miss Rona of Video Tapes, and Mr Blake, of DVDs, were caught canoodling behind a pillar.

Mr Smith of Video Tapes asked them quietly who the hell they thought they were, Miss Montague and Mr Capulet?, thereby showing that though he had a passing familiarity with Shakespeare, his had not been a completely thorough education. There was nothing wrong with his boxing technique however, and he let Mr Blake have it on the chin, at the same time bestowing a curse on his house.

The fight escalated, until broken bottles, can openers and furniture were employed, and the dance floor was littered with wounded warriors. Individuals from other departments were drawn into the rumpus, some never went home that night. One or two never went home again. The casualty departments of the hospitals worked overtime.

The following morning the first sign of really serious trouble came just after the ten o'clock coffee break, when a young man new to Men's Underwear accidentally got out of the elevator on the wrong floor. His own department first saw him again a few minutes later when the elevator doors opened and his lifeless body dropped at the feet of their sensitive Mr Williams, who screamed energetically until Mr Jones slapped his face. The corpse was wearing nothing, but a sequinned G-string, wound tightly around its throat.

'Lingerie!' cried the department manager, and despite the fact that Mr Williams said it could be a frame, that just because an item of ladies' undies was used as a weapon did not necessarily mean that Lingerie was responsible, the manager despatched a commando team to raid the guilty department. 'Shut your face, Williams,' cried the department manager, or you'll find yourself demoted from floor supervisor before you can say kiss my ass. I know your boyfriend works in Knickers and Bras, so don't give me that crap about how it might be somebody else! You're just trying to protect your Mr Simpson.'

This was true enough.

The commando team was led by a man who was a sergeant in the National Guard, their Mr Ackroyde, a high-flyer and rising star in Men's Underwear. His sales figures were magnificent and his fervour in promoting his department during coffee breaks was unequalled. There were four ex-marines with him, older men who had seen service in Afghanistan. Their first stop was Sporting Goods, where they rushed from the elevator into the room, grabbed some weapons, and back into the elevator before the doors closed. Each of them had snatched a golf club, or a climbing ax, and Mr Ackroyde himself had managed to grasp a crossbow with two bolts.

On route to the battle the elevator stopped to let on a white-haired bespectacled little man with the demeanour of a Swiss toy-maker. A ripple of fear went through the five-man attack force as they quickly made space for Mr Vandyne, a counter clerk from the most elite department in the building. He looked at their weapons and then into each of their faces with an expression of contempt. They coughed quietly and shuffled around staring at their feet until Mr Vandyne got out. Only then did they break into loud animated discussion again.

They came out of the elevator into Lingerie in true heroic style; yelling their famous battle cry of, 'Briefs and buggery!' they laid about them with their deadly tools. Mr Ackroyde pinned a Miss Feversham to the wall with one of his bolts, but unfortunately missed his target with his second shot. His team mates felled at least eleven counter staff before they were overpowered.

Rage is not a good companion in war. Unfortunately their blind anger had not allowed them sufficient time to plan their escape. One needs a cool head when forming strategy on the battlefield. Though it had not been their original intention to forfeit their lives, it was in the end a suicide mission. The women of Lingerie wrested the weapons from the hands of these border raiders and then carried out some unspeakable tortures on the poor individuals. There was no such thing as rules of war in Maccine's: you took no prisoners. The girls simply screeched, 'No quarter!' and proceeded to do inventive things with pins and clips on male skin. Once the blood began splashing the designer foundations, they ceased their cruelty and put the raiders out of their misery. The bodies were piled into the goods elevator and sent hurtling down to Packing with labels that read, 'To be despatched to the Dead Centre of the City. (Joke!)'.

In the meantime, Sporting Goods, (or Jock's, as they liked to call themselves), were incensed at the audacious theft of their items by the crew from 'Shreddies'. Being gentleman, they sent someone to Men's Underwear to complain.

The body came back wrapped in several, quite separate, thermal undershirts.

The Jocks armed themselves, but first they intended to pay back Shreddies on a one-for-one basis. Ronnie (the Jocks were on first names) rang down to Men's Underwear, using the outside phone, and pretended to be the Fire Officer. In thick accents Ronnie asked the callee to look out of his nearest window, to see if he could detect smoke from the lower floors. The poor schmuck did as he was asked and was almost decapitated by a medicine ball dropped from Sporting Goods. It certainly broke his neck and he flopped out of sight to a cheer from the Jocks.

One of the Four Horsemen was now in full gallop.

At fifteen minutes past ten, alliances were made. Sporting Goods phoned Lingerie and proposed that they join forces to wipe out Men's Underwear. The two departments had always been on reasonable terms due to the fact that Lingerie employed airhead females who were attracted to the kind of dim but muscled males in Sporting Goods.

Unknown to these two allies, Men's Underwear had contracted Kitchen Improvements and Bathroom Appliances. Now armed with bread knives and clubs fashioned from faucets, they waited to repel the onslaught expected from above.

Amazons from Lingerie used the fire escape and entered Men's Underwear from the windows screaming like banshees. The Jocks used the large service elevator, knowing their front rank would be cut down, but hoping the rear troops could use their bodies as a shield.

The ensuing battle was swift and vicious and blood flowed in rivulets down the glass showcases; splattered on the display figures (Men's Underwear called them 'manikins') wearing Hawaiian shorts and the new undershirts with the Macho 'drop armholes'; sprayed the counter busts of a male midsections wearing men's knickerbriefs. Lingerie and Sporting Goods finally retreated, having failed to take Men's Underwear by storm. They left many dead behind them, most of them wearing black silk underwear bearing designer labels.

All the departments in this battle regrouped afterwards and counted their losses. All declared they were by no means beaten, that they had a lot of fight left in them yet, by golly. Banners were fashioned. Pennants were raised. Soon they were ready to do battle again, and set about contacting other departments throughout the huge complex, to gain support for their causes.

At precisely eleven o'clock, the General Manager arrived at the store to find that practically every department in the building was either under attack, or in the process of an aggressive act. Only one solitary department had not yet joined the conflict, and this particular section held itself aloof from what was now a store war. The worst area was the roof, where a terrible carnage was still taking place.

Once in his office the General Manager became aware of bodies falling past his window. His secretary had been waiting for him to arrive for the last quarter of an hour. She said she was terrified and wanted to leave the battle zone, but had at the same time this inexplicable though undeniable urge to have sex with him.

War, he told her, did that to some people.

When they had finished, she said sadly as she buttoned her dress that they might never see one another again, but the General Manager made light of the situation, saying it would be over before next Christmas. Seriously, he told her, there will be peace before the twelve o'clock onslaught of customers. I hope so, she replied, throwing her laddered tights into the wastepaper basket, I sincerely hope so.

The General Manager then set about trying to restore order. He called in some of the Members of the Board of Directors to assist him in settling differences. The Unions too, were contacted, and sent representatives to form with the Directors a kind of peace-keeping force. This amalgamated group called themselves the Unprincipled Negotiators, or UN.

The UN risked their lives journeying through corridors, up and down elevators, along passageways, into rest rooms, looking for the leaders of the various factions. They carried a huge banner which read GENERAL MANAGEMENT AND UNION OFFICIALS to deter ambushers whose bloodlust blinded them to the fact that there were non-combatants still in the building.

At first the UN believed they were in search of department and floor managers, but the war had gone beyond that stage. New generals had arisen, popular leaders not chosen from the official hierarchy, but whose charismatic personalities made them prominent amongst their kind. The supreme leaders, one would have to call them Field Marshals at this point in the war, were— on one side—Hardware's strategist warrior queen, the iron lady of Pots and Pans, Bo Driscoll—and on the other—the cunning intellectual from Magazines and Periodicals, Fletcher J Jnr, whose left pinkie knew more about tactics than Julius Caesar and Napoleon put together.

The UN finally got these two sitting at a table together, the tall willowy figure of Bo Driscoll and the short but feisty Fletcher J, who glared at each other with such hatred the General Manager foresaw that the exercise would turn out to be a useless one. Indeed, both parties swore that the conflict had reached a stage where they could no longer control their armies, that the fighting would go on until the last counter assistant stood amongst the bodies of the enemy and planted a victory banner.

'Genocide!' cried one.

'Genocide!' repeated the other.

The General Manager saw only one path left to him. He telephoned the President of the company, who was on a business trip to the capital.

'We need your voice,' said the General Manager. 'We've done a hook-up to the speakers system throughout the building. You have to make a speech, plead with the two armies, get them to stop before they destroy all our stock...'

'Plead with them?' boomed the President. 'Never!'

Instead he made a dreadful mistake: a telephone call to the one department that had so far remained neutral, the department of which Mr Vandyne, the white-haired little man encountered by the Men's Underwear commando unit in the elevator, was proud to call himself a member.

The reason GUNS & RODS had not participated in the war so far was not because they were pacifists or anything wimpish like that. They had kept out of it because there was nothing in it for them. They were the ultimate department, in terms of force. Their firepower was unequalled, devastating. They were an utterly cold and ruthless breed, with contempt for all other mortals. The Department Manager would not recruit anyone whose medical report did not bear the words 'sociopathic tendencies' or 'history of psychopathic disturbances'. Their greatest pleasure, was in firing weapons on the indoor range. Their second greatest pleasure was in stripping down the guns afterwards, oiling them, and putting them back together again. Shooting things was their raison d'être, big game fishing their only hobby. When a customer came in and asked for anything smaller than a 12 gauge shotgun, a .45 handgun or said they wanted to fish for trout, the counter clerk would curl his top lip and openly sneer. Middle-aged grandmothers who had found themselves in the department by accident when looking for Babies' Clothes, had walked out with make-my-day magnums rather than continue to face the disdain of the staff.

The deadly beauty of the goods they sold, with their shiny blue gunmetal barrels and hardwood butts, was so superior to anything else the store had on offer that the counter clerks (who called themselves 'weapon salesmen' or 'gunsmiths' in the bars outside the store) looked with dreadful scorn on the rest of the company staff. The latter were as cockroaches to them.

The President's telephone call unleashed these hounds of hell, who came whooping and yelling from their cages, wearing baseball caps which said: 'Born to Decimate'. They brandished pump-action over-and-under 12-gauge shotguns, and waved vicious-looking hunting knives with blood-grooves on the blades. The poor misguided President of the company knew not what he had done in loosing these dogs of war.

Until this point, although there had been some damage to the goods, much of the stock was still in a saleable condition. Then GUNS & RODS began blasting their way through counters and doors, laying about them with wanton carelessness, peppering washing machines with bullets and shot, shattering televisions, puncturing pots and pans. GUNS & RODS had their berserkers who at the first sniff of a fired cartridge, leapt on counters in a frenzy and used their hunting knives to tear suits and dresses to shreds. They came in firing indiscriminately and went out blasting with abandon.

Not the least terrible amongst them was the maniacal figure of Mr Thornton Vandyne, the pupils of his eyes like tiny mad mosquitoes, as he emptied two .45 automatics at anything that resembled a human shape.

When Bert Wilkins, the Chief Security Officer, crawled mortally wounded to the main doors at noon and opened them as the clock struck twelve precisely, the waiting hordes trampled him underfoot. New friendships which had formed amongst the waiting customers now disintegrated. Fresh loyalties were crushed without hesitation or remorse. It was every man, woman and child for themselves.

The waves of customers kept coming until the store was full of people. At first they ran around with wild eyes, their minds tuned to bargains. Then gradually their feet slowed to a stop, their thoughts became more regulated. Slowly, slowly the idea came into their heads that all was not right with Maccine's. It settled like fine dust upon their feverish brains.

A kind of universal daze came over the crowd, as they stared about them at the smoking ruins, the soles of their shoes crunching fragments of crystal into the carpet. There was nothing left to buy. Nothing worth having, that is. All that remained, amongst the corpses, were the useless shards of a former shopper's paradise. The devastation had been total.

It was the end of all cheap goods.

Garry Kilworth

THE MEGOWL

(My father used to have a recurring nightmare about an owl that perched on his bedpost while he slept, this bird having the face of an old woman.)

TIM SULLY WAS DRESSED IN all black, with a luminous green skeleton painted on his front. His face was a grinning skull behind which his worried eyes flicked to and fro as he hurried past the wild thickets that separated the houses. It was Hallowe'en and he had been out trick-or-treating with friends. His pockets were full of sweets and he had eaten more cakes and biscuits than was good for him.

Tim walked the lane that led to his house. It was only a short distance, not more than two hundred metres, but it was overshadowed by trees on both sides and very dark. Every so often he passed a house, set back from the lane in the trees. The lights from their rooms gave him a little comfort. Listening to his heartbeat, which seemed louder than the wind in the trees, he suddenly came in sight of his own house.

Tim felt a sense of relief. They had been scaring so many people that night that he had finally worked himself up to a pitch of excitement from which it was hard to descend. At thirteen he believed himself to be too grown up to get scared on Hallowe'en, but once his friends had left him at the turning to his own lane, taking their high chattering voices with them and leaving him with the silence and darkness of the October night, it had been a different story.

When he was twenty metres from the house, Tim suddenly stopped dead, the skin on the back of his neck prickling in fear. Something was moving in the unkempt hedgerows. Slowly he turned and stared at the spot from which the noise was coming. It was a kind of rustling, skittering sound and he told himself it must be a bird.

'It's probably only a thrush or something,' he muttered.

To prove to himself that it was nothing out of the ordinary, he walked to the hedge and peered into the black foliage. With his heart pounding he reached out and gently parted the leaves. At that moment the moon found a gap in the clouds and illuminated a white object nestling in the fork in the hedgerow. The pale, ovoid shape seemed to invite Tim's touch as he reached out and, hesitating only for a moment, put his fingertips to the thing, which was an egg.

Tim's hand jerked back to his sides. The egg was warm. His common sense, as well as his instinct, told him this was very strange. It was October, the autumn leaves were falling and any eggs forgotten by birds in the spring should be stone cold by now. He could think of no birds that laid their eggs in October, just before the onset of winter, which would kill any newborn chicks. The egg of a wild bird, whatever it was, should not be warm. It should be dead, cold and rotten.

Was this someone's idea of a Hallowe'en joke? Perhaps it was a pullet's egg, or that of some other tame or domestic fowl. Maybe someone was hiding in the thicket, watching to see what Tim would do. Perhaps there would be a sudden gust of laughter in a moment and one of his school friends would come crashing through the trees shouting, 'Got you, Sully! Got you this time! Wait till I tell the others about this then!'

There was laughter, however. The wind played chasing games with the darkness in the trees and a few more leaves fell. Overhead, a cloud passed in front of the moon, causing a brief blackness to envelop the scene, then the light returned.

The egg was still there, inviting touch. Tim impulsively reached out and grasped it in his hand. Without really knowing why, he ran towards the house, clasping it to him. It seemed to pulse in his fingers as he dashed through the open gateway and hammered on the door with the iron knocker. The sound echoed through the hallway, then he heard his mother's quick footsteps. The door opened.

Tim's mother, a tall woman with a narrow face, gasped and stepped back, her hand to her breast.

'Oh, Tim!' she wheezed. 'I'd forgotten you were dressed like that!'

'Sorry, Mum,' he said, slipping past her. 'Didn't mean to frighten you. I'll go and change into my pyjamas'

Tim walked quickly to his bedroom, but stopped on the way to put the egg in a shoebox which he kept at the back of the airing cupboard, under a bundle of old newspapers. It was his hidey hole for treasures. Then he had a quick wash in the bathroom and took off the skeleton suit, replacing it with his pyjamas. He went to the living room to find his mother.

She was sitting by the gas fire, poring over some papers to do her work. Tim's parents were divorced and his father lived in Lancaster with a new wife while his mother, Deborah, worked in a local estate agent's office. Though Tim occasionally saw his father during the holidays, the meetings were becoming fewer. Mr Sully seemed more interested in Susan, his new wife, and appeared to want a complete break from his former wife and son.

Tim was an only child so he got a bit lonely at times. His mother was often too absorbed in her work to have much time for him. Sometimes he wished she didn't work quite so hard.

'Sorry about that, Mum,' Tim said again, as she looked up from her work.

'It's all right,' she replied in her abstracted way. 'I just wasn't expecting it. You off to bed now? Did you have a good time?'

'Yes. Dave was dressed in a sheet and Karen wore a witch's outfit.'

'That's lovely, dear,' she said vaguely.

Tim stared at his mother's wispy-haired head as she bent over her work and he sighed. She was a good mother in many ways but she lived in some hazy world which was hard to access.

'Night, Mum,' he said, kissing her cheek.

'Night, Tim.'

AFTERWARDS, LYING IN BED, TIM considered the egg. He had never robbed birds' nests before tonight and wondered why he had done so now. The egg had seemed strangely attractive and he had felt a sudden urge to possess it. It had been a feeling impossible to ignore. Then there was its strange warmth, as if it were still alive. That was not possible of course. Either someone was playing a trick or some animal or bird had warmed the egg by accident. He would throw it away in the morning. He fell asleep, staring into the darkness of the room around him.

The following day, however, he had forgotten about the egg, which nestled in the shoebox in the warmth of the airing cupboard. Unknown to him inside the shell there were signs of faint activity—activity which increased as time went on.

Occasionally, Tim heard a rustling noise on the landing, but thought little of it. He thought nothing too, of the strange dreams he had from time to time. Dreams in which he was flying, or hunting in the dark. He certainly never thought of the egg. Indeed, he had forgotten its very existence.

Time passed swiftly and it was soon Christmas. Tim was very excited. His cousins would be coming for Christmas Day and he was looking forward to receiving his presents.

ON CHRISTMAS MORNING TIM VISITED the shoebox again. Among the treasures inside it was a small present for his mother—a pair of sewing scissors. He had bought them in the summer, knowing the pair she already owned were getting rusty.

The scissors were there all right, but someone had been to his box. The lid had been removed and was lying upside down next to it. Tim was just considering remonstrating with his mother for going through 'his things' when he noticed the broken pieces of eggshell. He suddenly realised what had happened. Incredibly, the egg had hatched and the chick had pushed the lid off the shoebox to escape.

Tim stared into the depths of the cupboard, which housed the hot water tank and sheets, towels and pillow slips. He could see nothing—no signs of a bird of any kind. His mother would not be pleased to find droppings or feathers on her clean linen, that was certain. Finally he decided that the bird must have got out of the cupboard earlier, when his mother had opened the door. No doubt it was free, somewhere in the house. He would have to keep his eyes open for the creature.

WHEN TIM'S COUSINS AND VARIOUS relatives arrived the creature was soon forgotten in the excitement of exchanging presents. Tim got the pair of roller blades he'd wanted for ages, from his mother. They were the latest in roller skates and he and his cousins, who also had blades, went off to the local skateboard park to try them out.

Late in the evening the last guest left the house and Tim and his mother were alone again, clearing away and washing up together before going to bed.

'Have you enjoyed today?' asked his mother anxiously. 'I'm sorry the turkey was overdone. I don't think your uncle Jim liked it very much.'

'Never mind, Mum. Turkey's turkey—and the roast spuds were good.'

Her eyes lit up a little at these words.

'Were they, dear?'

'Brill, Mum—take my word for it. And the roller blades are ace! Thanks a million.'

She went to bed fairly happy after these words. Tim was always amazed at the power he had to make his mother cheerful or sad, and sometimes it frightened him. He did not want the responsibility for her happiness.

He put out the lights and went to his room at the back of the bungalow, where he stowed the roller blades in a cupboard before climbing wearily into his pyjamas. He tried to read a comic but his eyes kept closing, so he switched off the light and lay down to sleep.

It must have been about twenty minutes later that Tim woke to a strange sound. For a few moments he just stared into the darkness of the room, wondering what had roused him from his first sleep. Then he heard it again—a kind of rustling, scratching noise which seemed to be coming from the corner of the room. He peered into the dense shadow but his eyes could make out nothing except blackness. For a while nothing happened and Tim was dropping off to sleep again when there were further sounds.

He felt a trickle of fear go down his spine. What was it? Had a mouse got into his room? Maybe it had been attracted by

Christmas cake crumbs or something. He and his cousins had been eating in the bedroom that day.

He wanted to get out of bed and look but a stronger feeling of fright would not let him. He was afraid of what he might find. Late at night there were things that worried him more than they might have done during the day. Things were different in the dark, in the silence of the small hours.

Suddenly, Tim reached for a book on his bedside table. He threw it into the corner and buried his head under the bedclothes. After a few moments he listened hard for the sounds to return and when they didn't decided it must have been a mouse after all—now frightened back into its hole. He would search the room tomorrow and block the creature's lair, wherever it was. The fear-sweat that had covered him earlier now began to leave and he was able to go back to sleep.

Later, however, he had the sensation of being disturbed by a faint rustling in the bedsprings, but it was not loud enough to wake him thoroughly and in the morning Tim wondered if he'd fallen asleep and dreamed it after hearing the scratching in the corner. It was always difficult to sort the real from the unreal after night fears.

An inspection of the bedroom after breakfast revealed no holes in the skirting-board. Remembering the broken egg-shell, Tim searched for fur and feathers too, but found nothing and convinced himself he'd been dreaming as a result of too much Christmas dinner.

'Had a bad dream last night,' he told his mother.

'Did you, dear?' she replied vaguely. 'How upsetting for you.'

'Oh, it was no big deal,' Tim added. 'It wouldn't even seem scary if I told you now.'

'Fine,' she replied. 'Now I must get these papers finished before I go back to work tomorrow. Can you amuse yourself?'

'Sure,' said Tim, leaving his hard-working mother to her problems.

Boxing Day was spent walking the downs and using the roller blades. It was one of those sharp, crisp winter days, where a low sunset throws out bright rays to make the frost glisten on the meadows and pick out crystallised spiders' webs in the hedgerows.

That evening, on returning to the house, Tim found his mother still engrossed in her papers. She murmured something about 'lunch' and Tim told her lunchtime had long since gone and it was time for dinner.

'Oh dear,' she said, pushing her glasses up her nose and brushing away strands of hair from her eyes. 'Never mind, we'll have some turkey sandwiches in a moment. Will that be all right?'

'Fine, Mum.'

Time went to his room to put away his roller blades. It was gloomy in there, as the main bulb had blown and only his small bedside table lamp cast a pale light over the corner. He opened his wardrobe door and put the blades in the shoe rack inside. As he did so he glanced up at the hanging coats.

Something white stared out from amongst their dark folds.

Tim jumped backwards quickly, startled into uttering a sound much like the yelp of an injured puppy. Fear gripped him. It washed through his whole body like a wave of freezing water. His breath came out in short, sharp pants.

He was immobilised, rigid with terror, as he stared at the creature before him, perched on the coat rail.

It was a bird with the face of an old woman.

The creature's feathers were white. The complexion, with its tiny, shrewish features, was a pasty grey. Prehensile claws flexed on the coat rail. The creature spat at him viciously.

'Yetchhh!' it screeched.

Tim could do nothing but stare into the mean eyes of this nightmarish fiend. He wanted to scream for help, yell for his mother, but the eyes would not let him. They held him fast where he stood, their control over him complete. He could not even move his hands or feet.

'Eeerchh!' whined the owl, through the tiny, white, even teeth.

Tim's own teeth started chattering and he bit his tongue several times. Sensing his distress, the owl's human face produced a savage smile. Then some strange creaking words came from its mouth and Tim found to his horror that he understood them. Hypnotised, he closed the wardrobe door gently and went into the kitchen.

There he walked straight to the fridge and selected a piece of liver still swimming in a pool of blood. Taking some scissors from the cutlery drawer, he cut the raw liver into slivers and carried them back to his bedroom. He opened the wardrobe door again to find the terrible owl still there. Tim fed it the strips of raw liver, watching in disgust as it snatched them from his hand and swallowed them like worms.

When the creature was satisfied, it shuffled on its perch, said something in its dark, ugly tongue and closed its eyes. Tim shut the door on it and crept away, still chilled to the marrow by the encounter.

He went straight to the living room and stood in front of his mother. Her head was bend over her work but eventually she looked up at him.

'Goodness, Tim!' she cried. 'Are you all right? You look so pale.'

Tim wanted to tell her about the horrible thing in his wardrobe but his tongue would not let him. Instead he heard himself say, 'I'm fine, Mum. Just a bit tired. I think I'll skip dinner.'

'Skip dinner?' she said. 'You must be ill. Go to bed. I'll bring you something.'

He stumbled out of the living room, half in a dream, and went to his bedroom. There he changed into his pyjamas and got into bed. Later his mother brought him some turkey soup and he ate it. Then she pulled the curtains and left him alone.

That night he hardly slept at all.

OVER THE NEXT FEW WEEKS Tim was haunted by the owl. It sat on the headboard of his bed at night and kept him awake by whispering foul things in his ear. It made demands on him, urging him to bring it pieces of raw meat. The creature began to grow at an alarming rate, until it was as large as a pillow, its creased, wizened face becoming more evil-looking with every passing night. It devoured everything that Tim could find in the house, until eventually he had to begin begging for meat from other places.

Tim himself began to change too, both in appearance and attitude. He was morose and glum, avoiding his friends until they began to shun him. His teachers became worried about him and sent notes home to his mother, telling her that Tim was falling asleep in class. These he threw away on the way home from school.

Eventually a teacher went to Tim's house and had a long talk with his mother, who confessed that she had had a crisis at work and had not noticed that her son was looking unwell.

'I'll take him to the doctor in the morning,' she promised.

When she finally did take time to notice him, she saw how hunched he was, his head sunk between his shoulders and his arms dangling by his sides.

'Why are you standing like that?' she asked. 'Oh, Tim, you do look a bit grey and worn. We'll have to see what the doctor says.'

The doctor gave Tim a check-up but could find nothing wrong with him.

'It's probably one of these new viruses,' he said. 'They sap one's energy and leave one feeling listless and apathetic. Give him three of these tablets a day and see how we go on. If he needs rest, you'd better let him stay off school for a while. We'll have to play this one by ear. All right Tim?'

Tim gave the doctor a tight, wan smile, as weak as a winter sun. He had the words ready in his head to tell them all—the teachers, his mother, the doctor—but nothing would come out of his mouth. He longed to tell someone, to ask anyone what he could do about this dreadful creature which was destroying his life, but he couldn't. So he simply hunched deeper into himself and shuffled his feet, like an owl settling on a perch.

That night, when he took the owl some raw lights, the creature made Tim eat some too. Together, the human-faced creature and Tim tore at the soft giblets and intestines of animals which Tim had begged from the butcher, the juices dribbling down their chins and dripping on to the bedroom carpet. Tim had told the butcher that the raw innards were for his pet bird.

'What have you got? A kestrel hawk or something?'

Tim had nodded and muttered, 'Or something…'

He wanted to be sick when the slimy giblets slid down his throat but the owl stared into his eyes and he found he could not bring up the disgusting raw meats and had to digest them.

'I hate you,' he whispered to the owl and its old woman's face snarled and spat at him, telling him he was hers to use and he would have to eat far worse things before too long.

Anyone walking into Tim's room that night would have been shocked to the core at the scene. On one end of the bed sat the terrible owl, hunched into its feathers. On the other end of the bed sat the boy, hunched into his shoulders. Both creatures were uttering strange black words at each other, like two demons who despise each other yet are forced to live under the same roof. They hissed and spat and ground their teeth, the boy rippled his arms like wings and the owl shuffled her feet and sneered like a human. It was the most appalling and terrifying sight to witness.

Tim began to grow desperate. There was no one he could talk to about what was happening to him. No one would understand. He himself didn't understand. He began frequenting libraries and reading books on mythology, determined to discover what this creature was and where it had come from. Day after day he searched, but found nothing.

One day, Tim was lying on his bed trying to get some rest when his mother came into his room. She had his coat in her hands and she made straight for the wardrobe. Tim knew the owl was perched inside and he sat up expectantly as she opened the door.

She looked inside, gave a high-pitched scream, dropped the coat and ran from the room.

Tim followed her out a few moments later. At last, he thought, someone would do something to help him out of his nightmare. Instead, his mother was beside herself with anger. She was furious with Tim. He stood by helpless as she berated him.

'How could you?' she cried, shaking with annoyance.

'What?' pleaded Tim.

'You know very well—that horrible mask. You hung it in your wardrobe to frighten me. I don't know what's happening to you lately, Tim. You used to be such a nice boy. Now you're lazy and full of silly tricks like this. Mr James, the butcher, said you've been asking for meat from him for an eagle or something. I told him we hadn't got any kind of pet. What are you playing at?'

'I don't know,' said Tim, close to tears.

'Well, I certainly don't know either,' replied his mother. 'Now if you'll go to your room, I'll try to get on with earning us some money, though I'm sure I don't feel like it after that ugly scare.'

Tim lurched from the living-room, tears in his eyes. The owl seemed to have him trapped. He was its slave and he was becoming more owlish every day. He could no longer go to the butcher's so he would have to start trapping mice and rats. The owl's and, indeed, his own appetite was voracious. That evening he found some mouse traps in the garden shed and set them in likely places. Lately he had found his movements becoming quicker and his hearing and smell more acute. Perhaps he would soon be able to hunt without traps.

Just before the summer holidays, Tim finally discovered what he was up against. He found a book in the school library which somehow he'd missed before. It was entitled Local Myths and Folk lore. Delving into it he came across a section entitled THE MEGOWL. It seemed that King Arthur's half-sister, the witch Morgan le Fay, had once passed through a remote corner of Essex. She had become displeased with one of the local witches, an old woman named Meg Hopkins, whom she had changed into an owl.

The Megowl was a bird with a human face which laid one egg on Hallowe'en, then lived only until Christmas Day, dying the moment the new chick was born. It was, in fact, a rebirth—the old Megowl giving birth to herself through her own egg. Sometimes the egg lay dormant, waiting for centuries, for it had to be nurtured by a human child. Once the child was found, the Megowl gradually turned it into a creature like itself, so that it could more easily obtain food to feed her. And the worst thing of all, was that there was no way of destroying it.

Tim put the book back on its shelf and left the library, feeling bleak. He was indeed caught by a fiend, a demon who refused to let him go. Some of his former friends were off to the pitch to play football. They saw Tim staring after them and yelled cruelly, 'There's the boy-bird of Ashingdon! Why don't you flap your arms for us, Sully?' Tim bared his teeth like a savage animal and moved so swiftly towards the jeering youths that they ran off, leaving their football on the ground. Tim pierced it with his sharp fingernails, puncturing it. Then he made for the nearest ditch to hunt rats.

Several days later, Tim was called to the front of the class by the geography teacher.

'Tim, you don't seem to be paying attention. Are you sure you're well?'

'I'm never well,' muttered Tim, burying his head in his shoulders and flexing his clawlike fingers.

'I see. Well, if you're ill you'd better go home, but we hardly see you lately, do we…?'

The teacher stopped in mid-sentence, for Tim had begun a peculiar movement, now familiar to him but so far not witnessed by anyone else. His throat was pulsing and his chest heaving violently. A kind of shudder was going through his whole body.

'Are you going to be sick?' cried the teacher, stepping back in alarm.

Suddenly the boy gave a kind of strangled cough and spat a large pellet at the teacher's feet. The wad which had come out of his mouth was made of fur and bones, packed together into a tight wad. It was in fact the regurgitated remains of a mouse that Tim had eaten earlier that morning. He had been unable to digest this pellet and, just like an owl, his body had rejected it.

The teacher took Tim's hand and led him immediately from the room. His mother was called on the telephone and came to collect him half an hour later. On the drive home, she questioned him.

'What have you been eating, Tim?' she asked, her eyes fixed on the road.

'Nothing,' said Tim, sullenly.

'Tomorrow,' said his mother, nodding, 'tomorrow, we're going to the doctor's.'

Hope surged through Tim's breast. He had been eating mice, voles and other small creatures for several weeks now. He knew exactly what he needed to do.

That night he climbed out of his bedroom window, under the sharp, piercing eyes of the Megowl. He had told her in her own tongue that he was going hunting. This was true enough. Tim intended to catch several small mammals.

He crawled into the nearest ditch, on all fours like a wild animal, and waited in the moonlight. When he heard a rustling in the hedgerow, his hand flashed out and snatched the small creature. It was a vole. The speed of his strike would have electrified any human witnessing this scene. Tim's movements were as fast as any wild predator's. He waited for a second creature to come along. Animals tend to use pathways they have made for themselves rather than cross open country, and Tim was waiting by one of these busy highways.

When he had several small, limp bodies, he went back to his room where the wizened-faced owl was licking her lips in anticipation. Tim fed her three of the mammals and ate two himself.

The following morning he was driven to the doctors. In the waiting room, he felt like regurgitating the pellet of bones and fur, but held it down until he was ushered into the surgery. As soon as he was standing in front of the doctor he let go and vomited the bolt of waste matter on to the desk. As expected, the doctor jumped backwards out of his chair.

'Good God!' he exclaimed. At once he examined the pellet then made a phone call. Tim was to be taken to the hospital for observation.

After a check-up, the boy was found to be in a weak condition, with worms and various other intestinal infections caught from the raw meat he had been eating. He was admitted to hospital.

His plan was working. At last he was out of the clutches of the Megowl.

Tim's mother was distraught. She was convinced that her son was going mad.

'Is it because his father and I got divorced?' she asked the doctors. 'Is that why he's been eating these horrible things?'

The doctors were of the opinion that Tim was indeed deliberately trying to get attention.

'He probably feels rejected by his father,' they told her. 'And, as you say, you're very busy yourself, trying to earn a living. It's not an unusual situation. He needs to stay in our care for a while, until his physical health improves. Then we'll sort something out to help him mentally. He's not mad. He just needs some care and attention...'

That night Tim had the first real rest he had enjoyed in a long term. Snuggling down between starched white sheets, he felt cosseted by the hospital and its staff. The nurse called by every so often and there were three other patients in his room. It was like a fortress to him: a clean, stark fortress which would not permit entrance to a foul creature of the darkness. Tim was sealed inside a safe haven and he hoped that by the time he went home the Megowl would have either gone away or died of hunger. He thought of her vicious white face, ringed with feathers, and buried himself deeper under the bedclothes. She would be very angry. She would be spitting poison by now. He fell asleep.

Tim was kept in hospital for a fortnight, during which time he talked with the psychiatrist. He told the man that he had been having nightmares and after these dreams he ate things like mice and other small creatures. He still could not speak of the Megowl, for she had hypnotised him permanently, so that there was a blockage between his brain and his tongue. Every time he even attempted to tell someone about her, he experienced a kind of seizure during which his lips and tongue were locked and would not move. So he did the best he could, by laying the blame on nightmares.

The doctors were still convinced that the problem arose from his parents' divorce. His father was informed of his illness and came to visit him.

'I'm sorry to see you like this, Tim,' he said. 'Perhaps it's our fault—your mother's and mine—but sometimes people have to go their separate ways.'

'I know all that,' Tim said. 'You told me before.'

'Yes, well, it doesn't change with time. It's unfortunate you've taken it so hard—but I can't change, nor can your mother. We're as we are, and that's that. What I can do is see you a bit more. Would you like that?'

It was better than nothing and Tim nodded.

His father placed a hand on his shoulder. 'We can start by you coming to stay with me for a while,' he said. 'Susan, my new wife, has agreed that we need to see more of you.

'Would you like to come to Lancaster for a holiday?'

'I'm not deserting Mum,' said Tim fiercely.

'I don't expect you to. She agrees that a holiday will do you good and though we're divorced she still trusts me with your welfare. You are my son, after all. It'll just be for a holiday—nothing more. Then you can go back to your mother to live, but we'll still see a bit more of each other. What do you say?'

Tim nodded dumbly. He knew it would get him out of the house and away from that terrible creature.

THAT NIGHT, THE NIGHT BEFORE he was to be collected by his father and driven to Lancaster, there was a scratching on the hospital window pane. As if in a dream, Tim got out of bed and slowly crossed the room. The other patients who shared the room with him were fast asleep. He lifted his hand and pulled back a corner of the curtain. There on the sill sat the foul creature which had caused him so much misery. Her grey-white features sneered at him, as if to say, 'Did you think you could escape this easily?' She bared her white, even teeth and hissed some ugly words. Tim reached up, mesmerised, for the window catch. His fingers pulled at the handle but the window had not been opened for quite a time and it was stiff.

The Megowl screeched at him, jabbing the glass with her face, ordering him to pull harder so that she could get in. Her feathers were fluffed in fury and her owl-eyes blazed.

Just as Tim was about to give the handle a good hard wrench, a voice from behind him cried out,

'What do you think you're doing, young man?'

Tim whirled, to find the night sister watching him, amazed.

'I... I... er... nothing, Nurse.'

'Get back into bed,' she said, straightening the curtain, 'and let's have no more nonsense.'

Tim did as he was told.

Later that night there were more scratchings at the window, but Tim heard nothing. He had claimed that he could not sleep and the nurse given him a strong sedative.

The next day his father took him to Lancaster.

AWAY FROM THE MEGOWL, TIM gradually began to recover. He still looked fearfully at the window at night and waited for the scratching sounds which meant that the creature had caught up with him again, but the sounds never came. His father's flat was in the middle of town. There was the comforting noise of traffic well into the night, running below the bedroom window. In the centre of a city, amongst modern houses, machines and industry, the idea of a supernatural creature, especially a being of the woods and fields, seemed faintly ridiculous.

Tim stayed with his father and Susan for several weeks. He found Susan pleasant and willing to please him, but he had little real interest in her. She was not his mother and she had no children of her own, so she treated him like an adult, which suited Tim fine.

THE DAY TIM WENT BACK home, all his fears came rushing back. His mother was enormously pleased to see him, but he could hardly keep his attention on what she was saying.

'And how did you get on with… with Susan?'

'Oh, okay. She was all right…'

Tim then noticed his mother's worried look.

'She wasn't you, of course,' he added quickly. 'She was just someone else. You're my mum.'

His mother looked relieved to be told this and Tim was pleased he had said it.

Once his mother had satisfied herself that he was glad to be home, Tim went on a search of the bungalow. It was past Hallowe'en—he had deliberately remained with his father until after that date—and he hoped the Megowl had gone. It should have set out to trap some other adolescent by now but Tim wanted to be sure. He looked in all the likely places—under the bed, in the wardrobe, behind the curtains—until it seemed certain that the creature had fled in search of a new slave.

With an enormous sense of relief, equal to that of his mother when she learned he was well again and had missed her, Tim went back to his normal life. November the fifth arrived, with all the excitement of Bonfire Night, and then the days fell away like leaves from the trees, until it was December.

December crawled by, for both Tim and his mother were looking forward to Christmas. Deborah had met a man she liked, a divorcee like herself with a daughter and son both younger than Tim. They were all coming to stay for Christmas and arrived on the evening of the 24th.

Tim liked Edward, his mother's new friend, and though the children were shy he wanted to make friends with them quickly. He knew it was important to his mother and he had never had the pleasure of young companions living in the same house. Everyone said 'hello', smiled a lot, and went to bed early.

In the early morning Tim woke to hear noises in the kitchen. He crept downstairs to find Edward looking very sheepish.

'Sorry we woke you, Tim,' said Edward, 'I'm afraid I was a bit hungry and raided the fridge. I made myself an egg sandwich… I'm sure your mother won't mind.'

He held it up for Tim to see.

Egg sandwich… Egg. Something suddenly clicked in Tim's mind.

Leaving a surprised Edward, Tim dashed out of the kitchen and went straight to the airing cupboard. Flinging the door open, he reached underneath the tank and found his old shoebox. Even as he pulled it out he could feel a movement coming from within.

The Megowl had laid its egg inside the box and left it to be incubated by the hot water tank.

Tim grabbed the box. Then he ran out of the house in his pyjamas and bare feet and along the lane to the main road. There were sounds coming from the box. He held the lid on tightly, his chest heaving with the exertion of the run in the cold morning air.

The thing inside the box began to struggle. Tim stopped, pulled out his pyjama cord from his trousers and tied the lid down firmly. He could not allow it to look at him. Once it looked into his eyes, he would be its slave again. Then, one hand holding up his pyjama trousers and the other clutching the box, he finally ran the last few yards to the road.

He waited.

A car went by.

The chick inside the box began gnawing at the cardboard.

Another car went by.

It was furious. It scratched and tore at the bottom of the box. In a few moments it would be free.

An open-backed Land Rover came into sight. Tim waited until it was level, then threw his burden with all his might. The shoebox and its contents landed in the back of the Land Rover and were taken away along the winding road, out of sight.

He was free at last!

Garry Kilworth

THE SILVER COLLAR

(My daughter Chantelle actually dreamed this tale on the eve of her marriage to Mark, her husband now of twenty years. I have merely wrought her base dream into the written word. Readers will be pleased to know Mark is not a vampire but a fine family man and a son-in-law of whom we are all proud.)

THE REMOTE SCOTTISH ISLAND CAME into view as the sun was setting. Outside the natural harbour, the sea was kicking a little in its traces and tossing its white manes in the dying light. My small outboard motor struggled against the ebbing tide, sometimes whining as it raced in the air as a particularly low trough left it without water to push against the blades of its propeller. By the time I reached the jetty, the moon was up and casting its chill light upon the shore and purple-heather hills beyond. There was a smothered atmosphere to this lonely place of rock and thin soil, as if the coarse grass and hardy plants had descended as a complete layer to wrap the ruggedness in a faded cover, hiding the nakedness from mean, inquisitive eyes.

As the agents had promised, he was waiting on the quay, his tall, emaciated figure stark against the gentle upward slope of the hinterland: a splinter of granite from the rock on which he had made his home.

'I've brought the provisions,' I called, as he took the line and secured it.

'Good. Will you come up to the croft? There's a peat fire going—it's warm, and I have some scotch. Nothing like a dram before an open fire, with the smell of burning peat filling the room.'

'I could just make it out with the tide,' I said. 'Perhaps I should go now.' It was not that I was reluctant to accept the invitation from this eremite, this strange recluse—on the contrary, he interested me—but I had to be sure to get back to the mainland that night, since I was to crew a fishing vessel the next day.

'You have time for a dram,' his voice drifted away on the cold wind that had sprung up within minutes, like a breath from the mouth of the icy north. I had to admit to myself that a whisky, by the fire, would set me on my toes for the return trip, and his tone had a faintly insistent quality about it which made the offer difficult to refuse.

'Just a minute then—and thanks. You lead the way.'

I followed his lean, though my sea-socks. The path was obviously not well used and I imagined he spent his time in and around his croft, for even in the moonlight I could discern no other tracks incising the soft shape of the hill.

We reached his dwelling and he opened the wooden door, allowing me to enter first. Then, seating me in front of the fire, he poured me a generous whisky before sitting down himself. I listened to the wind, locked outside the timber and turf croft, and waited for him to speak.

He said, 'John, isn't it? They told me on the wireless.'

'Yes—and you're Samuel.'

'Sam. You must call me Sam.'

I told him I would and there was a period of silence while we regarded each other. Peat is not a consistent fuel, and tends to spurt and spit colourful plumes of flame as the gases escape, having been held prisoner from the seasons for God knows how long. Nevertheless, I was able to study my host in the brief periods of illumination that the fire afforded. He could have been any age, but I knew he was my senior by a great many years. The same thoughts must have been passing through his own head, for he remarked, 'John, how old are you? I would guess at twenty.'

'Nearer thirty, Sam. I was twenty-six last birthday.' He nodded, saying that those who live a solitary life, away from others, have great difficulty in assessing the ages of people they do meet. Recent events slipped from his memory quite quickly, while the past seemed so close.

He leaned forward, into the hissing fire, as if drawing a breath from the ancient atmospheres it released into the room. Behind him, the earthen walls of the croft, held together by rough timbers and unhewn stones, seemed to move closer to his shoulder, as if ready to support his words. I sensed a story coming. I recognised the pose from being in the company of sailors on long voyages and hoped he would finish before I had to leave.

'You're a good-looking boy,' he said. 'So was I, once upon a time.' He paused to stir the flames and a blue-green cough from the peat illuminated his face. The skin was taut over the high cheekbones and there was a wanness to it, no doubt brought about by the inclement weather of the isles—the lack of sunshine and the constant misty rain that comes in as white veils from the north. Yes, he had been handsome—still was. I was surprised by his youthful features and suspected that he was not as old as he implied.

'A long time ago,' he began, 'when we had horse-drawn vehicles and things were different, in more ways than one…'

A sharp whistling note—the wind squeezing through two tightly packed logs in the croft—distracted me. Horse-drawn vehicles? What was this? A second-hand tale, surely? Yet he continued in the first person.

…GAS LIGHTING IN THE STREET. A different set of values. A different set of beliefs. We were more pagan then. Still had our roots buried in dark thoughts. Machines have changed all that. Those sort of pagan, mystical ideas can't share a world with machines. Unnatural beings can only exist close to the natural world and nature's been displaced.

Yes, a different world—different things to fear. I was afraid as a young man—the reasons may seem trivial to you, now, in your time. I was afraid of, well, getting into something I couldn't get out of. Woman trouble, for instance—especially one not of my class. You understand?

I got involved once. Must have been about your age, or maybe a bit younger since I'd only just finished my apprenticeship and was a journeyman at the time. Silversmith. You knew that? No, of course you didn't. A silversmith, and a good one too. My master trusted me with one of his three shops, which puffed my pride a bit, I don't mind telling you. Anyway, it happened that I was working late one evening, when I heard the basement doorbell jangle.

I had just finished lighting the gas lamps in the workshop at the back, so I hurried to the counter where a customer was waiting. She had left the door open and the sounds from the street were distracting, the basement of course being on a level with the cobbled road. Coaches were rumbling by and the noise of street urchins and flower sellers was fighting for attention with the foghorns from the river. As politely as I could, I went behind the customer and closed the door. Then I turned to her and said, 'Yes madam? Can I be of service?'

She was wearing one of those large satin cloaks that only ladies of quality could afford and she threw back the hood to reveal one of the most beautiful faces I have ever seen in my life. There was purity to her complexion that went deeper than her flawless skin, much deeper. And her eyes—how can I describe her eyes?—they were like black mirrors and you felt you could see the reflection of your own soul in them. Her hair was dark—coiled on her head—and it contrasted sharply with that complexion, pale as a winter moon, and soft, soft as the velvet I used for polishing the silver.

'Yes,' she replied. 'You may be of service. You are the silversmith, are you not?'

'The journeyman, madam. I'm in charge of this shop.'

She seemed a little agitated, her fingers playing nervously with her reticule.

'I…' she faltered, then continued. 'I have a rather unusual request. Are you able to keep a secret, silversmith?'

'My work is confidential, if the customer wishes it so. Is it some special design you require? Something to surprise a loved one with? I have some very fine filigree work here.' I removed a tray from beneath the counter. 'There's something for both the lady and the gentleman. A cigar case, perhaps? This one has a crest wrought into the case in fine silver wire—an eagle, as you can see. It has been fashioned especially for a particular customer, but I can do something similar if you require…'

I stopped talking because she was shaking her head and seemed to be getting impatient with me.

'Nothing like that. Something very personal. I want you to make a collar—a silver collar. Is that possible?'

'All things are possible.' I smiled. 'Given the time of course. A torc of some kind?'

'No, you misunderstand me.' A small frown marred the ivory forehead and she glanced anxiously towards the shop door. 'Perhaps I made a mistake…?'

Worried, in case I lost her custom, I assured her that whatever was her request I should do my utmost to fulfil it. At the same time I told her that I could be trusted to keep the nature of the work to myself.

'No one shall know about this but the craftsman and the customer—you and I.'

She smiled at me then: a bewitching, spellbinding smile, and my heart melted within me. I would have done anything for her at that moment—I would have robbed my master—and I think she knew it.

'I'm sorry,' she said. 'I should have realised I could trust you. You have a kind face. A gentle face. One should learn to trust in faces.

'I want you—I want you to make me a collar which will cover my whole neck, especially the throat. I have a picture here, of some savages in Africa. The women have metal bands around their necks which envelop them from shoulder to chin. I want you to encase me in a similar fashion, except with one single piece of silver, do you understand? And I want it to fit tightly, so that not even your…' She took my hand in her own small gloved fingers. 'So that not even your little finger will be able to find its way beneath.'

I was, of course, extremely perturbed at such a request. I tried to explain to her that she would have to take the collar off quite frequently, or the skin beneath would become diseased. Her neck would certainly become very ugly.

'In any case, it will chafe and become quite sore. There will be constant irritation…'

She dropped my hand and said, no, I still misunderstood. The collar was to be worn permanently. She had no desire to remove it, once I had fashioned it around her neck. There was to be no locking device or anything of that sort. She wanted me to seal the metal.

'But?' I began, but she interrupted me in a firm voice.

'Silversmith, I have stated my request, my requirements. Will you carry out my wishes, or do I find another craftsman? I should be loath to do so, for I feel we have reached a level of understanding which might be difficult elsewhere. I'm going to be frank with you. This device, well—its purpose is protective. My husband-to-be is not—not like other men, but I love him just the same. I don't wish to embarrass you with talk that's not proper between strangers, and personal to my situation, but the collar is necessary to ensure my marriage is happy—a limited happiness. Limited to a lifetime. I'm sure you must understand now. If you want me to leave your shop, I shall do so, but I'm appealing to you because you are young and must know the pain of love—unfulfilled love. You are a handsome man and I don't doubt you have a young lady whom you adore. If she were suffering under some terrible affliction, a disease which you might contract from her, I'm sure it would make no difference to your feelings. You would strive to find a way in which you could live together, yet remain uncontaminated yourself. Am I right?'

I managed to breathe the word 'Yes' but at the time I was filled with visions of horror. Visions of this beautiful young woman being wooed by some foul creature of the night—a supernatural beast that had no right to be treading on the same earth, let alone touching that sacred skin, kissing—my mind reeled—kissing those soft, moist lips with its monstrous mouth. How could she? Even the thought of it made me shudder in revulsion.

'Ah,' she smiled, knowingly. 'You want to save me from him. You think he is ugly and that I've been hypnotised, somehow, into believing otherwise? You're quite wrong. He's handsome in a way that you'd surely understand—and sensitive, kind, gentle—those things a woman finds important. He's also very cultured. His blood…'

I winced and took a step backward, but she was lost in some kind of reverie as she listed his attributes and I'm sure was unaware of my presence for some time.

'…his blood is unimpeachable, reaching back through a royal lineage to the most notable of European families. I love him, yet I do not want to become one of his kind, for that would destroy my love…'

'And—he loves you of course,' l said daringly.

For a moment those bright eyes clouded over, but she replied, 'In his way. It's not important that we both feel the same kind of love. We want to be together, to share our lives. I prefer him to any man I have ever met and I will not be deterred by an obstacle that's neither his fault, nor mine. A barrier that's been placed in our way by the injustice of nature. He can't help the way he is—and I want to go with him. That's all there is to it.'

For a long time neither of us said anything. My throat felt too dry and constricted for words, and deep inside me I could feel something struggling, like a small creature fighting the folds of a net. The situation was beyond my comprehension: that is, I did not wish to allow it to enter my full understanding or I would have run screaming from the shop and made myself look foolish to my neighbours.

'Will you do it, silversmith?'

'But,' I said, 'a collar covers only the throat…' I left the rest unsaid, but I was concerned that she was not protecting herself fully: the other parts of her anatomy—the wrists, the thighs.

She became very angry. 'He isn't an animal. He's a gentleman. I'm merely guarding against—against moments of high passion. It's not just a matter of survival with him. The act is sensual and spiritual, as well as—as well as—what you're suggesting,' there was a note of loathing in her tone, 'is tantamount to rape.'

She was so incensed that I did not dare say that her lover must have satisfied his need somewhere, and therefore had compromised the manners and morals of a gentleman many times.

'Will you help me?' The eyes were pleading now. I tried to look out of the small, half-moon window, at the yellow-lighted streets, at the feet moving by on the pavement above, in an attempt to distract myself, but they were magnetic, those eyes, and they drew me back in less than a moment. I felt helpless—a trapped bird—in their unremitting gaze of anguish, and of course, I submitted.

I agreed. I just heard myself saying, 'Yes,' and led her into the back of the shop where I began the work. It was not a difficult task to actually fashion the collar, though the sealing of it was somewhat painful to her and had to be carried out in stages, which took us well into the night hours. I must have, subconsciously perhaps, continued to glance through the workshop door at the window, for she said once, very quietly, 'He will not come here.'

Such a beautiful throat she had too. Very long, and elegant. It seemed a sacrilege to encase such a beauty in metal, though I made the collar as attractive as I made any silver ornament which might adorn a pretty woman. On the outside of the metal I engraved centripetal designs and at her request, some representational forms: Christ on the cross, immediately over her jugular vein, but also Zeus and Europa, and Zeus and Leda, with the Greek god in his bestial forms of the bull and the swan. I think she had been seduced by the thought that she was marrying some kind of deity.

When I had finished, she paid me and left. I watched her walk out, into the early morning mists, with a heavy guilt in my heart.

What could I have done? I was just a common craftsman and had no right interfering in the lives of others. Perhaps I should have tried harder to dissuade her, but I doubt she would have listened to my impertinence for more than a few moments. Besides, I had, during those few short hours, fallen in love with her—utterly—and when she realised she had made a mistake, she would have to come back to me again, to have the collar removed.

I wanted desperately to see her again, though I knew that any chance of romance was impossible, hopeless. She was not of my class—or rather, I was not of hers, and her beauty was more than I could ever aspire to, though I knew myself to be a good-looking young man. Some had called me beautiful—it was that kind of handsomeness that I had been blessed with, rather than the rugged sort.

But despite my physical advantages, I had nothing which would attract a lady of quality from her own kind. The most I could ever hope for—the very most—was perhaps to serve her in some way.

THREE WEEKS LATER SHE WAS back, looking somewhat distraught.

'I want it to come off,' she said. 'It must be removed.'

My fingers trembled as I worked at cutting her free—a much simpler task than my previous one.

'You've left him,' I said. 'Won't he follow?'

'No, you're quite wrong.' There was a haunted look to her eyes which chilled me to the bone. 'It's not that. I was too mistrustful. I love him too much to withhold from him the very thing he desires. I must give myself to him—wholly and completely. I need him you see. And he needs me—yet like this I cannot give him the kind of love he has to have. I've been selfish. Very selfish. I must go to him…'

'Are you mad?' I cried, forgetting my position. 'You'll become like him—you'll become—'

'How dare you! How dare you preach to me? Just do your work, silversmith. Remove the collar!'

I was weak of course, as most of us are when confronted by a superior being. I cut the collar loose and put it aside. She rubbed her neck and complained loudly that flakes of skin were coming away in her hands.

'It's ugly,' she said. 'Scrawny. He'll never want me like this.'

'No—thank God,' I cried, gathering my courage.

At that moment she looked me full in the eyes and a strange expression came over her face.

'You're in love with me, aren't you? That's why you're so concerned, silversmith. Oh dear, I am dreadfully sorry. I thought you were just being meddlesome. It was a genuine concern for my welfare and I didn't recognise it at first. Dear man,' she touched my cheek. 'Don't look so sad. It cannot be, you know. You should find some nice girl and try to forget, because you'll never see me again after tonight. And don't worry about me. I know what I'm doing.'

With that, she gathered up her skirts and was gone again, down toward the river. The sun was just coming up, since she had arrived not long before the dawn, and I thought: At least she will have a few hours more of natural life.

After that I tried to follow her advice and put her out of my mind. I did my work, something I had always enjoyed, and rarely left the shop. I felt that if I could get over a few months without a change in my normal pattern of existence, I should be safe. There were nightmares of course, to be gone through after sunsets, but those I was able to cope with. I have always managed to keep my dreams at a respectable distance and not let them interfere with my normal activities.

Then, one day, as I was working on a pendant—a butterfly requested by a banker for his wife—a small boy brought me a message. Though it was unsigned, I knew it was from her and my hands trembled as I read the words.

They simply said, 'Come. I need you.'

Underneath this request was scrawled an address, which I knew to be located down by one of the wharves, south of the river.

She needed me—and I knew exactly what for. I touched my throat. I wanted her too, but for different reasons. I did not have the courage that she had—the kind of sacrificial courage that's produced by an overwhelming love. But I was not without strength. If there was a chance, just a chance, that I could meet with her and come away unscathed, then I was prepared to accept the risk.

But I didn't see how that was possible. Her kind, as she had become, possessed a physical strength which would make any escape fraught with difficulty.

I had no illusions about her being in love with me—or even fond of me. She wanted to use me for her own purposes, which were as far away from love as earth is from the stars. I remembered seeing deep gouges in the silver collar, the time she had come to have it removed. They were like the claw marks of some beast, incised into the trunk of a tree. No wonder she had asked to have it sealed. Whoever, whatever, had made those marks would have had the strength to tear away any hinges or lock. The frenzy to get at what lay beneath the silver must have been appalling to witness—experience—yet she had gone back to him, without the collar's protection.

I wanted her. I dreamed about having her, warm and close to me. That she had become something other than the beautiful woman who had entered my shop was no deterrent. I knew she would be just as lovely in her new form and I desired her above all things. For nights I lay awake, running different schemes over in my mind, trying to find a path which would allow us to make love together, just once, and yet let me walk away safely afterward. Even as I schemed, I saw her beauty laid before me, willingly, and my body and soul ached for her lovely form.

One chance. I had this once chance of loving a woman a dozen places above my station: a woman whose refined ways and manner of speech had captivated me from the moment I met her. A woman whose dignity, elegance, and gracefulness were without parallel. Whose form surpassed that of the finest silverwork figurine I had ever known.

I had to find a way.

Finally, I came up with a plan which seemed to suit my purposes, and taking my courage in both hands I wrote her a note which said, 'I'm waiting for you. You must come to me.' I found an urchin to carry it for me and told him to put it through the letter box of the address she had given me.

That afternoon I visited the church and a purveyor of medical instruments.

That evening I spent wandering the streets, alternatively praising myself for dreaming up such a clever plan and cursing myself for my foolhardiness in carrying it through. As I strolled through the back-streets, stepping around the gin-soaked drunks and tipping my hat to the factory girls as they hurried home from a sixteen-hour day in some garment manufacturer's sweatshop, I realised that for once I had allowed my emotions to overrule my intellect. I'm not saying I was an intelligent young man—not above the average—but I was wise enough to know that there was great danger in what I proposed to do, yet the force of my feelings was more powerful than fear. I could not deny them their expression. The heart has no reason, but its drive is stronger than sense dictates.

The barges on the river ploughed slowly against the current as I leaned on the wrought-iron balustrade overlooking the water. I could see the gas lamps reflected on the dark surface and thought about the shadow world that lived alongside our own, where nothing was rigid, set, but could be warped and twisted, like those lights in the water when the ripples from the barges passed through them. Would it take me and twist me into something, not ugly, but unsubstantial? Into something that has the appearance of the real thing, but which is evanescent in the daylight and can only make its appearance at night, when vacuous shapes and phantasms take on a semblance of life and mock it with their unreal forms?

When the smell of the mud below me began to waft upward, as the tide retreated and the river diminished, I made my way homeward. There was a sharpness to the air which cut into my confidence and I was glad to be leaving it behind for the warmth and security of my rooms. Security? I laughed at myself, having voluntarily exposed my vulnerability.

She came.

There was a scratching at the casement windowpane in the early hours of the morning and I opened it and let her in. She had not changed. If anything, she was more beautiful than ever, with a paler colour to her cheeks and a fuller red to her lips.

No words were exchanged between us. I lay on the bed naked and she joined me after removing her garments. She stroked my hair and the nape of my neck as I sank into her soft young body. I cannot describe the ecstasy. It was—unearthly. She allowed me—encouraged me—and the happiness of those moments was worth all the risks of entering Hell for a taste of Heaven.

Of course, the moment came when she lowered her head to the base of my throat. I felt the coils of her hair against my cheek: smelled their sweet fragrance. I could sense the pulse in my neck, throbbing with blood. Her body was warm against mine—deliciously warm. I wanted her to stay forever. There was just a hint of pain in my throat—a needle prick, no more, and then a feeling of drifting, floating on warm water, as if I had suddenly been transported to tropic seas and lay in the shallows of some sun-bleached island's beaches. I felt no fear—only, bliss.

Then, suddenly, she snorted, springing to her feet like no athlete I have ever seen. Her eyes were blazing and she spat and hissed into my face.

'What have you done?' she shrieked.

Then the fear came, rushing to my heart. I cowered at the bed-head, pulling my legs up to my chest in an effort to get as far away from her as possible.

Again she cried, 'What have you done?'

'Holy water, I said. 'I've injected holy water into my veins.'

She let out another wail which made my ears sing. Her hands reached for me and I saw those long nails, like talons, ready to slash at an artery, but the fear was gone from me. I just wanted her back in bed with me. I no longer cared for the consequences.

'Please?' I said, reaching for her. 'Help me? I want you to help me.'

She withdrew from me then and sprang to the window. It was getting close to dawn: The first rays of the sun were sliding over the horizon.

'You fool,' she said, and then she was gone, out into the murk. I jumped up and looked for her through the window, but all I could see was the mist on the river, curling its way around the rotten stumps of an old jetty.

Once I had recovered my common sense and was out of her influence, I remember thinking to myself that I would have to make a collar—a silver collar...

THE FIRE SPAT IN THE grate and I jerked upright. I had no idea how long Sam had been talking but the peat was almost all ashes.

'The tide,' I said, alarmed. 'I must leave.'

'I haven't finished,' he complained, but I was already on my feet. I opened the door and began to walk quickly down the narrow path we had made through the heather, to where my boat lay, but even as I approached it, I could see that it was lying on its side in the slick, glinting mud.

Angry, I looked back at the croft on the hillside. He must have known. He must have known. I was about to march back and take Sam to task, when I suddenly saw the croft in a new perspective. It was like most dwellings of its kind—timber framed, with sods of earth filling the cracks, and stones holding down the turf on the roof. But it was peculiar shape—more of a mound than the normal four walls and a roof—and was without windows.

My mind suddenly ran wild with frightening images of wood, earth, and rocks. The wooden coffin goes inside the earth and the headstone weights it down. A mound—a burial mound. He hadn't been able to stay away from her. The same trap had caught her...

I turned back to the boat and tried dragging it across the moonlit mud, toward the distant water, but it was too heavy. I could only inch it along, and rapidly became tired. The muscles in my arms and legs screamed at me. All the time I laboured, one side of my mind kept telling me not to be so foolish, while the other was equally insistent regarding the need to get away. I could hear myself repeating the words. 'He couldn't stay away from her. He couldn't stay away from her. He couldn't stay away.'

I had covered about six yards when I heard a voice at my shoulder—a soft, dry voice, full of concern.

'Here, John, let me help you...'

SAM DID HELP ME THAT day, more than I wished him to. I don't hate him for that, especially now that so many years have passed. Since then I have obtained this job, of night ferryman on the loch, helping young ladies like the one I have in the skiff with me now—a runaway, off to join her lover.

'Don't worry,' I try to reassure her, after telling her my story, 'we sailors are fond of our tales. Come and join me by the tiller. I'll show you how to manage the boat. Do I frighten you? I don't mean to. I only want to help you…'

Garry Kilworth

MOBY JACK

(*National Geographic* has been the source of ideas for many of my stories. One article even spawned a trilogy of novels [*The Navigator Kings*]. This one obviously came from an article on beluga whales, coupled with factual stories from an uncle who worked on a whaler in the early 1900s. Herman Melville had something to do with it as well.)

CALL ME CRAZY, BUT... WELL I guess I'd better tell you the story, then let you judge for yourselves who's crazy and who isn't in this tale of horror and destruction.

At this precise moment I'm standing on the bridge of the *Titan* staring out over the ice-littered Arctic Ocean, off Elwin Bay on Somerset Island. The wild seabirds are dipping and diving, their harsh cries like the screeching of banshees on the wind, symbols of that female spirit foretelling the many deaths that hang in the air above the chopped, cold sea. Deaths of whales, or deaths of men? The birds are uncaring as they drop brokenly to the surface to snatch at some unseen morsel of food, then to rise again smooth-flighted out of the white mouths of waves that snatch blindly at all, and nothing.

I am speaking quietly into a contraption, a black box the size of a Gideon's bible. The coxswain knows that I am muttering, but he can't hear what I'm saying from this distance. Occasionally he glances over at me, but I just smile and continue murmuring. I am one of the ship's most trusted personnel, being the man who knows where the whales are to be found.

If I look through a viewer in the direction of the island I can just make out the houses of native Inuvialuits, who traditionally hunt the mammals we ourselves are here to slaughter. The landscape around their homes is beautifully decorated with fiery saxifrages and cool pale yellow poppies. My current emotions reflect these colour suggestions, being on the one side passionate and angry, yet on the other calm and collected, coolly considering my position.

Above the dwellings I see areas of deep snow on the slopes where shadows remain, the whiteness stark against the purple and black of the folds of the hills.

To the east and west of the houses, on the broad, stony beaches below the cliffs are the blanched bones of thousands of whales, scattered widely, almost as if from a single mighty beast which has beached and fragmented itself over the years. You could walk over that ivory plain of skeletons for an hour and still be treading on bone. They are macabre reminders of another age of whaling, when the old Scottish sailing ships trapped beluga schools in shallow inlets and slaughtered them by the hundred. My great-great-grandfather was a harpooner on one of those vessels and I still have the carvings, scrimshaws from whalebone: little figures of men and beasts, whistles, albatross brooches and ships like the one in which he sailed.

The Canadian Inuvialuits themselves kill about 150 beluga whales each year, mainly for the vitamin-rich skin which they call *muktuk*. Even that number from an acceptable traditional hunt which supports a population at subsistence level, would tear the heart out of Jacqueline who feels deeply for every single whale life taken by mankind.

The average monthly hunt by the *Titan* is 800 to 1000 whales.

Out in the bay are the creatures themselves, the white beluga whales in their great schools, playing like dolphin amongst the lily-pad floes that decorate the slate-black surface of the sea. They form a huge flotilla, as they romp and sing as numerous as a whitebait shoal, churning the dark sea to a white and lime-green froth. They send giant plumes of spume up into chill air. They too are beautiful, but I am one of their hunters who see in their white numbers only profits on the world's black markets. Their oil may no longer light a thousand lamps, but their flesh is still desirable on the tables of gourmets, their bodily juices still required by many industries.

The *Titan* is of course the infamous gigantic pirate whaler which militant anti-whaling groups throughout the world have tried, unsuccessfully, to blow out of the water since the turn of the century. It is by far the largest and most expensive craft of its kind afloat. It is unique. Other pirate whalers are clam boats in comparison. It cost several billion dollars to build and is virtually irreplaceable. It also has an impressive array of anti-weapon systems. It isn't designed to attack, but it is able to protect itself and negate virtually any type of missile fired at it from land, sea, subsea or air. Since its setup is entirely defensive, its anti-weapon systems are legal on international waters.

The *Titan* is a floating island, self-sufficient, gleaning almost everything it needs from the sea, even the milk for seaweed coffee coming from cetaceans. Essentials which the sea cannot provide are flown in by helicopter. If the *Titan* sank the company who owns it would face financial ruin, since no half-respectable insurance company would touch it, let alone Lloyds of London. It sneaks in and out of its country of registration and never violates any other national waters, or it might be impounded or even sunk, its activities being illegal in almost every country in the world.

It is a factory ship, totally efficient, able to harvest thousands of whales every year.

The white beluga whales are shot by a bolt of high voltage electricity. If it hits them accurately in the brain, it usually kills them, but occasionally they are merely stunned. They are then hooked onto the deck of the *Titan* by rows of derricks running alongside the gunwales and guided whole to the slicing machines positioned amidships. The separated bones go to the fore, the flesh aft where the massive microwave cookers are situated. The deck between is awash with blood and gore, waste tissue from the slicing blades, oil and liquid fats. The seamen have to wear spiked shoes to prevent slipping on this deadly layer of slime. In the ship's wake is a shining trail of oils and fats, stained pink, like the track of some giant wounded creature crawling away to die. The stink outside is unbelievable and it's not often that I venture forth onto the open deck amongst the muck and filth.

At this precise moment we're not actually steering a course for the schools. In the captain's absence I've ordered the ship out to open waters. We're being pursued, and even as I record these words I see one white whale whom I call Moby Jack, break from the main school and head in our direction. Without any doubt Moby Jack has our destruction in mind. Moby Jack is without hate or malice, without even rancour, for as with his forerunner, Moby Jack's intentions are cast upon him by the shadows of the hunters.

However, unlike her forerunner, Moby Jack is not an act of God, but an act of Man.

I foresee only one survivor of this encounter, but this time he will not be called Ishmael. The survivor will be this black oblong box: an unsinkable device carrying my words. On contact with the water, the box will emit a signal which it is hoped will be tracked and the source discovered. Whoever you are, who has found my voice, I ask that you pass it on to Jacqueline Jones, my murderer, with the message that I love her.

I MET JACQUELINE WHILE AN undergraduate at the Bright's Institute for Marine Studies. I was doing an Honours Degree in Cetology, while she, I discovered, was doing a postgraduate paper on something called Ocean Political Studies. Her first degree was in Marine Engineering Design, so her Masters seemed to me to be a radical change in direction.

'What's with the Masters?' I said, over our first cup of coffee together in the student canteen. 'Are you going to organise fish shoals into democracies?'

'No,' she said, laughing. 'Although it's a good idea. What I'm interested in is the exploitation of the marine world by business organisations and countries, purely for profit.'

Jacqueline's high principles did not interest me at the time. She was, however, extremely attractive: dark-haired, high cheekbones, very dark eyes. I would guess Armenian by ancestry. She had wider hips than most men prefer, but not me. I have always been attracted to a hippy woman with a swivel to her walk. I also like my bed-fellows to be intelligent and clever too, with a touch of earthiness about them: bright she was and definitely of peasant stock. Her father was a bus driver and her mother a part-time waitress.

'So, you want to figure out some way of policing the seven seas?' I said.

'Something like that—I hope you're not sneering.'

'Who me?' I said, feigning surprise. 'I'm not a great believer in altruism or any of that crap, but if other people want to make the world a better place to live in, then I'm all for it. People have to understand that certain commercial activities are good for the ocean too.'

'Give me an example.'

'Okay—culling the seals allows certain shoals of fish to maintain their numbers to survival level. This keeps several types of predatory sea birds alive, as well as species of predatory fish which might die out if there's no prey.'

She grimaced. 'It also keeps a number of businessmen with fat wallets.'

'Don't knock it,' I replied. 'The sealskin industry keeps *people* in jobs, in food, with a roof over their heads, and therefore *alive*. Don't let's forget the most important animal on the planet— humans. They need to survive too.'

'I'm not sure I agree with that,' she muttered. 'I'm a few years older than you and I've seen what people do to the planet in the name of assisting humanity.'

'Oh God,' I cried in mock distress, 'a die-hard conservationist. How green is my soul!'

Several people in the canteen turned to stare at us and I immediately felt like a crass idiot. Jacqueline looked as if she wanted to leave straight away and I put my hand on her arm.

'I'm sorry,' I said, 'that was uncalled for. I tend to shock people for effect—that is, I try to be controversial. I find you learn more about things that way, rather than if you agree with everything everyone says.'

She stared at me doubtfully, then smiled. 'I suppose you're right. My younger brother was always doing that with my parents. One day he came in and said he thought a Fascist government might not a be a bad thing for a change, but he was just trying to shake them up and find out what their ideas about politics really were. He's about as far away from Fascism as you can get, really.'

'That's right. I mean, hey, if you just nod your head and say, "Ummm that's how I feel about things too," how are you going to get a good discussion going? You have to play Devil's Advocate sometimes, to get at the truth.'

By the time the evening was over we were on a better footing and I made a second date with her. Within three weeks we had been to bed and found, in that respect, we were very good together. The fact that she was seven years older than I was seemed to be a bonus. I mean, I was only twenty-two and I knew next to nothing about sex. Jacqueline taught me everything.

Lying together one summer afternoon, the sun shining through the open window and a sea breeze blowing the lace curtains over our naked sweaty bodies, Jacqueline said to me, 'You don't know how much I envy you, studying cetology. I just love whales, don't you? Magnificent creatures. All that weight and yet they are so graceful, so agile, their flukes kicking up spray—the utter delight on their faces as they roll and leap...'

'You're anthropomorphising. That smile of happiness on the face of dolphins and whales is not a smile at all, it's just the way their skin wrinkles. How can you know they're enjoying themselves?'

She turned on her side and began stroking my hair. 'The sheer joy in their movements. And the sounds they make. Look at the belugas, your favourite whales—the *sea canaries*. Look at the songs they sing, the range of sounds. From squawks, yelps, warbles, trills, chirps and whistles, to blats, snores, croaks, clicks, creaks and brays. How can you listen to the recordings and remain unconvinced?'

'The, er, sounds—most of them—originate from sacs and organs near the oil-filled melon in the beluga's forehead. There are fatty pouches through which they force the air to sputter. During the moulting season...'

'Oh, come on Danny, less of the biology—*why* do they do it? I think it's because they're full of the joy of life. By the way, have you chosen your special subject yet?'

I hesitated before answering, but finally told her, 'I'm studying the migrational routes of the belugas.'

She frowned when I said this, as I knew she would, but it would not have been any use lying to her.

'I hope your security is good. If those routes were to fall into the wrong hands it would endanger over a hundred-thousand white whales. I think…'

'Jacqueline,' I said, 'Professor Kinchmier is happy with the arrangements, so I don't think you need to worry. To enter the files and get at the charts you have to use five different codewords at each stage.'

'Who's supplying you with your source material?'

'The professor herself of course—who else has tracked the belugas across the Arctic? We all know they move with the ice fronts, staying ahead of the solidifying sea, but precisely *where* the processions of belugas travel along that front is known only to Kinchmier and a handful of her students. I'm to be one of them, as it happens, whether you like it or not.'

She sat up and stared at me for a moment, a trickle of sweat running down between her breasts, catching my attention. I licked it away, trying to divert her, but she was not to be distracted that easily.

'Oh God, Danny,' she said, 'I hope you're who I think you are—who I want you to be—under that skin. I'm in love with you—*really* in love with you—but if you should turn out to be a louse, I'd kill you, you know that don't you?'

I tried to laugh this off. 'The vegetarian animal lover, member of Greenpeace, Earthwatch and a dozen conservationist organisations, is in reality a cold-hearted killer who would destroy her lover at a stroke.'

'I would too, Danny—oh, darling, please be who I think you are. Please be you.'

I began to get annoyed with all this melodrama and pulled away from her to sit on the edge of the bed.

'Hell, what do you think I am, some kind of monster? Would I betray my own profession?'

'What *is* your profession, Danny? What do you want to do with your life?'

This irritated me even more. 'I don't *know* yet, Jacqueline. Shit, it's all right for you—you come from a family whose expectations for you are low—almost non-existent. Mine expect success—and success in their terms is money. My father was a millionaire by the time he was thirty. If I don't at least repeat that I'll be considered a failure. Actually my generation is supposed to do much better.'

She hooked an arm around my neck and hugged me to her.

'I know—I know. Just don't betray me, Danny, that's all, because I'm deadly when it comes to saving the creatures of the sea.'

It was a good time to tell her that my great-great-granddaddy was a whaler and my reason for choosing the creatures as my area of study. I was surprised to find she was not angry. In fact, she approved of my reasoning.

'It's right that you should study whales when your ancestor was a hunter of them. In hunting them he must have come to understand them a little. You want to deepen that understanding, in a more enlightened age.'

'You don't—disapprove of him?'

'Then was then, now is now. I haven't any patience with people who judge another age in retrospect. It's easy to look back and condemn the buffalo hunters, the foresters, the whalers, but they didn't know any better then. We shouldn't be ashamed of our ancestors for doing what was acceptable in their time. The fact is, it's unacceptable now. No one has an excuse in this day and age. We have proof of whale intelligence, we have proof of deforestation, we have proof of endangered species. What may have been right then, is wrong now.'

MOBY JACK IS STILL IN cold pursuit. Now that it has cut us away from the main school of belugas, it bears down hard on our stern. The distance between us is gradually increasing, but if I'm right about it, that won't make any difference to the eventual outcome.

The belugas are moving into the shallows of a river outlet from Somerset Island, presumably to feed on cod and squid. They fill the blue basin of water with their twelve-foot-long bodies, rubbing against each other, their flukes slapping the surface creating great gouts of water, which fly up and then fall to smack on the surface. The river delta is a writhing mass of white giants, thrashing and surging, spilling the flow over the alluvial plain where the wading birds are gathered. The birds protest but their complaints go unheeded. The whales are too full of themselves to notice that they're disturbing others: like a crowd of football fans when their team has won.

ONCE I HAD MY DEGREE, I went to work for a company making radar equipment for luxury yachts, but promotion was slow and I became dispirited. Jacqueline told me not to panic, to wait for a while before looking elsewhere. I did. I waited four years. The whole time my father was on my back, asking me when I was going to start making some 'real money' so that he could call me *his* son. 'You're just like your Uncle Timothy,' he told me on my twenty-sixth birthday, 'a slow loser. You'll be old and grey before your time, trudging to work with hunched shoulders, earning a pittance all your life, scared to say boo to anyone looking like an accountant.' Dad owned a stock-broking firm and was impatient of losers of any variety, slow, fast or medium, especially his progeny.

It was shortly after this birthday when I was contacted by an international company interested in my work on the beluga migration routes which they had heard about. I asked, where they had heard about it? 'Oh,' the voice on the end of the line said, 'we listen in the right places'. Was I interested? Yes, of course I was interested, and a meeting was arranged. The source of the information, as it turned out, was not as I imagined the result of industrial spying, but a clever remark of my father's at a businessman's dinner. 'My son studied whale spawning grounds during his time at university,' my father had said, 'can you imagine anything more bloody useless than charting the places where fish go to fuck?'

Apparently someone did not think it useless, because they offered me an enormous salary to work for them. I spent several weeks in making the most important decision of my life, walking the floor at night, weighing the consequences. Finally, I made my resolution and resigned myself to that decision.

I went the same night to say goodbye to Jacqueline.

Apart from negotiating an increase in the salary I had made the stipulation that if I was to hand over the information they required, I would do it on the spot, on the bridge of the ship. I was no fool, despite what my father thought of me. If I'd given them what they wanted straight away, they would have taken it and said thanks very much ta-ta fellah. I was going to eke it out to them, at the same time they would pump money into my account on an offshore bank on the Cayman Islands. I could make checks from the ship to the bank, regarding my account, using a codeword. I wasn't going to be cheated out of my earnings. They smiled knowingly and said they understood. If there was one thing they did understand, it was avarice.

Before joining the ship I went into hospital for a minor operation on my right leg.

Then I went off, without a companion Queegqueg, to hunt the white whale. Captain Jisteain was a weedy-looking man, with yellow-rimmed eyes and a heavy smoking habit. Unlike Ahab he had no passion driving his blood like hot mercury through his veins, no obsessive vengeance urging him on. He had no dark and wonderful oaths to scream into the wind, no skin that burned feverishly while he stared out at the wild sea. I could not imagine him lifting his streaming face to the storm and cursing God for sending a typhoon that robbed him of his kill, nor blaspheming with such marvellous inventiveness that it actually added to the depth and breadth of human thought and language. His eyes never strayed to where the crow's nest once reigned, nor did his ears listen for that heart-stopping 'Thar she blows!' which sent the captains of former whaling ships into shivers of excitement. Jisteain spent most of his time in his cabin, reading Regency novels and smoking Turkish cigarettes.

We were bound for the Arctic circle, where the white whale formed a hoop around the axis of the Earth. I spent my days staring at changing skies, interesting seas, that melded into one another at some times, and broke and separated cleanly at others. The horizon was on some days a line as sharp as the edge of typing paper and on others a mountainous seascape. The colours vary as much as the shapes of the waves: green, blue, purple, black, and with dozens of different shades between.

On the deck in the morning there would be fish which had tried to jump the ship and had struck an obstruction halfway across—or had simply not leaped strongly enough. We ate these for breakfast, along with seaweed and shellfish gathered during motion. The chef was resourceful. Even flotsam and jetsam were harvested from the sea: one evening we came across a whole armada of coconuts, presumably shaken into the sea during a hurricane somewhere in the tropics and carried by the currents towards the magnetic north.

Finally, the *Titan*, with its arsenal of defensive computers and anti-missile missiles, not to speak of its whale-killing potential, arrived in the Arctic and found the belugas. The school I led them to was not the largest in the area, but this particular school would, I knew from former intelligence, contain Moby Jack. I was in fact leading the ship to Moby Jack and its doom and not to the killing seas.

Captain Jisteain has come onto the bridge rubbing the sleep from his eyes. I'm leaving the black box running, so that it catches our conversation. Later, Jacqueline, when you transpose this into the written word, please fill in the gaps so that it flows like a narrative. It'll make much more interesting reading that way, for the members of our organisation. I am after all about to make the ultimate sacrifice: my life for that of my fellow creatures. Forgive me if I want to dramatise that moment to give it some power. I don't want to go out with a whimper, but with a bang. A hero's death deserves dramatic telling. My ego requires that the world recognise me and becomes emotional at the mention of my name. I am not a modest man, my darling.

'WHY AREN'T WE KILLING WHALES? Coxswain, why are we heading out to open waters?'

The coxswain looks towards me with a worried expression and the captain turns to stare.

Giving Jisteain a tight smile, I say, 'We're heading this way on my orders.'

He whirls on me, his little moustache twitching. 'Who gave you the bloody right to give orders?'

'You did,' I reply.

He stands there, smouldering, realising that yes, he *did* give me permission to steer the ship towards the belugas. I was the one who knew where they were, therefore he was superfluous on the bridge. I could take over until the school was found, he had stated.

'Turn the ship around,' he orders the coxswain. 'Now.'

Looking out over the sea and broken ice I notice Moby Jack is coming towards us at a high rate of knots.

'I think you'll find you're too late,' I say to the captain. 'Moby Jack is about to smash us to smithereens. You're no Captain Ahab, but I'm afraid you're destined for the same end. The white whale is about to destroy you and your ship. I ordered the ship away from the bay, so that the belugas would not be harmed when we get blown out of the water.'

The captain snarls, 'What the hell are you talking about? Moby Dick? Are you crazy?' He stares at the single white whale bearing down on the ship, its tail driving the water behind it, churning the ocean into a boiling wake. There's something about the determination of that whale which surprises even Jisteain. He doesn't know what to make of the situation and his face is a picture of perplexity and indecision.

'Not Moby Dick—his descendant, Moby Jack. I may be crazy,' I say. 'I probably am. I've sacrificed myself, my life, for a few thousand whales. Moby Jack is not a real whale, by the way. I think it's fair to tell you that at this stage of the deadly game. Moby Jack is a warship in the guise of a whale, designed by my girlfriend, Jacqueline Jones for the International Anti-whaling Activists…'

He interrupts me. 'The IAA? That bunch of bloody terrorists? Now I know you're mad,' he snorts. 'Those militant sons-of-bitches will get what's coming to them if they mess with me. I'll have them intercepted. They'll rot in some Canadian jail for the rest of their lives.'

'Believe me,' I tell him simply, 'the last few minutes of your life could be better spent in praying, or dictating a letter to your loved ones, or even cutting your toenails in preparation for the long journey to hell. Ranting and raving is an utterly useless activity at such a time. Even the deranged Ahab was calm and reflective just before his death. You *are* going to die. We all are. There's nothing that can save us now. I forgot to tell the company by the way—I'm a member of the IAA myself—have been ever since college.'

His eyes narrow. He picks up a pair of viewers and looks at the oncoming white whale. Something he sees convinces him that it is a device, not a living creature.

'Who's in that thing?' he asks.

'No one,' I reply. 'It's being run remotely.'

'There's nothing that monster can throw at us that I can't shoot down or blow out of the water,' he says with confidence. 'You know that, don't you?'

'It's a sad thing to be the bearer of rotten news,' I say in reply, 'but Moby Jack is armed with JAWS.'

Now he turns to stare at me with a worried expression.

'Justified Attack Weapons System,' he says. 'That bloody monstrous spray-launching invention of the anti-whalers? It doesn't matter how erratic their trajectories are, a JAWS missile needs a homing device physically located on the target vessel…'

'That's always been the IAAs' problem,' I say, 'until now of course.'

I give him a grim little smile.

He glares at me. 'You! You brought a fucking homing device on board. You bastard! I ought to throw you overboard, you bloody shit.'

I shrug. 'Be my guest. I stand a better chance in the ocean than I do on the *Titan*. I could survive perhaps three or four minutes in that freezing water, whereas you have rather less time…'

'We'll find it,' snaps Jisteain. 'We'll find the bloody thing and then you'll go over. Full steam ahead,' he orders the coxswain.

Then on the loudspeakers system, 'All hands - search the ship for a homing device. I want anything suspicious thrown over the side immediately. Anything, do you hear? Hang the expense of a mistake. All our lives are stake here. Just throw it over and we'll ask questions later.'

With full power we begin to pull away from Moby Jack rapidly, but we shall be in range for a time. Jisteain and I stare out over the choppy waves at the oncoming white whale, then something happens, it blossoms, opening like a flower blooming, and missiles are launched as a spray of seeds into the atmosphere. They are crazy pods, zipping around randomly, seeking the homing signal, difficult to shoot down in numbers because of their erratic movements, their unpredictable zig-zagging.

Around Moby Jack's belly the sea froths: ripples appear on the surface, heading every which-way. A clutch of torpedoes has also been launched, to dance along the wavetops, jumping and leaping impetuously. Jisteain goes white and for the first time reveals a little fear.

'My computers will seek out and destroy those,' says Jisteain quickly. 'We'll shoot them out of the sky—we'll blow them out of the water.'

He has none of the heroic stature of Ahab, none of his magnificent profanity, none of his demented rhetoric. But then Jisteain has never been torn apart by a whale, nor suffered his embittered soul to be disfigured by the mad spirit of a sea monster. He has all his limbs, his organs, his manhood. He has never drunk rum from a harpoon head, nor tempered steel with his own blood. Jisteain has only Ahab's cold determination, the unfeeling side of Ahab which allowed the mad captain to sail away from a ship searching its lost children. In truth, Jisteain is a poor sacrifice to Moby Jack.

'You can't possibly get them all,' I tell him, 'if you don't find the homing device. It only takes one to get through. Once they find the beam from the homing device, they'll come in like a swarm of mosquitoes after warm blood. One will be enough to blast us into so many fragments it'll be raining shards on Somerset Island for the next few days.'

'We'll find the homing device,' he says, with just a trace of doubt in his voice. 'We have a minute or two yet.'

His men are already dumping things into the ocean, my luggage, my camera, in fact everything belonging to me. They are also scanning the ship with homing device detectors. However, the inner bridge where I am standing, containing as it does the computer that runs the ship, its navigation devices, steering equipment, weather forecasting apparatus, and so on, is of course shielded. The shield that prevents penetration by enemy probes will protect the homing device from detection until it's too late. That's my gamble and it appears to be working, because they're running scared on the decks below me. Not even the *promise* of a shining gold Spanish doubloon nailed to the mast for these fellows: only the certainty of brilliance from a coin of plutonium.

They won't find the homing device. The reason is, it's inside *me*. I had it implanted within my thigh after I accepted the job with the company. Jistean's men can search the ship from stem to stern, they will find nothing. In a moment I will step outside the bridge and small missiles and torpedoes will rush joyfully in to be the first to give birth to heat, light and an explosion that will blast the ship to tiny fragments, startling the beluga whales.

Some of those little harpoons careening around the ship are exploding now as the *Titan's* computers desperately try to track them and detonate them. Small black spears, most of them not more than a foot in length, yet able to destroy ship such as ours with ease. They're twisting and turning erratically, crazily in the sky. They dance around the heavens in their dozens: agents of death telemarking at whim. Looking. Seeking. Then once they recognise the target, to spear it without compassion.

Irony: the little whale Moby Jack will have harpooned the mighty ship, for the target they're seeking is within *me*, standing on the bridge of the *Titan* waiting for death and glory. I have experienced love, what more can a man ask? I have sacrificed the mellowing, the ageing of that love for the sake of humankind as well as the whales, for whaling dehumanises us, debases us to a level lower than any creature on the Earth.

Call me crazy, but I believe there is a greater love at risk than just a relationship between two people. I would rather save the greater at the expense of the lesser, however potent the latter may feel. I am about to experience the ultimate mystery, to travel the last and longest journey. Don't be sad for me, Jacqueline. I look on such a death as a triumph, and I won't have my triumphs wept over like wretched failures.

And father—you are a poor, miserable man.

PUBLISHING HISTORY

'The Sculptor' (first published in *Interzone*, June 1992)

'Black Drongo' (first published in *Omni*, May 1994)

'Bonsai Tiger' (first published in *Spectrum SF1*, 2000)

'Attack of the Charlie Chaplins' (first published in *New Worlds* edited by David Garnett, 1997, White Wolf Publishing)

'When the Music Stopped' by Christian Lehmann and Garry Kilworth (first published in *Other Edens III* edited by Christopher Evans and Robert Holdstock, September 1989, Unwin Hyman)

'Cherub' (first published in *Heaven Sent*, edited by Peter Crowther, Daw Books, 1995)

'The Council of Beasts' (first published in *Interzone*, September 1996)

'The Frog Chauffeur' (first published in *Silver Birch, Blood Moon* edited by Terri Windling and Ellen Datlow, March 1999, Avon Books)

'Hamelin, Nebraska' (first published in *Interzone*, June 1991)

'Hunter's Hall' 1993 (first published in *Mysterious Christmas Tales*, Scholastic Books)

'Something's Wrong With The Sofa' (first published in *The Edge*, 1997)

'Exploding Sparrows' (first published as 'Punctuated Evolution' in *CRANK!*, Issue No 1, 1993)

'Death Of The Mocking Man' (first published in *Interzone* Magazine, September 1999)

'Wayang Kulit' (first published in *Interzone*, December 1994)

'Inside the Walled City' (first published in *Walls of Fear* edited by Kathryn Cramer, September 1990, William Morrow)

'My Lady Lygia' (first published in *REM*, Issue 2, 1992)

'Oracle Bones' (first published in *Touch Wood (Narrow Houses 2)* edited by Peter Crowther, Little Brown Publishers, 1993)

'Paper Moon' (first published in *Omni*, January 1986)

'Store Wars' (first published in *The Anthology of Fantasy and the Supernatural* edited by Stephen Jones and David Sutton, March 1994, Tiger Books International)

'The Megowl' (first published in *Chilling Christmas Tales*, Scholastic Books, 1992)

'The Silver Collar' (first published in *Blood Is Not Enough*, edited by Ellen Datlow, Morrow Books, 1989)

'Moby Jack' (first published in *The Edge*, 1997)